D0880411

Age of Rust

ISBN-10: 978-1-947578-37-1

Ink Smith Publishing
P.O. Box 361
Lakehurst, NJ 08733

`

AGE OF *Rust*

by Conrad Bair and Thaddeus Yeiser

Ink Smith Publishing
www.ink-smith.com

Dedicated to Maurice Yeiser, Robert Bair Sr., Frank Herring and George Patt.

Chapter One

March 2717
Southern Kentucky in the Town of Greenboro

Tavin

You don't truly know anyone until you've seen them in desperate moments. In that sense I don't really know who I am either. We tell ourselves that we've been through hard times, but we're painting a fantasy. Our fate has never truly hung in the balance. Not yet. How will we handle the moment of truth? Will we freeze? Will we make others proud? Will they do the same? Sometimes I feel foolish for coming here, but I can't leave and that shadow of fate is looming ever closer. My only comfort now are the words he taught me. I will keep my eyes on the horizon and when that pain arrives I will not feel it, but instead give it back, and I will not stop until I am on the other side.

The howl of a lone wolf found Tavin's ears, making them hum with the steady tone despite the miles between. As if to listen closer, Tavin pulled away from the girl, peeling his lips off hers and craning his neck to look out the chapel window. Hauntingly, the howling stopped, slipping off at the end of its note, but Tavin kept his gaze beyond the stone walls. Something about the timbre had snapped him to attention. Outside the night was cool and still, the moon and its light had disappeared behind the mountains around the town and on the horizon was the hint of sunrise.

"You don't like wolves?" asked the girl. "I can't imagine being afraid of something so beautiful."

Tavin turned to her again. She was soft in the gentle light of night, a thin thing who was admirably young and energetic.

"As cautious as I am with ordinary things, I'm even more cautious with beautiful things. They have a way of eroding one's judgement."

He flashed her a reassuring smile. It was his smile that people were always drawn to. They could not help but smile back. He touched the woman on the jaw and rubbed the same place she had been rubbing his beard moments earlier. Their eyes locked for a lingering, peaceful moment.

Feeling the hardness of the ground against his knees, Tavin stood to relieve it. He covered her kindly with the blanket they had borrowed from the chapel offices, and then walked to the window of their steeple hideaway. Tavin had looked forward to sneaking up here with a woman for the past week, but now something chewed at his stomach.

"Do you even remember my name?" she asked with charming accusation.

Tavin could feel the arrogance in his automatic grin.

"Of course, Marlies. Marlies, Marlies, Marlies," he

echoed.

"I'm impressed, we were drunk every time we saw each other."

"I may have been drunk, but I remember what I said, and I meant every word," Tavin said, his eyes, now adjusted to the moonlight, on the flickering lights in the distance. He propped his elbows on the cold hard surface and tried to look closer. Campfires, he assumed, but they looked different. The drift of chilled air through the window had an anxious scent.

"You know what drew me to you that first night? I thought you had such serious eyes for how much you danced around." She made room beneath her blanket and adjusted herself. "Here I'm cold, ignore the window and get under the blanket. You can't see their camps from here anyway."

Tavin paused, then turned and rejoined her as she requested. It was much warmer beneath the blanket and she was much softer than the stone walls.

"I know," he replied. "But something is different about this morning. Something about the air. You can always smell them cooking their morning stew, but not today."

"You guys are in over your heads aren't you?" she asked with a solemn expression.

Tavin sighed again. The horizon was a bright purple now but there would be another hour or two until the sun rose.

"Well, they don't exactly know how many of us there are, so… we'll let them take their time. At least until reinforcements can get here. As soon as that happens my friends and I can finally rotate to the fortress."

"It figures. I didn't think this was going to last long," she replied. "You and I, I mean; though the war as well. I suppose I never thought either would drag on like it has."

"Well the reinforcements still haven't come. And there's been no word to suggest they are coming soon. You might have to put up with me a little longer yet."

But there was a chewing at his stomach that made Tavin feel the beginnings of terror. The way his words reverberated off the stone walls of the chapel pinnacle, cold and hollow, he could feel that they were wrong. He stirred beneath the blanket again, agitated.

"What will happen if they take us?"

Tavin glanced to where his swords lay propped against the wall. For a second, he regretted having ever removed them. They were a defensive comfort in times where comforts were few.

"You will be fine if they beat us, probably. They're brutal on the battlefield, but I haven't known them to kill civilians. You will be good with or without me."

"You don't sound too sure," she replied, and he could feel himself losing his smile.

Before Tavin could form his answer there was a loud ringing from outside. He sprang from his blanket as if he had been expecting it. When he reached the window, the sound came clearly to him. It was a fast repetition of a brass bell, coming from the west of town, one of the alarm bells from a guard tower. Tavin listened to the echoes that spread through the valley of the town, each clashing note brought his heart into his throat. He felt like he was watching himself standing frozen in the window, as one watches a player upon the stage and frets over the poor man's ill-luck.

"Where is it coming from?" Marlies asked, standing and walking to his side at the window, still covered in the wool blanket.

"From the west of town."

"It's probably just another cave-in at the mines. It happens."

"No," Tavin said. "It's not."

In the dimmed light he reached for his gladius swords, two black, wickedly pointed twin blades. A brief thought flitted through his awareness. The swords had been his father's at one point and were the only thing that remained of the man. The steel was older than the bones of his body. With nimble fingers he lashed the scabbards across his back, and retrieved his battle knife from its place under his jacket. Then, he reached to his right calf to check for his dagger.

A voice suddenly called from the bottom of the staircase. A voice familiar to Tavin, and one that made Marlies nearly jump through her blanket.

"Hello!" the baritone words of his friend, Gannon, called. "Tavin, are you up here?"

"Yes," Tavin called in return, "I am coming down."

"Who is that?" Marlies asked, panicked, her eyes wide, "How did he know we were up here?"

"He doesn't," Tavin replied as he finished dressing. "He only knows that I am up here."

"But how—"

"If you are going to go home, then go now. Stay there and bolt the door." Tavin explained, rapidly. He knew he must have looked frantic and struggled to hide it, regretful that she would be further scared.

Hopefully, she will be fine, Tavin thought urgently.

"If you stay up here, then stay up here all day until it is safe, but do not go into the streets."

"Why not?" she asked, but he interrupted her with one last kiss upon the lips, full, nearly forceful.

Then he was sailing down the dark stone steps to where he knew Gannon awaited him in the chapel foyer.

"I hate when you're right," Gannon complained. He rushed behind Tavin into the first light of day, darting through long dark shadows of stone buildings.

Tents sat nestled on the north side of town behind most of the houses, now alive like an anthill with scurrying soldiers. The mines, the enterprise of the town, lay to the west up against the rocky hills. The south formed the main entrance of the town and to the east lay thick forest. Tavin followed his friend across the trampled paths of dirt. Shallow valleys of dried mud in what had once been a park in the middle of town. Following the hoarse shouts of the sergeants, they funneled in with a mass of soldiers onto the cobbled main road. A river of tawny, dusty uniforms, like a mudslide flowing to the southern entrance and blockhouse where the barrage of their archers were, was the only thing stalling the inevitable onslaught.

Tavin glanced around above the bobbing heads of his fellow soldiers. Tall stone houses lined the main road with shops beneath. He was still taken in by the sheer wealth of buildings in Greensboro: elegant houses of granite and slate. Most towns made due with log and thatch. But most towns were not a source of gold for the Republic, and now more than ever the town showed its haughtiness in the way it handled war. Tavin had been in other towns, defended them from similar situations. Most welcomed them and offered food and water to their defender, or came out to show moral support. But not Greensboro, here only the folks his age mingled. The elders kept away.

Everywhere the windows were shuttered. And Tavin sensed the doors were barred, though knew this to only be an assumption. How strange that a town would not bear witness to its defense. Beyond the steepled roofs the advancing sun illuminated clouds of slate.

Someone grabbed Tavin's shoulder as he jogged along the uneven street. A heartbeat of excitement turned him and he saw that Kendo had found them in the flow.

Kendo was a tall young man, much taller than Tavin, who found himself straining to walk taller in Kendo's presence. Blonde hair was matted to Kendo's forehead beneath the press of a half helm.

"I couldn't find Sen," Kendo said in a distressed way, slouching slightly to speak in Tavin's ear, a rule that Kendo's six-foot and five-inch frame always mandated. Tavin pushed Kendo's sword staff away slightly so it would not cut his cheek.

"They decided to finally attack us?" Tavin asked Kendo. "Why now?"

"Maybe they were tired of looking at us living comfortably," Gannon voiced over the tramping of feet. "I don't think we survive this."

Ahead of them, their fellow soldiers were already drawing steel. Tavin followed suit, withdrawing the two blades from behind his back as the sight of the ensuing battle exposed itself.

Where the path from the fields became the cobbled

road of town, the blockhouse was releasing shafts of arrows at a growing tide of red uniforms. The crimson waves of Western invaders were making steady progress against their growing pool of leather and steel-clad Eastern defenders. Cries and heavy grunts echoed across the valley of stone walls and houses. Clashing of steel and oaken shields clanged in Tavin's ears. They formed ranks and prepared to reinforce their comrades.

Tavin looked to see Gannon and Kendo were near and ready, and exchanged curt nods of approval, sensing the precipice of battle approaching.

"The mines! The mines have been breached!" cried out a voice, complicating an already precarious situation.

The screaming came from Sergeant Fallon, their own platoon's officer came sprinting into their group from the west of town—bruised, disheveled, and soaked from head to sword in blood of questionable origin.

"Turn men! Turn! They have us flanked!" the sergeant spewed as he gasped between breaths.

Tavin turned about toward the mines, the hills to the west of town that housed the gold from which Greensboro drew its great wealth. A ribbon was clamoring into town from that westward road; slithered downhill like a maroon snake twisting its way through the hills still brown from the winter frosts. Yelling and ruckus amongst the men around Tavin assaulted his ears as they turned to defend the flank now besieged by Westerners on two sides of town. Any guards at the mines were surely dead, and he hoped that was not where Oil'ib had been stationed. They had managed to keep their group of six friends alive to this point. Anxiety from the sudden attack wormed its way to the den of

Tavin's worries. He shook his head to dispel the burrows. No time to ask Kendo.

War calls of Western men were rapidly echoing through the streets until the first of them was upon their flank. With muddied crimson jackets, the long haired and wild eyes of the Western soldiers collided into their defenses. Tavin barely dodged the fierce passado of an enemy. Painful sinuous stretching of his abdomen took his breath as he backed away from the biting steel. He swung his own right-hand weapon around and was parried away. His opponent was sooty with the dark red dirt from the deep mines. Tavin's mind struggled with the puzzle this attack presented. The mines were the one place they had felt was impenetrable.

Another slash at his head and Tavin ducked, he brought both his blades shooting forwards at opposing angles. His left-hand weapon struck home in the man's chest. Tavin withdrew then whirled around to slash the hamstring of Kendo's opponent. The hobbling blow gave his friend an opening, and Kendo's killing blow lifted the Westerner into the air several inches upon his sword staff as Kendo used the leverage of his height to toss the enemy aside. Tavin sensed a presence behind him, a tingling pressure like an invisible finger tapping his mind from somewhere behind him and he used the break in enemies to scour the courtyard with his eyes.

Across the stony ground Tavin could see Seneca, the fighting doctor, his best friend, was engaging the penetrative forces from the south. Tavin's eyes were pulled away before he could help Seneca, and from his peripheral he saw his friend throwing his shield like a discus, his medic bag swinging on his back. The flanking maneuver had done its job and the initial invading forces were now sinking their steel teeth deeper into the defending lines. Tavin turned and found Gannon behind him.

"We need to work our way to Seneca!" he shouted noticing that Seneca was amongst some Easterners being funneled away in retreat, "There's no time!"

Gannon nodded and ran a hand across his balding head, sweat plastering the hair backwards. The main road was a scene of utter chaos as attacks from both sides were compressing the Eastern defenders into a thinner and thinner line. Tavin collected Kendo and, with Gannon, made the effort to pierce what was now becoming a frenzy of skirmishing.

Immediately their way was blocked by crimson forces. Chaos won the day as forces converged from all sides like a flood. Tavin caught a whistling blow between the cross of his two blades. The stinging reverberation of the clashing steel brought tears to his eyes. He blinked away a haze as he pushed his attacker backwards then gave a vicious kick to the man's gut. His enemy grunted and Tavin had made three slashes at his neck. Two merely rang the half helm about the face, but the third exposed a bloody gash. Regaining himself, Tavin looked beyond the jostling heads to where he had last spotted his friend, but Seneca was gone. Scanning the battle, Tavin avoided confrontation as he could, searching for the chestnut hair and dark green bag that was always strung across his friend's back. Tavin only saw the river of crimson enemies flooding into the muddy banks of their small army. His stomach sank as he knew it was over. All over for this place.

If only I could stop this avalanche and send it back to the mountains, he thought.

Tavin attacked the three men that had managed to engage Kendo and Gannon. As a team they cut down their foes with a series of sweeping swings. An onlooker might have assumed it was choreographed, but to Tavin it was like a flowing instinct. The thrusts, slashes, and parries came to him like the inspiration of a manic artist and he struck before he thought. When they had slain an opening through their attackers Tavin grabbed his friend's shoulders.

"It's over, we need to run!"

The southern blockhouse erupted in bright yellow flames. A thick black smoke churned its way to the sky. Without further encouragement, Kendo and Gannon followed his lead. They took their opening and retreated down an open alleyway, running toward the eastern wall of the town. In reality Eastern men were running in each direction, defending themselves where they could. Some were cut down as Tavin passed them in his sprint. Arrows flew at their backs, whistling overhead and across their path. Smoke filled the alleyways and the acrid smell of burning pitch made him cough. Guilt gnawed at his chest while his heart beat like a wild drum in his ears.

He was soon enveloped in banks of thicker smoke. It choked him as he tried to hold his breath. His eyes flooded with stinging water as he tried to keep pace with Kendo and Gannon. A hand grasped his left arm. Instinct forced him to fight the grip, but he knew it was Kendo and followed. Kendo pulled them left and Tavin saw that he would have run smack into a low wall had he kept running forward. They cleared the smoke as they found a side street with a breeze that blew the haze out across the rooftops. Kendo released his hold and the three of them continued to run.

Tavin pushed forward through the soreness in his legs, using the steady burn of the muscles as a motivational whip, cursing them all the while for becoming accustomed to comfortable cots.

Approaching the east of town, Tavin recognized Sergeant Fallon again, a tired looking sergeant with thinning curly black hair. After leading a group of survivors on a similar retreat the group must have been forced to stop at the low wall that separated the town from the quickly sloping hills and bramble that led to the distant mountains. Tavin's heart sank when he saw a group of Westerners had pursued the sergeant and his band of survivors and now pinned them to the town wall, holding onto their lives with a weakening grasp.

Despite the breeze nipping at his cold hands, Tavin gripped his swords with whitening knuckles. No words were needed to bring Kendo and Gannon with him on another charge. Surprise paid them a favor this time and Tavin swung his weapon around and sliced the nearest enemy across the back of his neck to bring the attackers attention away from the sergeant's men.

His opponent had a weight advantage, a rotund Western soldier with his jacket long gone and only blood-stained mail upon his barrel chest. He drove Tavin backwards, stumbling, until Tavin's heel struck a stone and he toppled on his back. Advancing with lustful force, the Westerner made to kill. When Gannon's clubbing morningstar blossomed upon the Westerner's temple in a bloody flower Tavin could only gape with relief.

"Soon your debt will be too large to repay," Gannon quipped.

"Only if we are measuring debt by the pound," Tavin replied rubbing his jaw, staring at the massive man on the ground.

As Kendo helped Tavin to his feet he turned to see the group of enemies retreating back to their main force in the center of town. But he knew they had little time to continue their retreat before a larger force would return to see to survivors like themselves.

Sounds of merry excitement were surprising to Tavin, and as Gannon called out with optimism Tavin followed to see what had made him exclaim thus. The vision gave him elation as well. Enough to forget about the bleeding gash in his tongue.

Seneca was amongst the men they had helped. The aquiline nose and thick dark beard were unmistakable. Yet as Tavin approached to give him cheer he saw that Seneca was busy helping an injured man, whose intestines were spilling out into the street.

Tavin could hear him addressing Sergeant Fallon.

"He's gone."

Tavin was hesitant to approach. Yet, when Seneca stood and saw him, Gannon, and Kendo, a smile flickered across his kind face.

Seneca was a simultaneously cynical and humorous man of the most practical education. An idealist and moral snob with a kind heart. They affectionately referred to him as "The Fighting Doctor."

"I thought for sure you would be dead," Seneca expelled as he embraced the three of them. "Have you seen Oil'ib? Praxis?"

"Neither," Tavin said, downtrodden, "I thought Praxis was with you."

"He was. But after the flanking from the mines we were separated."

"We can talk later," Tavin said, his joy in seeing his friend was muted by the possible loss of two more. "We have to go now."

"What about the townsfolk?" Kendo stated, causing the others to look upwards at shuttered windows and dark houses.

What about our friends, Praxis and Oil'ib? What about the men we dined with last night who no longer breathe? What about the blood? What about the ruin? Townsfolk will be nursed by those that wounded them. The prize is the pauper, for the West. For the townsfolk, a new king.

Sergeant Fallon, vapidly, as if ringed dry of all emotional nuance, sighed as smoke and flame engulfed more and more of the town. "The best thing we can do is reach the fortress and alert the main army and the general."

"Then those hills are our only chance," Seneca added pointing a blood-soaked hand toward the east.

Their small group, a residue of twenty-five men, squirmed over the town wall. Pushing and pulling each other over and then starting the climb up the hills. They followed goat paths in a winding trek up the steep, rocky ridges. Tavin supported himself by grasping onto the young saplings, his leather boots sliding with uncertainty on the gravel ledges. Silence was key to their escape, and nothing was said. Yet the sacking of the town continued without them. Screams from the remnants of the Eastern battalion as they were slaughtered in the streets. Tavin held his gaze on their hands and feet. Fingers gripping rough stone and leather boots sliding on loose topsoil. Only after they had climbed to the peak of the nearest hill did he stop to rest and peer out at the columns of smoke pouring from the blockhouses at the four corners of town.

Seneca approached Tavin, and he knew what his friend wanted before he asked.

"When was the last time you saw Oil'ib?" Seneca inquired.

Tavin shook his head.

"I was hoping you had. I thought he was on guard duty with you and Praxis?"

"He overslept. Like always. We left without him and I haven't seen him since. But he was gone when you woke this morning?"

"I don't know," Tavin replied, looking down at the town, at the tall stone spire of the chapel, untouched by violence. "I spent the night in the chapel."

"The chapel?" Seneca asked, stressing his confusion. Tavin did not explain, but kept his eyes roving the height of the spire and the streets below. For a second, he thought he saw a flash of brown hair in the distant window, and he felt the ecstasy of hope.

The scene in the streets tempered his elation though. He could see bands of men moving along the grey furrows of the town like fire ants through a maze.

"If we'd been stationed in the northern blockhouses, we wouldn't be sitting here," Tavin said pointing at a billowing of smoke in the background to punctuate the point.

It happened so fast. Like spilling water on a table full of papers. You can watch it as it happens but cannot move to stop the ruin.

Tavin sensed Gannon and Kendo settle in around them.

"Don't bother asking, Seneca didn't see them either," Tavin said speaking out the side of his mouth.

Gannon dropped his voice down low and spoke so only

they could hear.

"We need to be careful. Fallon's in over his head."

Tavin turned to look at him.

"We can cross that bridge if we get to it. For now—"

"Do we have time to wait and see if they appear?" Gannon asked.

Tavin did not answer. He touched the tip of a scabbard behind his waist, felt the firmness of the steel beneath. The man he had received these from had been a famous commander, a humble genius who had congealed an Eastern victory against poor odds in the last war. A man who found the means to rally passion and devotion in people who wanted nothing more than to drop their weapons and run home. A person who freely offered himself over and over again. Tavin's own head felt empty by comparison to the memory.

Father would have known what to do.

"Look below!" Kendo shouted, pointing to the wall they had climbed over but minutes before.

Tavin's gaze flew to the spot, hoping....

Below was a small group of Eastern survivors struggling over the wall. They barely made it over before their pursuers did the same. A giant, clad in glinting burnished gold armor, flew over the wall then, the tell-tale affluence of a Western officer. They knew this man; it was the Western devil that had terrorized their scouts for the past two weeks. A berserker who had risen high enough in the ranks of the enemy to become equally known in the Eastern mess halls. Clades, in his unmistakably hideous splendor, was hot on the trail of the escapees. Tavin moved closer to the edge of the gorge, where Kendo was watching like a waiting hawk, bow and arrow in hand.

Clades," Kendo confirmed, looking down with heavy concern.

"He doesn't look human," Seneca added.

Tavin could only watch as the Western forces overwhelmed the Eastern men that made to clamber up the goat paths and crumbling slopes.

"Cover them!" Tavin nearly shouted. His own volume surprised him as he nudged Kendo to raise his bow in defense.

"It's little use from here," Kendo retracted nervously, "I could just as well hit our own."

"They're fucked either way if we don't do something," Tavin slurred, "Fire! Anyone with a bow, give them a chance!"

Kendo lined up his shot, fired, and managed to fell one of the pursuing enemy, but another of his missiles found its home in a comrade.

There burst forth a small flame of blonde hair below. Its jostling movement caught Tavin's eye and he recognized Lieutenant Solly. One of the few females in the whole of their battalion, Solly had been one of a small number of kind-hearted officers, a guiding hand in the training camp. It was with a sinking in the pit of his stomach that Tavin realized the jostling of her flaxen hair had also caught the attention of the gold-clad brute. Clades was making powerful strides toward where she was negotiating violently with the ground, working around the twists and turns of the goat path, and leading his men on with the loping strides of a pack of wolves hot on the trail of easy game.

Tavin's legs yearned to run down the hill to help her, but the view of the path made it clear how impossible it would be. He would never get there in time, or he would inevitably fall to his own peril. Solly had already turned to face her enemies. One of the red ants fell in front of her quicker and skillful blade.

But the demon, as the men called him, stepped forward and knocked her sword away with one chop. Clades kicked her in the face when she bowed to reach her weapon and then knocked her to the ground with a strike to the chest. A desperate arrow struck one of Clades' men, and another bounced off of his own chest plate, but it failed to deter him.

As Solly lay helpless, Clades' remaining soldiers egging him on, he delivered the deathblow, taking her head off with a swing of his steel. The sheer sight sent an unearthly chill through Tavin's veins, the likes of which he thought had long since been extinct. Sensation caused him a moment's regret for joining the war as the heartache threw numbness away. They had never been close, but in that moment, watching her die alone and in fear, Tavin felt love for the Lieutenant, a sinking sad love, multiplied by the sheer cliff face. Tears formed in his eyes.

Love was replaced by icy venom, which raced through cold veins as he looked down at the glinting image of Clades. But as much as he wished to relinquish it upon his enemy, it merely saturated within himself. Why had he chosen this over school, over the happy middle-life that his father had prescribed him? The tired advice of his late father whispered in his head as he watched the carnage below.

I don't care what he told me; he'd be out here now. He would slay that monster. He wouldn't let this happen, Tavin thought.

Atop the hill there was only the sound of the breeze, a

rustling of the young buds on the scrub bush as the wind tossed over the pine trees that stood as sentinels upon the hill.

Far below, Clades reached down into the grass. The gray and cloud-hampered sunlight glinted off his burnished armor and a braided goatee swayed from his scarred face. The demon reached into the ground and retrieved the head of Lieutenant Solly. Even from their place atop the hill they could see the wicked smile that exposed the sparse white teeth. With slow ritual, Clades brought the head to his own, and kissed it fully upon the mouth, holding it there long enough for Tavin to question the reality of the image.

"What... the... fuck," Gannon muttered, holding his hand to his balding head and kicking himself away from the edge of their cliff-side view.

The demon then threw the head in their direction. It landed with a sickening thud a quarter way up the ledge. Wiping some blood from his mouth the beast loped away again toward town, disappeared over the town wall, a movement that his tremendous height and strength made appear easy.

It was not until they had begun wandering south along the ridgeline that Tavin spoke up.

"Fallon, how far is the fortress?"

"Illinois or Tennessee?" the nervous sergeant replied.

"Tennessee," Tavin replied with frustration. "It's the only one we have a shot at."

"May be a hundred miles. Give or take—"

"That's where we go," Tavin announced, looking around to the despondent faces, "What other choice do we have?"

No one replied.

"It's over. Greensboro is over, but we have to keep

moving. We have to find a way."

Seneca put a hand on his shoulder, nodded, but did not look into Tavin's eyes, only kept watching where his feet fell on the crags of granite.

Sergeant Fallon stopped, gazing at the town in the valley. "It's going to be a difficult hike."

Tavin caught the assumption. Clades had seen them on the cliff. Certainly, the Western army would send a platoon after their escape. Keeping the sacking of Greensboro a secret would make their invasion of the fortress much easier. Tavin knew with the honest pang in his stomach that it was not the last he would be seeing of the gold demon.

"*Why are you scared of the monsters? They only come out at night because they're afraid,*" again his father's words rang out in his mind.

"You heard of him from your childhood?" Tavin asked Kendo after catching up to his friend's long-legged pace.

Kendo, who had spent his childhood in the West, had explained the image that was Clades when first they had spied him from a blockhouse with a lens weeks ago.

"He earned his reputation. That is no longer in doubt."

"I'll pose a question. He takes you one on one. What do you do?" Tavin asked.

Tavin scratched at his own beard. Cinnamon whiskers grew thick upon his cheeks. Kendo sighed as he spoke.

"I would try my best."

Their group of survivors had trekked through the remainder of the morning and on into the afternoon. The sun had finally burnt through its gray cloak and its golden rays were warming the front of Tavin's body pleasantly. Ahead he could see where their trail over the hilltop would soon plunge into the valley and he savored the last of the sun's warmth before it would be diluted again by the boughs of sycamore trees.

A dichotomy waged an emotional war inside Tavin. On one side, a great sadness. This war should have been over by now. The loss of Greensboro meant that their conscription was nowhere near fulfillment. So many of them had expected to rotate to the fortress and then to be released home with an Eastern victory at the Mississippi River. But now there was little reason to believe that would happen. Many would not see home for a long time. Many may never return at all. But deeper inside this sadness, an unexpressed pleasure brewed in Tavin. The six of his group, Seneca, Kendo, Oil'ib, Gannon, Praxis, and himself, in the process of the war, had stumbled upon a great power. It was subtle, unnoticeable to others until the fray was upon them and one could see the perfection with which they fought together. It was sublime, it was just below cognition, and it taunted at Tavin seductively from the corner of his conscious. Tavin knew that they would never leave war now. But he could never admit it.

Chapter Two

March 2717
Southern Kentucky

Seneca

Why should we be unhappy, Seneca thought, we are the first of our kind. A race broken free from the bonds of predation. We mastered all the elements of the earth and all the creatures that dwell in it. Yet now we hunt our own. Where is blessed temperance? What craving leads me to kill my distant brother? When did the original tribe forget about those that traveled far away? Twisted bloody reunion! With what claim does my cousin's life become my property to dispose? Call him my enemy if you wish, there are worse things a man could have, but I sneer at the inheritance.

After his canteen gave up its last few drops of moisture, Seneca gave in. Until then his mood had remained afloat in a form of self-trickery, where getting out of Greensboro was falsely associated with an improvement. But after two days of hiking across the hilltops and a night of sleep that had seemed completely devoid of any rest, the foundation of that illusion had faltered. The rocks and roots dug in through the thinner shielding of his worn military boots and his Achilles tendon ached. He thought for sure he could hear it creaking as they stepped up the rocky stairs of a boulder and then down the other side.

The water was a problem, a serious problem. There was little, if any, that could be found in the meager pools along the hillside. And hiking down to the valley risked attack by predators or whatever humans may be trailing them. It would be predictable to follow the stream. Instead they took the harder road.

To divert his mind Seneca had been diagnosing himself for the better half of the day. Heightened pulse, dry mouth, a lack of sweat despite the warmth of his clothes, and he had not had a bowel movement since they had retreated, classic dehydration. He could hear his father drilling in the symptoms into his mind from a distant memory at the Finger Lakes clinic. He felt his pulse again, and it was fast. The anxiety of fleeing from death did not help either. The uptick in his nervous system was another factor.

Luckily, the dehydration will kill me long before I die of colonic rupture and sepsis, Seneca thought.

The other men were having trouble as well. Some had not had the advantage of the last breakfast served at the barracks before the attack. It had been a hearty meal, and Seneca had fortunately made use of it. He regretted every meal he had not made the most of and catalogued them in his memory. At his sixteenth birthday he had barely eaten any of the shortcake. What a waste.

They had divided what rations survived with the growing clarity that soon they would be in narrow straits. Some of the men had already eaten what was given them and now searched the ground for onion grass or chewed the bark of birch trees as their ragtag platoon scuffed along the thin trail through the thickening Tennessee forests. Despite their issues, Seneca could not help but feel bored. The problems of the day paled, in his mind, to the problems of the year. The problems of his occupation. His mind dwelled specifically on his home in the Finger Lakes and on the woman that he had left there. Seneca thought of the family he did not miss. Seeking analgesia in conversation, he outpaced the birch-chewing soldiers in front of him around a widening in the trail.

"You know… I used to love hiking," Seneca divulged.

"So did I," Kendo replied, glancing at Seneca with a welcome smile.

"Now I worry that it might be ruined for me forever."

"So do I."

"Do you suppose that everything in life can be spoiled?" Seneca asked with a slight grin.

"No not everything," Kendo replied. Scratching the back of his head and sauntering his awkward height forward at a pace that Seneca could keep up with.

"That's exactly what I hoped you would say, now if only you could show me some proof."

"I think I can. The things that the body needs, that the soul needs, I don't think certain things like that can be ruined."

"Do you mean like love? Or something along another platitude?"

"Yeah, sure, I think that would work. Love is kind of like

water, which you never lose the taste for. And I can give you proof. I am out of water, and I crave it more than I crave the ending of the war."

Kendo shook his canteen to show it was empty, and coughed out a sigh after.

Seneca could not help but laugh. While he shook his own empty canteen, Kendo chuckled as well.

"Maybe I worry too much," Seneca said facetiously. "In fact, if we can find some more water, the hiking might not even be so bad."

As the group entered another clearing on the top of a rolling hill, the marchers trickled to a stop at the edge of the shallow tree line. There Tavin and sergeant Fallon stood with their arms akimbo, eyeing the men as they landed for a rest.

"And that… was one ridge… well done," Tavin panted as he scanned the group.

Seneca could see sweat beading along his friend's brow line. Tavin sweated prodigiously, a fact that had been the source of jokes in the summer training camp. But here, Seneca's thoughts went to dehydration again and he approached Tavin to express his concerns.

"Make sure you're drinking water. You'll sweat yours out quicker than the rest of us. And I'm not sure I could carry you."

"Well," Tavin started before giving a sarcastic look. "I'll get started with my last three drops."

"You know what I mean," Seneca replied wishing Tavin would just accept the advice without insisting on qualifying everything. "Whenever we do get more."

Tavin nodded, still catching his breath after the ascent.

The sun had started the day as a welcome friend, warming them from the frosted and sleepless night spent stretched out upon the cold and unforgiving earth. Now it added to their burden and drained them of their remaining moisture.

"By the way, most everybody is out of water," Seneca said, making sure that he caught Tavin's eyes to get the point through.

The icy blue eyes of his friend flashed with an understanding and Seneca sensed the change of plans unfolding in Tavin's mind.

"We should head down into the valley and find the stream." Seneca added.

Tavin scratched at his cinnamon beard with apprehension but did not deny the advice.

"So, then it's downhill for a while?" one of the survivors asked aloud, catching wind of what Seneca had said.

Others still were sucking air through cracked circles of dry mouths.

"We can probably reach the valley in a couple hours, refill, and then follow the flat land for a while for a place to camp the night," Seneca explained.

"Seneca," Tavin said suddenly, turning toward him as if remembering something important, "Can you go check on Smith back there?"

Seneca turned around where Tavin's eyes gazed beneath his lowered brow. A soldier removed his boots and whined loudly to the others around him.

"He's been complaining for a while," Tavin admitted, "it might be something serious."

"Sure thing," Seneca said, and walked toward where the young man was whimpering on a fallen tree.

Seneca breathed deeply once and went through the brief seconds of wordless ritual that resulted in a mindset where he could speak from the pedestal of greater knowledge without disenfranchising the patient. A complete character transformation that was both insensible and expected.

"When was the last time you changed or washed your socks?" he asked the young man, gagging as the soldier removed them upon his order.

The young man, whom he was truly meeting for the first time, rolled his eyes up in pondering thought beneath eyebrows depressed with pain.

"You think I had time to wash up, man? My friends are all dead. They're all fucking dead," he stammered.

"I understand," Seneca stated, putting a hand on his shoulder.

Do not give in to the comfort of the void. Do not let this world beat you into the ground. Hold yourself up. Refuse to slip away.

"I won't make it if my foot's broken," Smith replied.

Seneca eyed the foot, which was erythematous across most of its surface. A blotchy rash covered the foot and gave off a particularly fetid odor. The nails looked thickened and dark.

"It's not broken," Seneca replied finally, standing and backing away from the terrible stench that had driven away the other soldiers.

"Looks like a serious case of trench foot. When we stop for the night, I want you to wash both socks and feet in the downstream. Then warm them by the fire. And thoroughly dry your socks. I mean thoroughly. Can you make it the rest of the day?"

He nodded with only the least bit of confidence, then clothed his feet as Seneca retreated to the front of the company again. A gentle breeze blew across the greening field and into the tree line where they rested. Seneca took in the fresh air in large gulps. It smelled of spring and of budding plants.

Let me sleep now. Let me move out of this nightmare. When I open my eyes you will be there in all your loveliness and grace. You will take my hands and walk beside me.

Seneca was making to sit down when another hand found his shoulder and he turned to see Tavin again.

"Can I speak with you in private?" Tavin asked.

"Can we sit?" Seneca asked, shielding his eyes from the sun as they walked a short way into the field.

"Hell yeah, we can." Tavin replied, and they took a seat in the shorter grass, still dry from the passing winter.

The sun was once again a blessing, its heat relieving some of the aches in Seneca's joints.

"What's wrong, huh?"

Tavin shook his head. "How do you know something's wrong?"

Seneca shrugged. "You're easy to read. What's right then?"

Tavin acknowledged the humor with a smirk, looked off over the edge of the hilltop and across the vast distance of rolling slopes.

"I saw you helping out the men from the back of the line. I just would like it if you stayed up front, ya know? It's fine, just keep the men coming to the front for their drugs so that we don't slow too much."

The tone of authority that laced Tavin's voice pricked Seneca. But the annoyance was faded by the humming soreness of his feet.

"I was only giving out beeswax for chapped lips. We really need water, like I said. There actually hasn't been a large call for opium since that older guy passed. Or at least, not a worthy call."

"Yeah, okay," Tavin responded forlornly. "I mean, it's not really that. I just would prefer to have you in front if we're ambushed. You and I operate better in tandem."

Seneca sighed. He wished that his role could be relegated to the position he had been hired for.

"I shouldn't have ever fought in the dueling rings," Seneca stated flatly.

"I don't think that was optional for any of us."

"Well I should have sucked at it."

"You shouldn't have eaten the bread with the rest of us." Tavin laughed.

Seneca glowered at this repetitive argument from over the last three months, that somehow a sixteen-hour hallucination from ergot poisoning had melded six minds. He glowered because the argument could not be disproven. It was something beyond experiment and deduction. And on top of its slipperiness, the argument was somewhat lucid. This frightened Seneca. Something *had* certainly changed since the six friends spent a week in the infirmary recovering from the poisoning. But the idea of being tethered beyond his own will made him uncomfortable, made him fear how much of life was out of his control. Ever since that week, and the particularly intense phase of the alkaloid induced hallucinations they had worked better as a team, communicated instinctually—as if thoughts passed wordlessly between them with no impetus needed. Whenever the adrenaline was running, the link seemed to go into high gear. They fought better, and *killed* better.

Maybe that's the worst part, Seneca thought.

"We don't know for sure it was the ergot that did it. And then, either way, I shouldn't have picked up a sword if I didn't want to fight," Seneca said on the verge of anger.

"Sen, you were drafted. Stop lamenting your decisions as if you had a choice. You, of all people, have no need for self-blame. I'm here on my own accord. I'll deal with that."

"But I could've said no."

"And what? Let the captain execute you?"

"Maybe," Seneca reasoned, "maybe to achieve any real change extreme action is needed, and that was the only option at my disposal."

"And yet here you stand." Tavin let his point linger. "Think of it this way. All our medics, all the men that never fought in the ring, they were trapped in the south blockhouse when it burned, so maybe things do work out sometimes."

"Yeah. I suppose that's one way of looking at it." He felt himself being torn between laughter and weeping. His throat was too dry to do either, and his head vacillated. He sighed.

"You're right though. We should take every advantage we have. Whatever this... gift is, we should use it." Seneca smiled, "Otherwise we would waste that time we spent on the edge of death—rolling in anguish on the floor of that shitty medical tent."

"I wouldn't call it a waste of time anyway," Tavin said. "The nurses made it all worth it."

"You were having them rub the pepper balm onto your junk, even though that area was fine."

"Well the joke was on me, that shit burned for hours," Tavin laughed. But I think she enjoyed it. I spent a whole weekend with her."

"You are a whimsical man, if nothing else. Even in pain." Seneca shook his head. "I hate how serious everyone has to be. There should always be time for silliness."

"There will be time when we reach the fortress," Tavin said with a smile.

"Here's to hoping, but it seems trouble is always on our heels. I'm ready if you are, the sooner we move the closer we get to water and shelter. Better to arrive exhausted then not at all."

"That's the spirit!" Tavin began shouting and the soldiers slowly rose to his calls.

Seneca pulled on some low hanging branches to raise himself to his feet then proceeded to stretch. His muscles fought the pulling. He slapped at his quadriceps.

Come on body, we've got to set the pace.

It was late afternoon when they finally reached the valley floor. There they were rewarded in the cool shadows, hooded by the looming hills and tall trees at the edge of the creek that traced the valley's crevice. They submerged their faces in cold, clear water and filled their canteens to the brim. Some of the men even unclothed and bathed downstream in the deeper waters. Seneca was pleased to see young Smith from before, washing his feet and socks further down. But he could not bring himself to bathe, as much as he yearned to rid himself of his own must, for he could not stand cold water and instead rubbed himself down with a cloth moistened in the creek. The cleansing coolness of the water refreshed him mightily.

When the watering was finished and the men had prepared to continue the march along the low-lying trails of the valley, Seneca saw a wolf for the first time since entering the wild. It was a black and ragged canine, barely standing out from the dark green shadows of the forest until Tavin brought it to the attention of the platoon. The men gathered around each other and watched as the beast bounded off through the underbrush, stopping to observe the men from the far side of the creek.

"Look at those eyes," Tavin muttered softly. "Look how it's watching us."

"We had best get going," Seneca replied. "Before we have to deal with all the crepuscular beasts. It would be good to gain a little altitude on the hills."

"Crepuscular, eh?" Tavin asked with a sarcastic smile.

"Fuck off."

Seneca had seen few beasts of the world at his home in the Finger Lakes. The town was large enough to keep the predators largely uninterested and afraid of noisy mankind. Life in the army had been a survey of the natural world. Upon the leftovers of a battlefield, one might see any number of opportunistic scavengers feasting on the kills of men. He had seen animals that were only talked about in stories around fires by eccentric grandfathers. Great mountain tigers and other wild cats that cracked the bones of the deceased in the night, a grizzly bear far out in a field with her cubs, giving their marching army a wide berth, and the ever-present howling of wolves that seemed to follow them on their tour of duty.

The oral traditions told of a time of man's dominance in the previous age, when animals such as these were kept for public interest after the wild had been thoroughly tamed. As his elders had explained, the fall of man allowed for a resurgence of the predator, and nature had long since laid claim to the skeletal remains of the old world.

He eyed the wolf suspiciously as it retreated from their position.

"It probably has friends—a lot of friends," Seneca mentioned.

"Let's hope it's a rogue," Tavin offered.

"Doubtful."

"In either case let's get everybody moving." Tavin stated, as he crept to the front of the men, drawing their gaze away from the forest underbelly.

That night the platoon allowed themselves some small campfires. Along a shelf of moss-covered rock that flattened out from its position a quarter way up the hillside, their fires pointed out like a small constellation in the deepening darkness of night. Overhead, the true stars were shielded out by the thickening canopy. Seneca rolled his jacket into a tight bundle for a pillow and laid himself supine beside the warmth, turning over now and then to warm the other side.

Exhaustion swelled in his body. Its ache keeping him hovering above sleep. For an hour he lay upon his back, thinking of home and of Chiara, thoughts he had not procured with the other soldiers when stories of women in waiting were drunkenly shared.

For him, the longing felt truer than he assumed it was in others and the idea of muddying its waters in conversation made him uneasy. Many of the men seemed to get by just fine in the taverns of Greensboro despite the stories of their own blushing brides awaiting their return. For Seneca, every thought could turn upon an axis that led invariably back to Chiara. The darkness of night and the warmth of fire were like so many loving and dark nights spent in a similar warmth, different only in its tenderness. Everything in the night's blackness was like her fine dark hair. The firewood smell was the musk of a natural perfume. His thoughts bled at last into a deep and twisting sleep. Seneca dreamt that he was home and flying around his father's house with Chiara on his back, trying to find a room where they could be alone but constantly being interrupted by intruders.

I am uprooted. But do we still inhabit each other?

He woke at the first sign of sunlight splitting the trees with invading shafts of gold, surprised at how rested he felt, at how quickly the morning had come. Seneca stretched the slight soreness from his back and made to the nearest bush to relieve himself. As the gentle stream came rushing outward he felt his thoughts drift inwards into a meditative state. The earth hung solid and ready under his feet. A cool breeze whisked against his cheeks causing his nose to scrunch up, and the sound of rustling leaves gave his mind just enough to focus on without overwhelming his silence.

"You shouldn't stand alone," Tavin said walking past him.

Seneca finished his business and pulled up his pants.

"I can't get one minute alone. Not one," he replied.

"No," Tavin stated with a deep drawl. "Not until we're behind walls again."

Seneca wanted so badly to smack his friend upside the head when he tried to pull a rank that didn't exist, but he had to admit Tavin was beginning to embody the absent role of leader. The man took visible pride in directing and guiding wherever he could and seemed to channel a second personality when the role of leadership was on his shoulders.

"You don't have to talk that way when it's just us," Seneca stated with tired cordiality.

Tavin turned and unclasped his hands allowing them to hang freely.

"I'm sorry. Sometimes I speak without thinking. It's just that we're so alone out here. I mean look out at the distance. There are shadows, underbrush and trees every possible place you can look." Tavin moved in a circle to demonstrate his point. "You ever notice how in bars I always take a seat on the back wall so I can see everything? I can't do that here. We're exposed on all sides."

"Not to mention Clades is obviously following us," Seneca stated, finally spilling the worry that had plagued him since the sacking. "I've thought it every time I look backwards. I can't explain it other than I feel something ominous. I don't want to worry the others."

Tavin merely dropped his head a moment and laughed softly.

"I knew he would come." He looked up at the morning sun allowing some light to catch his eyes. "I don't know if I'd rather face Clades or the wolves more. At least wolves would kill us quickly."

"You're right. I always told myself that if the worst should happen that at least the Westerners could be reasoned with, because they're people." Seneca rubbed some lingering sleep from his eyes. "But by now my optimism is spent. They fight like animals."

"So, can we," Tavin said, flashing a smile that threatened to inspire Seneca's spirit.

Some rustling drew both of their gazes back to camp as they realized the others were joining them.

"How'd you sleep?" Seneca asked Gannon who lumbered over to them while scratching his stomach.

Gannon offered only a gaping yawn as a response. Fallon, the powerless sergeant, strolled through the men with gaunt anticipation all over his face. He attempted to spark a lively morning debate but was silenced by Kendo, who now stood, slender as a reed and stern-faced. He gazed to the northeast where his eyes were fixed on the edge of the forest. An attempt to gain Kendo's attention failed so instead Seneca followed the line of vision. A long silence followed as the men remained fixed on this one direction.

The soft crack of twigs in the distance confirmed the shared suspicion, and a bead of sweat on the temple signaled the rising paranoia. Kendo met eyes with Tavin then—a slight twitch of the iris in the sockets of his hairless face—Tavin pulled swords from his back.

Seneca's sword drew from its sheath before he realized he was doing it.

What is it you seek? To let the world know who's stronger?

Tavin and Fallon pulled the soldiers along into a wedge forming from the outer edge of their camp. The cracking grew louder. From behind, Seneca heard the familiar stretching of the sinew on Kendo's bow, the whisper of a notch fitting the string. Bushes rustled in the distance. A closer sound, a faster and faster crashing. Sweat started to pool on Seneca's forehead in fresh beads. Leather on his hilt now felt softer and malleable under the strain of his grip. Chirping sounds from above that had been so prominent were now gone. His mind narrowed, the familiar tunneling of tension.

Breathe....

Seneca's muscles twitched forward as the strangers finally came into view, but at that instant his worry and fear melted away.

"Oil'ib?! Praxis?" Tavin exclaimed having spotted their friends leading at least a dozen soldiers from their lost battalion.

Fear gave way to mirth as men rushed forward to greet their friends and brothers that had been presumed dead.

Deep relief escaped Seneca's lungs as he sheathed his sword and pressed his hand and head against the bough of a tree.

Chapter Three

Tavin

At night I hold my breath. At night I look up at the sky and witness the universe mocking my limitations. It casts its abyss over all things, coats the world and engulfs us in its turbulence. I remain here, held fast to the earth beneath my back, a helpless tenant to gravity. In the abyss I see a veritable bounty of orbs and fire. The all-consuming darkness, thick enough to swallow me without a thought, reveals a light that I can never hold — and so, painfully admonishes me for simply being.

I am a man. I have nothing else. Even the greatest king, while safely assured of his power, will one day lose everything he's ever touched to the turmoil of the blackness. The sky demands that I look inward and feel that one beautiful thing that is my own. I grasp at my selfness, and then I breathe again. Everything from nothing.

Praxis and Oil'ib stood tall despite their limping and abrasions, looking as exasperated as Tavin felt. Joy filled his mind at their return and brought forth a litany of questions. At least for the moment he had all his closest friends with him.

"But how?" Tavin pressed.

Praxis sat and rubbed his face, "We just ran. We didn't have a choice."

"Where were you?" Kendo insisted, while still sporting a wide grin from the sudden turn of events.

"After we escaped the blockhouse they would have had us, but then the fires started and we were able to get away. Quite literally—we used a smokescreen."

"All twelve of you?" Tavin questioned.

"Mostly. There was another cluster that broke off from the main rank and we met up. Then we ran like hell and the smoke was blowing that direction and nobody noticed us. Two were lost last night. They never made it back to camp." Praxis sighed to catch his breath. Sweat ran like a river between his blond brow ridges as he spoke. "We went around past the mines and then snuck up into the forest. It took forever for Oil'ib to find your trail, but we eventually wheeled around and here we are."

"Oil'ib found our trail?" Tavin asked dubiously. "And here I thought we had made ourselves invisible."

"Clearly you didn't," Praxis smirked under his serious eyes.

They both knew what such a trail meant. It had brought him his friends, but it could also bring his enemies.

Chance smiles upon those that ignore him, Tavin thought.

"Did you see what happened at the town?" Gannon asked spitting upon the ground as he finished the sentence. "The way you went you would have had a better view than we did. Come, tell us what happened."

"They were cutting off heads," Praxis stated as mildly as a summer breeze, which would have unsettled Tavin were he not used to Praxis's candor.

The groans of the other soldiers, however, reminded Tavin that their sadness was fresher than his.

"Around the square. It did look like they were mostly killing soldiers. I didn't see civilians."

"That's comforting," said Fenlo, a venomous sting in the words of the hotshot archer.

Tavin and his five closest friends: Seneca, Kendo, Gannon, Oil'ib and Praxis encircled Fallon, who paced and kneaded his hands nervously.

"Well, Fenlo, I'm sure you'll like to know that Clades is following us," Praxis retorted to the archer, a man that Tavin had never gotten along with.

The groans grew louder.

Tavin shook his head. "Where did you see him?"

"Yesterday around twilight," Praxis reported. "Oil'ib kept us out of his reach until nightfall, and in the morning he was out of sight."

"How many does he have?" Gannon asked, sounding more alarmed each time he spoke.

"Maybe uh, maybe forty or fifty," Oil'ib mumbled before Praxis could speak.

Gannon cursed aloud in unison with some of the other

soldiers.

"So now we're retreating to a fortress we may never reach, with animals at our back, and he's chasing us too? Fuck!"

"What would you have us do? Climb the trees?" Tavin retorted. "We're obviously going to continue this march whatever its chances."

Still Gannon continued.

"Greensboro was fucked from the beginning. They couldn't see what was happening? None of them? What was the captain's job? What were they supposed to do if not to protect us from that exact thing?"

"Gannon, it's not like any of us could have known about the mines," Kendo insisted softly.

"Then we have no right fighting this war. We're not prepared. We're not ready. We're just making a mess of things. And if the West is so clever then maybe they *should* take this country."

Silence and the breeze overlapped the hot boiling anger that was building in Tavin's brain. All he wanted was for his people to pull together in one direction. But they could not keep their mouths shut long enough. He did his best to stay even-tempered, his words came out slower than usual.

"Gannon. Even without the ambush, the moment their forces arrived in the fields, we were finished. There is a victory to be had, but it's not *here*. We need to get moving and find the high ground—*then* we'll go at Clades." Tavin put a hand on Gannon's shoulder. "I had a dream last night that I killed him and it seemed real to me. Okay? I know just how I'd fight him."

"Every problem can be solved with those swords and a

dream, right?" Gannon retorted sarcastically.

Seneca laughed.

"We're being chased by a heralded Western invader who decapitates the heads of surrendering men," Praxis interjected as he cleaned his brow with a rag, "In this case a sword is probably the best tool for the job,"

"You're all fucking enjoying this?" Gannon asked, quieter now, and Tavin thought he saw a tear in his eyes and felt ashamed. "It's not fun. This isn't like training camp when Solly had us playing war games. People are dying, and you want to engage him again? Why?"

"What would you have us do?" Seneca asked, ever the devil's advocate.

"Run. Run *now*, but not for the Tennessee fortress. We run southwest past the fortress. Down where it's warm year-round. Where the war will never reach. Kendo's family lives near some islands in the Gulf. I'd rather wait there and let the insane sort out their land disputes. Am *I* crazy?"

"Were I unattached I would have to agree," Seneca stated. "But I am not. My path is that fortress. Then the northeast after, if I am lucky."

Tavin could see Gannon was shaking from fear and wished he could agree with him, if for no other reason than to calm him.

Tavin spoke loud enough for all to hear, "I'm taking this group to the fortress, and I hope that somehow our people will find a way to stop this bleeding, but right now our numbers are strong and we can make a push... right *now*. But it has to be now. I *need* you with us Gannon," he pleaded. "Aren't we the same battalion that has fought the West three times? Aren't we still standing here talking about it? We're alive."

"But for how much longer?" Gannon asked quietly, as he turned his back to Tavin, then, seeing the faces of the crowd that watched them, turned around again. "How much longer for any of us? Continuing in this way seals the fate of every single one of us. Even the last man standing still dies in the end," Gannon said in a near whisper as he walked closer to Tavin.

Oil'ib approached Gannon and squeezed his shoulder. Gannon gazed ahead with a look of quiet resignation.

"We gain nothing retreating," Kendo urged.

"Gannon. You know Clades will pursue us wherever we go," Tavin finally admitted. "Running isn't an option."

Gannon cracked a brief smile.

"Fine, let's go to the fortress," Gannon sighed, then moved close to Tavin again, close enough that only the six of them could hear his words, "If all is lost, I only trust you five. I will not be wasting my life on strangers"

Tavin sank his head.

"Off we go then," Tavin stated, and helping Praxis from his seat on the ground, pointed their direction down the valley floor. "Oil'ib... the trail is yours."

With a silent burst from his feet, Oil'ib, the quiet hunter, lifted off and pushed the group ahead to begin the day's march. It was only with the most modest sense of timidity that Tavin took upon himself the leadership of their platoon of ragged survivors; some things just run in the family. Sergeant Fallon, though officially the highest-ranking member of the troupe, often deferred to the better judgments of men around him. It was this quality

that had made him so likeable in the early days of war following
the training camp. The leadership of Fallon had always come
with its own sense of autonomy. Those underneath him largely
ran themselves, although they were forced to fall into the lines of
poor Lieutenant Solly and the late Captain Vencin, who was surely
destroyed in the sacking of Greensboro. Now, Fallon looked a
nervous wreck, and his reliance on the ability of others to keep his
own mind safe and secure had grown beyond his own control. So,
it was with great pity, and only a spoonful of pride, that Tavin took
the reins from the Sergeant.

I will not tell these people what to do, Tavin thought, *I
will show them. I will walk in steps that demand to be followed
and they will reach higher than they ever could on their own. Yes,
Mother, you were right. I did become my father.*

As the day waned, they followed Oil'ib's trail, or what
he judged to be a good one. There were several times where Tavin
could not wait any longer as Oil'ib stood staring a two separate
breaks in the trees and plowed ahead trusting nothing but his gut.
Often to the protests of Oil'ib.

"If you would have let me finish, I would have chosen the
left!"

"Well then next time choose the damn left," Tavin
seethed. "We don't have all day, you can do your best from here."

And Oil'ib would do his best. Their path was somewhat
smoother thanks to his eye for game trails.

"Deer are incredibly lazy," Oil'ib would insist. "If you
wanna know which way is easiest follow a deer trail."
Each night, huddled around the faint light of a campfire, Tavin
gathered Fallon, Oil'ib, and Praxis around their lone map of

the Tennessee region and pressed the compass gently upon its center, resting on whatever uneven surface they managed to make into a table. Fallon needed to be there. He had some additional knowledge of troop movements. Tavin needed Oil'ib for his instinctual knowledge of terrain, which he had gained through his years of childhood spent roaming in the Pennsylvania wilderness under the wing of his trapper father. Praxis possessed a genius perpendicular to Tavin's and would inevitably, if given long enough to study the maps and surroundings, come up with an idea or two that Tavin had not considered.

Praxis had that certain intelligence that was built up over a lifetime of study. He was not so adept at philosophical musings or on the fly conversation, which requires an inward wisdom: such things came out in Tavin's conversations with Seneca. Nor did Praxis have smarts that were bought from a school, such as Kendo, who was raised in a wealthy family and attended a school his whole childhood. Or like Gannon, who had attended the music conservatory in New England and could play any instrument he touched. Praxis had smarts built like a pyramid, with a foundation of long hours reading in the loft of his family farm. Knowledge that fermented into keen astuteness through longer hours of thinking while picking citrus. It could be seen in the deep tan skin that faded out from the edges of his face and into the folds around his eyes. Tavin could tell Praxis had an idea by how those sharp blue eyes cut about the map, flashing in the twinkling of the campfire. It was that same evasive motions that, when translated to the movement of the platoon across the rolling hills, kept Clades and his men at a distance. The flashes of crimson and burnished gold armor glinting between the trees had been a rare sight. But memories were enough to keep the platoon pressing forward at a near untenable pace, staying ahead of bloodshed.

It was a transcendent spring day when the platoon descended the mountains and into the grassy steppes that would need to be crossed to reach the Tennessee fortress and safety amongst the core of the Eastern forces in the territory. Somewhere in between lay the desolate ruins of the near-ancient city of Nashville. Though Tavin could not see the shadow of the ruins in the distance, he felt their approach in his joints. It was not until he faced the idea of passing through the heart of the ruins that he had actually noticed the pain. The idea had been Praxis's, of course, and Tavin was unable to deny the logic behind it around the fire the previous night. It was their hope that the gold demon would not follow into such a taboo and superstitious place. Then they could continue to the fortress without harassment.

The trail out of the mountains was steep and knotted, and the constant flexion of the joints was driving him mad, like a child that would not stop asking when they could sit down and rest. He cursed Praxis silently. But Praxis had brought them Oil'ib. And Oil'ib brought his skills as a hunter. His steady supply of forest hare, and the occasional white tail deer had saved the platoon from having to eat their boots.

As they reached the grassy expanse of the plains and steppes that would lead them to Nashville, Tavin gazed out across the flowing blades of green and glinting sunlight at the patchy forests that lay about the flat ground in the distance. The sunlight of the open ground was already making him sweaty and uncomfortable. Crossing the lake of grassland would be a hot affair in the midday sun, and though he was excited to reach the far tree line and the promise of clear creek water, he suggested to Fallon that the men be allowed to rest at the tree line before venturing out. Fallon was only too happy to oblige. Tavin was equally happy to sit down upon a sandy granite rock, kick out his heels and think about the turns of fortunes that had led them to this place.

Their training camp had been a grueling one, made of violent degradation and rebuilding of men throughout the humid overbearing summer months in Kentucky. Out of that strain, friendships blossomed with the five men that he now held as brothers in his heart. They had witnessed destruction and victory together, seeing themselves as successful defenders of numerous villages. Their closeness had been why all six of them ended up in the medical tent after eating the same loaf of bad bread from a tavern. They had struggled through it together on sick cots, tossing and turning with burning fevers and the clammy white flesh of ergot poisoning —hallucinating and drooling obscenities at invisible threats, screaming with joy and crying in painful hysteria. Allegedly it was that terrible fate that allowed a strange gift. A gift that had managed to keep them alive from there on out and had seen the six of them become a driving force for victory upon the battlefield. Tavin still found it hard to believe, but thought the looming shadow of their defeat in Greensboro had clouded his judgment.

Stretched out upon his cool rock in the shade of heavy sycamore trees, Tavin closed his eyes and peered into the black void of thought, keeping it as empty as he could with the expectancy of the gift—the vision that was more feeling than eyesight. He could sense Seneca tending to the foot of the soldier suffering from trench foot, and his nose crinkled just as Seneca's was. Out of sight behind the turn of trees, Praxis and Kendo stood debating the history of the Western theocracy and Tavin could feel their conversation without hearing it, like a rapping of fingertips upon his mind.

In the distance, Gannon was emptying his bladder, and Oil'ib was approaching from the back of the formation. Tavin opened his eyes expectantly and watched as his friend walked toward him with lumbering strides.

The gift left him as he allowed his thoughts to have voices again. He wanted badly to call it a fluke, a hallucination. But their experience on the battlefield argued against that. The two ideas didn't marry well in his mind. Perhaps other factors were at work. Perhaps their minds were slipping from so many days away from home.

"Have you guys ever thought we could just be crazy?" he had told them.

He kept that cynical mindset until the day he saw a blade without looking. No, felt it. Feeling the enemy's weapon cutting through the air at Seneca's neck, he had spun around to stop it, placing his own blade in between, as if on instinct. The advantage afforded was less than a second's time, a mere tremor of thought or twitch of muscle. But that had made all the difference to Seneca. Those moments, occurring more and more, forced his mind into a maze.

Oil'ib walked like a slow giant to where Tavin was seated. A simple man, Oil'ib walked like one. His long face and long nose were always pointed at the ground, as if he were looking for something he had misplaced in the tall grass. His height was looming and gawky despite the muscles of tough and knotted sinew. A dented and scraped silver ring was around one finger, and Oil'ib turned it anxiously in subconscious worry. He wore the stained dark jacket of an Eastern soldier around his shoulder like a cape, and in his pack kept the fur of a large grizzly bear, which had drawn the jealousy of every soldier when Oil'ib curled up inside it during fireless nights. A devoutly honest man, even honest about his psychological shortcomings, Oil'ib's awkward conversation skills, inability to read body language, and tendency to sleep in every morning, made him frustrating. But his honesty made it impossible to hate the man, and when he brought meat back to camp, he was celebrated and looked at his boots as he smiled with yellow crooked teeth.

Tavin wondered who had agreed to marry this man, but then also why any woman should not.

"Listen—Oil'ib," Tavin started, before Oil'ib had a chance to explain his approach. "I still don't fully understand how you guys found us, but I'm fairly certain we'd all be dead if you hadn't. I won't ever forget that," Tavin said, patting his friend on the back while Oil'ib joined him on the gritty granite stone.

"Oh, Praxis—uh—Praxis came up with the idea. I just followed your trail," Oil'ib remarked keeping his gaze upon his boots.

"You make it sound so easy?"

"Yeah. So, so, when it comes to hunting and trapping game you have to remember, you know, people—people behave like animals. And they are the easier to track,"
Tavin tried to draw Oil'ib's eyes away from his boots by sitting up but failed. "Well, we are animals after all…"

"Think about it. All animals run a certain way when

they're scared. They'll—what's the word…"

"So, we're about a quarter mile from our crossing point?" Tavin asked, trying to change the subject.

Oil'ib changed his gaze from boots to sky. He was silent.

Oil'ib required patience. Reclining further on the rock, watching the leaves above fluttering across the breeze, Tavin wondered whether Oil'ib ignored people or simply was thinking too hard to hear or interpret. The difference between the two bothered Tavin. In his mind's eye, he knew Oil'ib was staring off to the clouds and groping through his own mind in a clumsy search for words.

"So, they'll run to familiar ground, or friendly ground, whatever. They'll basically establish like—patterns. Over time you can predict an animal's movements, um— pretty easily. That's probably what Clades—Clades is doing with us."

Tavin laughed heartily.

"I'm sure you are right about Clades though. I've had the same thought myself, which is the only reason I agreed to Praxis's plan. My father used to talk about the old ruins a bit himself, they ended up playing a role in the first war. Deserters would escape persecution. Enemy cavalry would stop in and hide there while scouting. But most people are smart to avoid them, the unstable ground, pits, poisons, predators that like the darkness."

Tavin sat up straight, realizing fully just where they were headed, and for an instant considered a change of plans.

"Oh well," he said with enough optimism to cover his uneasiness. "That's why we have you anyway." He patted Oil'ib on the back, who remained stoic. "You'll see the predators before they see us, right?"

"Well, um…"

"Yes?"

"Well—there's stuff following us right now, kinda…"

"Like what?" Tavin was aghast with frustration. "What do you mean? What stuff? You just mean Clades?"

"Good god can we talk about something else?" Gannon said walking past them.

"Are we offending?" Tavin snapped back.

Gannon sat for a moment upon the boulder and pulled Tavin into a rough squeeze with one hairy arm.

"Stop worrying everybody," Gannon said under his breath. His tone was Gannon's signature brand of upbeat and cheery sarcasm.

"Who are we worrying? People weren't already worried? Oh, that's right— our talking is going to start worrying everyone."

Gannon lost interest and walked away. "It's bad karma."

Tavin shook his head. "Whatever. Oil'ib what were you saying?" Tavin urged, wanting as much information as possible before they attempted their trek across the open field.

"It's a bad time of year for this crossing. I mean there's— umm— a good amount of wolves around. And I think we attracted more since the first one," Oil'ib said.

Tavin took a moment and scanned his periphery.

"Sen and I spotted one yesterday, and another this morning," Oil'ib continued. "Wolves do a lot of—wolves like hunting in the grassy areas, kinda like this."

Tavin looked over to see that Oil'ib was smiling to himself faintly, and turning the thick silver ring on his finger with nervous twists of his dusty fingers. Tavin leaned forward so that only Oil'ib could hear him.

"We're crossing at the narrowest point we can find. Not much else we can do."

"We have to cross, there's no doubt, though, uh, if Clades is above on that ridge he'll see us a mile out. It would be, umm, nice to lose him here," Oil'ib lamented.

"Are you also nervous about the ruins?" Tavin pressed, sensing that he could get a real answer from Oil'ib now.

"My father, umm—dad just always said to stay away from them. He would never set traps in sight of—of 'em."

"And lord knows what our mothers would say," Tavin grinned somberly. "I'm going to start getting people around to move. I'll warn them to be extra aware too. Thanks, Oil'ib."

Upon hearing his name, Oil'ib finally made eye contact with Tavin for a brief moment. His eyes were two morose walnuts beneath a heavy brow and a receding line of straight black hair.

"You better start preparing to march now, especially if there's anything special you want to do about these wolves, so that you can be on time with all of us."

Oil'ib's only reply was a smirk over top of his recessive chin, as he scratched the patchy stubble of a goatee with his fingers and looked out again across the field.

Tavin roused the others from their brief respite and then led them down the rest of the slopes and entered the sea of long grass. His sore ankle was glad to find the even grade of flat land. The mass of men crept through the field in a thick line, their hands resting upon the hilts of their weapons, ready to draw at the slightest glimpse of strange movement. Oil'ib caught up to them as the last of the men were just entering the expanse. He complained about needing more time to get his boots straight, but Tavin was already tuning out everything, aside from the swishing of wool jackets upon the thick grass and the occasional creaking of a far-off tree.

"Your nine o'clock," Oil'ib said to Tavin, when they were no more than a quarter through the crossing.
Their target, a line of heavy green, another outcrop of forest, was still a ways ahead.

As he looked in the hinted direction, Tavin caught the shifting figures of several gray wolves, lurking in patchy shadows along the tree line behind them. He would have never noticed them, and though he dared not to raise his voice, Tavin nodded in recognition and inwardly blessed Oil'ib's father for providing the young man with such a skill.

"How far to that line of trees?" Fallon asked in a winded tone, pushing his porridge-pale face ahead to catch up with Tavin.

"Two miles?" Tavin posited.

"A little over," Oil'ib remarked.

Tavin looked back across the rank and file of haggard faces and paused upon Seneca's, whose trepidation was absent from his friendly face. But Seneca nervously snapped his fingers as he walked closer.

The road they had traveled was now barely a thin and dust-beaten compression on the long grass around them.

"There's thirty-three of us. Three columns of eleven is better than a long line. We move out together. Oil'ib and I will take point on the center column. Praxis take the left. Fallon take right. Let's haul ass! And we'll rest when we get to that next tree line."

"The wind is whipping like crazy out here," Fallon noted,

"Perhaps we wait."

Tavin considered, the gusts were growing stronger outside of the cover of boughs and leaf-burdened branches.

"Oil'ib how far behind is Clades?" he asked.

"Umm."

"You're best guess. Please," Tavin asked again.

"Can't be more than an hour," Oil'ib presented with hesitance.

"We've had the high ground the last couple days." Praxis said. "It never made sense for them to attack. If we wait here though they can run right down that hill and crush us."

Seneca offered only a shrug.

"We cannot wait for the wind," Tavin said aloud for all to hear. He was sorry that he had to directly subvert sergeant Fallon in front of the men.

The sergeant only gazed at him from worried eyes and tightened his lips. In the distance and off to the side, Tavin thought he saw a creeping motion in the long grass. The wind buffeted their group again, and following a spike in anxious energy, he led the men onward through a deepening chill in what had been a warm day. The wind was increasingly blowing away their comfort and staunching their voices, making conversation too difficult to keep up. Tavin saw the formation of men behind him falling to shambles. Some men were noticeably limping. and others were wandering to the edges of the path in the thrall of a daydream.

"No! Stay together! Keep moving!" His words, even from Tavin's substantial pipes, failed to pierce the wind.

It was with a steady quickness that the wolves took form in Tavin's eye. As he yelled for the men to circle up, the first of the four-legged beasts had already begun encircling the platoon. Men drew their steel and waved it warningly at huge grey dogs with gleaming canines. The wolves emerged like phantoms from the tawny grass, stopping to test the ankles, drooling a hideous hunger and yipping away from the blades of swinging men. Tavin motioned the men around him, and found himself between Oil'ib and Seneca at the edge of the circle of soldiers. He drew his own swords and kept them in front of him, the cruel points threatening to prick the first animal to test his vigor. He dared not separate his eyes from the beasts as they circled and circled, adding to their numbers from the tall grass in a constant stream.

Somewhere in his mind he knew that Gannon, Kendo, and Praxis were close by on his back left, but he couldn't peel his eyes from the large black wolf in front of him that bared his teeth. The pitch-dark fur of a creature accentuated the fury in its glowing cerulean eyes. Tavin could not help but wonder whether the scoundrel saw the same cold threat in his eyes. Look at you. *We are cut from the same cloth.*

The wolf dove for his feet so suddenly that Tavin thought his foot would be gone as he pulled it back in haste. He swung at its head, but only felt the gentle rasping of hair as his razor skimmed the outstanding fur at the scruff of the wolf's neck. The coal black menace recoiled as well and let loose a savage growl.

Tavin allowed himself to look back for a second. He saw Praxis straight behind him, struggling with a wolf of his own: a gray and white thing that jumped and skidded playfully before Praxis's blade. Another man had managed to connect his sword with the leg of a wolf, which sounded out with a splintering smack and a yelp before it limped away into the long grass.

Tavin turned toward the black fiend again, but it was gone. There were several more that were circling, but none addressed Tavin or his blades. He looked again to his rear in time to see the coal-colored streak of fur assaulting the back of their circle. The men there, strangers to Tavin, broke before the onslaught. Tavin cursed their luck as he joined the retreat to the far tree line, which was still a good six hundred meters away. There was no other choice once the others began to flee, and he fumed at the cowardice that had broken them. As he pumped his legs forward to catch up with the fleet-footed Seneca, Tavin knew a war of attrition was happening behind him. He could hear the ripping of flesh and shouts of men as the first victims were swarmed to the ground by the fearless and hungry masses of fur.

Swords swung about as man waged desperate battle with the animals.

Grass parted to his racing feet. The pounding resounded in his temples. Dry blades of grass whipped in the wind and pelted his chest. To his right, a wolf caught up to his pace and began nipping at Tavin's heels. He swung down hard with his right as he ran and connected with the beast's skull in a sickening thud. Ahead of him on his left, he saw Oil'ib trip, fall, and become immediately covered by the savaging pounce of gray and white. Tavin increased his speed, his legs tight with stress and threatening to snap like a taut rope. He swallowed the pain and increased his breathing, pumping hard against the uneven surface. The hair on the back of his neck stood on end from the snarling and screaming behind him. Then, he lurched forward in a sudden and vicious lunge and delivered a devastating upward kick to the ribs of Oil'ib's attacker. The wolf had latched on to Oil'ib's forearm, which, when wrenched free, revealed a blood-soaked sleeve. Tavin got his friend to his feet without a word between his heavy and straining breaths.

Tavin would not stop shaking. Even after they had reached the safety of the tree line and taken the time to rest and regroup. Even after Seneca had mended Oil'ib's arm with careful stitches and ample balm and bandage. Even after they had put more distance between themselves and the valley of the wolf attack and found shelter in a high rocky area bordered by pines. Even then, Tavin could feel the tremor in his feet and hands and tried to calm himself with deep breaths as he joined his friends at their campfire. He coughed when he inhaled some of the smoke, found a seat beside Seneca upon a decomposing log, and set his feet to warm by the low flames.

Across from them Oil'ib, Kendo, Praxis and Gannon were devouring the last of their dried meats and bread.

"Do you need to smoke or drink?" Seneca asked him, motioning to his backpack, which contained medical and recreational supplies.

"Cannabis, tobacco, opium?" Seneca offered again, "Are you in pain? I already got Oil'ib squared away."
Tavin looked across the fire at Oil'ib, who seemed to be sleeping sitting up, slouched upon a mound of rocks, a portrait of blissful exhaustion. In the hand of his bandaged arm was cradled Seneca's elegant dark wood pipe. A faint ember still glowing somewhere within.

"Why?" Tavin asked him.

"You're hurt."

Tavin looked down at his left calf and realized it was bleeding.

"Hadn't noticed."

Tavin took the pipe from Oil'ib and allowed Seneca to top it off. Seneca wrapped his calf tightly with cotton. He drew in a deep breath of smoke and after holding it a few seconds released a cloud with a cough. As quickly as he took in the smoke his mind relaxed. He felt secure. The soldiers were gathering around in a cluster of miniature fires. Kendo, the best archer, took his familiar perch in a nearby tree—scanning the surrounding forest with his bow at the ready. Before Tavin's leg began to hurt, the opium and cannabis had already leached to his brain, a pleasant melting sensation. He slid to the ground in a humming trance and let his head rest upon the log.

"That instinct keeps showing up. That feeling in your head that was never there before," Tavin intoned. The others nodded as if their thoughts had been on similar veins.

"When we were running?" Gannon surmised.

"Yeah," He replied. "I knew Praxis was going to swing at a wolf, and when the wolf was moving at him—I didn't need to see it. It's not always during fighting. Sometimes, just when I'm really relaxed, I feel like I know where each of you are in relation to myself. Or if my nerves are—I don't know. I know it's strange, but I can pick up on things. Not all the time, but it's gotten stronger since we left Greensboro. Maybe the panic increases it."

"It is strange," Seneca reassured him, "but I have been having the same symptoms. And every time it happens, it feels a little bit like when we were sick. That same sensation in my scalp and mouth and the world seems to…breathe." Seneca threw his arms up in a desperate explanation.

"Things that wouldn't normally breathe," Praxis

exclaimed. "Like the trunk of a tree, or your own hand."
Kendo shifted his weight forward, finding a way to somehow look even taller.

"It keeps getting louder," Kendo said, as if wanting to add his thoughts but not knowing how.

"I know," Seneca said. "And it's never anyone else. Just you guys. That first battle we were in last spring. It was just sort of a feeling, but it keeps growing like a painless migraine. Mostly in battle, it seems. I think Tavin's right about the panic and struggle."

"Well if it stays like this, then it's an advantage, but if it gets worse. I mean, I don't want it to get out of control. I don't want to forget about the things I love," Gannon said, a tone of resistance in his voice.

Gannon's eyes seemed a little desperate to Tavin and his hand groped subconsciously to his mandolin, usually amongst his belongings, only to find that it had been left in Greensboro.

"I have to get a new mandolin, too," Gannon bemoaned.

Tavin smiled. "I don't think it'll affect your ability to play music," he said with a laugh, coughing when he did. "It's too subtle. It's the strangest fucking thing and I'm guessing that's why we're all so worried about it, still—it's tiny, minute. It probably wouldn't matter if we weren't pushing ourselves as hard as we have been."

"And yet I wouldn't be alive without it," Praxis stated. "None of us. Seneca saved my life that second battle in Kentucky. I can't get it out of my head."

Tavin craned his neck to see down the ridge into the valley and saw campfires lighting up.

"Look," he said.

Peering over the edge, they saw the twinkling of their pursuers farther down in the black wrinkle.

"I hope they made friends with the wolves, too." Tavin mused remembering the black wolf with cerulean eyes.

He rolled into his makeshift bedding then, too tired and disappointed to continue talking further. While he tossed and turned before finally finding sleep, Tavin worried blindly about their destination. He imagined the ruins of Nashville without being able to see them, a feeling of being lost in a maze of high stone walls.

Chapter Four

March 2717
Just North of Nashville, Tennessee

Seneca

Life is such exhausting work. Eat, sleep, shit, wash, run around, and repeat. Pile anything on top and it can be too much. Sometimes death sounds restful. To not exist, no worries, no fears, no enemies—how nice it would be to not have to fight every day to keep the body from deteriorating. The damn thing wouldn't let me anyway though. The minute the blade is held to my throat it will kick and bite—scream for its survival. We talk of the mind having control over the body, but maybe the mind is just along for the ride.

Seneca breathed deeply, held it, sat up and glanced in all directions. His bed was a soft mound of pine needles in the nook of an old tree that cradled him comfortably. The sun had not been up long, its golden rays barely pierced the canopy of dark green pine boughs enough to cast shafts of ethereal light upon the glen.

His heart still beat heavily from the excitement of a dream. In the deep slumber, he had been captured by Clades, who stood larger than life and wore armor rusted to death. Clades had been about to torture him when, in a fortunate twist, he managed to release his hands from their binds. The dream had been turbulent and violent, with Seneca flinging himself upon the giant brute and punching with all his mental might. Yet no matter how hard he struck, his dream-world fists never landed a solid blow. Clades had laughed a deep and rasping laugh before plunging his beautiful sword into Seneca's abdomen. Rather than die he had awoken, remembering where he was.

Seneca stretched and counted his friends. They lay close by, huddled within their sleeping furs, forming a line between him and the other men at the center of the camp. He recognized Kendo, stirring a little farther off, the restless hawk-faced archer laying his head upon his quiver of arrows. There were only twenty-four survivors left now. How many had they started with? Thirty-four? A man lost for every day on the run. Despite all the effort and sacrifice, they were barely halfway to the fortress in Tennessee. Crossing the territory from the western edge, where they had been charged with guarding Greensboro, seemed to Seneca like an endless odyssey and he yearned to reach the destination as much as he craved returning home.

Such hopes were best left unspoken, even disregarded if possible. Already he felt himself becoming tough to the death that he witnessed. The deaths that he caused had accelerated the process. As he stared up through the shafts of early morning light he wondered if he would ever give into such apathy toward his own death. Surely, that thought carried immediate disaster. Surely, one was already dead if such thought patterns took over. He swore to himself to never fall into such a trap. However far his psyche deteriorated in the bath of war, he would never let it take his will. A general soreness blanketed his body and he pulled his thick bear fur, a generous gift from Oil'ib, tighter around him and adjusted his position in the nook of tree trunks. By savoring however many minutes of rest remained before Tavin or Fallon roused the men, he hoped to quell the numbness in his head and the soreness in his body.

Somewhere out there that golden demon is hot on our trail. I wonder how long they sleep in after first light. No matter, we all sleep with our swords.

His breath steamed out of the hole in the fur where his face hid, he watched the vapor dissipate in the cool morning air. Up here where they had made camp the ground was dry and chilled and the earth smelled of pine needles and dust. When Tavin's muted calls finally found his ears, Seneca hid his head in the furs one last time, soaking in his own warmth and humidity. Then he lunged upward to greet his friend before Tavin could shake him and ruin his composure.

"Why so nervous?" Tavin asked, as Seneca bounded up.

"*Why so nervous,*" Seneca mocked, smiling though he tried to suppress it. "Is it the wolves, or the guy who chops off heads, *Seneca?*"

Tavin laughed and his chuckling brought forth Seneca's laughter as well.

"Alright, alright." Seneca slapped Tavin's back. "Let's get these guys moving before they sleep to death."

Having escaped from the bulk of the wolf threat, the

survivors had travelled eight days southward through thick forests, constantly thinking of the shadow of Clades close behind. A few times they had seen scouts running ahead of the larger group at their heels, reporting on their movements. Many arrows had been wasted on such scouts, and only Kendo, whose skill with the bow could not be denied, had managed to bring one down. Clades and his battalion were of unnatural stamina. No matter how hard they pushed themselves, it seemed they never gained any ground between their pursuers. Around the nightly campfires they often shared admiration for their chaser, who would stop at nothing to keep them from warning the East about Greensboro.

Unable to rest anymore in the growing brightness, Seneca removed himself from his sleeping furs and began packing them away in his sack. He sipped water from his canteen and chewed upon salted venison. He nudged at Tavin, who sprang up as if he had been seeing the same dream. His friend rubbed his eyes and grumbled about water. Seneca told him to wake the others while he checked upon the various wounds amongst the men. Tavin nodded and was soon out of his nest.

Seneca spent an hour going from soldier to soldier, inspecting wounds for infection and giving away the last of his Sulphur salve. Soon his supplies would be gone. He had already been forced to perform two amputations to remove infected limbs. Both had been caused by the wolves and festered over the week. The men would have died if the infection were allowed to spread; but unfortunately, they died anyway, too weak to properly heal from such a surgery.

I'm hardly a surgeon anymore. I don't think like a surgeon. I don't act like a surgeon. I am more and more like the patient, in desperate need for something of which I have no knowledge, Seneca scolded himself.

The other men were packing their things and wetting their palates while Seneca approached the last of his patients. Oil'ib had barely survived with his arm—which would no doubt be horribly scarred—but Oil'ib had been healing without infection. Seneca was quite proud of his work on the sutures. And he was happy that he need not amputate, for it had been the last of his sutures and would have been a sad waste to cut off the arm.

"How is it feeling today Oil'ib?"

Oil'ib was still in bed, stretched out languidly beneath his own collection of pelts. His eyes were open and gazing at the sky beyond the trees. When Oil'ib did not answer, Seneca gave him a soft kick in the leg, tapping with the toe of his leather boot.

"You should get out of bed," Seneca added, "you don't want to fall behind the retreat again."

"It feels better," Oil'ib said, ignoring the latter statement. "It still burns, but not all the time."

"That's good to hear. Do you want the last of the salve? Why not do the honors?"

Oil'ib thought silently.

"You might as well use it. It would be nice for at least one arm to survive."

"Umm. Okay," Oil'ib said. "Thank you."

Seneca handed Oil'ib the nearly empty tin, then looked around to see that the rest of the group was almost ready to form up and begin the day's hike.

"Hurry up though," he added to Oil'ib. "Looks like we'll be leaving soon."

Oil'ib's procrastination in the mornings, something which happened almost every morning, was annoying to Seneca. However, Oil'ib always seemed to catch up, even if he fell far behind initially, and sometimes when he caught up he did so carrying fresh game. This made it hard to fault him for his sloth. Instead, he focused on his contentedness to help his friend with a wound and proceeded to prepare himself for the day's retreat, sure that there was nothing he could do to prevent his friend's tardiness.

Replacing his scant medical supplies in his bag and stuffing the furs around the more fragile possessions, Seneca listened. Tavin, Praxis, and Fallon were having a serious conversation.

"City is coming up, we're almost on it now," Praxis offered.

Tavin paced. "I'm still on the edge about it."

"We're already so close," Praxis replied, perplexed. "We don't have the luxury of options. Plus, in the ruins we could set up an ambush. At least have a better chance than out here in the woods." He traced a line along the map the trio had spread out upon the flat of a boulder.

"How do you know it's called Nashville?" Seneca asked as he approached. "There is no name on the map."

Praxis looked up at him and smiled, a nostalgic twinkle in his eyes.

"My mother was a collector of history books. Some of the first books I learned to read were old geographies."

"Oh," Seneca replied, interested. "You never tell us these things."

"It wasn't relevant until now," Praxis stated.

"Tavin," Fallon pressed with an assertiveness he was not

known for. "What would your *father* do?"

"My father?" Tavin repeated, biting on his thumbnail. "He would never have gotten himself into this situation in the first place."

Seneca laughed aloud. "He would fly away before getting stuck like this."

"Let's assume he did. Let's assume for a moment he's like the rest of us," Fallon insisted.

Tavin thought, shrugged. "He would end this retreat. He would go into that city, and he'd wait for them. And if they showed—he'd destroy them—and never speak of it again."

By this time Fenlo, Gannon, and Kendo had joined them, attracted to the sounds of conversation. Fallon sighed and agreed; the young sergeant looked many years older than when the war started. He pouted at Seneca with a face of flaccid resignation and ran his hand through his thinning black curls.

"Let's move out sergeant," Tavin told him, patting him on the back before striding off.

The sergeant resigned to the gathering of the men, and he even swatted at Oil'ib to make him hurry. Seneca looked down at the map where Tavin's finger had just been pointing. A gray blob showing the paths in and out of its center. A tiny skull had been drawn on the gray.

Seneca had never seen one of the Old World ruins before. The cities were the last time capsules of a forgotten age. Awe inspiring and mind bending, they were rarely visited by sane people. Just like everyone else, Seneca had heard the stories since he was a boy. His grandfather would tell him dark tales when they would sit around the fire at night: tales of how the old cities were the place where society first collapsed—the epicenter of the fall—where all constructs and social graces were stripped down to instinct and violence. The ghosts of destruction haunted overgrown roads and collapsed towers. Perhaps there was something to the superstitious fear, or perhaps it was merely the overarching reminder that man had failed before and could fail again that kept people away. There *were* the practical fears as well, which existed alongside the supernatural.

Still, he could not disagree that the plan to lose Clades' pursuit was a good one. If they ever planned on making it to the fortress, decisive action was necessary. They lost ground to the beast every day and continuing at their current pace would be deadly.

"I suppose if the Westerners are as afraid of the old cities as we are, then perhaps Clades won't follow," Praxis said, reiterating his feelings as they fell in beside the others.

They marched through the warming morning, watching the leaves begin to glow with a richer green. As the morning turned to noon, it became clear they were approaching the ruins. The ground leveled into a nearly flat grade, uneven clusters of strange mounds and rises scattered throughout thinning undergrowth. It looked as if giants slept beneath the layers of plants and soil. The trees themselves were growing sparser and the number of species more diverse. Trees that Seneca had never seen before lined a now wide and grassy road on which they walked—trees that lacked a single branch but grew in circular sections to great height before terminating in tufts of fern-like branches.

A long stretch of flat grass and low-lying shrubs cut a straight line north where, in the distance ahead, they could see the ruins awaiting them. Many green and gray irregular monoliths stretched up from the ground like a crown of shattered glass.

"We follow this I assume?" Seneca said, motioning to the road.

Praxis nodded and the group continued cautiously down the path, the rest of the battalion following in silent horror. When Fallon had let them know of their destination there had been no demur, which had surprised Seneca. Yet it was clear by the tepid silence and sidelong glances at each other's swords that the men were unsure of the plan. Years of stories and lessons were crashing against twenty-four minds, and the men walked with counterfeited boldness. As the road led them on, the scenery continued to change in jagged breaks. Small buildings rose alongside the road with no windows and no roofs, made of thick heavy blocks covered in lichen, mold, and moss. Inside the naked walls, lived shadows where the light was blocked by the branches of opportunistic trees. The soldiers looked in upon the darkness but stayed close to the middle of the path, not wanting to find out if anything more lived inside.

"We don't have anything like this where I'm from," said one of them.

It was true the only building material around was log, brick, and stone. This gray and seamless material that formed smashed domes, crinkled blocks, and cracked walls was a mystery to Seneca. He longed to get closer and examine these strange structures, which were growing more frequent as they paced the miles to the heart of the city.

Inside each shaded outcropping lurked strange noises and a hollow breeze. Some structures looked as if the stone had been poured into one complete shape, while others seemed to have been made by stacking gray rocks of perfectly identical proportion into various designs. The sights only became more terrifyingly wondrous as they marched deeper into the city ruins and Seneca gazed up and around as if he were seeing the world for the first time.

"Come on, we have to keep our pace up," Tavin said, still half dazed himself. "Kendo, if anything moves shoot it."

Moss and ivy grew like robes over the broken bones of the ancient structures. Here and there steel beams jutted from the ground or from the cloaked buildings. They could see different metals as well, some seeming to shine like silver though lacking the correct form, but most had long since tarnished. The buildings stretched even taller until finally, in a moment he would never forget, they saw the cityscape emerge in its towering and broken glory.

"Holy hell," Seneca muttered.

All of them stood in a line at the crest of a hill where the road came to the climax of its slope before easing down into the heart of the ruins. Beyond and around it stood the massive towers from childhood imaginations. Only a couple retained an upright posture. Most were broken or floundered upon each other at shifting angles.

Hundreds of years had made a graveyard of giants, their skeletons reclaimed by the green nets of nature, glinting dimly in the bright noon sun. In his mind's eye, Seneca was sure he could see the ghost of a pristine city with unspeakable technology. And for a moment he was saddened, as if he had lost something he had never owned.

People are a failed experiment. What are we clinging to? Seneca thought as he gazed at the rotting cityscape.

Their inspection of the scenery was disrupted when they heard shouting in the distance behind them. There were not many sources that could have made the noise, and the group doubled their pace, remembering why they had entered the ruins in the first place. They were lightly jogging now, a mass of men breathing loudly through the exertion of overworked limbs, climbing over twisted obstacles and turning down corridors hooded by the shadows. The road took a downward turn until it was broken completely in half, a deep chasm separating them from the other side of the road.

"Looks like we gotta jump," Oil'ib said, taking a leap across the gap and making it with plenty of room.

The gap was only five feet or so, easily clearable, but the depth was undeterminable and threatening. Seneca peered over the edge, saw the layers of black rock that had split to form the cavern. He watched as a crumb of it fell and disappeared into the inky void. Backing up for momentum he took a breath, held it, and sprinted forward, his final step landing closer to the edge than he meant. As he hit the far side, Tavin grabbed him and pulled him to a safe distance as he released his breath. The rest of the soldiers followed suit, jumping across onto the path below. Their knees buckled as they made their landing. Every soldier was absolutely quiet, reverent as if attending a funeral. Their slapping boots echoed against high walls and the depths of slanted caves beneath them. Seneca jerked his head around at every distant sound, each crumbling grain of rock and rustling of birds taking off from their advance scrambled his nerves.

They reached the denser center of the ruins. It was here that a vast grove of elm trees had taken root. Even amongst the towering ruins the trees were imposing, a massive coronet. There was a stream of water trickling from the center of the grove, where a spring was gushing forth from a perfectly circular hole in the ground. Seneca figured the abundance of water had led to the massive population of flora, and led their wave of exploration into the grove with keen interest.

"Let's see them follow us here," Praxis said with a satisfied smile.

Tavin gripped his knees to catch his breath. "I figure there are three routes they could reach us from." He motioned with his arm at the intersection of two artificial valleys between looming scaffolds.

"Splinter off by fours and keep watch," Tavin ordered to the men with a nod. "The sun's out. It's warming up—this is a good spot."

Seneca did not splinter off. Instead, he watched from below the elm boughs as Kendo traversed a narrow staircase of crumbling stone to a high platform, which gave him at least twenty-five feet of elevation. Like a willing falcon, the archer scanned the streets below, throwing hand signals to Tavin accounting for every sound and movement. His bow and sharp eye offered an advantage on any surprise attacks.

Seneca hoped that the Western men held ruins in the same distaste as Easterners. He had the sudden urge to ask Kendo more about this but did not wish to break the tranquil silence or the white noise of wind whispering through the colossus. Rations were passed around in similar quiet. They gathered at the base of an elm tree that had sprouted a little deeper into the grove, comfortable with their initial scout to meander back together. While Tavin passed their dry rations around, Fallon was nice enough to throw some food up to Kendo, lest he yield his position. Seneca finished his meal of jerky and bread quicker than he meant. The alien nature of the skeleton city was enough displacement to cause a general anxiety. Yet, there was also a warm breeze and the smell of plants upon the air that was inviting and filled him with a conflicting desire for exploration.

"Anyone want to scout around a bit?" he asked. "I'm not going alone."

"I'll come," Praxis volunteered.

Everyone else declined, opting instead to get some sleep while the sun warmed the area. The first spring birds were chirping and flitting around the heights. Squirrels and rabbits could be seen if one held still long enough to observe the creases between trees and the stony remains. Seneca and Praxis meandered with care across the sunlit turf before coming upon a sloped archway, the remains of some long-lost grotto.

"Over here," Seneca said, cocking his head at an angle to peer into the shattered domicile before walking in on tempered feet.

Praxis followed with wonder and amusement lighting his face, and he brushed his growing sandy hair from his brow. The cave-like hovel received enough sunlight to warrant exploration but was checkered with shadow from what had once been a ceiling. They stepped into the cool space between two crumbled mortar columns and saw a staircase leading down under the road.

"Maybe we could find something preserved?" Seneca surmised, sniffing the air for a clue.

"I don't doubt we could. I'll wager we're the first ones down here in decades," Praxis replied as they stepped slowly into the dim and dank area. "On second thought, maybe that means we shouldn't be exploring it."

"Too late, I'm already intrigued," Seneca replied with a smile.

The air smelled of moss and stone. A mixture that flooded their sinuses with moist sensations. As their eyes adjusted the interior slowly came into focus. The room was maybe thirty feet by twenty feet and featured stone walls that were in decent condition considering the mass of roots and ivy that penetrated between the cracks. The sunlight came in at an angle from the road and lightly illuminated a little space, set apart from the main room by a long and thin altar that stretched parallel with the wall. It was too rectangular and straight to not be man-made, and as Seneca and Praxis dug at the thin layers of soil and meek vegetation, the marred granite of the structure became apparent. Seneca found rusted metal slats that formed a small cabinet upon the side of the smooth granite table. He cut at them with the bowie knife from his hip, the same knife that Tavin had bestowed on him months earlier, and after slicing away the roots and tangles the rusted doors fell away. Inside revealed rows upon rows of glass bottles, covered in thick layers of dust and mildew, which, when wiped away, revealed amber liquids within.

"Here's something," he said to Praxis.

He wet his shirt sleeve with some water and cleaned a few of the bottles enough to see the opaque glass beneath. It was a simple green hue that obscured the color of the drink. The bottle was corked. Seneca opened one of them by breaking the top off with his knife in a sliding fashion. It was louder than either of them had wanted, and caused a moment of startled worry. After a brief silence their hearts stopped filling their ears and Seneca sniffed the contents. The sweet and spiced aromas of whiskey wafted through his nose. He took a little into his mouth and swished it around before finally swallowing and handing the bottle to Praxis who did the same.

"It's pretty bad," Seneca said. "But good enough to drink, I suppose."

"All whiskey is good enough to drink." Praxis lit up with quiet excitement. "This trip has already paid dividends."

Seneca laughed. "This would cost us two silvers in the towns, so you're not wrong."

A bottle fit nicely in his bag without taking up too much space. They were going through provisions much quicker now so he had more space to work with. This thought made him forlorn as he considered the many deaths and injuries that had emptied the space in his medic pack. He cradled the whiskey between his sleeping fur, as to shelter it. When he looked up, Praxis had already wandered away. Holding bottle in hand, the blonde soldier sauntered through the room.

"Come, check this out," Praxis said beckoning Seneca into the darker side area.

Seneca pulled his worn jacket tighter around his shoulders and paced slowly across the damp floor and into a room almost as big as the first. There was a water leak on the far left corner of the room that had led to the wall collapse. Crumbled pieces of stone littered the floor. A thick layer of dust made a muffling carpet.

"Look at this," Praxis said staring down at his feet.

Praxis bent down and retrieved what seemed to be a small statue. It was in need of cleaning, which Praxis carried out with some of the opened liquor. When he was done, his efforts revealed a stone statue of marble. It depicted a wolf. The snowy white mane of the statue cleaned up well with minimal erosion or chipping. It sat upon its haunches and its detailed eyes seemed patient and lifelike.

"What about that?" Seneca asked of Praxis.

"He kinda looks like my dog back home. You know, dogs are the same species as wolves. The only difference is human breeding."

"You read that in your books too?"

Praxis nodded, there was a faraway look in the young farmer's eye as he gazed at the statuette. Seneca sensed a misplaced nostalgia there. Certainly not for the Old Age of human superiority, Praxis was not so infinitely old nor wise. It was something warmer, which filled Seneca with empathetic sentimentality.

"Everything was so gray back then," Seneca muttered, eyeing the statue and walls around them. "How did your mother find these books?"

"She—well," Praxis explained, "she never told me how, and I guess I never really asked."

Seneca watched his friend fumble with the little statue, feeling that he had more to say. Praxis' mouth twitched back and forth in pinched expressions of thought, blinking heavily. Drawing forth the memories brought deep wrinkles to his young face, darkened by years of sun.

"As early as I can remember she read to me. But they

weren't our books. They belonged to another age." He chuckled to himself. "She treasured those books above everything, and never allowed us to tell anyone about them. Father, he couldn't read and never seemed to want to try. But those books were—I don't know—they were a window into a different world."

"What kinds did she have?"

"Everything. History books, geography books, fables," Praxis replied. "They were in rough shape. The more you read them, the more they fell apart. Sometimes she'd try and tell people what she knew and they'd listen. More often they'd get angry or they wouldn't believe her. So, she stopped trying. When I was older, she let me read them whenever I wanted. I spent more time doing that than anything else. I learned everything I could. So much was written about the earth that used to be, except how it all went away. That part was never in there."

"Everyone has their theory," Seneca repeated the old epigram.

"Sure, and who knows, but it is interesting to see what people are capable of. We did incredible things," Praxis stated. "That is, if you trust the books."

"The only ancient book I ever read was a medical one," Seneca said, remembering a similar experience in one of the lectures before his drafting, "Most of the pages were missing. But I realized how far those people got. They had figured out how to fix so many problems." He laughed lightly as they walked around the musty room toward the exit, their voices resounding off the thick stone.

"My father once told me that long ago, people could take a heart out of a dead person and put it into a living person who needed a better one."

Praxis leaned against the wall and nodded.

"But they also fought wars back then too," Praxis replied. "I have a small idea of how powerful those people were, I'm scared to think how efficiently they might have destroyed each other."

Praxis shook his head, as if he had more to add to the conversation but not enough time to go into proper depth. The cold air of the room was starting to make its presence felt, and they mutually adjourned toward the entrance.

Ascending the steps up to street level, Seneca was immediately greeted with a host of violent sounds around the corners in the direction of camp. Metal clanging against metal and whining screams were all too familiar sounds by now. The ruckus grew louder and louder as they made haste to where the others had been resting.

They exclaimed curses together when they realized the source.

Seneca sprinted the rest of the way back to camp, Praxis keeping time behind him. When they turned the final corner, they lost momentum at sight of the brawl. A mass of tattered Westerners, in their dirty red uniforms, were dueling the ragged bunch of the remaining battalion. Seneca looked for recognizable faces, but it all was a blur of battle and he saw only violent strangers.

Seneca cursed inside his head as he drew his sword.

Praxis drew metal likewise and together they ran into the fray. They found a wizened Westerner upon the fringe of the din and Seneca pulled his enemy from confrontation with a wounded comrade, tossing him backwards. With a full-bodied swing, Praxis forced the man to parry and as the Westerner threw a block, Seneca ran him through, coating his beard in blood. He followed Praxis further and engaged the first that came to him upon the tide of battle.

Two hard swings at a Westerner's sword broke his defense. Before the man could adjust his parry, Praxis was on him, his sword jutting into the enemy's belly just under the ribs. The Westerner howled and threw his arm forward, dropping slightly to cup at the wound.

Seneca dodged charges from two more wild men, offering swings that failed to reach the passing target. However, none stayed long enough to partake in true conflict. He backed up, wanting to stay on the edge of the battle and not get surrounded. Using one of the thick elm trees for balance, he caught his breath and adjusted his grip. In an eerily growing familiarity, he could sense his friends' presence dotted throughout the mess of bodies. Tavin and Oil'ib felt closer, and he knew they were outnumbered. He knew it as surely as if he had actually seen them with his own eyes. Seneca made for their position across the grove, swiveling between boughs and flying blades. But before he could reach his friends, he felt a great presence closing behind him.

Seneca whipped around with a jerk and saw none other than Clades, bearing down on him, brandishing his glittering sword back and forth, forcing Seneca to retreat hastily. All at once, his dream from the night prior came pouring into his conscious mind, and he felt terrible fear and a wary rage that pitted like lead in his stomach. The massive man's burnished armor had been lost but his face was armored in dried blood. He looked like the true demon they called him. His golden hair hung ragged, and the tips of his long-braided beard were a gory rouge. Sunken eyes burned with an abominable blood lust. Seneca stood as a tree flexing beneath the fury of a storm, bending before his massive opponent.

Their swords met in a cross and Clades clenched teeth were close to him, revealing a grin full of blood. The brute used his strength to his advantage and pushed Seneca backwards and out of the grove of trees, separating him slowly from any reinforcement that his comrades could offer. The hair on the back of his neck bristled. Creaking, gloved fingers twisted an even harder grip around the leather handle of his sword, the weight balanced with the tension in his trapezius.

As Seneca measured his surroundings, Clades faked to swing and when Seneca stumbled sideways, Clades kicked him in the chest and sent him backward upon his rear. The air left his chest in a rush and a crunch of pain replaced the breath. Seneca was able to stand up and point his sword enough to stall the monster's advances. He parried a slash at his ribs then an overhead hammering blow. Clades now took up his entire view. The man was massive, mountainous shoulders that propelled his sword knocked Seneca back across the root-laden grass. The sun glinted off the collisions of steel.

Clades used his advantage well, swung his sword without dexterity, but his swings were heavy and powerful enough that Seneca could not find an opening. Every parry jarred his sword too far to one side and hurt his arm to the shoulder with a reverberating clash. One after another met Seneca's blade with only enough time to keep from being cut in two. Then Clades managed to outmaneuver Seneca again, stepping forward over the matted grass, parrying his sword to the side. He backhanded Seneca across the jaw with his free hand. Seneca fell to the ground, and his face was numb.

He's a giant, Seneca thought desperately, *I have to be quicker*.

He spun backwards as quickly as his frame would allow, just avoiding a swing at his back. Jumping backward he righted himself and this time took the offensive to the enemy. He swung high, forcing Clades to expose himself and they clashed twice more. Seneca was able to use his faster hands to take a slight advantage. He dodged a side slash by Clades and used the opportunity to drive his elbow into his gut. Before his enemy could catch his breath, Seneca uppercut the hilt of his sword into Clades' jaw in the narrow space between them. He spun for room and stabbed his sword through the air hard enough to kill, but Clades parried the blade aside and returned another backhand slap. Seneca tasted blood.

Pain awoke the terrible primal core of Seneca's heart. He felt desperate rage with an inhumane intensity. Rabid grunts reverberated from his chest. Seneca bared his teeth at his opponent, feeling his own blood drip from his canines. Clades smiled brutally, mocking, revealing his own gory grin and twisted the grip upon his sword. Seneca's vision tunneled and he felt a strange willingness to destroy his entire life if it was necessary to obliterate this enemy.

The physical pain that the man had caused him drove this inward torment and Seneca charged with a frenzy of blows. He howled in fury, the deep call echoing up the towers of dead men. He threw himself at the demon. Clades rebounded, pushing Seneca backwards until he executed another kick to Seneca's midsection sending him through a space between two columns of a ruined entranceway. He stumbled between rocky surfaces and came to a painful stop.

The sun shone warmly on his face. He was aware of his own panting and the sweat that was soaking into his shirt. Seneca could feel every nerve in his body firing at the sudden peril he was facing. No longer could he see the others, only a ringing could be heard in his ears. He was oppressively far from help, and he struggled to cover a bead of doubt within his aching stomach.

Clades charged through the archway, forcing Seneca back, deeper into the torn and roofless walls of a gray and grainy ruin. The walls dripped with green water and the soil was eroded away, exposing the dark black gravel foundation. With no time to think Clades was on him again and swung around. Seneca blocked him, taking the advantage. This time he found an opening to drive his own fist into Clades' cheek and made a hard kick at a knee, attempting to cripple the leg and break the ligaments. The giant winced and sprawled to the side but was not incapacitated.

Clades reached out and grabbed Seneca's sword hand with an iron grip, balanced himself, and lowered Seneca's sword by force. The shock at having his arm moved against his own effort caused Seneca to roar. Attempting to break free, he shot out with his left fist but his target moved backwards and reared his sword for a finishing blow. Seneca kicked up into his groin as hard as he could and squinted when his foot struck a steel codpiece. It was enough for Clades to release his grip, but not enough to stop the whistling sword, which managed to cut Seneca deep across the thigh. Pain shot through the limb. But as Clades was still reeling, Seneca kicked again with his good leg and sent his enemy's sword clattering across the rough floor. His cut leg burned under his weight and he tumbled backwards, catching himself on a crumbling pillar.

Damn him, he's no more skilled than the least of us, Seneca thought, panic setting in. *He will strong arm me to death.*

Frustrated and exhausted, Seneca felt acceptance of the end creeping through his mind and struggled against it. The laceration on his thigh burned and hobbled him greatly. The muscle beneath was spasming. Seneca moved in circles as best as he could around broken structures and collapsed walls, trying to follow the slanted light to the outside, where his friends might help him end the giant. Heavy footsteps were moving to flank him. Seneca spun around to try and counter the next attack but was stunned when Clades stabbed him in the stomach with a short knife, hardly visible in his fist.

All the feeling left Seneca's body as the foreign object sliced into him and came to rest between his organs. The world moved slowly and he felt instantly cold; he struggled to control his numbed limbs. His mind raced ahead of his physical being, and he started to realize he was never going to see home again. The grief became impossible to choke back and his rage turned to a feral gasp.

In his mind he felt the minds of his friends, and he knew that they knew of his pain. He knew it with an instinctual jolt. Clades pulled the knife back and threw Seneca again, sending him tripping over low rising rubble and onto a bed of green moss—his head outside of the grotto and in the warm sun, his legs still in the cool of the murky shadow. For the moment he could not make his legs function and he gripped at the incision in his gut.

"Hey!" came a shout that broke Seneca out of his stupor.

He turned on his side and saw Fallon running into the roofless room of broken walls. The sergeant threw himself at Clades, who happily accepted the challenge with a whooping yell and dodged the attempts by the slack sergeant to make contact. After three failed attacks, Clades grabbed Fallon's sword hand and broke his arm viciously, snapping down with his own arm and exposing the bone through Fallon's skin.

"No!" Seneca shouted, but he was sure it sounded more like a whisper.

Fallon fell backwards with a scream, and his pale face faded into an even whiter gray. Clades punched him with a hard, left hook. Fallon's face was covered in blood as he hit a wall. Another brutal punch sent teeth flying out of his mouth. Fumbling, Fallon pulled his knife and tried to lunge at the beast but Clades easily grabbed his off-hand and reversed the attack.

Seneca could not stop looking in Fallon's eyes, though he would have liked to, as Clades placed the knife and then slowly drove it through the sergeant's jaw. Fallon kicked wildly, struggling to free himself. Seneca's chest felt numb. Blood poured out of Fallon's mouth as the knife was driven back through his skull before he was finally dropped to the floor, twisting and jolting in agony. On the dank wall a smear of dark red remained.

Seneca finally looked away, and noticed his bowie knife, five feet in front of him under some broken pieces of cinder stone. For a fraction of time, no longer than a blink, he could see the pattern of his life in the glinting steel. With sputtering strength, he crawled forward and secured the weapon. The seemingly fated luck of the knife's presence suddenly filled him with hope. His condition was weakening but there was an explosion of energy left at his disposal, and he lay with the knife tucked lengthwise under his arm and out of obvious sight.

He could hear Clades approaching him and waited for his opening, wondering if it would come. As his attacker drew closer, Seneca was reminded of the day Tavin had given him the knife, all those months before, and what Tavin had said during camp.

"Everyone needs a 'Plan B.' Keep it close. That sword is no good when they're six inches in front of your face."

Clades' hand was rooting on his back then, grabbing his hair and pulling him up. The tug upon Seneca's scalp was excruciating, and he cried out. The blade spun around in his hand as he thrust it into Clades' side with all of his remaining strength. The blade slid surprisingly well under Clades' right arm, between a couple of ribs, and into the space where his lung awaited. The demon gave a gentle gasp. Seneca felt the grip on his hair release and he fell back upon the ground.

Clades tripped over his own feet, stumbled, and fell backwards onto and through a soft spot in the floor, crashing into the lower levels of the building. Seneca wanted so badly to look down and see Clades' lifeless body but time was running out for him. After securing his weapons he fled, limping, his hand pressing at the wound.

"Somebody, help me," he murmured.

Panic crept closer. The world raced as he made his way back through the tortured building to where the battle had been.

Why had there been no help for me? Where was the gift for battle this time? I don't want to die alone in this place, he thought wildly.

Upon leaving the grotto, Seneca expected to turn the corner and see Clades' men, in their greater numbers, finishing off the rest of his friends. It might not matter; he would bleed out if he failed to find someone. He felt the wound and surmised that it would not be fatal if he could close it in time. His arteries had been spared and his bleeding was slowing under the pressure of his fist. Still, he needed to act quickly.

He finally reached the decrepit entrance and stumbled out into the light. Outside lay a hell worse than the one he had faced alone. There were butchered corpses everywhere that leaked blood across the stones. The temporarily peaceful ruins were a wasteland of human agony once again. Nearby, a Western infantryman lay gasping in a twisted mess. He was curled up against one of their comrades and, though he couldn't speak, his expressions told a nightmarish tale. The insides of his stomach snaked out onto the cobblestone like a silent serpent despite his feeble attempts to guide them back inside his gut. Seneca thrust his sword through the man's heart, relieving him of his torture.

He heard a sharp cry, and the intuition he felt during battle returned. They weren't dead, he knew that now. They had to be alive. He pushed his failing body onward.

Seneca turned a corner back to the elm trees and saw his five friends. The hairs stood on the back of his neck like quills as he took in the predicament. Their number, boxed in by a force twice their own, formed a pentagram of defense and every blade that could be wielded stuck outwards like shiny death. Each one's eyes held a distant gaze, a strong and leveling instinctual precision. The irises flicked like insects at every movement. Their blades moved in surreal synchronicity, as if orchestrated to each other's movements. Seneca moved forward to help them but instead found his body collapsing next to one of the trees that had grown out of the ruin.

The enemy, numbering nine now, closed in. Seneca's mind flew unwittingly to Praxis. He could sense him flexing a throwing knife in his left hand ever so slightly. Sure enough, Praxis spun his right leg backwards and, in a full turn, slung his knife across their circle. Just as the knife left his hand Tavin ducked downwards, allowing the weapon to pass over his head and pierce an enemy through the throat. Then Tavin spun back around and thrust his sword forward stunning his own opponent with a quick death through the thorax.

Seneca mouthed in wonder.

A numbing and feverish feeling, the familiar breathing of the hands, and the clearing of the internal vision overtook him. It was there like a finger upon his forehead, a solid structure in his mind. Here it was like never before. Seneca's eyes closed but in his mind the battle unfolded. Feeling every sinuous synaptic reflex, Seneca fell into a meditative state and experienced the dancing, beautiful battle scene until his friends had finished off the last Western soldier. After the final, efficient kill the heart of the ruins quieted again.

Seneca was terrified at the sudden presence of a predator that had surely been lying in wait for the carcasses. Out of the shadows, the powerful jaws of a lion were drawing the limp body of a soldier into a cave. A sickening cold enveloped his back. The startling fear helped him regain some presence and nerve.

"Help me," Seneca called, as his friends turned and saw him.

"Look for the medic's bag," he heard one of them say aloud.

They rushed over and surrounded him, their presence overwhelming and calming him at the same time.

"He had fresh supplies. Here!" Praxis yelled, bringing forth the bag of a Western medic.

Tavin opened the sack and emptied supplies onto the ground.

"Tell us what to do," Tavin said.

Seneca lay back and started talking, unsure if he was giving proper instruction, his tongue tripping over the fog in his mind and the pain as Tavin cleaned the wound. Giving desperate direction, he guided Praxis in making a rambling suture for the wound in his gut and a wrap for his leg.

"Its—ahhh!" he seethed, "just like… sewing cloth…."

"Stay with me!" Kendo kept shouting when Seneca would begin to pass into the daze. The towering skeletons above him drew his eyes to the bright sky. His vision tunneled slightly, then he focused his eyes upon Kendo's and gave further direction for pressure and tincture and tying the knot, opium if it was available.

Seneca fought everything in him that was telling him to faint. But his words would not come and his vision faded. When Praxis straightened his broken nose, and Seneca felt the bones snapping back into place, the world went dark.

Chapter Five

April 2717
South Nashville, Tennessee

Tavin

Six of us left. The six that I would choose with a knife to my throat, Tavin thought as he threw a stone down a ravine of rust. Oil'ib would say its divine and Kendo would cite some higher calling. At least Seneca and Praxis have the reason to call it skill. But damn it all if it's not sheer luck. No amount of skill puts you in the right place at the right time, just look at those guards in the burning blockhouses of Greensboro. And no divinity is out there saving the kind people, just look at the sergeant, poor bastard, I can't imagine the pain. No, we are on a run of insanely good luck, even if it only duped us out here on an empty road. But if there's one thing more important than luck it's what you do with the opportunity when it presents itself. Damn it if we don't owe it to ourselves to milk every last drop of luck out of life.

The glinting towers of the Nashville ruins were still in sight when Tavin turned his head behind and glimpsed the sunlight twinkling off the shattered giants. In front of him stretched the expansive thoroughfare, now covered in seven-hundred-years' worth of vegetation but still largely sparse compared to the thick masses of forest that walled-in their road to the south. They walked in three pairs: Tavin and Oil'ib in the front, Praxis and Seneca in the middle, and Gannon and Kendo in the rear, seeking to maximize their visual size as a way of warding off predators. The rest of the battalion had all perished in the bloody battle with Clades and his men. Only the six of them had managed to survive. Survival had not come without its own misgivings. Seneca still walked lightly upon his left leg, the slash from Clades' sword not yet healed. Tavin suffered from a chronic headache he hoped would dissipate soon and was consistently surprised to find a new bruise every time someone bumped into him or his rucksack rubbed him the wrong way.

Not until the sun began to sink did they halt their travel along the grassy road. In the distance Tavin felt a quiet reverberation upon the breeze, flirting with their ears and hinting of an approaching something.

"Sh—someone's coming," Kendo whispered from his rear position, and the six of them halted their shuffling feet, pricked their ears to the road behind them.

Around the corner, formed by waving branches, came the sound of quickening hoofbeats. A rider gained ground so quickly that Tavin lamented how long it had taken them to cover the same distance on foot. They drew their steel in order to bring the man to a halt, though he showed no signs of being armed, and feathered out into a straight line perpendicular with the road, forcing the rider to pull up quite abruptly when he reached them.

"Stop!" Tavin bellowed, holding up his hand.

For a second, Tavin had thought the stranger would blow right through them and his heart thudded dull aches in his head. The rider was an older man, perhaps middle aged, but at a vague point in his life impossible to tell how far back his life spanned. His skin was a dark brown, almost black and his eyes were similarly dark with heavy gray brows above. The man looked down at them from his horse with stern amusement, measuring each of them for but a second.

He pulled back the hood of his humble gray cloak to reveal a dome shaved clean and gleaming like polished ebony. Beneath his cloak was an even simpler tunic and his cotton pants showed signs of kneeling in dirt. Tavin saw only an old hunter's knife at the hip, its leather sheath tattered and stained.

"Good evening. I'm just passing through," he stated authoritatively as he dismounted his horse in a youthful spring. "My name is Bok. I can see that you are Eastern soldiers."

He began walking his horse forward, closer to the six of them when Tavin stepped in front.

"Stop. Show us your hands," he insisted.

Bok hesitated then complied, showing his palms, the skin a lighter color from the friction of many years and calloused with hard work.

"Open the coat."

Bok did so and revealed a crossbow slung behind his back. Tavin felt Seneca moving closer to him for support. Seneca winced at the movement, and Bok's eyes immediately flickered down to Seneca's wounded leg.

"I can see your concern. These war zones move farther east every day. Nowhere feels safe anymore, but I assure you I'm Eastern. More specifically New England. The Cape Cod region, if you are familiar. I lived there most of my life, when I wasn't traveling."

Bok's voice was a deep bass that demanded attention. He had hardly said anything at all but Tavin could sense the compulsion in himself and his friends. There was something heavy in Bok's movements and graces. With a sweep of his arm he removed their doubts and there was a deepening in his eyes that stirred their interest.

"I am from the same region myself actually," Gannon mentioned, stepping forward next to Tavin and looking over Bok with a feigned distrust. "If what you say is true, then you will know the name of the tavern two blocks off Washington Pier?"

"Two blocks? Hmm… well now, what if I'm not a drinker?" He smiled. "But, in any case it's called The Dog's Bone, and I've only been inside once. The barkeep at the time owed me some money, but I knew he didn't have it, so I worked behind the bar all night and whatever tips I got were mine… and then I went home. The barkeep was Rick Waters."

Gannon smiled with surprise, a good sign in Tavin's mind. He had been keeping his hand upon the hilt of his knife the whole while, but now let his grasp relax, straightened his back and let his hands lay at his side.

"He's right. He's Eastern, or an excellent spy," Gannon awarded.

"At least a well-travelled one," Kendo commented, his

arms still crossed in quasi-judgment, his steely eyes leveled at Bok, who stood a little taller than himself.

Tavin looked Bok over with a discrete intensity and saw that Seneca was watching him do so, as if to glean information from Tavin's observations. They had been friends for nearly a year now, and in that time, Seneca had come to know Tavin's mind down to minute machinations, perhaps to a level even stronger than any of the others. Their ability to anticipate each other's thoughts and actions played no small role in their survival to this point. There was something about this Bok. He moved and spoke with deliberate dedication to an invisible ideal. He was limber, yet his limbs and hands spoke of wild strength reigned in through ritualistic practice.

"What did you say your name was?" Kendo asked.

"Bok."

"Well, I am Kendo. I am from the Gulf of Mississippi. Most recently, anyway. This is Seneca—from the Finger Lakes, Tavin—from Carolina, Praxis—of Florida, Gannon you know already, and that is our quiet friend Oil'ib—from the Pennsylvania."

Oil'ib bowed awkwardly at hearing his name.

"I assume you gentlemen are heading down to the fortress?" Bok asked, through the hint of a smile on his dry lips.

"Yeah. That's right," Gannon responded.

"And you? Where are you headed?" Tavin inquired, incredulously.

"The same place as a matter of fact. I haven't been away from it long either. I was out looking for my students."

"Students?"

"I mean, that's more or less what I'd call them," Bok tugged on the horse's reins to keep it in line. The dappled mare grunted and pawed the ground.

"They were supposed to meet me in the ruins. They're a week late."

He began walking the horse down the road.

"I'm headed the same way you are. Would you mind if I walk along?"

The six of them exchanged glances just long enough to avoid awkward silence.

"I don't see why not," Seneca said, welcoming Bok with a curt nod and smile. "After all, it would be helpful to have someone who knows the way to the fortress, as I assume you do."

"That I do." Bok smiled in return, his eyes glinting like flakes of obsidian in the sunlight.

"You boys wouldn't be offended if I trot along on my horse, would you?" he asked. "I've already done a lot of walking today."

They shook their heads in deference, and the group of them followed Bok, who led the way down the steepening road to where the path narrowed slightly and once again rose and fell with the hills in the land.

"Don't take my words in any wrong fashion, but you boys look like you were in hell for a while," Bok offered.

Tavin caught Seneca sending him a look of disquiet after this break in the silence from the older man. The limp in Seneca's leg was slight but certainly noticeable. He tried to straighten his gait, but failed and clutched at his side when a shooting pain made him slow down.

"Maybe we were," Praxis mused.

"And maybe you weren't, eh?" Bok chuckled. "Do not feel pressured to tell me of your battles. Every soldier has his scars, every scar a story, each story only heard in the right setting."

"True enough," Seneca stated. "But what if we weren't in a battle? What if we just finished fighting off a lion?"

Bok let out a brief guffaw.

"That look in your eyes doesn't come from fighting lions. It comes from killing people."

Tavin saw Seneca wince again. Bok rode his dappled mare ahead of them, speaking loudly enough for them to hear from behind. His back straight as an arrow upon the saddle, he swayed with every flexion of force and kept a perfect balance.

"Looking at you men," Bok continued, "if I may be so bold, I am reminded of myself at your age. Timorously poised at the edge of endurance. It is a hard sacrifice that you have made. You will never be the same again. I never was. I *think* differently now."

"And would you say you are worse off for it?" Praxis asked, playing into Bok's bold way of speaking.

"No. I would not say that. I just have memories, but they're my own and I wouldn't share them without the proper... setting. Which is why I won't ask you to share yours. Not until you are comfortable with me."

The hard expression on Praxis's golden face softened. He found a place at Seneca's side, helping him with the rucksack Seneca carried, relieving some of the burden.

"I assume you were in the first war?" Tavin asked.

"First, tenth, hundredth, whatever you want to call it.

People have been fighting since we could throw rocks, but yes that's the one I was known for," Bok replied airily, giving a brief waving of his hand to the breeze. "You know it's interesting, because back then they called us Easterners the bad guys. Isn't that strange?"

Bok turned as if checking the road behind them, or the setting sun. "Funny thing is, in war everyone is the bad guy. But no one ever talks about that."

"Did you know my father? Lavin Weber?" Tavin asked. "He was a Commander from Carolina."

"Lavin Weber?" Bok turned in his saddle, his spine surprisingly flexible for a man of his years. "How interesting. I did hear his name often in those days, though I am afraid I never had the pleasure of his acquaintance. He would've been involved in the final defense along the Mississippi. A good officer, your father. From what I heard anyway. Damn good officer. The generals spoke highly. You know there was one story I remember about his particular style of warfare. One of the generals of the army was an avid fan."

"What did he say exactly?" Tavin urged.

"This was a long time ago."

"I'm sorry to press. I haven't seen him in years."

Bok's upbeat demeanor waned a moment, his eyes looked like they were searching a well for a penny.

"We were studying some tactics in the south where I was stationed and the General brought up your father, as an example. He was complimentary, no question. Mentioned how Weber had a knack for taking smaller contingents away from his main group and holing up in dense woods. They'd wait in ambush until the enemy was almost kissing distance and then they'd spring the trap. The enemy would run and end up in front of the whole battalion. Brilliant tactics. I'll always admire that."

The answer contented Tavin greatly. Stories of his father rarely found him anymore. Most had been lost when the first war was won. Few enough men had returned, and of those that did, few had stories to share with Tavin of his father. Those that did have stories, preferred not to share. Tavin thought about what Bok had said about setting. It made some sense to him now. Why would he want to tell anyone of the battle with Clades? And even if he did, who would ever understand? People are naturally selfish in thought to begin with and to ask someone to consider something they have never seen is a pointless endeavor.

"He left for the last time when I was ten," Tavin said. "He was always teaching. Always instructing. I loved him for it."

"What was your role in the last war exactly?" Gannon wondered aloud as he patted Tavin warmly upon the back, directing his question toward Bok.

"I went into their camps, their towns. I was supposed to suppress riots. Take out rabble-rousers. It didn't do anything beyond pissing people off and making a lot of enemies.

"When I was in enemy lands I would camp out in the old cities, the old ruins. No one would bother us. Unlike everyone else on this planet, the ruins don't frighten me. To the contrary, I find them quite inviting. Graveyards have always been the most peaceful places in the world. From great violence inevitably springs great peace."

Praxis spoke up. "Is that why you are out here now?"

"Like I said," Bok replied without turning from his view

of the stone littered road ahead, "I was searching for my students. It was a logical place to look, but one could spend his whole life searching those ruins, and would likely lose it in the process."

"He's right on that," Seneca sighed.

"Do you guys know why the Old World fell?" Bok asked, turning around again to smirk in their direction, the age-old question lilting from his mouth like so many philosophical teachers in so many places.

"Everyone has their theory," Seneca and Tavin said concordantly.

This brought a deep chuckle from Bok before he turned back to the road in front of him to answer.

"It is the great poison," he mused. "Mankind cannot make any decision without first tasting that poison. You all know what I mean."

"What of the other theories," Praxis interjected. "Starvation, drought, desertification and a changing climate? What about floods?"

"A realist. I like that, Praxis," Bok replied. "There's always a concrete reason for things. I can respect that opinion."

"Don't forget plagues and pandemics," Seneca added.

"All means to an end," Bok replied coolly. "Those things may spark the fire that consumes the people, but it is the fire that ultimately destroys them, and mankind's unwillingness to douse it. Violence is the all-consuming fire. And where do we find ourselves now? One might fairly ask if we are the ones seeking to end the fire, or if we are merely the fire itself."

"You say we," Kendo said, breaking his meditative silence.

Bok laughed again.

"Yes, I suppose I did… Unfortunately, my role in this conflict is not yet over. Indeed, you may find it is but half way."

"Um. You mentioned you went west before," Oil'ib asked of Bok. "Did you uh—travel with anybody?"

There was a long pause after Oil'ib's question, and the men looked at Bok, awaiting an answer. But Bok only gazed ahead of him, suddenly absent from the conversation.

"I'm sorry, excuse me gentlemen, but I must run ahead."

Before Tavin could ask for an explanation, their newfound acquaintance had nudged his mare into a gallop and stampeded down the dirt road ahead, kicking up small clouds of dust into the hot spring air. Tavin batted the dust away and blinked it from his eyes. He watched Bok grow smaller in the distance until he appeared to come to a stop and dismount at some twisted objects along the side of the road in a clearing.

"No rush, but we might as well catch up with him and see what that was about," he said to the others. He put his hand to his eyes to block out the sun as he strained to see Bok's motions in the distance.

"Are you ok to keep walking, Sen?"

"I'm fine."

After some time, they reached the clearing, where the main road widened out before continuing on again. When they caught up with Bok, he was already at work building a large fire. The smoke was just beginning to rise from some kindling that had been set alight with a spark from his flint. At first, Tavin was greatly confused. The fire would be immense. Then he saw what was weaved in between the branches and dried grasses. He grabbed

Oil'ib's attention, and motioned behind them indicating Oil'ib should keep a lookout on their rear while they approached the scene. Bok seemed completely oblivious to their approach as he worked the fire. Tavin could smell the foul stench of rotting bodies.

From between the limbs of wood and flesh, Tavin caught the glimpse of a pale white hand stiff with death, it looked to have been dead for at least a couple days. Bok sighed in exasperation, picking something shining and golden off one of the bodies before the pyre could come ablaze. The smoke was thick and reeked of death as it began to burn. The older man continued to throw branches on top of the fire as the six soldiers retreated from the thickening gray smoke and heat, which was doubly oppressive in the heat of the fading day.

"I'm sorry," Bok uttered, placing the shiny object inside the pocket of his robes. "If I had waited for you to walk with me, we would only just be building the pyre and it is nearly time for you to rest as it is."

"Is there anything we can do?" Tavin offered. "How did they die?"

Bok stood straight, shook his head with obvious care. His eyes were misty and he motioned for them to follow him as he took the reins of his mare. She had been grazing upon the greener grasses at the forest edge, and Bok tugged her away from her meal and led them all away from the place of death. There was an agonizing wait as Bok took a deep breath.

"Thank you, but there's nothing to be done anymore. These were my students if you haven't already guessed. I had sent them out on a mission to find a marauder. A marauder who is more dangerous than anyone will admit."

"Should we be forming a defense?" Tavin asked in a hurry, withdrawing one of his swords from its sheath in his back and looking about the tree lines on each side of the road.

There was no movement. No sounds but for the chirping of robins and the occasional rustling of the warm breeze through the emerald leaves. He squinted into the reddening horizon.

"You are in no danger," Bok said calmly, resting his hand on Tavin's shoulder.

Despite the lack of evidence, Tavin believed him. His voice was vacant of all threat and worry, and the firm pressure upon his shoulder transmitted only an inner peace.

"I know who did this. I spotted them fleeing through the ruins a few days ago. It is not in their leader's nature to take the roads. And my students…This marauder showed his true nature in their death. They were not killed quickly."

"Clades?" Seneca questioned passionately. "Did he do this?"

"No, but how do you know Clades?" Bok replied.

"We destroyed him, and his men. Back in those ruins."

"You did all that?"

"With the help of those who did not survive, yes we did. When he took Greensboro there were a couple dozen survivors that made it out, and he came for us himself. Over twenty of us reached that city, but now it's just us," Tavin explained.

"Clades was a great warrior. His soldiers, especially his veterans he kept close by were renowned. You defeated them?"

They all nodded.

"How?" Bok wondered. "If I may be so bold as to ask."

"Can't really explain it. We were lucky," Tavin replied.

"It takes more than luck to defeat an enemy like that," Bok reasoned. "That was one of our biggest threats in the Southern Theatre."

"If your men weren't after Clades, then who were they following?" Kendo asked.

"A man named Kayzitt."

"Is this Kayzitt a Westerner? I spent my childhood in the West," Kendo continued peering down at Bok from his lean height. "Where I'm from I've never heard that name."

"I doubt you would have. He's likely not much older than you gentlemen. He was initially spotted attacking small villages near the Mississippi, but things have escalated since we evacuated the region. The rumor I heard was Kayzitt and his men were heading east through our lines. I sent the best soldiers from the fortress, my students, to find him. I wish now that I hadn't."

Bok led them in a sad march while bowing his perfect posture in subtle grief. Tavin looked behind them to where the pyre was now blazing in the distance. Its smoke funneled into the sky in thick plumes. He worried about this Kayzitt and hoped that Bok was right and this smoke would not bring an enemy to their heels.

"I'm sorry this happened," Praxis lamented.

"It's in the past. I'm heading to the fortress still," Bok said while jockeying his horse forward with a tug on the reins as he walked. "Are you coming?"

They walked in silence while there was still light in the sky. Even Tavin felt too embarrassed in the presence of Bok for conversation, knowing that he must be grieving, though his stoic nature gave nothing away. Tavin wished he had a horse, his feet hurt just watching Bok swaying in the saddle. When Praxis mentioned that the growing darkness signaled a good time to stop for the night, he was glad to have a break in the silence so he could ignore his aches. The mood lightened when they set about the work of it and Bok seemed happy to help.

Night dropped its pitch-black curtains by the time they had set up their camp. They had followed Bok's lead and made what, according to him, had been good distance for the day.

"You are but one more day's walk from the fortress," he promised.

A blanket of stars had coated the clear night sky and Tavin allowed himself to relax as he stretched out beside their generous fire. He knew that he was taking a risk believing that they were safe and could allow such a blaze, or that he could rest easy with his boots off and his swords resting behind him. But there was something about Bok that encouraged trust. Though he had only been able to observe him for a day, Tavin had no doubts that Bok was someone of truth. He munched contentedly upon some jerky. His mouth salivated heavily with the eager expectation of food.

"Here. This is a special arrangement I always keep with me. It's a little homemade mixture," Bok said taking a swig from his flask.

They passed the flask around the fire, taking turns sipping a bit at a time. It was a stiff drink that burned with satisfaction all the way down to Tavin's stomach. He felt immediately refreshed. The heat from the orange flames of the fire soothed his aching feet. The splendor of the heavens stared down at him.

Across the fire, Praxis was engaged with Kendo and Bok in a murmuring discussion on Eastern politics, the shortage of draftees from richer households, and timid assertions of bold actions that the Chancellor should take. Through the fire, Tavin noticed Gannon seemed unable to stop looking into the thicket of tree line. Ever since the battalion had been attacked by wolves, Gannon had spent most hours before bed staring into the closest forest with sincere expectation.

The poor man is truly lost without his mandolin to distract him, Tavin thought.

Gannon was a different animal. He had become a traveling musician after his schooling, working a circuit of towns around New England and earning good silver playing at the local taverns and summer festivals. He was someone of no commitments to any one job, town, or woman. He lived for smiles and music, frivolity and promiscuity. Tavin was still unsure exactly why Gannon had left such a life for the seriousness and danger of the army. After all, Gannon had joined voluntarily.

Tavin watched the light flickering off Gannon's pale skin which showed slightly beneath the thinning, tawny hair on his round head. Gannon was no athlete, though he carried his own, and had made up for the rest by taking full advantage of the skill that had followed them since their fever illness during training camp. His face was glazed without expression and his hazel-brown eyes continued to penetrate into the inscrutable tangles of night-darkened evergreen.

"Gannon. Oil'ib checked these woods, and there are no tracks," Tavin said.

"That's not what I'm thinking about."

"What troubles you?" Bok requested, as if he had been listening to Tavin's thoughts.

Gannon was silent still for another moment and Tavin wondered if he was going to simply ignore Bok, who waited patiently with a half-smile, the firelight flickering off his onyx eyes. Gannon took a swig of the flask as Oil'ib passed it to him, wiped his mouth, then turned back around and spoke.

"I was just thinking, you know...We don't have to go to the fortress...We don't have to go," he stated. "Who's to say we didn't all die in that city? How would anyone know?"

Tavin glanced over at Seneca, aware of the effects that such thinking might have on his friend. Seneca had voiced the same thoughts of desertion to Tavin, during a walk in the summer of training camp. It seemed like an eternity ago. But now, Seneca wore only a look of honest confusion. Gannon continued.

"If we die in the wild at least it's our choice." He glanced around at his friends. "I was just thinking that's all."

Bok nodded his head and seemed to take sincere appreciation of Gannon's words. Tavin always felt like people generally displayed a modicum of false understanding in life, but Bok, despite whatever he felt inside, seemed to take seriously every word.

"You have a family?" Bok asked.

Gannon nodded.

"You would want to find them, I'm sure?"

"Of course."

"I'm almost sixty, if you couldn't tell. I've seen more than I ever wanted to. It occurred to me during the last war, while captured by Western forces, that there is a fluidity of war's violence. The violence moves like a flood. Covering everything and anything in no particular order or pattern," Bok explained in his calm and collected basso voice. "There's no guarantee the people who run, or the people who stay, will be any safer than the people who fight."

Bok's statement made Tavin think of the red flood of the Westerners into Greensboro. He wondered what had happened with the townspeople. He wondered if the girl he had left in the church had stayed safe.

"Well it certainly doesn't seem right," Gannon muttered.

Tavin could not be quiet.

"It's cold out here, and it's not just the weather," Tavin said as he huddled closer to the fire and added a few sticks. "I want to get to this fort. As quickly as we can. Being alone out on the frontier starts to fuck with you. You forget things. You can never stop moving and you feel like there's this need to turn your head every ten seconds and make sure something isn't flying toward it. I think we will benefit greatly from being behind some stone walls."

"Having real food will mean everything," Praxis said, leaning back upon a rolled-up fur to stretch before the fire. "No offense Oil'ib."

"Thank you—uh—you're, you're welcome, yeah," Oil'ib said quietly, smiling, his crooked teeth glinting proudly against the firelight. "By the way, I consider squirrel to be real food."

"I don't care about the food as much. What I need is to restock my medical supplies," Seneca confessed. "Maybe the fortress has some decent hashish and maybe you can get a new mandolin, Gannon."

Gannon attempted a smile as he nodded in concordance.

"Just be sure to take it easy on the hash there," Bok expressed with a stern friendliness. "Too much can dull the senses and slow the reaction time."

The flask reached Bok and he finished it with one last swig.

"Yeah, sure, of course," Seneca agreed with a nervous laugh. "It is for medical purposes. I am a medic after all."

"A medic who kills great warriors?" Bok laughed.

"Or at least I was supposed to be," Seneca continued. "I trained as a doctor at the Finger Lakes Clinic before being drafted. Now, I'm here."

Tavin coughed. "It took all of us to have the chance to sit around this fire."

Tavin saw that Bok was listening keenly to what they were saying. Tavin was careful not to outwardly mention the strange gift, the enigmatic battle vision, that had not only saved their skins but turned them into a fighting team that could at least pose a challenge to the Western elites. It was a team that he hoped, with every inch of his being, to keep together. Tavin was unsure of what glory or honor might come of their resolve and determination, but he knew that there was life-changing good to be found. He was sure of it. The men slowly drifted off to sleep and Tavin took a moment to appreciate the quiet serenity.

As he lay on his back, the heat from the glowing coals warmed his right and balanced perfectly the cool dewy air on his left. The firmament above was smeared with stars. Tavin counted the ones that shot through the sky as he fell asleep.

What an exhilarating life they have, he thought. Such a short one, and traversed so fast. But how brightly do they shine for it.

The next morning, he was awakened with the breaking

of sunlight over the far hills in the east and by Kendo shaking him forcibly on the shoulder. Tavin roused easily and sat up so fast that he almost slammed his face into Kendo's knee. He looked about through eyes blurry with sleep and rubbed them to clarity. He could smell the smoldering ash of the fire. A pleasant smell of pine wafted in on the cool morning breeze from the forest.

"He's not here," Kendo stated matter-of-factly while the others stood to attention.

"He left us?" Gannon wondered aloud with calm dubiety. "What the fuck is wrong with that guy?"

Tavin and Oil'ib searched the surrounding grounds for half an hour but returned only with dew-soaked boots and no sign of the peculiar man.

"Could be an ambush coming," Gannon stated, wringing his hands together.

"If so, it would have already come," Tavin replied. "What do we need to gather?"

"Nothing. We have water, provisions, everything," Seneca assured. "We should leave though."

"He left this," Oil'ib said suddenly, holding up a golden medallion that had been under Oil'ib's canteen.

"Give it here," Tavin said, and Oil'ib tossed it.

He examined the coin closely, turning it between his fingers. It was a beautifully intricate gold piece, pressed with the symbolic eagle of the East on one side and a picture of a grand building on the other. A braided border followed along the edge. It was only when they were ready to leave, and Tavin had buttoned the medallion safely into his jacket pocket, that he recognized the glinting piece of gold.

"This is the thing he retrieved from his... from his students!" Tavin concluded, remembering the same glint of gold disappearing into the old man's pocket.

"But why would he leave it here with us?"

"An accident."

"Impossible, it was placed purposely under Oil'ib's canteen. It couldn't have fallen out of his pocket either," Tavin concluded.

"We can return it to him. He said he was going to the fortress."

"Yeah, true," Tavin agreed, turning to lead them away again. If he was truly headed there.

They were a ragged crew. Tavin looked at himself and his friends now, as Bok must have seen them: quiet, cold, tired, hungry, almost out of food, low on water, clothing in tatters. They kept talking to a minimum to conserve their energy, walking against the resistance of their aches, pains, and mending wounds. Kendo set the pace when Tavin no longer could. His long strides led everyone else's much quicker footsteps. Beaten leather boots hit the hard ground and scuffed against rock and root, following the road exactly as Bok had described to them and avoiding the longer route through a village—empty and abandoned for the safety of the high-walled fortress. When at last they heard the sounds of human activity off in the distance they celebrated their arrival, gliding along the stretched road to the front gate at a meager march. It took every ounce of remaining energy to keep their postures and to look more like the victors they were and not the waifs they resembled. Tavin felt the dirt and grime on his skin and struggled to keep his inward composure.

"Oh my god it's real," Seneca said with a laugh, the first words anyone had said for hours.

The gate was made of thick and dark lumber planks. The outer walls were of overwhelming size. Massive blocks of glittering gray granite had been stacked in nearly seamless perfection. Tavin knew that it was the largest fortress east of the Great River, a consequence of the convenient location of a nearby granite quarry, as his father had taught him years ago. But he had not expected to be so awed by its size. He could not realize the entirety of its circumference from where they stood at the entrance. Two towns could have easily fit inside. Towers pointed to the heavens at uniform distances along the outer wall. Above, on the battlements, he could see Eastern soldiers in fresh uniforms marching in similar fashion. The bulwark was completely impenetrable in its thickness. Only the ruins of the old city and its skeleton towers had been more awe inspiring. But the Tennessee fortress contained more immediate implications.

As Tavin approached the gate, a voice from above ordered them to halt. Before he could complain, a view-slot was opened at eye level in the massive gate and the eyes of an older soldier, wrinkled with crow's feet and with a thick gray brow, were exposed to him.

"Halt your advance! What brings you here?"

"We are Eastern soldiers of the eighth battalion under Captain Vencin of Kentucky. We were defending Greensboro—it's fallen! We bring news and are in need of refreshment. Open this door before the fortress becomes the next to fall!"

Tavin surprised himself by yelling. Then he whispered back to his friends. "We're getting inside or I swear…"

The eyes disappeared and there was a moment of silence before a great grating noise and creaking of massive chains signaled the raising of an inner portcullis. A while longer and the great doors of dark lumber swung inward just enough for the six of them to enter one at a time. As Tavin led them in, his senses were immediately barraged by the grandeur. Several flights of granite stairs to the top of the battlements surrounded a long and winding courtyard of cobblestone. Farther on he could see the beginnings of thatch roof tops, barracks and stables, gardens farther off still, and blocking his view any further was the indomitable bulk of the keep, its buttresses and gargoyles protected by a short inner wall and topped with its own high battlements. Weaved around them were thin slits for archers to use.

Some archers were already approaching the wall by descending the stairs of the outer battlements while the main gate slowly closed behind them. A group of guards waved them into the courtyard across the threshold. Tavin's feet rejoiced to feel the familiar pain of cobblestones beneath leather boots. He longed for new boots. When he saw a man in an officer's uniform approaching, he made a mental note to request some.

"My name's Captain Keller. I hear you're from Greensboro?"

Tavin nodded. The captain was a pale, dapper looking man with light red hair and an air of formality that spread across his demeanor like thick butter.

Tavin doubted the man had seen any action yet.

"We are from Greensboro, most recently," Tavin motioned to the five exhausted friends behind him. "We have news and are in desperate need of provisions. We would like to speak to the authority of the fortress."

At this the captain merely smiled at the men behind him, who returned it in jest.

"I'm afraid I'll have to be enough *authority* for you for now. I'll examine you myself and make sure that you are who you say you are. We will see to your provisions eventually. First you must answer my questions."

Tavin felt his heart sinking into his stomach. His arms grew weak and he stuffed his hands in his jacket pockets to hide how he clenched them. That was when he felt the cool presence of the gold medallion in his pocket. Hoping for the best, he withdrew and presented it to the captain's face.

"Perhaps this will expedite the process," Tavin said aloud, gathering the stares of the many around them.

Captain Keller turned and frowned at the gold coin. He then approached with several quick strides before eyeing it closer, but refrained from touching either it or Tavin's dirty hands.

"I see," the captain said, both confused and abashed. "I'll take you to General Thom."

Keller drew one hand through his fine red hair as he beckoned them to follow. The other he kept constantly upon the pommel of an ornate katana. On his back was a quiver of arrows and a sleek black bow that told Tavin that he was the captain of the guard, and likely one of several at this position. He motioned again for them to follow, unaware of their exhaustion as he gave a verbal tour of the fortress on their way to the general.

"Were you gentlemen in the first wave?" he asked, to which the six friends nodded.

"I assume then that you've never seen this fortress. It

was built two-hundred years ago. It's twice the size of the fortress in Illinois. Designed solely for the purpose of blocking armies, withstanding sieges, and providing safe haven for travelers. Those outer walls are newer stone, reinforced with logs. In total it's about five feet thick, seventy-five feet high, impenetrable to trebuchets or projectiles. Six reinforced towers allow us to cover every inch of these walls, and the viewing tower atop the keep gives us an extra one hundred yards of visibility across the field. The inner fort alone would be as big as most strongholds in this continent. The whole structure has a spring underneath for a relatively unlimited supply of fresh water. We have storehouses with more food than anyone could eat in a lifetime."

The suddenly cordial captain took them through a series of hallways and then up a spiral staircase into the officer's quarters, a homely four-story building of granite stones and mortar. A lumber balcony overlooked the cobblestone passageway and there was evidence of a backyard garden between the house and the other places of residence. He pushed through two heavy doors and their arrival stopped short a lively conversation around a gentle cottage-like fireplace. At the center on a large red velvet armchair was a man wearing a gold-trimmed, dark green jacket. The various golden stars upon his breast and ruddy complexion introduced him immediately as the general they had been promised. The general had just finished laughing with a group of various officers, who were seated upon simple wooden chairs at a central table, leaning in obsequiously around the general, who looked up and examined the group behind Captain Keller.

"General Thom," Keller said with a salute. "May I introduce the surviving defenders from Greensboro."

The general stood immediately, returned the salute, and put the captain and the others at ease. He stood a little over six feet by Tavin's estimate. His thick black hair was shaved short and his skin had a rich olive color. He gave the impression of a man of unique athletic ability, who had perhaps allowed his waistline to enjoy the finer things of late but was young and strong enough to hold authority—with a quick-twitch physicality to back it up.

"You made it all the way here?" the general asked as he found his seat again and beckoned the group to be seated at the other side of the table.

Keller motioned for the medallion to be shown, and Tavin obliged, placing it on the table before General Thom.

The general gazed at the golden medallion for but a second before motioning to one of the lieutenants in attendance. The lieutenant came quickly to the beckon. The general whispered something in his ear and then turned to listen to Tavin's explanations as the lieutenant ran briskly from the room and up the stairs of the spacious house.

"They ambushed us almost a month ago," Tavin started, realizing he wanted already to be done with the story. "The town fell in an hour. We didn't have a chance. There's going to be an army here soon. They sent a contingent after our retreat but—"

"Who was leading them?" Thom interrupted with steepening interest, gazing sternly into Tavin's eyes with grave seriousness so strange on his previously laughing and blushing cheeks.

"Clades," Seneca added from his seat next to Tavin. "He and some of his men chased us south. We destroyed them in the Nashville ruins, but the rest of our group was slain."

"You killed him? His name is known to us. He and his men were great warriors."

"They were just men," Seneca replied.

Tavin noticed that Seneca was holding a pain in his flank as he spoke. Thom smiled at this comment and looked around at his officers who immediately smiled as well. A few even laughed.

"I must say we're short on inspiring stories right now, and that might be the best one I've heard. As you already know, I am General Thom. This is Captain Franzen, he's my second-in-command. This is Captain Keller who you've already met. He's in charge of the wall, the archers, everything that happens there. And these are my lieutenants Cody, Jans, and Tanner."

Thom continued, "I'll have six beds put together in one of the empty apartments. I'll keep you together, as I'm sure you have much to talk about amongst yourselves. I will be wanting to hear more as well, but for now I can only imagine how tired you must be. You can sharpen up your weapons, get some fresh provisions, whatever you need," he said while maintaining his commanding presence over his table.

"Cody captured some scouts a couple days ago, and it sounds like you men are correct. Interrogations hinted that the Westies are moving a massive army across the south here. Likely much bigger than the one that attacked Greensboro, if I had to put my money on it. They're sending everything they have across this continent. Their best warriors stand at the front. Now, I'm sorry, but what did you say your name was?"

"Tavin Weber, sir."

"Weber, hmm? Was your father, Lavin?"

"Yes."

Thom warmed up at the connection.

"I knew him! I did. He was a good man, and he'd more than likely be leading the defense of this fortress if he were still alive today! And I would gladly give him the job!" Thom laughed exuberantly. "We lost too many men like him this past decade. I was just a pup when he was making a name for himself, but he made us feel important. Leaders like that are few now. In either case you all have gone above what we could ask of any soldier. Interestingly enough, that's exactly what the Chancellor is looking for these days, and it's exactly what I'm looking for. You saw what someone like Clades is capable of. Now I hear talk of Kayzitt, the marauder making his way east, so we're building our own elite squads. We need to take out their leaders, their specialists, their assassins and brutes. We need units capable of destroying their heroes and morale before they can do the same."

"And you want us?" Gannon asked, his voice flecked with grief.

"It's my prerogative to recruit where I see fit. It's a great honor I haven't offered many. I like to meet people, talk with them for a while, but you all are different...." He rubbed his chin. "I can see that."

"Where will we go?" Praxis asked.

"For now, you'll stay here and rest. Train. I'll surely use you as long as I can, but if a mission calls from the capital, a mission that would require men of your ability, then I'll have no choice but to send you out to do the will of the Chancellor."

"Train?" Oil'ib inquired.

"Well, the Chancellor has given myself and General Nairobi the authority to mold these squads down here. They're doing the same up north. You already have quite a trophy under your belts. I'd be lying if I said I've found anyone more qualified. It seems to me that Nairobi has already given you his vote."

The six friends looked each other up and down the table in bewilderment. It was not until Bok came down the stairs wearing the same decorated uniform as General Thom that Tavin put the situation together in his head.

"Yes, indeed I have," the familiar basso voice droned as Bok entered the room from the far doorway.

As he approached the table, Tavin felt understanding spread across the minds of his friends. Bok stepped forward to the table. His demeanor was sharper and even more refined. He might have been completely unrecognizable if not for the eccentric twinkle in his eye.

"My students are dead. It's time I take on some new ones. I'll have you ready for this calling, I promise. I see immense potential in you men. The type of potential that, when unfettered from improper constraints, could end this war. You will be the Chancellor's finest men, the East's finest soldiers."

Chapter Six

May 2717
Tennessee Fortress

Gannon

Mother forgive the lost child.
Father protect the lost home.
Kindness and mercy are mild.
Our duty chills to the bone.

A week had come and gone within the massive granite walls of the Tennessee fortress. General Thom still awaited the Western army and prepared his men and fortress with diligent abruptness. Even the non-military citizens inside the walls ran their lives with the steady measure of a metronome. Crops were planted within gardens that fit snugly near the center of the fortress-town. Irrigation canals were fixed and fresh wells were dug in the city spring. Where things could not be built out, they were built-up from the endless supply of stone quarried nearby. Further agricultural works were maintained outside of the walls, but the general knew these could not be relied upon when siege came, and made the necessary preparations of stocking supplies. The military men were a quiet and constant presence. They exchanged guard duties, drill work, and civilian chores in seamless transitions. Gannon had never been in such a place in his life.

Even a year into his service, the regimented world of a soldier was difficult for his mind to accept. He had grown up in a languid world of ambiguous time in New England. Musical practice had been regimented, but mostly revolved around the striking inspirations of the spirit. After his schooling the most regimented part of his life had been lighting the fire of the lighthouse, in which his family lived and was charged with upkeep. When he left home for the life of the musical bard there had been no regiment at all. Life moved like his slow bumpy carriage rides from town to town, like his passing from tavern to tavern on old boots and just enough money. The peaks of excitement had been the occasional bar brawl or the thrill of successfully seducing a local woman. Never before had consternation come at such scheduled intervals.

For Gannon and his friends, the past week had been mostly empty of the rest he had craved. General Nairobi, who allowed them to continue calling him Bok, had taken the task of their "re-education" quite seriously. Every morning was physical endurance exercises of various forms. Bok would then test them on the use of arms. They learned a new array of holds and pins, jams and jabs, bars and breaks. They learned techniques that had been only glossed over in training camp. He taught them how to control a sword, an axe, a staff, or a knife as one controls his thoughts and how to keep the mind free. The others took to the training with an eager passion. Even Seneca, whom Gannon had trusted to share his views about the war, seemed to show a disturbing amount of pride in each accomplishment. Gannon could not secure that same passion.

By the time the noon break had arrived, Gannon had been too weak to hold his bowl of oats, and his arms shook as he reached with his spoon to feed himself. In the afternoon, they sparred—against each other and against Bok himself. It quickly became clear why this older man was in a position to teach them the art of combat. Bok was a master and a graceful fighter. If an example needed to be made, Bok would show each of them by pinning or binding, slapping or jabbing, disarming or defeating each of them in due order.

If he put such practice into the arts, this Bok would be immortalized.

Bok had taken it upon himself to teach most seriously, and accepted no error without eventual success, and no success without seeing out every single error. He denounced them and praised them. He augmented their form and destroyed their stigmas and assumptions. He built a new respect for the martial arts in each of them. He made them doubt and then he instilled belief. In the evenings, they would discuss what they had learned and what they had forgotten. They would ask him questions and he would ask questions in return. They would meditate and stretch their minds and bodies. And every evening when he left Bok's presence, Gannon left with his body on the brink of falling apart, his mind on the brink of discovering a nirvana he never asked for.

The combat master had given them a day of respite.

Gannon rejoiced at the news of the intermission and determined to spend the majority of the day alone. He made two discoveries during his time in the gigantic fortress that had distracted his fancy with great ecstasy. The first was a quiet area inside an apple orchard at the border of the wheat fields. Here, Gannon sat underneath a shady tree and watched the flowers fall to the ground.

The pink petals fluttered around at random intervals and his heart sang with each beautiful surprise. The second discovery had been the mandolin for sale at the trader's shop. While walking along the cobbled road on his way to training one morning, Gannon had taken a different route and been surprised by the instrument displayed upon a stand in the shop's window. The following day he bought it. They had received a large stipend in return for their agreement to be the Chancellor's men. Indeed, it had been the main reason Gannon agreed to such a dangerous job. Though he would never tell the others. He knew they joined for other reasons. Tavin for some sense of honor and pride, Seneca for the sake of his friends, and Oil'ib took the money for the hope of supporting a woman back home. Only Gannon felt he might be accepting for purely selfish reasons. He had never been paid in gold before, and even after his purchase he had plenty of coin leftover.

Under his favorite tree he began strumming a familiar melody upon the delicate copper strings, trying to shake the thoughts of economy from his mind. His fingers traced familiar patterns on the unfamiliar fretboard. The pressure of the strings hurt his fingertips; he was surprised at how quickly those callouses had disappeared and been replaced by the thickening of skin upon the pads of his palms, where knife, sword, and morning star had become the usual instrument. Fingers skipped and jumped from chord to chord. He closed his eyes and let his hands lead his mind as the lilting notes floated through the boughs of the apple tree. Then a dissonant note appeared and his fingers stuttered at the error. He started again from the beginning. Again, his flowing music jumped away at the same spot. Each chord he tried seemed wrong. His chest was tight with frustration. He breathed deep, the sweet smell of apple blossoms on the air, warmed by the humid heat and the sunlight that broke through the boughs. Gannon rustled in his seat at the trunk and began a different song, one that was easier and he had known since childhood.

After finishing he opened his eyes to see Bok standing ten feet away, still and pleasant as the trunk of the apple tree by which he stood. Gannon was not startled by him, nor surprised at how silently the master had managed to find him in the orchard. Yet part of him could not help but be annoyed by Bok's presence.

"That was lovely. I doubt you've picked up an instrument in weeks and yet it seems so natural for you."

"I found one in the shop and I couldn't help myself."

Bok sat down against the tree across from Gannon.

"You love music. I envy your skill. I could never play anything," Bok said.

"Thank you," Gannon replied, rubbing the back of his head in flattery. "Music has always been easy for me. I might say that I envy your skills in the martial arts."

"Would you say training is tedious for you?"

Gannon sighed. Over the past week he had come to find Bok's cryptic questioning tedious in itself.

"Yeah. It is," he said curtly.

"I'm sorry you feel that way."

"Bok, I should thank you for what you're doing for us. I mean it. But at the end of the day my friends are better suited than me. Maybe it's because they're younger, certainly Tavin lives for this shit, but I just don't have the same *zeal* that they have. I know what it takes to master something. I'm not sure I'm prepared to offer it."

Gannon picked up the mandolin slightly to make his point. Its sleek, dark cherry wood caught a shaft of light in its red undertones.

"They do it so fluidly. I can't. It's like I'm forcing it just to keep up sometimes."

"But you do," Bok's tone was patient and understanding in his deep voice. "You do keep up. It's not always beautiful but you seem to find a way."

Gannon picked at the mandolin again, allowing a few notes to flutter away.

"I hope I didn't offend you with what I said on the road and all. What about leaving the war and everything—I don't actually plan on deserting."

"Did you think this life would be different?"

Gannon thought for a second before answering the battle master. Bok had worn his simple gray robes to find Gannon, the same robes he had been wearing when they first met out on the road. He wondered if this was on purpose, or if Bok really was dressing for comfort. Compared to the simple linen shirt and cotton pants that Gannon wore, Bok looked like a burnt cinder in the sun, his ebony skin peeking out from the simple grey robe and tunic.

"When I was thinking of signing up for the service,"

Gannon finally answered, "I had heard about everything that was going on and I felt left out. I came west because I thought it would be fun... *fun*! Looking back, I don't know why in the world I would have such a thought. I suppose, I thought I would still be free to enjoy most of what I considered normal life. I just never realized how consuming it would be. For instance, when we were in training camp, back in Pennsylvania, I took my friends to this bar the next town over. We'd all just met, and I wanted to get everyone comfortable with each other. The next day the captain *beat* Oil'ib for being off campgrounds without permission. Apparently, somebody told on us, but Oil'ib took the blame. The captain always hated him, for being slow and everything. But that's not fair. How could you beat a man that might be dying for his country?" Gannon gently plucked a few strings. "Or at least dying for something. Maybe...maybe even dying for nothing. That was the first time I thought about running away."

Tell a man he can't control anything and he'll snap, Gannon thought.

"We've all thought about running away," Bok replied.

"Why didn't you?" Gannon leaned forward.

Bok hesitated. His brow wrinkled around the thick gray eyebrows as if he had never expected to be asked that question. It was the first time Gannon had seen Bok make such a face.

"It's not that easy. Sometimes I think I should have. But it wasn't just about me, it's always been about passing on an artistic tradition. I merely happened to be pulled higher because of my skill in this regard. Remember, not everybody's here for a cause. Do I support liberty and freedom? Of course, I do. But I am in favor of whatever gets us to liberty and justice with the least possible deaths."

"That's all good, but there certainly are people here for the cause," Gannon said, picking at the grass with his fingers. "Take Tavin for instance. He won't ever take his mind off it. Everything is so fucking heroic to him. We all have a part to play in his great adventure. And yes, I know he wants the best out of us, but some days I don't want to be bothered with being a part in a grand story. It's like he enjoys this and wants me to be one of his sidekicks while he runs around playing hero."

"One might say that all good things start out as something heroic," Bok mused, sitting up a little straighter to stretch his back. "Maybe Tavin has realized something that you still struggle to accept. You could have left, but you didn't. It's that you want to avoid letting your friends down. You wondered why you were coming to this fort and why you keep pushing on. But I think you've had five reasons with you all along."

Gannon felt a cold cross over him. In a way, Bok was right. More than right, he was able to know Gannon's reasons for staying even when Gannon was blind to them himself. Upon realizing this, he grew sad. It would be so hard to choose between saving his own future and saving the future of his friends. He hoped that the two were not mutually exclusive.

"I wish I could protect them, but I can't." Gannon felt tears welling up inside him.

Bok's demeanor calmed.

"Still worried about fighting? After all you've been through?" Bok replied. "After all this time you think it's because you can't fight like they do. Your head is always in the wrong place. You said it yourself. You don't think about music; you just play it. But when it comes to fighting you can't get out of your own mind long enough to do it. Look at Oil'ib."

"Oil'ib barely has a mind."

Bok laughed louder than Gannon had thought him capable.

"Strong words for a friend, but your cynicism might serve better if it were tempered. Look at the way he fights," Bok continued. "Everything moves together. Everything flows. Just like that mandolin. There's a rhythm to everything, Gannon. There's a rhythm for your feet, for the way they point, for the way your knees bend, for how you twist your hips."

Bok rotated his torso upon his hips as he sat, the folds of his robe rustling softly against the verdant grass of the orchard.

"All the movement leads up into your arms. You keep them balanced and your body stays balanced. Everything moves together—the strike, the block, the return strike, your feet backpedal, but your arms don't drop. Every stage of the fight, no matter how short, there's a coordination. Just like in music, that instrument you play, both hands working together with your mind, and then your voice joins in. It's all a rhythm. It's *just* a rhythm. Now, I can't make you want to do anything, and I cannot make you hear the rhythm, but if you want to get better. There's a way."

Gannon picked the ending chord he had been searching for the last two hours.

"There it is," he said finally.

"What's that?" Bok asked.

"That chord," Gannon smiled. "When was the first time you picked up a sword?"

"I was five," the battle master replied with eyes misted in

the past.

"You see. Tavin and Oil'ib are the same way. I was sixteen. And I was only doing it because my brother wanted to spar with me before he left for training. He almost dislocated my shoulder flipping me over!"

Bok chuckled. "How did you men survive the wild?"

Gannon moved with uncomfortable agitation. The mere hint of their ability made him feel naked and naive. Gannon disliked discussing it. It was too foreign and intimate at the same time.

"Together," he replied.

Bok stood, "Very good."

"Well, maybe you can tell Tavin to not hit so hard in practice. He means well, but god, he hits hard."

"It's because you're taller than him," Bok stated with a smile.

Gannon laughed.

"It's true! He'd rip out a man's throat with his teeth just to win. He's like a starving badger."

Gannon stood and turned toward the fort. He walked with Bok through the pink and white blossoms of the orchard at a leisurely pace. Gannon found himself happy for Bok's company. There was a deep-seated peace when talking to Bok and a calmness in his presence. Gannon realized that he had been misjudging him at every turn.

"So, the Western forces were spotted south of here along the Evergreen Pass? I only needed to be told once, but Thom seems to find the need to remind us every time we walk past him," Gannon said.

"He annoys me too," Bok replied with a knowing smile. "Don't get too comfortable here. I think that before either army falls you and your friends will be off on a different mission. The breaks in between the Capitol's correspondence are few and, usually, short. I will do the best I can, of course, to give you the sum of my help before then."

Gannon shuttered and rubbed at the thin hair atop his head.

"I was just starting to feel at ease again."

"I'm only reminding you to be ready. You men aren't being trained to stand guard. You will be asked to do great things."

Chapter Seven

(Day 2717
Canyontown, Pennsylvania

Dahli

So many young girls dream of marriage.
How lucky then, for a woman to be married.
For a man, it is often enough to be born.

      The seasons had changed five times since Oil'ib left town. Throughout all of them, Dahli felt she had stayed exactly the same. She never wavered from her routine despite the falling of the leaves, the migration of the summer sun, the coming of the snowy blankets that folded over the garden, or the return of spring's gentle breeze. Every facet of her life, every movement and thought that was hers seemed placid, stagnant. Around her, the world changed in its wandering orbit. She woke up every morning, looked over at her nightstand where a hand-drawn portrait of Oil'ib stood. The portrait showed no smile. She would smile, think of him ceremoniously, and leave for the day.

Outwardly she could not complain. Not a single thing was going wrong for her, yet she felt stuck, and some days, knew that she *must* be stuck. Something internal was missing from her life and it was difficult to figure out what. After all she was saving a considerable amount of money living in her father's mansion and reaped the benefits of being there. Her social life had been healthy and she was gaining more confidence and experience at the family business. When she thought about what her husband must be enduring, she felt guilty—even spoiled. How could she be so morose when he was in a war and she was cradled in comfort? Dahli missed him desperately, his reassurance and presence. However, these feelings were different and had their own separate origin.

A noticeable void had opened up in her life. Not just the missing lover, something more uncertain. Every morning she went down to breakfast with her father, who would lay out the day's agenda to her with stern good humor, and then she would ride with him in the carriage to the factory office to complete her duties. Listening to the wheels rolling over the rasping dust, she would watch as the houses disappeared behind the window and the looming mass of bricks that was the factory approached. By the time they were inside the building she would be torn between thankfulness for the cool air and chagrin at being trapped inside.

This morning found her sitting alone at the family's long dining room table, picking at the frayed edge of the fine, hand-printed tablecloth. It was her favorite tablecloth in the house, a loose, white fabric printed with red cherries and gold leaves. She was hungry and stared at her hot eggs and porridge in front of her, while she waited for her father to arrive.

Here I am, she thought, waiting for him to come down so I may eat. What beguiles me to do this?

She missed making decisions, especially ones that affected her directly. Tapping her finger against her temple, she stared at the steam rising off the eggs. When was the last time she had made a life decision? She searched for one that was not some mathematical calculation according to the success of her business. Nothing came to mind.

Her job, her wage, where she lived, and her future; her parents had dreamed up a life for her and had done a fabulous job of seeing that path executed. The one wild card she had managed to find was Oil'ib; but the longer the war went on, the more fleeting that independence felt and the more distant became that escape. Even the thought of him reminded her of her own inaction. She had to admire his determination, even if it did not serve either of them in the short term. Leaving for war had been a duty to Oil'ib that he followed blindly. After all, her father could have come up with an excuse for Oil'ib, or even bought off the draft sergeant. But Oil'ib had not wanted her to ask him. She did not blame him.

She waited for her father. The house sat so quiet that even the new kiss of spring could not bring it to life. As she gazed about the manor, she came to realize that so much of the house went unused, merely filled with stuff—the collections and hobbies of her father. Entire bedrooms existed between her own and her parents'. The overall effect was chilling isolation, and seeking comfort in her parents was not a significant cure. Father was predictable, obstinate, and busy. Mother, poor mother, seemed merely a diluted reflection of her father. If she wanted to know what her father thought of a thing, she could just as easily ask her mother.

Suddenly she was possessed by an inspiring idea. Dahli ate her eggs as the thought solidified, stuffing them into her mouth in gluttonous heaps with no one around to look upon her with judgment, as well as most of her porridge, burning the roof of her mouth a little in her rush. Before the servant could clear her place she was upstairs, forgoing her drab work outfit for something more flowery. Then she was downstairs again, heading for the ornate main door, rather than the back where her father would see her leave by carriage.

"Leaving early miss?"

Their butler, a sprig and wiry man of indeterminate old age stood in the hallway. Jeffer was his name, and he was a kindly sight when she turned, startled by the inquiry.

"Yes, Jeffer. You may inform my father that I walked to work. I… I wish to get an early start."

"Very good miss. Are you sure you would not like a horse made ready?"

"In this dress? No, but thank you Jeffer, breakfast was quite lovely."

"My pleasure, miss."

Her walk to the factory was not long. She had only one road to follow. There were several houses in between her father's and his factory, along with their yards and properties. The houses were for the factory employees and each one was rented to capacity by the different smiths and their families. Sometimes her father would joke that he nearly made back all the money he spent on payroll in silver from rent alone.

The breeze twisted gently on her morning walk and the sun burned a hole through the clouds to remind the town of its presence. Aromas from the fresh flowers made her walk more tolerable, the tepid smell of earth and roots exuding from the ground and carried by the breeze. In a couple months the season would change again. She was determined to do something before it did.

In time she came to the factory. The foreman of the early shift had already opened the building and she entered by the large rising door at the back of the massive brick structure. Deliveries and shipments were gathered here and a wave of heat engulfed her as she stepped inside. The smiths were already burning coal and their apprentices worked the bellows with continual thrusting of their young elbows. Dahli looked about the work, trying to find something new in the routine that they engaged in. Nothing came to mind. She sighed and found the grate-iron stairs to the offices above the factory floor.

Upon entering the spartan office space, with its lone window, brick walls around maple furniture, Dahli was pacified in relief that Jeremiah was not yet at work along with her father. It was not that her fellow assistant offended her, but he was the newest partner with the company and her father's gushing over him had been overwhelming. The only time he praised someone beneath him was when he was making plans of his own for that person's life. With a quickened pace she strode to her desk and pulled the latest files from her drawer, so as to look busy. Then, glancing once more out the small window, and again out the door to the office, she returned to her desk and bent down to where a floorboard was loose and pulled up the small board to reveal a space.

She opened a gap between the floor and the paneling of the ceiling of the lower works. The space was only six inches deep and the board only a foot wide. Inside was a metal case. She pulled it up from the warm and musty gap and placed it on her desk. A small black skeleton key opened the box and revealed the riches she had been able to squirrel away. A handful of gold, another of silver, it was a fortune in the eyes of any local layperson, and took two years to acquire.

After counting her money, sure that it would be enough for what she required, Dahli stowed it back in her secret compartment and smiled to herself. As her father and Jeremiah came through the door of the office, caught up in some bantering about raw iron shipments, she knew they would only see her smirking at the paperwork strewn about her desk—never suspecting she was looking through the work, the table, and the floor.

"It is nice to see you so happy to be at work," Jeremiah proclaimed with a wink that made Dahli uncomfortable. "Work is easier when colleagues are happy."

"Though I would have enjoyed your company in the carriage," her father said, as if the break from convention had hurt his feelings. "I do hope you still plan on joining me for lunch with the crew."

The crew was her father's euphemism for his small group of aristocratic friends. They were a collection of fine diners and whisky drinkers, who had become diluted in their own self-worth.

"Oh yes," she replied. "You didn't think I could forget something I do every day did you?"

"Well I just like to ask."

She began arranging the papers on her desk and straightening her thoughts so as to truly start her work. Aware of Jeremiah's eyes upon her, she resisted looking up, so as not to start a conversation. She knew there would be plenty more attempts throughout the day that she would have to curtail in some fashion. No reason to start now.

The excitement for her plan made the morning hours drag by. Her work held little attention from her and progress was slow. When lunch time finally arrived, she was relieved for the break from her own daydreaming, even if it was to spend an hour with her father and his stuffy friends. Escorted by Jeremiah and his conversation about dog breeding, the three of them made their way to the carriage.

"I don't care for it honestly," he stated with a tone of determination, "and the prices my father can charge for a purebred are asinine…but people will always pay."

"I'm sure they're lovely animals. I know I can't afford one," she replied.

"Nonsense. I'll bring you by the barn someday and let you pick one out for yourself. If my dad says anything, I'll remind him that it was I who delivered his last litter."

"That's sweet of you," she smiled, but said nothing further on the subject.

Another short drive and they were in the town center, with the driver tying up the horses at the gate of her father's favorite eatery. The place was an old billiards club, which charged a monthly fee for membership and also served hot sandwiches for lunch. Her father remained a member, out of show more than necessity, and hardly ever touched a stick at the billiards table.

"Gambling is a loser's sport," he was want to say. "Only ever risk money when you're in control."

The three of them took their seats at the table by the window where the view of town's main road was as good as the view of the perpetually drunk well-to-do's inside. Dahli tapped the dirt from her boots and allowed Jeremiah to seat her. The room was musty and smelled of roast beef. Cigar smoke curled lightly over their heads from a table of old men behind them. Through the haze she saw two of her childhood classmates, who looked to have fallen on hard times, sitting on the laps of two older men. Their shirts were cut low at the chest. The two older men seemed thrilled. The sudden clap of billiards colliding drew her gaze away.

A stale waiter, Jules, took their orders promptly and filled their goblets with tea. Just before Jules could leave for the kitchen the rest of their party arrived and placed their orders while joining the table. Dahli recognized and exchanged pleasantries with Mr. Owen Crumb, a local money lender; a flat and vapid looking man who parted his hair down the middle and peered at her through narrow spectacles. She did the same with Mr. Frederick Browning. He was a rotund one, who wheezed slightly beneath a wide forehead and simple hair-cut, straight across like a bowl—making his forehead appear all the wider. Mr. Browning's story was well known among the townsfolk. As a simple farmer, a series of successful deals had made him an owner of much of the local farmland, which he now rented out to poorer farmers in exchange for a hefty portion of the crop profits. He had changed his name from Fred to Frederick long ago at the change of his fortune.

"Finally, Demen, you've emerged from your brick castle

to spend some time with the common folk," Frederick wheezed. "I'm glad success hasn't changed you."

"You are hardly the common folk," Dahli's father replied, "but yes, I must apologize for my recent absence. We have more work than I bargained for. It's a lot to handle even with Jeremiah pitching in."

Her father clapped Jeremiah on the shoulder in a gesture of solidarity.

"Ah yes, Jeremiah," Owen chimed in with his soft voice. "Your father is Jeremy Stenton, is it not? The glass-blower from Middlebury?"

"As a matter of fact, he is," Jeremiah said, as if greatly pleased. "How did you know?"

"I was one of his first investors. One of the best investments I ever made. People do love the fragile convenience of glass."

"Indeed. Then I must thank you for helping to finance my childhood."

Owen Crumb nodded his head, a minute gesture in the way his short neck bowed his flat long nose forward.

"Dahli," Frederick said, leaning forward on the table, "you must be happy to have such a lad to help you with your," he wheezed, "your duties. Especially with business booming as it is."

Dahli blushed slightly at the mention of Jeremiah affecting her own world in any tangible way. But she nodded, bringing her chin high before dropping it, while fiddling with the silverware at her place, realigning the knife and the fork.

"Yes, the piles of ledgers that usually weigh on my desk have been halved. And for that I am quite thankful."

I'm no different than those girls at that next table.

The three older men nodded, as if agreeing to her thoughts.

At that moment the sandwiches were served by the stooping waiter and another man who worked in the kitchen. Dahli was happy for the momentary relief from conversation that eating brought. Though her appetite was small, she made sure to keep her mouth full, so as to possibly avoid further questions. As she ate, the conversation continued without her, the men came to discussing the war between mouthfuls of roast beef and sauerkraut.

"One might not guess, but the lending business has been rewarded with the continued fighting," Owen was explaining. "A fear of destitution brings a lot of families into our midst. Of course, I always charge military families a reasonable interest—cheaper than any other I might say. But even still, when it comes time to collect, I will not regret having parted with the money for a time."

"You can speak for yourself," Frederick huffed, putting down his sandwich and mopping his face with his napkin. "With all the farm men I stand to lose to the draft, I will be forced to hire out for the harvests. And the only men left are... well, not as *efficient*."

He swallowed and breathed quite intensely, catching up on the air he had lost while speaking.

"But you Demen, you have struck while the iron is hot! Tell me, what news do your," he pitched his wheezing voice lower for their ears alone, "your connections in the Capitol give you?"

Dahli watched her father, and she saw that Jeremiah watched him with intense interest while chewing away at his own sandwich, brushing a lock of hair back into position. Her father leaned back in his chair, inhaling as he tightened his grip on the armrests. For a second, Dahli was sure that Demen was going to reprimand the farm manager for asking such a question. But he leaned forward again, inclining his head and raising his brow so that the wrinkles formed on his balding hairline. There was a twinkle in his scheming eyes that Dahli recognized.

"I'll tell you this, and only this," her father said between glances at Dahli and Jeremiah. "With the way things are going I am considering opening up a second plant in Middleburgh."

"That well?" exclaimed Owen, his voice pitching high with excitement. "Or should I say, that long? Well—if you are in need of coin for this new factory…"

"Oh, trust me," Demen smiled, "I am in no need of a loan, in fact, the only thing I need are more people to hire. Lately it seems my potential workforce is the only thing that has thinned."

At this Frederick gave vigorous nods.

"But, besides that," Demen continued, "this company has never had a brighter future."

Dahli could not smile along with the others at the table. She instinctively clutched at the black metal box that she had smuggled along in her purse, now heavy with the secret. Her stomach was turning upon itself with her father's words, she looked repulsively at the roast beef on her plate, its flesh frayed and hacked by her knife.

Dahli seemed to be the only one at the table capable of seeing the people in the town were growing poor and indebted. She saw them hungry and unable to afford the food that they grew themselves. She glanced again at her former friends that both smiled with pretend joy as the business men groped their curves.

They were feeling the full effects of this dying economy. Still, she could not argue with her father about the war. How could she argue when she was living off the fat of the war herself? She was comfortable in her rich bed at night and eating the finest steaks for dinner. War was the only force she was willing to admit could end her time with Oil'ib. Her father could not have cared less. He was happy again.

"If you'll please excuse me," she said suddenly, capturing the gaze of the four men. "I have some, um, business to attend to downtown. I apologize for my rudeness, I only just remembered." Frederick and Owen stood with her and bowed their farewell, Frederick taking a little longer to do so. However, Jeremiah and her father seemed taken aback.

"Business during lunch Dahli? What possibly could it be?" Demen pressed.

Her father peered suspiciously over his vulture-like nose. His brow wrinkled again as his thin eyebrows lifted into thinner scalp.

"Are you feeling okay?" Jeremiah asked, looking at her unfinished meal.

"Oh yes, yes, I am fine," she explained. "Really it is a chore that I promised mother I would carry out." She looked sternly as she could upon her father as she said this.

If he had one weak spot, it was for the precarious temperament of her mother. Perhaps he might even suppose she was going to shop for his birthday, which was approaching in the summer.

"Very well, as you must," he assented. "Will you be ok getting back to the office?"

"Yes, please don't wait for me." She smiled generously at the others and was out the door before she could hear Jeremiah asking if she desired him to join her.

Jeremiah was a handsome thing. Certainly, that was why her father had hired him, besides his family heritage in business. His full coal-black hair, strong jawline, and patrician nose seemed to mock the man who had asked for her hand in marriage. In another lifetime she would have gladly accepted Jeremiah's advances. It was this knowledge of herself that made him all the more detestable. She cursed him for being so perfect in her father's eyes and so taunting in her own. Who was she to attract such things? In the windows of the passing shops she saw herself as little more than the short and stout woman that she knew herself to be. Her brow was that of her father's, broader than she wanted. Her nose was a feminized version of her father's as well and it displeased her. Her mother's hair had been kind enough to find her, but it seemed limp and lifeless in its tawny shoots.

Wood planks gave way to cobblestone, and threatened to trip her into a passing gentleman. The light stumble shook her free of her brooding. She walked briskly through the warm afternoon air, her stylish yet none-too-practical boots slipping slightly over the glazed cobblestones. A resolute goal had settled into her consciousness, and now she knew she must accomplish it before she could find the time to doubt herself and tear the idea asunder. Dahli also knew that she had some leverage over her father because of how valuable she had become at her position. He hardly ever looked at the financial books any more, and when the tax collector came, he allowed her to handle the transaction. Demen had even spoken of allowing her to take over control of purchasing. He found the work boring. He could not part with her even if she opposed him. She realized however, that the biggest challenge in confronting her father would not come from him, but rather from a small place within herself—a pit that festered with childlike fear and threatened to send her back to her room in a fit of dismay.

The work of the day had driven most people indoors or to their respective fields. The streets were still but for a driver feeding oats to the horses. In the afternoon sun, the chill of the morning had been sent away and along the roads could be heard the sounds of people opening their shutters and taking in the sweet air. The destination was not far. Dahli turned off the cobblestone road onto a brick walkway of the center street, home to all the major businesses in town.

The destination was Mr. Avery's house. Mr. Avery was a kind man, who was into the age that most kind old men had retired. Yet he was fond of making vapid excuses for not retiring, saying that his work was what kept him going. It was his self-invented responsibility to help sell and trade most of the land around the area. People would bring him their land claim and he would help them get a fair price from potential suitors. Years earlier, when Dahli was a small child, her own family had dealt with Mr. Avery when they negotiated for the hundred acres that the factory currently sat upon. If anyone could help her, it was him.

The walk up to Mr. Avery's place was one of Dahli's favorite walks in Canyontown. After passing the market shops she would take a right by the Red Cafe and slowly the colors of the brick blended from beige to red and then to beige again. Years ago, a large supply of red paint had been spilled upon the road while making the Red Cafe red. Now, the faded colors made a pretty cobblestone mural. When she was young the neighborhood girls would play games, skipping down the bricks—trying to only touch the red colored squares. Fond memories and the jingle of the gold within her lock box made her giggle to herself in the quiet street.

"Miss Perot," said Mr. Avery, surprising her as she entered his modest place of business. "Still playing at the *Red Cafe*?"

Mr. Avery was a handsome looking man for his age. He had short salt and pepper hair that managed to avoid recession far longer than his peers, and he always smelled like tobacco smoke, but was never smoking.

"Almost forgot how," she replied.

The entrance gave way to a darkened room. There were maps of the surrounding lands upon the walls and benches for people to sit upon as they waited to see him. To the left, a lone office made the throne of his business. A candle in the room was smoking as if it had just been snuffed out. To the right, a thin staircase led to his living quarters above. He had a stack of papers under his arm and appeared to be about to leave for another part of the town. She gave him a look of need and he decided to pause.

"Can I help you?" he asked.

"I hope you can," she said pulling out the tin that contained her savings.

He gave her a nod, and motioned for her to follow him to his desk. As the door opened, she was immediately hit with the familiar and strong aroma of coffee beans and tobacco. There were deer heads hung on the wall over the fireplace, the office doubling as his living room. A pair of black cats sat silently next to each other by the big table that he used both of entertaining and as his desk. Dahli paused to eye the cats wearily, they seemed to do the same to her.

"You never liked cats did you," Mr. Avery said astutely.

She nodded. Cats, especially black cats, had been a source of anxiety. It was the way they stared, as if reading you and knowing your thoughts. In all her years she never played with his cats and now she found herself especially fretful of them. She shook the thought from her head.

"Please have a seat," he said pulling an oak chair out for her. Then he proceeded to relight the candle that had been recently snuffed as well as several others.

She sat down across the table from him and he fixed his gaze. He looked at her like an elder, with his kind, sun-wrinkled face smiling and she took the moment to sit up as straight as she could.

"I know there have been a lot of newcomers to town with my father's factory," she said garnering a nod from Mr. Avery. "I know good land has been hard to come by recently, but I need your help."

"Dahli I'm having a meeting with your father on Thursday. We can all talk then if that would be easier," he said in a veiled attempt to reassure her, but she asserted otherwise.

"No, sir. This is between you and me." She opened the package and revealed her savings.

"I'm impressed," he said with a raise of the eyebrows.

"This is every gold piece I've saved. Every gift I had. I want to know how much land I can get and what I can build there."

Avery rubbed his brow a bit and exhaled deeply.

"Near town?" he asked.

"Of course. I'm the assistant to the owner of the biggest weapons manufacturer in the East. I'm not riding my horse to work every day," she tried at a joke.

Mr. Avery failed to laugh, but responded with his own curt nod of acceptance. He pulled out some papers from his stack and looked them over. Excitement flooded her mind as she began contextualizing all the details. He was actually taking her seriously. Mr. Avery seemed to ponder a certain sheet with great intent, but then was quickly onto another and then a different set of several papers.

"Sir," she said, looking out the slats of shuttered window and seeing her father's carriage being pulled toward the billiards club, "I just want you to know I am short on time."

He glanced over to her and discreetly put the page away.

"Perhaps you could narrow down what you are looking for?"

"I would like twelve acres and good soil," she replied.

"Twelve acres is impossible," he stated bluntly.

"Why?" she retorted, "I have more than enough of a payment and with my job and money I have coming to me. I could pay off a loan in—"

"Honey—"

"It's Ms. Perot," she said cutting him off. "Why can't you get me a deal?"

He moved the candle over which was blocking their view of each other, no doubt thanks to the fact that she stood barely five feet tall.

"Look, it's not as simple as you think."

Mr. Avery closed her lock-box and set it down upon his

desk with a rattling thump. He rubbed his face and eyes with his palms and then leveled his light eyes upon Dahli again.

"The truth is, Ms. Perot, that I am under instruction by your father already to—"

"Instruction by my father?" Dahli interrupted vehemently. She felt herself going white with shock.

There is no way that father could have known of my plan! Is there? I have been so safe and careful! Dahli thought, as panic rose in her chest.

"It's not what you think, perhaps," Mr. Avery said in a startled explanation, his eyes wide at the intrusion. "You see, your father has been making the plans for his umm, second factory, and in doing so he has paid me to put in a controlling bid on any land in the town that is for sale. As soon as something comes up, your father wishes to purchase it. Some will be land for the second factory, but most will be housing for those workers and homes that he will rent out, etcetera…."

"That damn man!" she nearly shouted, pulling at the hem of her winter skirts. "He wants to own the entire goddamn town!" Mr. Avery smiled as if he had said the same thing earlier.

"It might appear that way miss. I'm sorry, but if you put in a bid on a piece of land in town then your father will only automatically put in a higher bid. Times are hard, what with the war and all and I'm afraid I cannot turn my back on making the most out of my own percentage fees."

Mr. Avery petted his salt and pepper mustache nervously. Dahli could tell he felt bad about denying her claim. For a minute, she considered leaving the office and retreating back to work. Perhaps she could convince her father to sell her one of his new properties after she had earned a little more of his money for herself.

No, he will only say no. He'll tell me to be wise and save my money. He'll say I should live at home, where I have a room already for free, and a butler, and parents, and food prepared for me, and all the damn trappings of an aristocratic slavery of my own.

She threw her head out of her thoughts again, put her chin in the air and demanded Mr. Avery's attention once more, which the old friend gave willingly.

"If you help me, I'll give you seven percent of our rental profits," she said tossing her secret weapon at him.

Mr. Avery stood up, his pepper mustache twitching side to side as he started pacing around the room.

"Your father doesn't know about this?" he asked, wringing his hands.

"He trusts me with everything. We have tons of farming pieces at the end of the month and I rent them off to local farmers and such. Father never even sees that money. He's overcharging them as is," she said, standing up as well.

After a long pause he turned.

"I can get you five acres, but that's it."

"If you do, I won't give you more than two percent of the rentals, and the only way you're touching my money is if you can take it from me and if Oil'ib ever found out he'd beat you like a drum," she fired back. "Please Mr. Avery, I have never asked you for anything in my life, but this is the only thing that I have ever truly wanted. Would you stand between me and all of my life-long happiness? Surely, you would not want your own sons so undersold if they were in my situation. My father will own all the land one way or another."

"Ten acres," he stated, and Dahli could tell by the remorseful expression on the pouting old skin of his face that she had deeply affected him.

"Three percent then," she replied.

He put his face in his hands before taking a moment to stare down this girl who was suddenly a woman.

"Fine, twelve acres it is, but I want you to know that I am probably leaving a better offer on the table."

"I acknowledge that as the truth," she said, her heart already pounding with the growing joy alight in her chest. "You are always hard-working and fair, Mr. Avery, and a dear friend as well. And I thank you again, truly, this is more important to me than you know."

Dahli left after some small talk about the family and how Mr. Avery's son had been drafted into the army. Before leaving, she kissed her old friend kindly upon the cheek and thought she felt the cold ghost of a drying tear amongst the aroma of tobacco. As she walked with a brisk pace along the cobblestones toward home, her heart was rising with the excitement over what lay before her. She felt like the spirit of spring itself being blown forward by the west wind, warm and expectant, through the streets of the town.

Chapter Eight

Ϣay 2717
Tennessee Fortress

Tavin

Imagine how lonely life would be, if one had all the gold he could handle, but not a friend to share it with. What an empty existence! Give me my boon companions and the open world. We will make a kingdom from the dirt.

Plant matter seared with crackling heat in the bowl of the dark wood pipe as Tavin filled his mouth with the earthy smoke. The sweet haze lingered lazily from his lips as he opened and pushed it out in gentle plumes. He passed the pipe back to Gannon. The group of six laughed about a comment that Oil'ib had made. Though they had been relieved of their training today, in lieu of preparation for approaching Western forces, the friends had awoken early out of routine, dressed in their battle mail and weapons, and then retired to the haystacks around the inner wall of the fortress. Across the courtyard, the sun warmed their faces above the eastern wall.

They passed the morning making light of their situation. From the weeks of strenuous training under Bok, the approach of siege was surprisingly restful. Tavin kept the laughter coming by making ridiculous faces as he puffed the tobacco smoke above their reclined positions and performed his imitations of General Thom.

"I'm telling you *Nairobi*, the key to proper defense is a strong *ballistic* force!" he mimed, accentuating with the airy aristocratic voice that was General Thom's idiosyncrasy.

When he decided that it was time to go into the privy across the courtyard and empty his bladder, the conversation kicked up again as Tavin roused himself and stood. The muscles in his legs were still sore from Bok's incessant conditioning and sparring routines, but they felt springy and strong and Tavin had never been more pleased with how his life had turned out.

"Where's um—where's Bok?" Oil'ib asked drowsily from his seat in the straw.

"He walked by an hour ago. Didn't seem like he was in a rush," Praxis answered.

"The scouts said they saw advance cavalry on the move. Probably arriving on Tuesday."

"What day is it?" Tavin inquired.

Kendo exhaled smoke. "Tuesday."

The group began standing and stretching after Tavin made the move to do so. They patted the straw from their jerkins and tightened the belts of their scabbards. Along the high walls of the fortress, the reinforced guard marched in steady order like a line of insects silhouetted by the morning sun.

"I'm sorry. I was so tired from beating you in sparring that I forgot the day," Tavin said, while he picked an apple from a nearby tree. Its skin was fresh and crimson red. He tossed it at Kendo.

Kendo grabbed the fruit and bit into the crisp skin.

"I could use a *real* day off," Seneca said, as they walked across the courtyard.

They began to climb the granite steps to the overlook of the central keep. Tavin was slightly relieved not to find Bok upon the wide-open balcony of the keep's overlook. Instead there was only the sprawling view of the Tennessee wilderness. To the west lay the slightly inclining hill on which the enormous fortress was nestled. In the distance it leveled onto a high plain before being swallowed by the dome of the blue horizon. To the east, the heavy forest swept in like a dark green wave, coming ever so close to the eastern wall of the fortress bulwarks before sweeping back into the distance.

Behind him the inner sanctum of the fortress bustled with officers coming and going. Tavin could picture General Thom and Bok, strategizing across from each other at the wide tables in the keep's main room, arguing politely and giving orders. The lieutenants which came from that doorway walked past the six men of the Chancellor as if they were setting out to see to detailed instructions, saluting them with curt nods before carrying on.

"Good morning gentlemen. No training today?"

The cool voice of General Thom startled Tavin and he turned reflexively into a salute with the others. The general put them at ease and inhaled the morning air heavily as he stepped forward from the heavy door and out onto the open granite floor of the overlook.

"Bok gave us a day off," Tavin replied.

"Well, I know you boys have a habit of wandering around outside, but keep in mind no one's leaving the fortress. Not unless it's my scouts." The general let his gaze drift past Oil'ib as he spoke.

"The enemy should be here soon. If our scouts have correctly adjusted our expectations," Thom stated. "Unfortunately, the off days never last."

Seneca leaned against the battlements, "What will you have us do when they arrive?" he asked.

"I haven't figured that out yet."

Tavin let his imagination slip. The weight of his swords upon his back made him restless. He found it much more agreeable outside the walls than trapped inside the fortress awaiting a chance to play defense. The high walls gave him a great sense of advantage, but he hated heights. In his mind's eye, he imagined shadows crawling up the high walls of the fortress and felt a great tension in his chest, the feeling of something watching him from behind. His head felt strangely light, yet there was a pressure near the center of his forehead. As if a finger were poking him and pressing the picture deeper into his mind.

"Sir," Lieutenant Jans said suddenly, appearing behind General Thom and startling Tavin out of his daydream.

The lieutenant pointed to the wall.

The men upon the overlook turned in unison to see Captain Keller running along the far wall to the south. Keller was barely discernible from the lines of men along the wall, if not for the maroon flag he was waving in jerking motions above his head as he ran. The whipping red fabric, a piece of Western uniform donated generously from an enemy at some point, stood out in the banking sunlight like a beacon.

"Welcome to the show everyone," the general sighed in his airy tone. "It starts early today."

The general summoned the rest of his lieutenants from the keep. Jans, Cody, and Tanner surrounded him like children around their stalwart father. He beckoned them, commanded their attention, and delineated his orders to each. One took charge of the trebuchets arranged along the wider parts of the high first wall. Another took charge of the archers, running them up the various granite stairs to arrange in rows along the wall. The last was given charge of the infantry below, set to organize them along the staircases and main entrance, ready to support the archers or defend the heavy palisade as needed.

In the distance, Keller, the captain of the guard, appeared to be listening to a scout barking from beyond the wall. In due course, the captain began waving a different flag from his station along the southern ramparts. This one was white with a red 'X'.

"Advance cavalry," Cody interpreted aloud.

"Have archers fire sweeping volleys," Thom instructed, his countenance calm as he scanned the horizon.

A trickling of crimson could be seen emerging in the distance down from the mile-long grade to the south of the fortress. From their spot above the wall on the overlook, Tavin could see a small rivulet of Western forces diverging from the main at a slightly faster clip.

In little time, the forces of the Western army could be

seen breaking into three prongs of a scepter, while the advanced cavalry approached the fortress. The men and horses could be seen individually now. It was an appreciable force. Much larger, it seemed, than the totality of souls defending the fortress. Tavin felt the first pangs of anxiety ripping through him and hoped sincerely that their walls would even the odds. The fortress felt claustrophobic, even atop the high keep.

Tavin disliked being unable to maneuver about his enemy and he found himself annoyed that neither Thom nor Bok had taken the time to involve them in any way. He understood that at this point the fortress was being reactive and not proactive but itched for something, anything to do. As if Thom had sensed his inner turmoil, the general put his hand upon Tavin's shoulder, shaking him again from his own distraction. As he turned, he saw Thom was smiling ever so slightly and nodded to a cabinet on the wall of the overlook.

"Take the flag in there and give him three waves," he said.

Tavin did as he was told. He took the green flag in the tall wooden cabinet and waved it three times, relaying the order to fire to Keller. The archers along the wall began firing their weapons upon the enemy cavalry. The dusty stomping of hooves upon the earth poured over the fortress to reach Tavin's ears as muffled rumbling. Whining horses and the shouts of men pierced through. Tavin fidgeted nervously. His arms trembled to reach to the handle of his swords. He would have run along the wall to reach a better view of the action if not for the collected eyes of General Thom which seemed to be against his straying without orders of some kind.

After a few minutes a return volley sprayed from the

Western cavalry. Several guards around the battlements were pricked savagely, falling to their death or squirming upon the ground until their fellow archers could help them. A manic energy pervaded their group of six. They had become accustomed to the adrenaline rush of battle, and to be relegated to the peaks of leadership in the observation deck of the keep was to be a fish out of the water.

Captain Franzen, allegedly Thom's favorite officer, approached from along the wall. A leader among the lookouts, he was a sturdy young man of sandy disposition and an honest face. He sought general Thom in a hurry, giving no acknowledgement of the others.

"They're circling us, sir. Fairly close to the wall," Franzen surmised, "Likely they are just getting the feel of us. What are your orders?"

"Keep the pressure on them. Show them we're not intimidated," Thom stated. "We have to force them backwards in this first engagement, or it will never end."

"Yes sir."

The captain was off again to the far southern end of the high wall, shouting the order as he passed.

Captain Keller eventually re-entered the spacious balcony of the keep for a report, and saluted Thom, his dapper red hair and pale face unfazed and formal.

"Advance cavalry. They've circled off into the woods. No telling how far back the infantry is."

"Casualties?" Thom inquired.

"Minimal—both sides."

"Before they approach again, I want some hoardings upon

the battlements, just in case. And make sure the trebuchets have ample ammunition when they come into range."

"Any word on the reinforcements?" Keller inquired hopefully.

"I would not count on any."

"I'm heading to the wall, with your leave, sir. Anything you need reported?" Tavin asked, hoping that this formality would gain him his leave onto the forward bulwarks, his inspiration and curiosity no longer able to be contained.

Thom shook his head and dismissed the six of them to their perusal. They left the observatory in earnest order and stepped with excited interest along the high wall. The battlefield was in quiet intermission as they crossed the wooden bridges between walls and found the forward battlements. They walked along rows of archers exchanging their shifts and bows and greeted them with approving nods. Across the sloping fields to the south, the Western forces were retreating into a more permanent camp along the edge of the forest that swept in from the east and provided a break from the wind. The general's orders still drifted from mouth to mouth as officers prepared the men for the afternoon guard.

"How fast were they?" Kendo asked one of the soldiers standing post.

"Very fast. They were hard to hit. Fastest horses I've ever seen," the archer replied.

Tavin gazed over the edge of the wall and down the looming stone to the patchy earth below. It was rocky and populated by only the occasional bush or shrub. Horses that could move quickly across such terrain were sure-footed indeed. The land was its own defense and what the fortress lacked in a moat the ground made up for in its uneven, stony landscape. Tavin was comforted by this and spit over the side of the wall, watching as his projectile was tossed by the breeze and fell to a miniscule drop below.

Tavin tried to stay on the battlements longer, hoping that more excitement would find them, but after a couple hours it became obvious that he was wasting his time and the beckoning of his friends brought him back down into the fortress. There they passed the evening playing cards with the lieutenants and ate dinner at their table. He gathered that many of them had not yet seen any real action and was surprised at how many officers were fresh from the academy. This made Tavin uneasy, and it was all he could do not to start lecturing on his experiences like a grouchy old general. But he resisted and they had a good time, sharing port and playing poker until they dispersed to their rooms.

The night came and went for Tavin with no memory of sleep. He awoke somewhat agitated and upon entering the main room of the barracks was informed that one of the night shift guards upon the wall had fallen to his death after being struck by an arrow.

"Likely some ballsy Westie, felt like taking some shots in the night," General Thom concluded when he passed through the barracks at lunch.

Another day passed in similar manner. A portion of the Western cavalry would approach the wall, fire a volley or two and then dissipate back into the Western camp to the south, safely out of range of arrows. General Thom expressed his pleasure with the showing, fancying they had enough defenses and provisions to outlast the Westerners at this pace. After all, the archers on the wall had begun beating out the invading cavalry archers: three for every one Eastern defender. But Bok had reminded Thom that the West would try something new soon.

"They did not cross the great river to play games with us," he urged them.

On the next night, Bok was proven correct.

It was in the pitch dark of their barracks, a six-bed loft in a town house for officers, that Tavin awoke to muffled screaming; the sound slipped in through the shuttered window. He sat up into a cool, damp air, condensed from the heat of the day. The grainy wood floors were humid, and the sweat that had gathered on Tavin's lower back felt cold as he opened the window to the breeze. He pricked his ears again for the noise, assuming that he must have dreamt it.

The night was quiet. Only the torches up high illuminated the wall across the courtyard of dark houses. The sky was empty of any moonlight and only the blanket of stars twinkled upon the rooftops. Tavin shrugged and shuttered the windows again, hearing one of the others turn in his bunk as he did so. He returned to sleep.

He could hardly remember closing his eyes when he was shaken awake by the arms of Captain Franzen.

"I need all of you at the wall!" the sandy-haired man expressed consternation. "Last night several of the guards on the high wall were murdered."

He found that last word odd given the circumstances.

"Murdered?" Tavin questioned the captain, exasperated.

"They were found at the base of the wall. But it wasn't from cavalry arrows. Their throats were slit!"

Tavin jumped out of bed and began dressing into his jacket and pants, put on his swords as Franzen began shaking the others awake.

"What? Who?" Oil'ib asked in sluggish pity.

Seneca and Praxis joined Tavin upon the cool floor and dressed enough to be presentable, telling Frenzen they would be there shortly.

It was atop the same high overlook of the keep. Tavin felt trapped again, as he received his briefing in front of Bok and General Thom. Bok, who had put off any further training to focus on writing a series of letters to the capital, now questioned one of the night shift guards in the main room of the keep. They had seen him for but a minute before he had left and allowed Thom to brief them on the situation.

"It was brought to my attention that last night, probably around three in the morning, several of the guards on the wall were killed—throats slit where they stood. I'm trying to downplay this because I can't have a panic two and a half days into a siege," Thom said in his normal airy and calm voice. Tavin sensed a touch of nervous energy in the way the general kept running the palm of one hand against the short trimmed black hair atop his head.

Tavin could see a tremor in the muscle above the cheek, beneath the sharp features.

"Now, the survivors weren't able to offer much. Just that whoever it was moved quickly. They couldn't be seen. They did their damage and left. No one was able to get a good look. When pressed, the men only report seeing…" the general sighed as he turned his flint dark eyes upon Tavin and sweeping his gaze across the others. "Seeing shadows."

"Human shadows, I hope?" Tavin quipped.

"What you men did in Nashville was impressive to say the least. Therefore, I am assigning you to the night guard. I would be pleased if whoever is responsible for this attack did not return. Logic tells me that will not be the case." The general leaned back on the wall of the keep and pressed his fingertips. "You are to wait for them to come back, and eliminate whoever did this."

They were silent.

"I know this is a bit of a drastic change, but I told you I would use you. It'll be dangerous but the security of this wall has to be a priority. Am I clear?"

They all nodded their ascent. Thom made a motion with his hand and Captain Keller, came forward from the inner sanctum of the keep.

"Shall I sir?".

"Well, they're no good standing in here," Thom responded.

Keller motioned for the six men to follow him and led them out onto the outer wall of the fortress. They walked six abreast upon the wide battlements as the fire-haired captain detailed their assignment.

"Bok has been speaking highly of you men. Says you're the kind of people to have around for this type of problem."

"Where did they attack?" Kendo inquired.

"Four different spots. They must've scaled the walls. It is the only way such an attack could be made. This is where the first guard was killed," Keller pointed down to a corner. "I'm telling you, they had to scale these walls."

"Yeah they did," Praxis said.

Tavin crossed over to see where Praxis was pointing at scratch marks along the stone. White lines like the claws of a massive wild cat showed where steel had slid and then bit into the granite of the battlements.

"There you go. At some point they worked their way up. I'm afraid we didn't see them coming," Keller stated with regret. "And that's the problem. This part of the fortress is incredibly hard to monitor. It's the darkest area and there's simply too much we have to lookout for. The sheer size of this place makes it difficult to monitor everything. We will add another torch or two before tonight."

They spent the early morning walking along the wall with the captain, becoming familiar with the guard towers, the lay of the battlements, and the action of the main gate—just in case. When they had finally made a full circle of the fortress, the sun was already at high noon and Tavin had peeled off his jacket. He gazed out at where the Western camp was stirring in the distance. A few plumes of smoke paid witness to the enemy's lunch hour.

"Get some sleep this afternoon, as best you can. It would be good if you men are well rested before your duty tonight," Keller stated. "I will expect you up here at the changing of the guard. You'll be briefed in more detail then. Good day."

With that they walked down to the main barracks to have lunch before returning to their beds for the day. They ate much and talked little. Tavin's mind imagined cloaked figures stalking along the wall at night and the pitch-black abyss of the land beyond the light. He put his hand to his own neck as he swallowed his lunch of beans, pork, and onion. He felt his Adam's apple move up and down as the food passed and imagined the cold sharpness of a blade spilling it from his throat.

After hours spent tossing and turning, the sun finally faded. Their room within the officer's house turned to a dimmer gray and they awoke to a ruddy-faced sergeant calling the shift. Tavin was unsure if he had even slept for a minute. He felt like he had merely been within a worried daydream for a few hours and the rest had been spent staring at the shuttered window and watching the shafts of light change angle.

"My name's Sergeant Klemper. You gentlemen are the ones working for the Chancellor?"

The sergeant's remark surprised Tavin and even the others failed to answer. He had the blushed face of a man addicted to wine and eyes that squinted between swollen cheeks. Tavin remembered that they were, in fact, under the direct employ of the Chancellor. For a brief moment his tired eyes were energized by this thought and his head swooned with pride.

The arm of the Chancellor. What would father think of that, eh?

"Yes. We heard about last night. Keller gave us a little tour earlier today," Tavin stated with a touch of satisfaction. "I think it was earlier today. The days are sort of running together."

The sergeant, yet another face in the passing kaleidoscope of his life, nodded to the thought.

"I haven't remembered a date in years," he stated gruffly. "In any case, are you boys ready?"

"Absolutely. We just want to blend in. Get a feel for what's going on," Praxis responded, "It would be best if we were not saluted or treated any differently from the other guards while up there."

"Well, every two hours I rotate the archers out so they can get a break. It hurts the eyes... scanning for that long in the dark," Klemper said, leading them outside after they were dressed and then across the cobblestone courtyard to the flight of stone stairs. "Men on the walls should be moving and looking at all times. We're here to spot any enemy advances and protect against raiders. It sounds easy, but the tedium gets to everyone. There isn't a man here who hasn't missed something."

"That's what we've been told," Gannon said dryly.

Klemper turned to offer Gannon a look of disapproval.

"Well you know about last night of course. If they come back, we're ready. And listen, I know you all must be good friends, seeing as how you came together from another outfit. But on the wall, you can't get distracted. Don't get mixed up in conversations. Be vigilant. That's the best advice I can offer."

"Sergeant. What should we do if there's a breach?" Kendo asked.

"Don't die. I'm serious. That's as much as we can do. Don't die and you'll have help soon enough. And the only alarm you will have is your voice. So, shout and scream before anyone slits your fuckin' throat, yeah?"

The last gasps of twilight were fading. Already pinpricks of the brighter stars were standing out upon the velvet sky. The moon was visible but only as the smallest sliver above the horizon. Around the wall, a guard was placed every fifty yards. Two torches were lit between every man and soon the wall was illuminated in the faint and flickering light of the oil fires upon their sturdy posts. Tavin and the others began a wandering circle of the wall, greeting the other guards with wordless expressions as they passed.

Each guard had a short sword, knife, and spear to protect himself. Tavin remarked inwardly at the trading of a bow for a spear, realizing the uselessness of an arrow in this setting. Past the dome of light that each torch created, the world beyond and inside the wall was darkness on all sides. As the night deepened, only shadows could be seen around the mile loop of granite protection.

Tavin broke off from the group and lingered to the front of the southern wall, where one of the attacks had reportedly happened. He examined down the wall but could not make anything out amongst the black sea beneath. Taking the nearest torch in his hands, Tavin held it aloft in front of him and began to lean against a high block in the battlements. He noticed a smudge of dried blood upon the square dip where one might climb over the wall. For a moment, he was sure he could hear a rustling in the grass at the far bottom. Suddenly stricken with fear of the unseen, he straightened his back and stepped away. His back pressed against an unexpected presence and he gave a small shout, turning around and grasping for his sword. When the torch in his left hand illuminated the face of Praxis—his friend's hollowed eyes widened at Tavin's shock—he composed himself shame-faced.

Praxis held up a finger.

"What?" Tavin whispered.

"Nothing. You're just loud sometimes," Praxis whispered back.

Tavin pointed down the wall.

"Did you see that?"

Praxis followed Tavin's finger to the blood stain and nodded. Some talking could be heard between two of the guards and then a whistle as Klemper ordered their silence. Tavin could see the other four of his friends pacing slowly around the wall. He replaced the torch and stood in silence with Praxis, trying to tune his ears to the world around him. With his eyes closed he shunned useless distractions. He allowed his mind to wander, to be sensitive, to analyze on an instinct without the useless waste of thought.

Nothing.

Peepers were filling the air with their chirps from the field and forest. They made a cacophony in the night. The breeze was a howl. Tavin reached past these things. The music of crickets formed another layer. Somewhere in the distance of the forest to the east, coyotes howled and yelped in a frenzy. The occasional noise from the enemy forces sitting tucked away at the forest edge required a diligent calm to hear. Somewhere below a bush was rustled, but the sound was gone before Tavin opened his eyes to see Seneca returning across one of the gangways from the lower wall. He had taken one of their few breaks already and was chewing upon a piece of jerky.

"Why would they come back the next night?" Seneca whispered as he passed by Tavin. "That would be too predictable, don't you think?"

Around two in the morning, Tavin began to lose his composure. He was falling asleep while walking, catching his head falling forward and springing it back up in spasmodic jerks. He splashed his face with water from a canteen in one of the guard towers and slapped himself three times. The stinging upon his cheeks put him in a bad mood but it brought what remained of his energy back to the forefront.

As he paced again around the eastern edge of the wall, the chorus of crickets grew louder. The breeze passed through the trees, which were much closer on this side, and made Tavin feel an incredible sense of loneliness. He increased his pace, determined to reach the guard that stood twenty yards in front of him and just beyond the light of a torch, the guard's silhouette outlined by the next lamp farther on. Glancing around the length of the wall, he saw that Seneca and Kendo were in a whispering discussion and had fallen far behind him, the other three were somewhere amongst the other silhouettes. Tavin was determined to greet the guard ahead of him and wait for Seneca and Kendo to catch up in his company. The way the breeze rustled the leaves and the shuffling of boots upon the gritty stone had peaked his fear of the darkness beyond. He was glad to see that the guard was walking toward him as well. Tavin prepared himself to say something that would not give away his exhaustion.

But the thought was soon gone as he realized the man was not walking, but stumbling toward him. Tavin stood still. As the guard slipped into the orb of golden torchlight, he saw a weeping bloody gash on his throat and heard the choking gurgling gasps as he clutched for air and fell upon the ground to squirm and die. A pool of blood formed, before Tavin found his voice.

"To arms!" Tavin shouted. "To arms!"

He roared at the top of his voice, cracked with panic. Then spun around to see Kendo and Seneca rushing onward as he drew his swords in a gliding accuracy. His voice echoed across the canyon of the fortress. Everywhere, guards clumped into groups and came rushing out of the towers. Ahead of him in the shifting darkness between torches, Tavin saw the movement of shadows, then, as his eyes focused, a human form garbed in tightly wrapped vestments as dark as the night sky. The flashing blade of a knife disappeared somewhere within the form, its silvery menace reflecting the dancing flames of the torch for the length of an eyeblink.

The courage to charge filled Tavin out of an animalistic necessity. He clashed his teeth and growled as he sprang forward, his two blades held sinisterly in the ready. But as he approached, the shadow lifted upon the wall and vanished. Tavin reached the darkness beyond the torchlight. Kendo was soon next to him, wielding a spear.

"He's gone?" Kendo asked in shock, then, pointed to the wall where a hook held a taut rope against a straining weight in the darkness below.

Kendo traced the line into the inky blackness and leveled his spear. With a grunt, he heaved it, a harpoon into the sea of night below; it was a fantastic throw. Tavin's heart sank when he heard the clatter of the spear ricocheting off of a rock below. Suddenly, the rope was waving and jostling, the hook sprang free from the motion and fell into the darkness. Tavin cursed loudly as he reached to catch it but was too late.

"The others!" he shouted, and grabbed his taller friend firmly about the arm as he sheathed one sword.

They took off along the wall. Tavin's body was caked in the sweat of fear and exertion, chilled by the cool night air. They passed torch after torch and several groups of armed guards that had clustered and were pacing the wall in search of the enemy

When they passed two more bodies in pools of their own blood, Tavin's heart jumped into his throat. The floor of his

173

stomach fell and his body felt like it floated upon sluggish feet. He finally found Seneca, Praxis, and Oil'ib along the western length of battlements. In Seneca's pallid face and dilated eyes he saw the same thoughts that he knew must be expressed upon his own profile. In wordless expression, they came to understand the sinister threat of their assignment.

Sweat trickled down his face. The archer towers covered the area surrounding the fortress with a barrage of shots, but eventually the exercise was deemed pointless. Tavin looked down over the wall. A tension chilled him as he imagined that an enemy was dangling just below, but saw nothing.

For two more nights they manned the walls. For two more nights men were lost in similar manner. And General Thom could no longer keep his men from worrying about the threat. The general waxed and waned in his fury. The only evidence they had managed to capture of the enemy had been a mere shred of white cotton shirt. It had been nailed hastily into the crenulations of the high wall for them to find by light of day. Upon the scrap of cloth the word, *Nashville* was written in blood. The writing was sloppy and almost illegible as the blood had soaked along the length of the threads. Tavin had nearly bit off his tongue when Bok had shown him the note.

"They're playing a good game. I admire their strategy," was all Thom said.

When Tavin managed to sleep he dreamt of the black vestments and the silver gleam of a knife disappearing in the darkness. Every evening, when the sergeant woke them for their shift, he thought he could feel a blade pressing against his throat and choking his breath. In desperate hours he would waste his time away thinking of ways to thwart the Nightstalkers, as they were being called upon the wall.

"We'll catch up," Seneca said to the other four as they made their way up the stairs from the courtyard of the fortress.

Heading toward another shift on the wall, Tavin had been quieter than usual. Seneca turned and confronted Tavin upon the stair.

"What is it?" Tavin asked, already guessing at what concerned his friend.

"I saw that you ate almost none of your dinner. You're thinking about carrying out your plan tonight I'm guessing?"

Tavin grimaced, "I think it's the only way."

Seneca looked over his shoulder and up the stair. They were not being watched.

"And I'm saying you're wrong and you're acting dumb."

"Why?" Tavin complained in a near shout. "What would you have us do?"

Seneca attempted to speak but Tavin cut him off.

"It's Clades out there right now. I'm telling you. He's going to find a way in here no matter what we do and now we're just waiting for him!"

"What's your idea then? Go after him?" Seneca replied.

"Whatever must be done. I'm not getting my throat slit while my back is turned! If he kills me, I will look him in the eyes!"

"I already have. Remember?" Seneca spit back. "I *killed* him!"

"Yeah? Then why did the cloth say *Nashville*? Who else

was there? The lion? It's him Seneca, and even if it's not, you heard the general. After this mission they'll have another for us to fight. That marauder Bok talked about—Kayzitt or whatever his name was," Tavin blurted. "This is our life now, so when they come back tonight, I will follow them, and I will make that fucker stand up to me."

"Why?" Seneca muttered. Tavin knew Seneca wanted him to lower his voice. "This mission on the fortress wall is already the most dangerous place we can be," Seneca explained. "Am I right? We'll have to do our absolute best not to get picked off while we're up there, and you want to guarantee our demise by going beyond the wall? That's probably what they're hoping for. They have an army outside these walls bigger than our own. Our only advantage is these walls and staying on *this* side of them!" he waved his arms at the inner fortress.

Tavin followed and saw the gardens, the plants still young and tended to, the orchard, with its ripening flowers, the barracks, and many houses surrounding them. All of it was a reminder of the sheer mass of lives within the walls.

"We're limited in here. It's a win-win for them if you go out there. It's the opposite for us."

Tavin found himself angered by this logic. Not because it was unsound, but because it was Seneca that used it. Just as their deep friendship had been born of an initial dislike of each other, their discussions could vacillate so swiftly between enjoyable or vexing. Seneca himself was a man who prided himself on his mind. Problem solving, memory, tact, wit—all were sharp as the bridge of his aquiline nose. But he had a habit of using his skill for arguing and tearing apart ideals that Tavin saw as moot. Seneca was smart but unsure, a strong fighter and unmatched grappler but got caught up in the fights within his own head. He was an idealist with too many ideals, so many that he was unable to follow all of them himself. Tavin loved to talk whenever they agreed.

"Seneca, they're animals. Every single one I've ever met. They attack us like wolves. You don't reason with a wolf. You can't outlast a wolf. You can't outrun a wolf. The only thing you can do is lash out at it." Tavin took a deep breath and steadied himself upon the wall of the stair, "And I have to do this my way. I just have to. Even if it's alone."

Seneca shook his head. His moss green eyes searched Tavin for an ounce of insincerity.

"Don't leave the fort. I'm telling you."

"Seneca," Tavin sat down upon the stairs. "Did you kill Clades?"

"Of course." Seneca replied. "He fell through the floor—I saw him fall."

"Did he die?" Tavin pursued his answer. "Did you watch him die?"

Tavin's stomach sank a fraction more with each second that Seneca remained silent.

"No…"

Tavin left, walking around his friend in cold defiance and up the steps. He felt badly, guilting his friend in such a way. But his fevered thoughts of the past two days had driven him in a fury to one conclusion. Seneca had only left him further frustrated and he wished to be alone in his thoughts. As the hours wore on, he reflected on the conversation and broiled in his anger that Seneca could not see the way of things.

Does he want more men to die while we just sit here and provide them with the fodder? No, that's not fair. That's not what he wants. But he needn't act so enlightened. Always giving advice like he's thought of everything and come to conclusions on every aspect of life. Damn him. I need his help and hate it at the same time!

He put aside his emotions and joined his friends atop the wall. The tension between the men was worse than previous nights; he and Seneca could not look at each other. Seneca remained on one side of the fort and Tavin occupied the other.

When he saw Seneca approaching hours later, Tavin found himself welcoming his friend's company. Nights alone on the wall made one shake in his own skin and Seneca seemed to be of the same disposition. He approached the torchlight in front of Tavin, poking his face into the light and making a ridiculous expression. It forced Tavin to laugh. Snickering relieved Tavin of his brooding and he sighed deeply.

The moon laughed with them, slowly growing brighter off the horizon. Each night it's silver light waxed by the smallest degree and added a faint glow to the ground below. If he used his peripheral vision, Tavin could make out the darker outlines of shrubs and bushes when he approached the edge. He rarely got so close to the fringe, instead he listened and watched for the flying motion of hooks and the clanking of steel upon stone.

"Arrows!" the gruff voice of sergeant Klemper could be heard yelling from one of the towers on the western side, a shortways from where Tavin stood with Seneca.

Flaming arrows were suddenly flying over the same

tower. Tavin and Seneca ducked behind the battlements. Tavin watched as the hellish darts arced over the high wall. Some glanced off the lower inner wall or the guard tower itself. Others managed to find their way into a guard or two, the flame swallowed in their flesh as they screamed in agony. As more and more poured over the wall, a hay cart in the courtyard was struck and was devoured by flames. The men from the barracks were roused and poured from their sleeping quarters to douse the flames. Tavin could see them, running to-and-fro in little circles in their sleeping linens. Some were even naked as they clamored for more water, lest the fire spread to the thatch rooftops.

Tavin, sitting with anxious eyes scanning the wall in front of him, noticed Kendo. The awareness hit him like the snap of fingers within his psyche. Without hesitating he drew his steel and turned to where Kendo was backing toward them, engaged in combat with a shadow wielding a large sword.

Their friend was yelling against the attack and barely parrying blows that came from the darkness. Kendo dodged a high swing, contorting his body to get his tall frame below the glistening blade, but could not avoid a kick that sent him backwards onto a wooden gangway between the two walls, sliding down the sloping ramp.

Tavin shouted and ran to intercede.

One of the regular guards was already upon the shadow. The guard gallantly clanged steel with the assailant, who towered over him. Before Tavin could reach the scuffle, the guard was overpowered and stumbled over into the torchlight. A dagger stuck from his neck at a cruel angle. The dancing light of the torch was blown slightly by the breeze and its flitting shifted to show the enemy in greater detail.

For a second, Tavin saw the long, bulky frame wrapped in the tight black vestments. All but the eyes were covered in inky cloth—flecks of familiar gray. The eyes made contact with Tavin's for less than a heartbeat, a knowing, expressionless, and taunting gaze. Tavin reached the spot, the figure already over the wall and out of sight. Sheathing his swords, Tavin scurried to catch the rope. He had the cold steel of the hook in his hands when a forceful charge tackled him to the ground.

Tavin panicked and tried to reach his knife. But when he recognized that it was Seneca that had kept him from the rope, he howled in anger and wrested away from his friend with a furious push. Tavin made to stand when a swarm of flaming arrows whistled inches over the battlements where they lay. And Tavin swallowed his anger as they covered their heads.

Chapter Nine

May 2717
Canyontown, Pennsylvania

Dahli

Think about the conversations we have. When husbands gather, they talk about quests and callings. They spend hours on end discussing all the ways they can become kings in their time. When wives gather together, they talk about responsibilities and duties. Their hours are spent dwelling on all the things that keep them at home. I cannot be a part of that self-imposed oppression. I have my own mission, and my own quest. Screw duty, let me talk of myself for a change.

Dahli stood in wide-eyed shock at her father's anger. She knew his wrath would be swift upon hearing the news of her venture, but in her heart, she knew he had no leg to stand on. Her righteousness and truth in the face of his otherwise accusatory barbs gave her an elevated feeling she had never experienced before. A feeling of being right.

"And so, you just decided to buy property?" he exclaimed, as they continued to talk in circles.

"Why do you care? What does it matter? It won't affect my work. It won't affect your factory."

Arguing with him was something she had so seldom engaged in that every exclamation made her stammer a bit.

"It's because of Oil'ib. That's what it is. That's what it always is. You think I did this because of him?"

"Did you not?" he demanded.

"I want a life with him. He's my husband." That phrase still made her father recoil. "It's what we dreamed about before he left, and I'm not letting a war stop a dream. He'll be happy when he comes home."

Her father looked away. She could watch his thinking in the way his eyebrows twitched in and out of frowns. His balding head wrinkled, perplexed; and his eyes avoided hers. As her father stared off into the back garden behind his manor, Dahli circled around the flowers. She had decided to have this conversation in the garden and lured her father in with the promise of a quiet walk beneath the cherry blossoms. It was a promise she knew would be futile, but the green grass and oak boughs calmed her, if not him. The blossoming tulips and daffodils beside the fish pond made his anger easier to bear. When the tightness of fear gripped her chest, she petted the high stem of a lavender flower.

"And I don't appreciate you throwing Jeremiah at me either," she added, deciding to cover as much ground as possible now that she had his ear. "I know when you are trying to get me to look for an alternative."

Her father took a couple measured paces in front of her, scratching his chin while he thought.

"Every man in the world is an alternative to your little soldier friend. I will not be accused of placing one in front of you deliberately, when any single man you pass on your way here should be in your consideration."

He always knew how to put her on her heels.

"I accuse you of ignoring the fact that I am already in love with someone."

"Dahli." He turned his steel eyes upon her, and the remorse that was on his face made it hard for her to meet his gaze. She looked in contempt upon the flowers again.

"You are as smart as they come," he said softly. "I didn't hire you because you're my daughter. I hired you because you can do the job. But I won't have any eighteen-year-old tell me about love. You are too young to understand what is important in a marriage."

"Yes, I'm young, but I know who I want to be with. And even entertaining the idea of another man while Oil'ib is away? How can I *do* that?" she said with more than a little disgust in her voice.

She stopped walking and awaited her father's reply. He eyed her with scrutiny through his small framed glasses. His brow wrinkled and he drew himself up with a breath.

"Let's not talk about these things here," he said.

She hated when he would stall. The tactic remained a staple of his for as long as she could remember. He would buy time, build up a better argument, and come back later when his opponent was too off-guard to counter. It would not work this time.

There's no leaving now. Not while I have the high ground.

"No," she stated. "I'm tired of you not answering me on this. Why should I look away from Oil'ib? Why can't you accept my decision?"

She found herself ill-prepared for his answer.

"You shouldn't have married him," he replied.

"Wow. I'm *shocked* to hear you say that," she replied with sarcasm lacing her every word.

"Dahli this has nothing to do with him. I don't prefer him—obviously." He then spat forth with vindictive force, "He does more than bother me however. He's slow. He doesn't take any direction or invest an ounce of his time in improving his lot in life and you can't even say that he has the motivation to come to dinner on time. He'll have you living in regret your entire life. You don't see it now, no. Perhaps you even think it's romantic. You're not old enough to see how predictable your unhappiness will be! And you are too naive to heed my advice."

A rage was boiling inside her now, but she knew if she became disheveled it would only weaken her argument with emotion. A canary chirping in the tree above them made her feel like crying.

"You used to say that money is not what matters, that the years you worked in the shipyards were the most fun you ever had."

Now she had caught him, she thought, in a trap of his own words.

"That's true. When you are young and you don't rely on means for your health, one can be quite happy. But hear me on this," he pressed closer to her now as if grabbing her with his

184

own gravity, "happiness will all vanish the day you have children and realize that the choices *you* have made have pinned *them* to a certain life, or that you are responsible for their squalor. Do you wish to have children of your own some day? Hm? Then you would be well to think about your happiness as you watch your children grow up cold and hungry and far from the life that they might have had. The life that you are accustomed to."

Dahli was quiet. Hot tears were beginning to announce their presence upon the corners of her eyes. She wished dearly to have a seat, to let them flow freely into her hands, but remained standing. She had not been ready for such an angle and needed time to think. She hated him for being so adamant.

"Your feelings are your own, Dahli, and I cannot change them for you, but…" her father looked as gray and hard as the mortar in the brick walls of his factory. "But you should acquaint yourself with the idea that your… husband… is not coming back."

Dahli had almost dismissed her father's argument until he cast forth that barb and forced her mind to pause. She drew her breath together.

"What are you saying?" she finally shot back.

"Dahli, please don't think on this too much. Just take the day off. I'll have Jeremiah finish the rest of your work. It's not a big deal," Demen said taking her by the shoulder.

She knew she might regret pursuing the answer so vehemently, but she had to know.

"Father I'm not leaving until you explain such—such *ugly* talk!"

Demen let out a deep sigh and walked her over to the long stone bench beside the fish pond. She remembered numerous times as a child when he would have her read his books to him while sitting upon the same bench. Eventually, he would always dismiss her back to the house, staying a while longer himself, seemingly to play with the thorns upon the rose bushes.

"Oil'ib is not coming home. None of those men are," he leaned back against a cool stone as the news escaped his mouth. Dahli could say nothing, but only waited for him to continue an explanation. Her mouth opened slightly in disbelief. Surely it was a joke in bad spirit, nothing more.

"The government knows full well we don't stand a chance of stopping the enemy until they reach the Appalachians, but the Chancellor has to buy time. We have to stall them until they get a larger draft of men trained and ready. Until we have a force strong enough to push back across the Mississippi," he muttered the name from pinched lips as if it tasted sour. "Oil'ib went in the first wave. There's no plan to bring them back. The projections for loss of life say only ten percent may come home someday."

"What are you saying? That it's… a *suicide* mission?"

"I don't think they would ever call it that but… they know. I see some of the letters going out. I have connections. I hear things. You yourself see the orders we get. Those generals are ordering more and more steel with each month, and it's not going to the men that already left. The damned capitol hasn't even sent reinforcements out there."

Hot tears were melting from her eyes and chilling her cheeks. "Please, I'm begging you, my beautiful daughter, please… don't give your soul to him."

She wept openly. Even her father's thin mouth drooped at the corners.

"Daddy, it's not true. Tell me it's not true," she pleaded.

He hugged her as lightly as a father does in sympathy. Dahli was equally repulsed as she was comforted.

"There are miracles, but I would not hope for one, the pain may only be worse. Please consider what I'm saying."

Screaming out became difficult to stifle. Logic was the only weapon she had against it. On one hand, Oil'ib was not necessarily dead. Anything could happen. Perhaps he would run away. Maybe they would send him home. Perhaps her father was wrong, or even a liar. The Oil'ib she knew was impossible to predict. He could walk a hundred miles in unknown soil and find his way back to civilization. He could kill anything that walked and camouflage himself for days. But the pit in her stomach said Oil'ib's fate was not his own to control.

Suicide mission.

She hugged her father goodbye and agreed to stay home for the day. But she only made it a short way to the house before she broke down and crouched against a nearby supply shed. Fresh tears streamed down her face with unchecked fury. Her husband was gone. His comrades would be fodder for a greater good, and everything she had ever grown to love would be taken away. She looked up at the sky for something. The way mankind has always looked up, the urge of final desperation unwittingly and without exception drawing her to search for the creator. The only recourse.

"Please," she cried. "I don't even care if I don't see him again, but please just let him live. Let him escape this conflict and find peace. If that means I have to sacrifice my life with him I will gladly do it. I will willingly sacrifice my love for his, but please... don't take him away from this life. Protect him like he protected

187

me. I would give *everything*."

Night passed slowly and daytime found Dahli at her desk in the hot confines of the brick office. The heat from the forges in the works below seemed more intolerable than ever before. With the coming of spring, the heat had become humid and clung to the sweat that gathered on the nape of her neck with a thin layer of coal dust. Closing the office door did not help and the lone window was ill-suited to dealing with the heat. She wondered why her father had designed the space into such a hell hole. He'd managed to avoid it most of the day. After their conversation in the garden the previous day, he had acted aloof and overly formal—as was his nature whenever he sensed even a whiff of melodrama against him. While she had toiled over the account papers, her father had taken an extra-long lunch and then left early for home on some pretext that she had not bothered to hear.

She was far too stoic. The depression in her mood had made her into an automaton capable of accounting and balancing and signing papers and little else. When her mind turned to another person outside of herself it recoiled with pain. Lines of thought were too dangerous. Each one might eventually turn to Oil'ib, which in turn drew out thoughts of his death, alone somewhere in a wilderness, his body left to…

She sighed, casting a longing look to where her lockbox was hidden again under the floorboard—now empty. The entirety of her savings had been spent on a house on the far edge of the main road into town, pleasantly close to all the shops, yet not a far walk from her father's factory and enough land to make an honest garden of her own. Dahli wished that she could take more joy in her purchase. Before yesterday it had taken up her entire being with an oozing happiness. Now, that well of good fortune seemed as dry and barren as her lockbox, its contents exchanged for vague hopes.

Jeremiah entered the office. He moved in a hurry, grabbing something from his desk across the room from her own, a pair of keys jingled into his fine jacket pocket. He looked as pristine as ever, the dark shadow of his facial hair shaved smooth against a sharp and prominent chin. The searching eyes beneath his jet black and combed hair seemed not to see her at first, but when she moved slightly in her seat, he looked up. She had never realized how penetrating his onyx eyes were till he looked at her with a startled expression.

"Hey, Jeremiah."

"Hey," he smiled, a glistening white smile.

His teeth were so straight that it hurt.

"I'm happy to see that you're still here. I umm…" he sauntered over to her quite casually, his hands in the pockets of his pressed trousers. "I wanted to apologize actually. You did a good job today. I know things got really busy, and—well, me leaving to have a two-hour lunch with your dad probably didn't help."

"I'm used to it."

She was not in the mood to be overly forgiving, but Dahli was not the type of person to take her frustrations out on an innocent, no matter how mocking his existence might be.

"You shouldn't be. I'm sorry. I wasn't very helpful this week."

He moved closer still, and she wondered how close he was going to get until he seated himself upon her desk, the only corner not covered in pencils or loose papers. She was unsure how to react to such an intimate distance. Her back straightened and she held her chin high enough to meet his eyes. A reflexive smile crossed her lips before the anxiety that palpitated her heart wiped it away.

"Listen. I was talking to him, and he was saying you bought a house?"

"Yeah?"

"Yeah. He— he didn't seem to be that into it. But I think that's great! Really! Not many women your age would do that, and more of them should."

"Thank you. It wasn't easy."

"I'm sure. I mean there's a lot of upkeep. Lot of work to do, I'm sure. So, if you ever need help with anything, or getting set up and all, I don't mind helping out. You kind of pick up my slack at this place so I feel like I owe you."

"Oh. Thank you. I'll be fine, really. I'm kind of excited to have a personal project to be honest. But if you really are that *bored...* I suppose a little help never hurt. Just warn me when you're going to come over so that I can be appropriate."

Jeremiah smiled and nodded, removed himself from her desk and began to help her gather up the loose papers. He handed her the stack in a crisp bundle.

"And where exactly are you calling home now?" he asked her as they walked out of the office together.

Dahli thought it funny he had come to the office just in time to leave at closing. The men in the works below were already dousing their fires as they made their way down the wrought iron gate. The blasts of humidity and smoke made her cough. She usually tried to avoid this part of the day, even if it meant staying later. But being alone with Jeremiah in the office had made the stifling heat of the office doubly unbearable.

"It's by the old bridge next to the mill. I love the place. I used to play in the same area as a child."

"I envy that about you."

"What?" she asked.

"Having one place you could call home. We were always moving around. I never got to stay in the same place for very long. Sometimes I wish I could say I had a hometown," he offered her a sincere smile. "It does sound lovely. I'll have to drop by and say hello sometime. Have a good night, Dahli."

Before she could find an excuse to uninvite him, Jeremiah had already gone, finding the stables near the factory where his own small carriage waited. In her honesty with herself, Dahli doubted she would have found an excuse. She felt ashamed, but her cheeks burned with a heat that had outstripped the radiance of the coal burners.

"Good night, Jeremiah," she called.

Chapter Ten

Seneca

Both the soldier and the physician share a similar type of psychosis. To be either willingly, one must wish to be in a position of power over the life and/or death of another. Both roles may be used for good or for evil and both are open for interpretation. But the position of power, there's the test of a person's character. What does it say of me to be both the soldier and the physician? Am I merely a narcissist grabbing at leverage? Can one balance the sword and the scalpel without cutting himself?

The night shifts were beginning to wear on Seneca, and so was Tavin's argument to go over the wall. Seneca could see the foolishness in a war of attrition. By day, the Western forces bombarded the fortress with intermittent trebuchet projectiles and the East, from their own trebuchets, returned fire. The sunlit hours were now a cacophony of creaking wood and slinging stone. Within the sanctum of their apartment near the barracks, sleep was hard to come by. Paranoia of a stray boulder finding them came easily. Though it seemed they were safely out of range, one of the closer barracks had already been shaved on one side by a rolling projectile.

By night, the phantom enemy continued to terrorize the wall. Tavin acted like a caged bull missing his chance to chase the matador. There was a debate as to whether Clades was the leader. Seneca and Tavin had managed to corner two of the attackers atop the wall and brawl with them until those men were reinforced by a man in similar garb but of obviously greater martial skill, a man with tremendous bulk and sprouts of golden hair peeking out from beneath his black headwraps. When this figure attacked, he managed to carve a path for the three to get away. Tavin felt resolute in his conclusion that the large figure was their leader and Clades himself. Seneca did not want to be convinced. Tavin insisted upon following the enemy over the wall next time. Seneca did not have enough energy to fight his friend on this notion.

None of them had enough energy anymore. Gannon never touched his mandolin, Praxis never read, and Kendo never had time for meditation. They all went straight to bed at the end of each shift, tossed and turned throughout the daylight noise, and then left their beds to bathe before finding their way to the wall again—unsure if sleep had ever come or if they were still dreaming.

Seneca had just closed his eyes when he was awakened by fists pounding on the door to their dormitory. When Praxis opened the door to let in a flustered medic, the sun was brighter and coming in through the shutters in pallid shafts from a different angle. The room was warm with a dank humidity.

"What's going on?" Praxis demanded, scratching at his sandy blond hair, exhausted.

"We need to talk with Seneca."

"Everything alright?" Seneca asked, trying to be patient.

"General Thom needs you to dress and come to the ward right away."

Seneca sighed. He knew what this meant and that there was no resisting. He dressed as quickly as he could. The medic, in a silent rush to bring Seneca to the ward, walked him across to the eastern side of the fortress. They entered a large building with a high ceiling and tall windows along its western side. About twenty patient beds and a few surgical tables were interspersed along three even columns. Half were occupied by injured men—some already white with death, and many somewhere in between. General Thom was leaning against a table, his arms crossed.

"How'd you sleep?" the general asked, beckoning him forward.

"Not bad, considering."

Thom nodded, then looked over to a lone physician who was washing his bloody hands in a steel basin.

"Things could be better. A lot better. I've never seen a group of warriors so melancholy. They feel like we're holding back a flood with a raincoat." The general twisted his neck to one side, cracking it with terrible popping sounds. "Early this morning two of our physicians were strolling around the courtyard. It was after dawn, sun was coming up, and we just changed guard. That's when a few stones managed to crest the wall. One of the physicians died, the other will live but he can't perform surgery. At least not for a while, so… that's where you come in."

Seneca felt the inertia of another sudden change, like pulling himself out of quicksand only to fall into a mine shaft.

"Eventually, we'll be back up and running when the other doctor heals, but for a while we'll need your help down here."

"So, I'm being taken off guard duty?" Seneca asked, trying to judge what Thom's motivations might be for separating them.

"For now. I realize that you men have made some progress. But your friends will have to make due without you I think. That Tavin, he is every bit what his father was if you hear Bok tell it. He will catch their leader or die trying."

"That's exactly why I'm concerned. Sir. I can't leave my friends alone. We always fight together."

"I understand that, but we all have to serve where we are most useful. I talked to Bok. I know your background. I know your training."

Thom walked closer and put a large hand on Seneca's shoulder.

"I'm glad you boys showed up. We need some life in this place. Just like Tavin. The way he rants and raves each night in the mess hall, going on about catching their leader. There's a need for that energy. We're playing a long game here."

"I'll get it done," Seneca assured him.

"I know you will. Not many people would have made it all the way here from Kentucky." Thom shook his head. "That's still amazing to me. How old are you?"

"Twenty-one, sir."

As he dressed for surgery, donning the white linen pants and shirt before washing his hands in another steel basin, Seneca tried to review his gross anatomy. He thought about the surgical procedures he had learned, which felt like a different lifetime. His mind strayed to his first surgery. More specifically, he remembered the first time he had been allowed to lead, while his father watched from a short distance—no longer giving clues as to where to cut or ligate, but watching in judgmental silence as Seneca took the patient's life into his hands. It had been a simple surgery, only an appendectomy. But the care that Seneca had forced himself to take in removing the swollen organ, like a bloated purple slug being cut away from the intestines, would be in his memory forever. He had felt so much pressure then, yet his father had been uncharacteristically trusting. Not a single correction in the entire procedure was needed. His father's only contribution was a nodding sign of approval after the young man had been closed up again.

What General Thom had said about Tavin being like his father had bugged Seneca. Did he mirror his own father in ways that he was unaware of? What idiosyncrasies were showing through in his everyday demeanor? Did he display the same casual distrust, the lack of transparency, or a propensity for discipline— even the physical and reactionary punishment that his father practiced? He hoped he did not, but knew with regretful conviction that he could never really know. Only others might, and they may never tell him. As Seneca turned back from scrubbing and saw the medics preparing the surgical table in front of him, freshly cleaned he realized that in some ways he missed his father. But he was unsure why.

Sounds of violence pricked his ears, the noise echoing in through the tall windows. The thunderclaps of stone striking the granite bulwarks of the west wall chased in behind the warm afternoon sunlight, filtered by the smell of death around him.

"I think they're attacking again," said one of the medics who was administering a fresh bandage to one of the patients.

"Well they're consistent, I'll give them that," Seneca quipped while helping the medics set out instruments.

Outside the double-wide doors to the ward, a group of soldiers rushed past to reinforce the efforts atop the wall. Each recoil of the trebuchets firing came in a repetitive chorus of the swinging timbers releasing their projectile to the wind and halting their forward motion.

KERTHUP.

KERTHUP.

KERTHUP.

Seneca stood at attention, awaiting the coming of a storm. The minutes melted at a snail's pace.

KERTHUP.

KERTHUP.

KERTHUP.

One of the patients somewhere in the echoing chamber moaned for opium. A medic turned and provided for him.

KERTHUP.

KERTHUP.

KERTHUP.

Seneca's mind raced to the apartment where his friends were sleeping. Their place lay away from the danger of the western wall, but still much closer than the medical ward, protected as it was on the eastern side by the thick sweeping forest beyond the wall. Against his will, his mind showed him images of a quarried stone, a massive projectile smashing into the room where they slept and crushing it all in an explosion of stone, timber, and dust. He cleared it from his mind. In turn it showed him Clades snaking silently behind Tavin in the darkness of the forest, silent and poised like a scorpion to strike, then slitting his friend's throat with menacing ease. He shook his head and squeezed his eyes to press away the visions.

KERTHUP.

KERTHUP.

KERTHUP.

Beneath the steady tumult outside the walls, he could hear footsteps coming down the far hall, and then two soldiers appeared carrying a fallen comrade.

"They moved their trebuchets up. He was fragged," said the taller one.

"Took some shrapnel when the wagons broke apart," explained a bulkier soldier.

"Over here."

Seneca directed them to one of the larger tables in the back of the infirmary and a medic followed, preparing the steel instruments and gauze in an efficient and stoic manner. As he turned to the patient, who was now strapped onto the heavy table of softwood, he felt a sense of detachment slip over him.

He had only just begun observing the wound in the patient's upper right abdominal quadrant when another injured man was carted into the ward on a stretcher. The medics were quick to intercept.

"What is their condition?" Seneca yelled across the hall over the moaning and war, attempting to assess which injuries would require first priority.

"Limbs," shouted back one of the medics, and Seneca continued with the man in front of him.

The patient looked to be around his age, perhaps a year his senior, with a thick stubble of beard and an increasingly paling face.

The medic cut off the remnants of his shirt, revealing the grizzly wound in his abdomen. Deep wine-red blood was seeping in steady pulses from a tear in the white flesh.

"Laudanum," Seneca ordered.

The medic, a sun-tanned young man with red and tired eyes, dipped a shallow glass dropper into the dark brown jar, making a tinkling sound upon the glass. He then proceeded to administer splashes into the patient's mouth, taking care to hold the man's head still with one hand while the other aimed the drops with stern deliberateness underneath the tongue.

Seneca retrieved his scalpel, the razor-sharp edge glinting off the sunlight that poured in from the high windows. Taking a deep breath, he ceased to allow any hesitation and began by opening the wound slightly at the corner, creating a basic laparotomy. The incision drew protest and a slight struggle from the patient against the leather belts that held him to the table. Seneca saw a few lodged splinters as he opened the wound with a blunt-toothed retractor and removed them after switching the blade for forceps.

"Cloth."

The medic tamped at the injury site. With a brief pause in

blood flow, Seneca could see the source of the loss.

"Deep liver laceration."

He wiped a dampness from his brow with his forearm. It suddenly seemed humid in the lofty chamber of the medical ward.

"I need you to lift up when I say. Okay?" Seneca paused. "Lift."

The medic did and in doing so, better exposed the site of the leak from around the torn flesh. Seneca secured a small steel clamp around the hepatoduodenal ligament and watched as the tear in the hepatic artery spurted less blood and then finally none at all. With fresh cotton gauze, he and the medic cleaned the wound and washed it with salted water.

"Hold this." Seneca gave the medic a fresh pad of gauze and directed him to blot at the wound when necessary, as the smaller vessels still bled in slight rebellion.

When Seneca looked to see how the patient was doing, as he had been lying quite still after the clamp was secured, he saw that the man had passed out long ago. It was for the best, he convinced himself, and hastened to finish before he risked losing too much circulation of precious blood to his brain.

The medic, a solemn but helpful assistant, handed him the pre-threaded suture needle. With the gentlest of manipulations, Seneca retrieved the severed artery from the depths of the liver, moving his head at angles to keep the light where he needed it to shine through the dark red pit of abdomen. The artery was torn vertically down the side. He felt a cold sweat breaking out upon his own torso as he slipped the thin needle in through the two edges of the tear and then looped it back through. The repair required a tight and close suture to prevent leakage and the moaning of the other men awaiting his attention threatened to rush his hands over the exposed viscera. Seneca's mouth twitched back and forth as he worked, his brow furrowed in painstaking focus. He was inwardly terrified that the other injured soldiers were dying while he tried, perhaps in vain, to save the one before him.

The cure for the blade is the needle.

The patient flailed reactionarily as Seneca finished his repair and cut off the suture.

"Swab!" Seneca demanded.

The medic cleared some remaining blood from the area as Seneca worked with a fresh suture to close the wound in the liver. When he looked up into the dampened shafts of afternoon light, he saw that other medics were preparing the newer patient for surgery. He was on another table further down the rows of the groaning injured in their white linen beds and stained bandages. After several long minutes Seneca finished and released the clamp. There seemed to be no more leaking and the liver had not lost too much color. Seneca sighed in relief, his torso was now caked in sweat. Somewhere, someone was smoking. He had only time to give the go ahead for the medic to start his work stitching the exterior of the wound before he was already scrubbing for the next surgery. The soapy water in the steel basin turned pink with the gore that left his slippery hands.

"Deep tissue wound. Let's cauterize," he informed this new medic after looking at the legs of the patient in question.

There was no questioning from this medic as well. Seneca realized that he could have just as easily amputated the patient's legs and there wouldn't have been a single rebellion from this crew. They seemed numb to the strain of long hours and paying witness to suffering and slow deaths. This patient was bound a little tighter in the thick leather belts. He was a raven-haired man, equally young as the last. When the laudanum was brought, he drank it down greedily, but when the stick was presented for him to bite and the red-hot steel cautery was brought from the coal fire, the man shrieked and fought against his restraints. The medic's attempts to soothe the soldier were futile. But Seneca could not risk waiting for him to lose more blood. He instructed the medic to strap the knees as well, the wound was a bite out of each thigh. It was done, and soon Seneca smelled the putrid odor of burning flesh as he pressed the cherry-red steel into the wound.

The patient howled. Seneca allowed him more laudanum when he begged, then doused the second wound in alcohol before bringing the iron against the flesh once more. It crisped and singed and smoked in stomach-turning hisses against the bloody hole. Before the ointment and bandages had been slathered upon his wounds, he too had found comfort in a timely blackout.

For Seneca, comfort did not come till the next evening. Although the only other physician in tow had taken over duties for the night, Seneca had been unable to rest. These experiences tugged at him and his worries for his friends upon the high wall were too strong. The night passed him by in eerie silence. As he tossed and turned in the dark, warm apartment, he wished that he could hear something happening on the far wall—if just to know that something was happening at all. Every minute of silence was another minute that his friends could be lying upon the cold battlements with their throats slit into cruel smiles by the stalkers in the night.

The morning found him in the medical ward again, barely

rested, sitting down in a chair near the entrance of the infirmary. Seneca had left the apartment before the others had returned, which made him nervous. Though he fought hard to stay awake after his nearly sleepless night, there was solace in the absence of the usual morning bombardments. No bodies had arrived from the night shift with the Nightstalker's signature on their necks. The fortress had fallen silent.

Seneca's head began to nod forward in the welcoming blanket of sleep. In the sinking stillness of his reality he thought he heard a familiar voice, its soothingly rich contralto tones cradled him. In the beginning ecstasy of the dream he was sure he saw her calling his name. For a moment he thought he could hear his Chiara calling him from down the hall. The sound seemed to travel down the stonework toward his ear.

"Chiara?"

"Sir?" said a medic who was passing by.

"Nothing. It's nothing."

Chapter Eleven

May 2717
Tennessee Fortress

Tavin

This war is my inheritance. These swords are my dowry.
I'm looking at you now, two swords with a legacy, and I reminisce
of the time I stole you off my father's mantle. He came home right
after I had gotten one of you stuck in the trunk of a maple tree. I
feared his wrath, when he saw it. But instead he dislodged you,
returned your hilt to my hand, and taught me how to harness you.
As I carry you, I carry him.

Morale seeped out of the fortress as unchecked as a fog.
Even Tavin found it arduous to not let his enthusiasm die. When
Gannon had reported that a bombardment of Western trebuchets
had destroyed his favorite tree in the apple orchard, Tavin felt
an apple-sized lump in his throat. The orchard had been a pure
and sacred respite to Gannon and the others. Sitting amongst its

blossoms and listening to Gannon play upon his mandolin had been one of the few ways left to avoid unwelcome thoughts. Now garish lumps of granite lay across the torn brown earth like statues of violence. The trunks of two trees had been completely splintered, their tops laying in the dust, waiting for their funeral pyre. The inhabitants of the fortress bemoaned the lost fruits and beauty with somber gray faces when they passed the desecrated orchard.

There was little else to attach hope to in those days. Weeks had passed since the last communication with the capital or generals along the Eastern front. Men in the barracks talked of the dwindling odds of seeing reinforcements or fresh supplies, and the town looked upon the remaining crops in the fortress's central gardens as a meager reminder of what their life had been like before the invasion. The rations left from the fall harvest were dwindling and spring had yet to be fruitful. With the presence of the Western armies, there was little chance to tend the fields outside the walls. Scouts brave enough to venture out— and lucky enough to return— told of rampant weeds in the wheat fields to the north. But even fewer men were brazen enough to leave and tend to the fields. The Nightstalkers had succeeded at bringing fear into the heart of the fortress. Shadows were distrusted. People startled easily when others came around corners. Even in daylight, few allowed themselves to be alone.

The Nightstalkers' success chewed at Tavin. He nurtured a seething vengeance for the men in black vestments and dreamt of digging his thumbs into their eyes. He was surprised every morning at the profound hatred in his heart, ashamed that such strong feelings could be provoked within him and be so out of his control.

On the surface, he managed his composure. But wondered if everyone could see the fretting, sleepless glaze in his eyes and hear the disenchantment in his voice. How many more would die upon the wall before someone did something rash, something necessary, something drastic? How long would they continue to let this game play out according to the West's plans? What would it take to finally change the tone?

With Seneca distracted by duties in the medical ward, Tavin thought his time for action had come. But without Seneca, Tavin felt too uneasy, too unsure, and hesitated to plunge beyond the wall. His vacillation infuriated him. None of the others would go beyond the wall. Seneca had been his only hope and when Seneca opposed the idea so vehemently, Tavin lost his temper. He practiced the breathing exercises that Bok had prescribed him. Slowly in, hold, slowly out; he diligently focused upon an empty mind. He hoped that the spark of inspiration necessary to revive morale into the men of the fortress would appear to him in the darkness of his mind.

It was another evening of humid spring air in which Tavin led Gannon, Kendo, Praxis, and Oil'ib along the steps up to the high outlook of the keep. Having taken their supper, they had decided to watch the sunset from the pinnacle overlook before beginning another shift. As they reached the wide granite overlook, Tavin breathed deeply of the heavy air. Perfumes of budding flowers were dissolved in the damp smell of earth brought forth by the rain during the early morning. The rain had been a blessing. It had furloughed the bombardment of trebuchets for the day and allowed them to sleep well. For the first time in days, he felt rested.

In the quiet of his head, he thought he heard the spark or saw a whisper in a deeper realm. Tavin smiled at where the last golden crescent of sun was kissing the rounded mounds in the horizon. The sky, in its dark azure gown, blushed pink on its clouded cheeks.

"Heading back out?" Bok said stepping out of the shadowed doorway to the keep.

"Every night until the deed is done," Tavin replied.

He turned to watch as Bok strode gracefully across the granite overlook to where they awaited him at the crest. His countenance was dark and he wore his plain gray traveler's robes. Beneath that peaceful gray brow, Tavin sensed the potential for deadly action that never showed its head. The mystery of Bok's duality intrigued Tavin.

"Come here. All of you," Bok motioned them around him, and paused a moment for everyone to focus. "Look at everyone's face. This whole fortress is afraid. Isn't it obvious?"

"Yes," Gannon answered, a touch of sadness beneath his serious voice. "Evidently we can do nothing about that."

Tavin patted him on the back knowing he was going along with everyone else. Out of the corner of his eye, beyond where they huddled as a group, there was a motion of someone mounting the stairs to the overlook. As a group, they turned to see Seneca standing there in his full fighting uniform. His leather jerkin was pulled over freshly cleaned mail.

"Look at that," Kendo laughed.

"I have the night off from the infirmary so I thought I'd join you. I slept well enough this afternoon anyway, so there's no hoping for more."

Tavin found himself joyfully pleased at the return of Seneca to their ranks. Inside, he could not shake the feeling that it was to be a night of change.

"So, what's the plan?" Bok continued. "Just head back out? Wait for them to show up again?"

Nobody could reply, suddenly ashamed that the battle-master might be mocking their lack of success. Bok allowed the mood to become awkward in the silence, passing his heavy gaze around to each of them, as if to test their eyes.

Bok scratched at his jawline before breathing deeply and speaking again.
"I've heard you talk about this ability. Maybe, ability is too strong a word?"

Everyone nodded.

"It's not the same when we're just sitting around, but yes, it's there," Kendo explained with hesitation.

"It seems to only exist in combat," Seneca reasoned. "I felt nothing in the infirmary. Though..." he allowed himself to chuckle incredulously. "Sometimes I know what these guys are doing or thinking, or where they are, without being able to explain how I know. Sometimes, when we're just hanging out, I will be thinking the same thought as, say, Tavin, right before he talks about it."

"It happens to all of us," Praxis continued for him. "I couldn't put any faith in it at first, but it happens too much and feels too real to be coincidence."

"As if something is poking you in the forehead and feeding you a thought," Gannon remarked. "It just kind of springs up."

"We agree it's something," Bok mused, putting his elbows upon the wall of the keep and gazing out at the town within the fortress below. "Let me tell you. Those people I went west with? My friends, my comrades. We trained together for years. Spent years at the academy, years in the army, and time on the road before we accepted our first real mission. It took an incredible amount of effort to attain anything resembling that space you all seem to dwell in," Bok pulled a small leather wine flask from somewhere within the sleeve of his robes and sipped upon it lightly.

"You don't quite seem to understand how lucky this is. I'm not saying you've been given a free pass, but you're at the front of a line I spent years waiting through."

"This vision doesn't make me any stronger," Oil'ib said, breaking out of the quiet shell he occupied when authorities were around.

"No. Maybe you only get a split second extra. Am I right? Maybe your instincts are just a fraction of an inch more attuned than your opponent, but it's there and it gives us a little something to work with. I know you boys know what I'm talking about," Bok said, then sipped again. "Tonight, on the wall I want you to stop searching, stop looking for answers, and just quiet your mind. Trust that, if the threat appears, you will react the right way."

"Very well. But why don't you come with us?" Tavin asked.

His question seemed to take the others off guard. They glanced at Bok with sheepish expectancy for rebuke. But Bok simply shook his head, drew another sip from his flask, and continued to look out at where the final stretches of pink were fading into twilight in the sky. Venus winked at the battle-master with the same twinkle that lived in his old endearing eyes.

"I don't fight anymore. I don't even carry a sword."

"Why not?" Gannon pressed.

"That is a story for another time." He finished the contents of his flask and replaced it in the hidden pocket deep within his robes. "Tonight, is about you six. The future is about the men and women of your age. Take my advice. Block everything out, let your enemy show himself."

As the sky deepened into night, the six friends walked along the wide battlements of the high wall. They said little, only enough to prepare each other for the stresses of battle. They watched the dancing lights of the torches come to life along the long loop of wall. As Tavin led them on in the perusal of their surroundings, he caught the edge of a conversation among the spotters in one of the wall towers.

"We don't stand a chance just sitting in here waiting for them to kill us. This whole engagement is foolish." Tavin chose not to respond, his own thoughts similar.

After a long walk along the granite ridge, they reached the southern edge of the battlements, the section of wall closest to the enemy's camp. The full moon had already found its perch in the night sky. Tavin passed wearily by the area where he had first seen the Nightstalkers take the life of a guard with his own eyes. Bloodstains still remained in dried rusty splotches. The image of blood pooling on stone as the guard's life leaked from the stiletto jammed in his neck. Tavin girded himself against what he knew he had to do.

"It's going to be a long night," said a shadow.

Tavin looked up from staring at the dried blood to see who addressed them. He saw Sergeant Klemper walking over from the shadows between torchlights. The black outlines of the trebuchets upon the high wall behind him stood out like inky statues in front of the bright moon. Klemper's ruddy cheeks finally became visible in the flickering light of the nearby fire. The man looked like he had been drinking again before the shift started. His breath smelled sweet and volatile even from a distance of several paces. The sergeant gave Tavin a nod and leaned over to Gannon on his right.

"Full moon is out," he said.

"So are the wolves," Gannon replied, to which Tavin smiled.

"You think tonight will be different?"

"I think so," Gannon replied, "I'm ready to stop being afraid of these bastards."

"Well, if you want some good news, the morning crew managed to knock out a few of their trebuchets before the rain kicked in. So, we might have a couple days of good sleep before they're up and running again."

After meandering for ten minutes, Tavin led his friends to the eastern side of the wall. It was a different kind of quiet there. The trees below absorbed the man-made noises from the fortress and replaced it with the sultry rustling of branches and the creaking of heavy boughs. Even in the pitch black of night, it was a blanket of deeper black in those woods. Tavin's gaze dove into it for a second as he peered over the cavernous depths of granite, but was pulled back to the light of the torches by a ruckus at the far west side of the wall. There was a sound of iron tips ricocheting off the granite battlements and the whistling of fletched shafts zipping through the crisp night air before the alarm went up.

"Archers below! Take cover!" called the tower guards from the west, the yells echoing off the rooftops.

Everywhere, men took cover behind the battlements.

"Should we go over there?" Gannon asked, worried.

"Not yet," Tavin said.

"There's nothing we can do about archers in this darkness," Praxis added, his voice just above a whisper at the center of their entourage. "We know who we're waiting for."

Tavin concurred. He was bristling with anxious excitement for his opportunity. His eyes peered again into the darkness beyond the torchlight, searching, delving, peeling back the layers of blackness and shadows with desperate driving flicks of the eyeballs. It was here that the Nightstalkers thrived. He knew it as sure as he knew of his own existence. It was here in the confusion and turmoil that his enemy made himself known. Tavin could feel his impending presence like an electric charge on the breeze—it whispered of coming violence and danger. A chill shook him down his spine as Tavin turned away from the wall. He walked several paces ahead, into the darkness between the torchlight, away from the whispering planning of his friends. In his mind he saw the ebony flakes of Bok's eyes and remembered the advice of his master.

With two deep breaths he found his center. A third, and Tavin's mind floated on the whispers of the night. Each sound was dissected away from its source in this meditative state. With his eyes closed, his mind delineated the sounds and smells of the high

wall into an invisible order. Each scratching boot and creaking
bough was unattached to its source and drew no weighted notice
from him. The world outside expanded and covered him in an even
coating. The smallest dropping of a leaf was equal to the shouts
from the far wall for men to take cover. They passed through him
undisturbed, each one implicitly recognized amongst the chorus,
catalogued and ignored simultaneously. His awareness waited on
the edge of a knife for something, though he knew not what, to
push it over the side and into action.

A stronger breeze rustled his lengthening cinnamon hair
and swept it across his brow. It pushed him into the depths of
the forest and wall, rocking him on his feet and erasing the other
noises. When it was done, there was silence. The noises he had
recognized had taken a backseat to his present awareness.

Brush... tap... brush... tap....

Then he heard an oh-so-very-light thumping and the
sound of leather boots scratching against rough granite, dampened
by the angle of the wall.

"Ahhhh!"

Tavin unsheathed one of his swords in a singular
movement and buried its blade into the belly of a Western fighter
in black vestments, caught unaware after slipping over the wall on
their right. The enemy's eyes were wide and distraught—one of the
lesser Nightstalkers, not the leader himself. He was too short, too
slight.

"The wall!" As Tavin shouted he looked down the line
and saw Oil'ib intercepting an attacker.

At the alarm, the guards of the eastern side took arms
and Seneca leapt to the side of Oil'ib as several invaders crawled

over the battlements from where their silent hooks had sunken in. This attack was more visceral, more prolific. The enemies were everywhere.

Tavin kicked his victim off his blade and turned to join the growing fray. As he ran along the wall, the torches passed by in bright flashes. His eyes struggled to adjust from light to dark, to light again, and then finally to dark as he passed over Gannon and struck at a black figure pulling himself up over the wall.

The invader, a large brute, managed to avoid his sword with a deft maneuver and a lurch that sent him rolling past Tavin's blade and onto the wide walkway atop the wall. The black wrapping of his hood fell back slightly as he kicked backwards, Tavin's blade landing again only inches from where his legs had been. Tavin spat and drew his second blade giving each a reassuring twirl in his hands as he cocked his arms to attack the invader again. The wall had grown into a chorus of steel and grunting men. Through the spaces of light and shadow passed figures battling with the darkness. Swords glinted in the light of the torches only to disappear again into the ink of the night. The enemy had surely attacked with more men than ever before. All along the eastern wall, guards were exchanging blows with the dark shadows of the enemy and in the distance Tavin could see Praxis and Gannon cutting down an assailant in stumbling precision.

As his own opponent began striding toward him, Tavin saw the sprigs of blonde hair as he passed through the dancing torchlight. The leader, and his recognizable frame, emerged from the darkness. He moved to strike him again, but was intercepted by a tardy assailant rolling over the wall and in front of the leader.

The assailant blocked the path and Tavin faked a swing low before taking a hard backhand and chopping the man's head clean off. He had hoped the leader would be stunned, but he was instead busy tossing one of the guards over the wall into the courtyard with ease. Tavin recognized the movements, the brutal strength and elegant brutality.

With his heart in his throat, Tavin swallowed hard and gripped his swords all the harder. He rushed forward, his voice a rumbling growl as he charged. The leader sent a lengthy kick forward, keeping Tavin away. There was chaos on all sides at this point and Tavin ducked through a high slash of a sword before he came back in. The enemy awaited him with a broadsword, which made him appear even larger.

Tavin moved with agile paces and danced inside his opponent's guard; feigning with his left sword, he came slashing across with the blade in his right. The leader parried and sidestepped with awkward success, rewarding Tavin with a retaliatory upward strike. Tavin barely parried in time and his forearm suffered a cut for his slowness. But as the leader made to strike again, Tavin moved inside the blow and used his lower center of gravity to gain advantage. He blocked a strike from the enemy and then dropped his left blade and grabbed his opponent's right wrist, seeking to twist the blade from his hand. He plowed his leg forward for a kick to the knee. But as soon as he had, the Westerner stopped Tavin's pull with sheer strength and threw him backwards against the ground. In the light from a torch Tavin could see his head wrappings had fallen and Clades' visage emerged like bronze from soot.

Tavin jumped up, but Clades rained two kicks from above

onto Tavin's face and chest, pushing him farther back. His eyes stung, he squinted through the pain to keep his main hand weapon ready to parry.

But as Tavin struggled to gaze through his tears, he saw that the shadowed forces were disappearing. The ground behind him was littered with the bodies of black-garbed enemies and the cold faces of the Eastern guard alike. Ahead of him, he saw the shadow of Clades disappearing over the edge of the wall.

"Arrows!" he heard a hollow voice call in warning.

Soon the air was alive with the whistle of the diving missiles. Tavin lunged forward with desperate haste, sheathing his one sword; retrieving his second, he sheathed it as well as he plunged headfirst to the wall where the leader had disembarked. His heart leapt when he saw that the hook was still there—a cruel piece of curved steel that anchored his descent from the battlements. Without time for another breath, Tavin swung himself over the wall and grasped the rope he knew was there. Its strong hempen fibers creaked slightly from his weight. Kicking against the hard the granite, he repelled down the depths of the wall, torchlight draining from his view as he slid down into the consuming darkness. Below he now heard the rustling of feet and felt the rope beneath him being waved and tugged.

Arrows arced and whistled over him. One came so close that he froze for a second before continuing down the rope. For a second Tavin panicked, realizing his comrades would not know his location. He wondered if they had survived the attack and subsequent volley themselves. But against the panic in his chest, he continued down. The rope's sliding roughness heated his hands through the friction of his gloves. As he came under the shadow of the wall and high boughs of the trees, he relaxed his grip and sped to the bottom where his feet met the ground with a sudden stop. Tavin gazed back up at the high wall. He was alone, and felt it. The hairs on his neck sent a shiver down his spine. His heart beat like a hammer in his chest and his ears pricked for the slightest noise of an attack. Carefully, he gazed into the blackness, feeling his eyes slowly adjusting to the limited light of the moon that filtered through the treetops.

The snapping of a twig jolted into Tavin's ears from a clearing beneath the trees. He walked toward the sound, determined to not linger and let death come to him. Slipping behind the dark tower of a tree trunk, he pressed his back into the firm safety of the wood. Gazing into the shadows around him, he listened and focused his mind. There was nothing for a long moment. Only the slow movement of air through the forest and the fluttering of bats. Closing his eyes, Tavin breathed deep in a slow and quiet draw. There was a breath from behind the tree as well, quiet as a leaf falling to the forest floor, but slowly growing in volume. Tightening his grip on the leather around his sword handles, Tavin drew his steel and whipped around the tree to see the shadow that approached him from the depth of the darkness. He crossed his blades in an X just in time to stop a strike that would have ended him. He countered and Clades blocked in turn. They retracted back into the clearing; the moonlight that broke through the boughs overhead illuminated the fight.

"I know your face," Clades voice hissed threateningly through the shadows. "I've followed you long enough."

Tavin circled Clades wearily. He turned his head to each side, looking for an ambush from behind.

"Leave it. We're alone here," Clades continued, answering his glances. "I needn't any help."

"You should go home," Tavin said back to him.

Clades said nothing in return. The only sounds came from his hand as he rustled behind his back. Tavin's breath began to push out with frightened pauses and then the monster's hand lurched forward.

Tavin cursed aloud as he smacked the flung dagger away. Instinctively he paced backwards as the colossus charged straight for him. Tavin feigned a step to the left before rolling to the ground right at Clades' feet, sending the enemy toppling over him. The ground reverberated. Both men rose quickly, but Tavin had won the initiative. A few charging strikes pushed Clades backwards into the darkness and forced Tavin to withdraw. It was too dark under the thicker brush.

As Clades reemerged, he swung his sword tauntingly out in front. The length of the blade put considerable distance between the combatants. Tavin could tell when he was being toyed with. Clades took a few broad swings, forcing Tavin away.

"You have a funny culture," Clades mocked. "They send so few of you to fight their wars. If you would all just leave your jobs and descend on us, we could never win."

Clades whipped his blade around, taking crossing swings which Tavin could only dodge. One after another threatened to finish him, but then Clades' boot came flying forward and knocked Tavin backwards into the shadows.

I can't breathe...

Air came into his chest in painful gasps. The temptation to run was bearing down on him.

"There you go. Just like your people. Hiding from me," Clades stated as Tavin quietly shuffled backwards and around some of the trees, keeping Clades at a non-threatening distance. "You hide behind your walls but you will all die eventually. Whether by my hand or another's."

As soon as he had himself positioned perfectly, Tavin sprung forward from the shadows and swung hard with his right hand, slicing deep into Clades' left triceps. A terrifying cry escaped Clades' lips. Tavin turned at the sound to prepare his next attack and found himself blocking an ambitious assault. After slapping away several thrusting stabs, his opponent's sword hilt flung forward connecting on his forehead, and then a punch to the chest sent Tavin sprawling to the soil. He felt a fresh stream of blood drip down his face. Clades swung down hard. The attack just missed as Tavin flailed out of the way, returning with a kick to Clades' knee and buying him a short reprieve.

"I'm not afraid of you," Tavin stated.

His father's lessons were pounding through his mind like a drum.

A man who has mastered the sword needs no shield.

Clades charged him again and their blades crossed up high before swinging around. Tavin's weapons lacked the requisite weight to keep Clades' sword at bay and eventually Tavin was sent backwards into a tree. A wide swing by Clades just caught Tavin's pectoral and he felt the air rush out of him in a gust. Time slowed. He knew his chest was cut deeply. The stillness of blackout was just ahead, but his father's words tethered him to reality.

Don't stand still boy. Don't be afraid. Lunge out at me, come on!

Clades swung high and Tavin ducked down, just missing as the sword chopped into the tree. Tavin rolled away, slicing Clades' left quad as he went past. Then, before he could surface, he felt Clades strike him hard in the back of the head. All sounds evaporated save for a sharp ringing. Two more solid punches struck his back. Clades picked him up and clocked him, sending him to the ground in a heap, causing one of his swords to spin off into the shadows.

Blood was soaking through Tavin's jerkin. He coughed and it sounded like death. He looked up in a daze as Clades pulled his sword from the tree it had become lodged in. Tavin attempted to stand, but that had only made everything worse. His body now burned as the rush of adrenaline dissipated; his wounds demanding attention. As Clades approached him, he felt all his memories rushing back to him. He saw his dad sitting in the living room of their childhood home stoking the fire. He remembered his mother laughing in the kitchen with his sisters while they baked bread together. Suddenly a familiar presence pulled him from the daze.

Gannon, with blood upon his sword, emerged out of the darkness and pointed his weapon at their enemy. He was panting and looked exhausted himself. Clades wasted no time with introductions and with a wide swing to his right he nearly took Gannon's head off. Tavin could feel Gannon's heart racing as he narrowly avoided the blade. He couldn't waste the opening provided and shot to his feet, sending a sharp pain to his head.

In unison they sprang forward and merged their assaults upon the overwhelming warrior. Clades simultaneously sent a kick over to Gannon and blocked Tavin. Now the three men were dancing about each other with exhausted attacks. Tavin dropped low and sliced Clades' forearm but the giant spun about and maneuvered Gannon in such a way that he and Tavin crashed into each other. Clades kicked Tavin backwards and assaulted Gannon, taking swing after swing at his head. Gannon danced to his left and clubbed the giant on his head with the flat of his blade as Clades overstepped his attack. Clades charged but Tavin had resurfaced and along with Gannon harassed him with quick chops at his sword.

Tavin finally found home, driving his remaining sword through Clades' leg. Clades cried out and swung around in what should have been a killing blow. Tavin's skin felt the blade approaching as he desperately recoiled. A breath left his lungs as he realized he couldn't move in time. Death was here. Instead, Gannon's weapon knocked the sword away. Clades reacted by headbutting Gannon twice and dropping him to the dirt.

Tavin somersaulted backwards to get some space, but was disarmed except for his bowie knife. He watched Clades regain his focus and hobble toward him. Tavin withdrew the blade, backstepping. The weapon felt light and springy compared to his swords and his forearms twitched reflexively. As Clades charged, Tavin flung the weapon with all his might. Clades' eyes narrowed and waxed as the knife went into his gut. The giant sank to his knees.

"Gannon are you alright?" Tavin asked slinking off to search for his missing blade.

Gannon had recovered to his knees, but couldn't speak. Tavin's eyes scanned the ground. He retrieved the blade only to see Clades stumbling over toward them with Tavin's other sword still sticking through his leg. He looked like a sleepwalker, gingerly negotiating the ground. Tavin could not help but admire the warrior attempting with little success to lift his sword for a final attack. Springing out of his stance Tavin lunged ahead and buried his sword under Clades' sternum. The warrior dropped again to his knees.

Tavin stood in front of him clutching his chest. Clades' eyes strained, almost popped out of his head. As the enemy struggled and clutched at his center, he finally succumbed and toppled over. His final movement was the instinctual clutching of grassy sprouts in front of him. Clades broad fingers weaved through the blades of grass for a moment, then ceased.

Without sound or a thought Tavin took Clades' vestments and removed the tunic, then with a solid blow removed the head as well. He wrapped the head in the black shirt and tied the whole thing, like a satchel, around his waist. He and Gannon secured their weapons and arm in arm they helped each other back toward safety. The fortress wall awaited them in silent stoicism like a welcoming giant. They stumbled over to a rope that was still dangling.

"You first. You're losing a lot of blood," Gannon urge him.

Tavin knew the severity as he gripped the rope to ascend to the heights of the wall, he moaned in pain. His own protests made him realize that he might yet die beneath the wall if he could not climb it. He made it twenty feet when he realized he was no longer pulling himself up.

"Keep going we got him." he heard a voice shouting from the wall above.

Tavin looked up and saw his friends dragging him up. As

he finally crested the battlements and was welcomed by the warm glow of the torchlight again, he dropped into their arms like an old man. Gannon was next and when he emerged the group embraced for a dumbfounded moment.

"You are a crazy asshole. Both of you are," Seneca said while looking straight at Tavin. "How bad is it?"

"I'll be okay. But this one is not going to make it."

Tavin threw the sack with Clades' head from behind him and into the torchlight, where it rolled out of its garments and exposed the hairy, bloody visage.

Seneca gave a sigh that was equal parts relief and disgust.

"You can be mad later," Tavin said, as he stepped gingerly to his feet and then crossed the battlements and retrieved the head. He looked down into the courtyard and saw some of the Nightstalkers bound and being ushered inside the keep under the light of torches. Along the wall soldiers were recovering. Many were making their way along the battlements to where they stood. The men of the barracks had heard of the commotion and word of Tavin and Gannon's arrival from beyond the wall spread fast. Soon the entirety of the fortress was standing along the battlements to see them. The courtyard filled with blank expressions.

"Why so quiet?" Tavin asked his friends.

"We're all tired," Praxis responded, sarcastically.

Tavin walked over to the edge of the battlements facing the courtyard beneath. He grabbed a nearby torch to illuminate himself. As he did so, he winced from the wound on his chest and saw that he was pallid and covered in sweat and dirt.

"Where is your nightmare?!" he shouted to those that had gathered.

The soldiers in the courtyard stood without a word. All eyes were upon the grisly visage that Tavin knew he must be. He felt like a barbarian.

"He's right here!" Tavin yelled.

He pulled the head from behind him and held Clades' in the light of the torch. The head's pale skin was like another moon upon the dark sky. The gaping mouth and full blonde beard beneath his vicious visage made all the men take a pause in their breathing. Then a sea of murmuring voices. Tavin tossed the head down into the courtyard where it landed with a moist thud upon the cobblestone

"That is your nightmare! Look at him! He can't frighten anyone. He *bleeds* just like us. He *dies* just like us. Those invaders in the fields are the same! What reason have we to fear them? They don't come from some far-off planet. They are *men.* They fall when you strike them. They will kneel if you beat them! They are not gods! If they come into these lands looking for our predecessors, they will be disappointed!"

The men around him fed off Tavin's energy. Murmurings from below began to swell. As Tavin stood before them, a bloody fury, he could sense his own pain more and more, and yet he did not flinch. He knew that the Western forces could hear the echo of their victory. Men were standing and watching him intently, even the silhouette of General Thom could be seen in the tall balcony of the central keep. The crowd, in their celebratory frenzy, began to construct a bonfire. Their hoots and hollers echoing inside the walls.

Tavin stumbled backwards without realizing he'd lost his footing. As his friends caught him, Tavin floated upon a sea of nirvana.

"Nice speech," Praxis said from somewhere behind him.

"How bad is it?" Tavin asked Seneca, tilting his head forward a little to examine his wound. Seneca grunted and pressed an alcohol-soaked rag against the hole.

"It's reasonable, but stop moving." Tavin barely felt the pain of the sutures, as Seneca set to work.

"Don't you know, Seneca," Tavin smiled as he settled back down upon a cot that Oil'ib had brought forward. "I can never stop moving."

As the sun rose over the fortress, Tavin knew that their own star was doing the same.

Chapter Twelve

(Day 2717
Southern West Virginia

Kayzitt

Do not declare war and then tell me about rules of engagement. You do not ask a barn cat to be judicious when dealing with a rat, nor do you ask a warrior to temper its rage against the enemy. The powers that be have decided that this land should be warred upon and as such they have no right to attempt to contain the results of that decision. A warlord accepts the penalties that come from war when the bargain is struck. Do not point your finger at me and claim atrocity! Point that finger back at you oh tax-paying citizen!

The young woman was barren. Kayzitt knew that. It might have been the first detail he had learned about her, he could not remember, but it allowed him great leeway. The last spasmodic lurches of passion washed over him and she held his head as their rhythmic love making churned to a stop. He grew tired and rolled over in their sleeping furs to catch his breath. Too many nights had he gone without good sleep. Tonight, would be different; this night he would sleep well. But now it was morning and the golden light of day was already shining brightly into the earthy smell of the cave in which he and Sal had made their bed. Outside, Kayzitt could hear his men already packing up their limited trappings, enough to make their spartan camps in between villages and towns.

Kayzitt grabbed his clothes and threw them on with a spark of renewed zest. The fabric was cool from the night and damp with the morning dew. It invigorated his skin and made him feel fresh. As he stood, a hand shot out from the mess of sheets and furs and pulled his arm back down into the musky warmth from which he had emerged. Sal cooed soothingly and rubbed his arm as if to tempt him back to bed.

"You're not supposed to leave so soon," she said.

"And I'm also not supposed to have any attachments. But I fucked you, didn't I?"

She jolted up to hit him. Her perky breasts bounced lightly with her limber movements. When she saw that he was deliberately annoying her, she rolled her eyes and pulled him close again. Her brown skin was getting even darker now that the sun was strong with the spring heat. Its smooth warmth invited him and Kayzitt reached out to feel the texture of it. He then worked his fingers into the tight black curls atop her head. She was a tall and strong woman with a fine body, a body that could be sculpted out of stone. Her muscles were toned with use and the few scars upon her shoulders were badges of her service. Kayzitt cared for her as much as he was capable of caring for another person.

Finally, he stood and motioned that she should also prepare herself for the day ahead. He tightened his pants and put on his light jacket. He tied his long red hair behind him in a braid then retrieved his canteen and drained it of its cool water.

"We're fighting today, aren't we?" Sal inquired. "Kayzitt, last night you told me we'd have a break for a while."

"We will have a break. But not today, Sal," he stated, giving her a knowing look. "I've told you from the beginning, if this isn't the life for you then you're welcome to go back to the infantry."

He kept his eyes on her to see the effect of his words. She looked down at her navel with thoughtful disappointment. He found himself again admiring her dark curves and rich chestnut eyes.

From the side of their hovel he retrieved his effects, including two long oaken handled tomahawks with cruel steel heads on them—sharp, not ornate in any way. Upon one of the edges he spied a fleck of dried blood that had missed his cleaning from the day before. This irked him, but he thought there was no point in cleaning it again now.

"I'm not going back to the infantry. I'm not spending my life in a cold fortress being lusted after every time I bend down to pick something up."

"You'd rather be on the frontier to be lusted after?" Kayzitt replied as he strapped the tomahawks into the holsters at his hips.

"Your men respect me."

"That's because the last time a man fucked with you he died without his balls. Remember Quint? I know you do. You snapped his neck like a chicken." Kayzitt laughed. "People should respect someone who can give others what they deserve. Mine do anyway. They've always seen you as an equal."

She stood and dressed in the various layers that made up her battle garb, finishing with a thick leather cuirass that covered her torso nicely without hampering her joints. He watched her adorn her quiver and bow and secure her boots. Seeing her bring all the pieces together into the final presentation gave him a pleasing satisfaction.

"Do you have the sacrament?" he asked stolidly.

She nodded.

"I would never dare to lose it," she replied, showing him a drawstring bag of dark leather.

He nodded.

"That is why I trust it to you alone."

Kayzitt exited into the blazing light of the early morning sun, wincing as his eyes adjusted. His troupe of fifty men were busy packing. Some were eating a light breakfast, others were jostling together for amusement. One of the larger men approached him; a good head taller than Kayzitt and of a burly build, with a long brown beard and hair that draped over his shoulders in shaggy curtains.

"Juno," Kayzitt said in quiet salutation.

"You must be the only person here who's not hungover," Juno said, rubbing his temple to accentuate his own pain.

"I'm the only person here who doesn't drink."

"Can you give me an hour before we hit the next town?"

"Have five. It will be your loss. I suppose someone will need to guard the supplies while we are busy though."

Juno frowned and then moved on past the remark, walking to keep up with Kayzitt.

"You think this town will be ready for us?"

"Juno, I have no idea. When I got the information from the farmer he told me where the place was and whether or not they had militia. Then he died. I didn't get to ask him about their mood." Kayzitt kicked some dirt off his boots as he finished his sentence. "It looks like the boys are about packed up. Let everyone get some food in their belly and then line them up. Let me know when everyone is ready."

While his troops ate, Kayzitt opted to go into the woods and be alone with his thoughts. He cleared his mind and allowed whatever drifted by to inhabit his mind. He imagined how it sounds when wind rolls over a sandy dune, the sound of the minute grains that trickle over and down the curves.

Home.

As the wind rolled down the dune it hit some sawgrass. He heard the grass whisking back and forth and the wind rolling farther down, down and over, over and down, until it reached the shore. The wind picked up pace at the shore and whipped across the sand in hectic gusts. His mind fell into beautiful calm as his thoughts rolled into each other like waves in the surf.

Home.

"Kayzitt?"

He opened his eyes and saw all his men standing in a line in front of where he perched upon a moss-covered log.

"Shall we?" Sal asked, handing him the dark leather drawstring bag.

"We shall."

Opening the bag, Kayzitt carefully put in his hand. The inside was cool and earthy and he grabbed at the contents. Slowly, he withdrew two mushrooms of a dark and desiccated brown. The tips were tiny black nipples upon a skinny stalk. He handed one to Sal and together they held a mushroom to each other's lips.

"For the glory of the conquest," Kayzitt intoned.

"May Sol watch us shine," Sal replied.

Together they chewed and swallowed their mushrooms. The taste was earthy and stale. But in his head Kayzitt felt the lighting of a spark that would soon become a fire. With great formality Sal and Kayzitt distributed the sacrament to the rest of the platoon, repeating the incantation with each soldier. When it was done, Sal presented them with a jar of a thick crimson liquid, which she pulled from the same knapsack that she had kept the drawstring bag. She gave the jar to Kayzitt. Reaching into the jar with three fingers, he withdrew a small portion of the viscous paint, then smeared it down one half of his face. At seeing their leader do this, the men began pounding their chests and made exclamations to the sky.

"Let me see those faces," Kayzitt roared as he passed the jar to Sal and on to the men.

In turn they each painted their faces with various streaks and stripes, handprints and jagged smears. Before they reached the village along the main road, the sacrament had already begun taking effect. If Kayzitt stared at a tree its roots became alive like snakes and bled themselves into the ground around them. Clouds breathed and squirmed in the sky above. The sun's rays sparkled down and heated his face as the paint began to dry and crack. It was a good omen. His legs grew impatient and at times weak. Then

231

he would get a burst of energy as the spark within his head spread like wildfire through his body.

He stopped his men short of where a small stone gate led to the entrance of the village. It was a quiet day on the dirt road that ran amongst the homes and shops. Along the center were several reigned horses awaiting their owners to finish their business. From a nearby chimney some smoke could be seen floating lazily to the sky. Somewhere a group of women gossiped around a garden wall, their voices floating above and around them. Kayzitt turned to where his men were waiting for his word. They were wide-eyed and breathing heavily; others stomped the ground. Kayzitt smiled.

The West Virginia hills around the village were thick with the green of spring. The rolling slopes danced and breathed with a life of their own. He thumbed the handles of oak that were strapped to his hips and the woven leather thong that held the steel heads in place. Inside the dark leather cuirass that he wore over his thin jacket, his heart was beating rapidly. With his finger, he tapped the emblem of the sun that was stamped over the left breast upon the cuirass. He was ready.

Kayzitt started screaming. His bellows brought forth shouts and shoving and echoing chants from the men in front of him. With him they began to jump up and down wildly, stamping their feet upon the dusty road. The sounds of the village were gone.

"We are the chosen! We are the cleansing fire!" he screamed in a deep voice that sprang up to high pitches in wild tremor.

"Take everything!" his wild and crimson streaked platoon screamed back.

Kayzitt whipped his group into a frenzy. They foamed and beat their chests and released their weapons from leather prisons with untamed zeal. Sal's eyes were rolling in her head and she yelled and bucked in a focus of deranged intensity. She was even more beautiful now with her spirit uninhibited, chaos incarnate. Kayzitt let his swooning mind go and fed it to his wildfire temper.

Yelling and gnashing his teeth, he tore loose down the road in a headlong sprint, leading the fifty-odd soldiers behind him into the village. His first victim was an older man, shocked by the raucous, who had left his wood chopping to investigate the village entrance. He stroked his thinning gray hair back over his eyes wide with misunderstanding. As Kayzitt bore down upon him, the old man attempted to run. But Kayzitt caught him with a vicious swing of his tomahawk. The heavy steel head entered the man's skull with a shattering blow. The same happened for several men of the town who were exiting the various buildings to investigate. Kayzitt's raiders descended upon them40.

They poured through the village at breakneck pace, attacking everything and everyone. Kayzitt picked a house at the far corner of the village. He kicked open the wooden door from its frame and entered into a rustic kitchen. A smell of stew was in the air and a modest fire burned beneath a stone hearth. A woman screamed when she saw him. How wild he must have looked to her. A middle-aged man wielding a club rushed down the stairs. He was half-dressed and his hair lay sparse and tawny. His age showed in the bags under his eyes and the pot of fat that hung above his hips. Kayzitt could not help but laugh at seeing this man and his fearful wife. Their assumed innocence was funny to him, they so believed it was real.

"Who the fuck are you?" the man demanded, as he swung at Kayzitt with the heavy club.

He dodged the attack easily and collapsed the back of the man's head with the end of his tomahawk. The woman screamed anew; her voice hung like cobwebs inside Kayzitt's mind. As he made his way toward her she threw her wooden spoon. It ricocheted quite nicely off of his shoulder, like a tickle, and Kayzitt laughed again. He slapped her to the ground and was about to end her life when two of his soldiers—hands and faces covered in red and their eyes wild with gore—burst into the doorway, stopping when they saw Kayzitt. They were both smiling fantastically wild grins and they zeroed in on the woman, awaiting Kazitt's command.

"Take her outside," Kayzitt said, pointing at her. "I'd rather not watch." He laughed a little at that. "I'm not done with this house."

The two were on the woman before she had started screaming again. They grabbed her by her arms and pulled her outside into the garden. Her pleas slowly became muffled, wordless whimpers as Kayzitt searched the kitchen for anything useful.

He had noticed the woman's eyes settled upon the stairs after he had slapped her to the ground, and he decided to investigate. They were creaky old stairs, worn smooth with use. At the top were two rooms, one empty and the other closed to the thin hallway. As he pushed the slatted door open, the light of the sun spilt through the crack. Inside was a young boy sitting in his room, playing with blocks.

The boy had the same mousy brown hair as the woman

below, her cries barely audible now. He must have been about five years old, Kayzitt guessed. The room was simple with plaster walls, covered in an array of colorful, wax drawing. and loose boarded floors. The bright colors bled into each other and dripped away down to the floor, into eternity. Kayzitt closed the door, the sound of his men's whoops and yells coming from the kitchen were drowned. As Kayzitt approached the young boy, he appeared to be quite welcoming and unafraid. He offered Kayzitt one of the green wooden blocks with which he played.

"Who are you?" the child asked, staring at Kayzitt's red-painted face with curiosity.

"Friend of your parents."

The boy nodded.

"You building a house?"

"Mm-hm," he said. "See?"

The boy pointed out the green house. It swayed nicely in Kayzitt's eyes. It grew and shrank and grew again, and Kayzitt sat upon the floor.

"That looks pretty good. In fact, it's only missing one thing," Kayzitt took a cylindrical piece and clinked it up against the house.

"No house is complete without a chimney."

The boy demolished the house with a blow that startled Kayzitt and then sat down and started building another one.

"You didn't like that one?" he asked.

The boy shook his head.

"Where's my mommy?"

"She's finding your dad."

"Are you staying for dinner?"

"No, I don't think so," Kayzitt shook his head. "What's your name?"

"Ben."

"Ben. Nice to meet you. I'm Kayzitt," he pulled a dagger from his left boot. "I'm going to ask you a silly question, but I'd love for you to give me as honest an answer as you can. Do you think you can kill me?"

The boy looked up at him and smiled.

"I can fight!"

"Good! Can you kill me?" Kayzitt asked again.

The boy danced off the floor and over to the corner by a simple bed. He came back with a wooden toy sword held together by leather straps and smacked Kayzitt on the arm and then smiled.

"Dead," he sung aloud.

"I wish it was that easy."

As Kayzitt left the house for the village center, he stared at the red all over his hands. It was dripping and crawling and slithering off of his palms into a puddle in the dirt. The sun was hot now and he could feel the blood drying. On the street, the remaining villagers were being slaughtered by his men. The bodies of the local population were scattered where they had fallen. As he walked by a garden Kayzitt saw one of his men, covered in red, having his way with a portly woman who was bound and gagged with rope. Kayzitt laughed aloud. Where was the need for rope? Where was there time for rope?

"Rope, rope, rope," he chanted giddily as he worked his way to the center of the town. His men were already beginning to converge there.

"What about rope, sir?" one asked him, matching Kayzitt's smile.

"When we are done, there is some stew in that house that I would like to eat."

"Excellent!" the man replied, clapping his hands together.

"Is there anyone left?"

He received no response.

"We've checked everywhere?" he asked as he saw Juno and Sal approaching from across the small street.

They nodded.

"That's what you said at the last town."

"Kayzitt," Juno began to explain in a cautious voice, "I think Tenzin would like to speak with you when you get a chance."

Juno jerked his thumb behind his burly body to where Tenzin, the youngest amongst their ranks, was walking in a beeline for Kayzitt.His sword was out and Kayzitt noticed that there was no blood anywhere upon the blade or the young man himself. Indeed, there was nothing different about him from when he had left camp.

"Whoa, whoa, whoa," some of the soldiers muttered as Tenzin pushed past them and approached Kayzitt directly.

"Something I can help you with, Tenzin?"

"This isn't right" Tenzin replied. "We're not fucking helping anybody! You think these people deserved this?"

"They do!" Juno yelled back.

"And you think this is helping anyone? What are we doing?" Tenzin shouted in return.

"Why did you come with us?" Kayzitt inquired.

"To be a part of something! That last town… I can't get

it out of my head," Tenzin started to weep. "I can't get any of it out. They keep screaming at me! All night I keep hearing them screaming and crying and I can't stop it. I—I—can't stop it."

"So that's it?" Kayzitt asked.

"Yeah. Yeah, that's fucking it. I'm fucking done with you! I never should have come along."

Juno and Sal snickered. Tenzin only grew noticeably angrier and stamped his foot on the dusty ground. The dust danced and swirled and Kayzitt marveled at its beauty.

"Look at me Kayzitt! I'm fucking done with you! I challenge your leadership and your honor!" The young man spit at the ground and managed to hit the leather on the toe of Kayzitt's roughly worn boot. The saliva looked strange and alien there. It irked Kayzitt terribly.

"Very well."

Tenzin readied his sword. The other marauders gathered around the pair as the sounds and words floated through the dead village. Soon a solid ring of Kayzitt's men had assembled around them. Many were laughing. Some were busy in frenzied conversation and seemed to pay no mind to the young rebel and their leader. Others seemed genuinely worried.

Tenzin lurched before Kayzitt had finished retrieving his tomahawks from their slings. The boy swung wildly at Kayzitt's head and missed badly as Kayzitt stepped backwards. Tenzin readjusted and drove forward again, pushing him farther back toward the ring of men. But Kayzitt sidestepped and skipped in a circle away from the young man. He noticed that the saliva upon his boot had gathered dust and was now a thick slime of mud. He freed his weapons and beckoned Tenzin toward him.

"Come on boy! I'll show you the fun in it!"

He met Tenzin's charge with his own and deflected a swing with his weapons before kneeing the boy in the stomach and knocking him to the ground with a heel kick. Tenzin spit out blood from his mouth but turned and swung again. Kayzitt easily dodged the heavy-handed blow and rapped the young man's knuckles with the side of his tomahawk. Tenzin dropped his sword and Kayzitt smashed his knee-cap with another heavy blow. The boy screamed and crumpled to the dust.

"A leader must be able to walk, boy," Kayzitt surmised loudly.

"Please. Please wait."

"There is no time to wait," Kayzitt scolded back, "Our entire mission hangs in the balance, Tenzin! Did you not hear me say that a thousand times? This is bigger than you and I."

The young man tried to stammer a reply but Kayzitt swung around and sliced him across the neck, opening a cruel gash that gushed a deep red out onto the dust.

His soldiers let out a loud battle cry.

"Gentlemen!" Kayzitt laughed, "We've got a *lot* of work to do."

Chapter Thirteen

June 2717
Canyontown, Pennsylvania

Dahli

*Why do we hold ourselves to an impossible standard?
Why do the urges of the flesh always take second stage to the
expectations of others? Is there anything more psychopathic than
trying to tell another person what they can and cannot do with
their own body?*

Dahli wiped beads of sweat from her forehead. On her
hand, the smear of moistness glistened in the bright afternoon sun.
A locust roused itself in a tree and pitched its tune to the heat of
the day. Her new house had sprung a leak in the roof during the
previous rainfall and this day she had put aside to fix the problem
herself. With her large tin of tar, she climbed a tall ladder to the
roof where she had stripped down the rotten wooden shingles and
prepared to apply fresh ones. Buying the shingles, tar, and brush

had been a chore in itself. Waving off the supplicants of men who insisted upon helping her, all for the mere cost of a few coins, had taken most of the morning. It was only with a scrap of remaining pride that she extricated herself from the local tool shop and returned home. Dahli sighed as she straddled the high frame of the roof and settled the bucket of tar alongside stacks of shingles. Getting all the supplies up to the roof had been another chore.

But where was the brush? She put her hand to her face and blocked out the sun to scan the area. At last she spied it, sitting tauntingly alone on the grass below. She sighed again as she swung her legs back around toward the ladder, her thick canvas work pants scraping against the rough wood shingles

"I can run my dad's company, but I can't remember a simple brush," she mumbled.

Thoughts of her father still made her intestines curdle with a mixture of paternal love and acidic resentment. The words he spewed about Oil'ib still clung to her chest like an illness. But there was something more than that, something deeper and more a part of herself. In the presence of her father, Dahli also felt a resentment toward herself. She felt like a vulnerable leach, sucking its sustenance from the blood of the society around her, from the hearty people of the Pennsylvania villages that worked tirelessly day in and day out for survival, money, warmth, food. What did she do to deserve living in such luxury? What had she done to be able to enjoy living in such a grand mansion and eating the freshest beef and finest herbs? Certainly, she thought, the paperwork that metered the minutes of her life did not mean so much.

Dahli longed to escape from that resentment; the strong and heavy beams of the house underneath her buttocks felt like a sturdy ship, sailing her away from her own guilt and misgivings. Her skin felt dirty with her inheritance, just as it was sticky with the sweet clear sweat that sparkled as she climbed down the ladder toward the brush.

Finally, she was on the roof again, and with the thick horsehair brush dipping into the viscous pull of the pitch-black tar, she began smearing it over the fresh wooden underlayment. The way the bristles streaked the blackness over the wood reminded her of Oil'ib's hair. It made her think of him being scalped. She shook her head to change her track. The thoughts were exhausting. Forcibly, she attempted to be more joyful. A better thought emerged at last. A memory of the first time she had felt love for Oil'ib. And as she remembered it, she looked out across the lush treetops, soaking in the sun in her wide back yard.

They had been exploring at the canyon to the west of town and had climbed to the top of one of the mountains to view the gorge below. In his naive flirtations, Oil'ib had strayed to the edge of a large rock jutting out from the overlooking ridge and over the gorge. Sitting right at the fringe, he had spent the next half hour tempting her to join him. When at last she had overcome her fear enough to sit beside him, she had been glad for doing so. He held her waist with his arms and pulled her near. In that moment she was not afraid of falling. She knew Oil'ib would never let it happen. She could almost smell the wooden aroma of furs and smoke that lived in her husband's hair as she imagined it. All the world had been beneath them.

"House is looking good!"

Jeremiah's familiar voice sung out and startled Dahli from her woolgathering. The young man must not have been in the office, for he was dressed in only a thin white cotton shirt and cut-off brown pants. His hair was mussed as if by friendly fingers. He looked trim and cute in his summer wear. It would not have been a long walk from the factory to her house, but she wondered where he had come from. His coal-black hair was also like the tar. Dahli put her brush down with some vigor, unsure if she was annoyed or merely wanting to pretend that she was annoyed.

"Well look at you," she said. "No vest?"

He looked down at himself and laughed benignly.

"You just moved in and I thought you might need some help."

"Oh, really?"

"Yes, so I dressed the part."

"It's sweet that you came over here, but I'm okay, really I am," she called down from the roof, half hoping he might leave and half hoping that he would need more convincing.

"Well I was in the area, and I felt—"

"Jeremiah, you're really being too sweet, but if I don't do this myself how will I escape my father's insistence that I'm not independent enough to—"

"Oh, I didn't mean to impose. I'm just paying you back for all the times you've covered for me," he insisted, covering his eyes from the sun while he peered up at her.

She made oblivious strokes with the brush. "Thank you. It means a lot, but you know that I have a husband and maybe he's not here right now, but I just think there's certain situations I shouldn't put myself in. That's all." Just mentioning, indirectly, the idea of sexual tension between her and him made her blush and she tried to hide it by turning her head.

"Dahli you misunderstand. I'm not trying to take advantage of you. I've liked you since the day I first met you—it's true— but my intentions coming over here weren't to make you like me back. In fact, I spoke to your father yesterday and he told me how sad you'd seemed the last few days. I couldn't understand why. I couldn't understand why this perfect woman would be sad all the time. That's when I found out about Oil'ib's, um… situation. I'm really sorry. If I could be a friend and someone you could talk to I would gladly do it."

She sighed and wondered why she should even entertain him.

"You ever tar a roof?" she called.

"Believe it or not, I did my dad's sailboat last summer," Jeremiah mentioned as he ascended the ladder. "It was more of a pitch than a tar, but I think I get the general idea."

"I don't even think I have a second brush," she laughed delicately.

"It's okay. I'll relieve you."

He was up the ladder before she could think of something else to say and took the brush gently from her hand. He dipped it in the can. Then he spread the tar in wide sweeping motions, covering much more with one stroke than Dahli had been doing. She exhaled through her nose. The tar was beginning to dampen her sense of smell. In silence, she watched as Jeremiah spread the tar across the portion of the roof. More than once she falsely gazed away at the sparrows playing in the far apple tree when he would look over. His triceps moved nicely up and down his arm as he extended the brush, pulled it back, dipped, dragged, extended, and pulled it back again. His onyx eyes, watching his work with gentle accuracy, were a pleasant dichotomy to his skin, still pale from the cold of winter. She resisted slapping herself.

"I'll say this for you. You're getting good reviews at the factory," she said to fill the air.

"Oh yeah? From who?"

"The foreman mainly. But they all like how you listen. It's something my dad doesn't do well anymore."

"I've gotten to know your dad a lot since I started. He's a nicer guy than anyone gives him credit for."

"Yeah and he's also profiting off a war and not thinking twice."

"Well. That may be, but he's pretty damn proud of you."

"How do you know?"

"He talks about you all the time. Always saying how you're better with people than he is. He talks about how strong you are and how much you push everybody. I think he's right."

Dahli waved her hand at his sycophantic treatment.

"He didn't want me to buy this house."

"Of course not. He's not used to people going against him. But at the same time, I bet he didn't try to stop you either."

"How do you know?"

"Well," he dipped the brush again, "like you said I just listen to people."

Dahli sat up on her heels. "That's perceptive of you."

Again, he dipped into the ever-diminishing supply of tar.

"You're not alone in your hesitations though. Sometimes the things he says aren't always right. Sometimes it can sound like he doesn't care about the world, but I think deep down inside he cares. It's you and your mom, that is his world. I don't think he started this business to become powerful. He started it to give you two a better life than most."

Bittersweet lumps began building inside her throat until a solitary tear escaped the corners of her eyes.

"He tells you so much?" she uttered softly.

He shook his head.

"I just know. He's pretty easy to read. He mentions the two of you more than he probably realizes." Jeremiah smiled at her before returning to his brush.

The sun continued to bear down hard on the pitch-black roof. Sweat started to bead and drip from his brow. A crystal drop hit the tar. He wiped the sweat away and continued his work.

"Here," Dahli said, wiping his forehead with a cloth she had brought for the purpose. "You look like you're melting."

"I'm not used to the heat, yet," he replied with a laugh, which became a mild cough. "Wow, okay that's a dry throat. The good news is, I think the tar is good to go for a while."

"Come inside. I pumped some water this morning. I'm dying, too."

She swung her legs over the climax of the roof again and shimmied to where the ladder was propped against it. After they stepped down in tandem, she opened the door to him and motioned him inside with apologies for the mess. Moving crates were all over the downstairs and the straw was strewn about the hardwood floor in much of the house.

"I like your style. Very boxy."

"Oh my god. Shut up. It's just a mess right now. Here, a quick tour," she touched his arm gently and he followed with his gleaming smile.

"Two bedrooms. This one is mine in the back. One bedroom here off the side. Living room, obviously. Kitchen, and of course just off the kitchen is a work area."

"Damn, he's a hell of a hunter," Jeremiah said as he motioned at the pelts, traps and hunting supplies in the room. Dahli closed the door to the work area with some hesitation.

"Yes, he is… Oh yeah, the water."

They walked into the kitchen simultaneously, colliding their shoulders and the door frame together, which brought forth warm and hearty chuckles. Then Jeremiah put out his arm ceremoniously and allowed her to lead him to the kitchen. There was strength in the shoulders that she had felt. And there was a spark of awakening between her own. In that collision she realized how long it had been since she had touched anyone at all, even by circumstance. The thought pursued her and made her blush. She was giddy with embarrassment and hid it behind her search for a drinking glass in one of the crates upon the floor. After a moment she ceased her bending and appeared with two stout glasses of sparkling crystal. Without looking to Jeremiah, she filled it from the copper pitcher on the counter. Only hours ago, had she worked herself into a fevered blush manhandling the water from the long cast iron arm of the well pump.

"Here you go," she handed him the clear cool water.

Jeremiah made a sound of refreshment as he drank. And for the briefest of moments, their eyes met wordlessly. The moment seemed to linger even though Dahli looked away.

"I'm really glad I came to this town," he said with a smile. "There's good people everywhere."

"That is sweet," she replied. "I am glad you came as

well."

The lingering stares returned, and Dahli was suddenly hyper aware of her body– desperately aware, dreadfully, urgently, and ecstatically aware of her vulnerable tangibility. She was warm and knew she must be blushing and even as Jeremiah began to lean into her she could not recoil.

Closer and closer they moved.

I'm not going to do this.

Suddenly, his coal-black hair, and the pink lips in his beautifully pale face were upon hers. Her body became paralyzed by the touch. Everything was warm, warmer still, and there was a sinking, shocking pleasure before her mind that sprang from its cushions and her eyes peeled open so fast that she had not realized she had closed them. She backed away and his grasp on her wilted immediately, she hardly had to push.

"Okay. Jeremiah, thank you so much for coming over. Honestly, thank you. Why don't we call it a day," she half stuttered as she led him, without looking at him, toward the door.

"Okay." he said with invisible smile.

He put the glass down gently upon the counter and followed her to the door. She could hear the tenuous, halting movements in his shoes against the hardwood floor. Then, his shoes were outside and the door was already closing. He spoke through its shrinking opening.

"Should I not have done that?"

"It's okay. Umm, I'll see you at the office, okay? Okay. Okay..."

She closed the door. Its latch clicked with finality, and she took a deep breath as she listened for his footsteps to disappear.

Chapter Fourteen

June 2717
Central West Virginia

Kayzitt

Adults never do what they're told. They're worse than children in this regard. Children will at least defer to the adult in heavy situations, but an adult always fancies themselves as infallible. It has always been my pleasure, in these times, to force them to see how wrong they are. And low and behold, most of them start acting like children again.

"There aren't many black-skinned people in this part of the world," Sal said as they stepped over the soft carpet of pine needles.

The noises of the rest of the troop were fading behind them, waiting in the growing darkness of the woods for Kayzitt's signal.

"Perhaps you were right that I should have stayed

behind."

"No need to get nervous now," Kayzitt explained.

He was purposefully aloof. If one was to keep a woman, it was better not to get too involved in her worries. The deeper you traveled down that road, the more would come to catch her in spite of your effort. His mind was on the signal, how to make it, and what to do for fun first. But still, there was a playful urgency in finding the best way to have fun before it all. Acting like someone you are not can be quite exciting.

"You can pretend to be a whore that I bought. Whores travel a lot. No one will think twice," he explained.

She turned her body toward him and slapped him hard on the face.

"I'll fuck you up," she said, drawing a laugh from Kayzitt. "I will stand out."

"You always stand out," Kayzitt said, and he reached over and stroked the smooth skin where it showed above the nape of her neck.

"You are going to embarrass Juno if you keep touching me."

Kayzitt looked to his left where his brute of a friend was walking beside them, seemingly absorbed in his own hands as he turned them around and over against each other, flexing the digits. His burly nature, thick hair, and long brown beard would help him fit in perfectly to this town full of trappers, hunters, and prostitutes.

"I don't think Juno is capable of being embarrassed." They approached the edge of the trading post. Buildings loomed overhead on the waves of a hill. The smell of burning wood was thick in the air.

"Remind me to leave here with some tallow candles," Kayzitt said to his two companions.

Sal rubbed her hands. "You're crazy, but that is a splendid idea."

They followed a small road that led through the trading post. On one side was a large, squat tavern. Its roof looked like the melted butt of a candle, as if some giant had sat upon it and squished the wooden beams beneath its weight. Across the road were the small and mostly open shops of the tanners and butchers, with skinned carcasses of deer, elk, and even a moose on a giant iron chain hanging from the rafters above the working men. There was a building of a tradesman, which the fur-lined men of the profession entered and exited in a solemn manner. They came in with pieces of paper in their hands and left with clinking coins in their pockets, walking toward the tavern across the way. Farther down the road was a brothel. It was well lit and from it came the muffled calls of girls through the shuttered windows. All its three stories smelled of perfume and the hazy heat of a brazier.

A shame we cannot bring them with us.

The air felt more like an autumn day and Kayzitt knew it was why the smoke was so heavy in the air. A smell of piss and diluted alcohol wafted from the mud to Kayzitt's twitching nose as he led his two comrades toward the tavern. As they entered into the warm and hazy place, a thin and bearded man, who stunk of whiskey stumbled outside. Singing like a lunatic up toward the fading light of the sun upon the far horizon, he wavered and then collapsed upon the porch.

"This town is all transients and passersby," Sal quietly mentioned to Kayzitt.

"So, I guess we're home."

He maneuvered them over to the bar and they seated themselves in the last of three empty seats. High stools creaked under the weight of heavy use: leather-bound cushions long flattened and polished smooth by a thousand asses.

Kayzitt tossed a handful of copper pieces onto the polished dark wood of the bar as he sat to the right of Sal. The tinkling sound of the metal pricked the barkeeper's ears and drew him over from the far end. The barkeep had a flat nose and wide cheekbones. His eyes were beady and dark, his eyelids puffy and hung low over what little eye showed. When he asked Kayzitt what it would be, his breath was heavy with the smell of alcohol.

"Three pints please," Kayzitt said, exuding happiness.

Never before had he been so long behind the lines of his targets without exposing himself. Kayzitt reached down to his hips and was reassured when he felt the rough leather that bound the handles of his tomahawks. His heart was beating with exuberance. One finger fidgeted with a lock of his long, bright red hair while he watched the faces of the men in the room. Each one was a spell-binding mystery, hideously interesting. Their mouths gaped like endless sinkholes into faces that stretched forward on craning necks. Every nose was a mountain and their lines of broken teeth were the edges of old rusty saw blades. The collective sound of their voices was a nonsense that sung like a deranged chorus in his head and their faces continued to move and mutate with no more meaning than the elbows that flexed and fingers that groped at women's skirts. Every blush was a heartbeat's worth of blood. Kayzitt caught it all and found himself pleased.

What do they produce in all this chaos and turmoil? Do

they create or merely consume?

Quiet conversations overwhelmed the occasional loud outburst. Men muttered over faces full of hair with breath full of onions and meat. In the air hung the smell of carefully contented acceptance. Would the spring bring the elk back down from the north in great numbers? What of the beavers in the nearby river? Someone had surely seen the many dams and hauled in their fortune for the winter. The conversations smelled as dank as the wet furs, muddy aroma of boots, and moistened leather. In one corner a man groped at a prostitute that he had managed to lure in with some coins, and in another a man stared blankly into the bottom of his mug and twirled the long whiskers at the end of his mustache. The latter was more finely dressed but the former had the finer company. It was refreshing.

The bartender returned with the cool drinks. Kayzitt sipped upon the foam until the liquid rushed into his mouth. It was bitter but pleasant. It mixed with the sacrament that already sat in his stomach and his eyes widened with the sensitivity of a mad dog. He felt like the feral beast amongst so many broken house animals; he thought himself a fox. Kayzitt pushed back the long lock of red hair from his head and smiled at himself. To his right slouched a man with a shaved head and a beaver pelt hat upon his lap, his skin dry at every corner and cheeks rosy with his drink. The small vessels upon this neighbor's nose were like a spider web and he sat his insolent bulk upon his bar stool. Finally, his eyes met with Kayzitt's, and the stranger nodded and scratched at the stubble on his round face.

"Lost a bear the other day. Would've been my biggest catch in a month," Kayzitt said to the stranger. "The name's

Kayzitt."

They shook hands, and Kayzitt's skin crawled when he found the man's hands to be covered in a thin clammy sweat. Then he realized it was his own.

"Duff," said the burly, barrel-chested hunter sipping down some ale from his hefty mug. "This region's been pretty good for most of us. That's a tough loss, though."

"How long have you been in this life?" Kayzitt asked, quietly wiping his hand upon his leather framed pants.

"Been hunting since I was a boy. This isn't the sort of thing you start doing later in life. We're all stuck with it."

"Well, yeah that's true… But there's a certain thrill in the chase. Proving that you can outwit the prey. Am I right?"

Duff finished his beer and motioned for the bartender to get him another. Kayzitt took a sip on his own but could not drink too much.

"Well, I just try to put food on the table. I think that's what everyone here is doing," Duff responded at last.

"Sure. That's what we all have to do in life. I'm doing the same thing, but I try to enjoy what I do. See, I initially felt bad for the prey. As most people do early on. I didn't think it was sporting but then, one day, I realized I'm hunting a game that's much smarter and stronger than I gave it credit for. It became a challenge the more I delved into it."

"That's strange. The longer I hunt the easier it's gotten."

"Not for me," Kayzitt said, smiling at the man and his blushed cheeks. "No, no, not for me. I find that the further in I go with this the more the prey fights back. It doesn't get easier. The prey starts to get angry, starts to take offense. So, now I prefer trapping. I find that I'm back to the days where I feel a little sorry for the poor things. After all, they were fooled so... *completely.* But I catch my prey a lot easier."

"Yeah?" The hunter shifted uncomfortably in his stool.

"The only problem is when they're trapped, they squirm, and cry, and moan." Kayzitt realized he was smiling widely and stopped, "It's pathetic and dreadfully sad, so sometimes I try to end their suffering quickly. But, some of my other trappers, they don't see it that way. They like to have fun before it's all over. And really, who can blame them. I mean the animal is going to die anyway and it's going to die soon. Why not use it for what it is you know? Why not?"

"I'm afraid I can't follow. You got a lot of people in your outfit?" Duff said, glancing down the bar to the other hunters before sipping on his drink again and facing back to Kayzitt.

"Oh plenty. I'd say we have almost fifty in just our one outfit alone. We want to empty this whole region of every last catch we can find."

"Well that—" Duff said with a grimace, straightening himself in his chair, "that would be a right shit thing to do. I'm just trying to feed my family."

"Oh, come on. In this town? Everyone's trying to get their dicks wet!" Kayzitt blurted out, causing the bartender to look over. "Nobody's worried about their family here. I'm sure you had fun down at the working house, right?"

"Hey pal, shut your mouth, okay?"

Duff was beginning to breathe quickly and glanced down the bar. His loud words drawing the glances from others in the tavern.

"I saw that big-titted one in the window, shaking her ass at everybody. She knows none of you have your wives around."

"Listen, I don't know what you are on about, but why don't you just talk to your friends over there, eh?"

"No need to get all offended friend," Kayzitt gushed. "Did I strike a nerve? Is the whore your wife or something?"

The guy turned and slugged Kayzitt in the face with a heavy fist as he lurched from his barstool. The blow was nothing much to Kayzitt, who had experienced much worse in his day and Duff was an aging specimen if nothing else, but it sent him back into Sal's waiting arms. She had undoubtedly watched the whole scene with a snickering Juno. Kayzitt knew there was little more provocation needed.

"Woo! I love getting hit!" Kayzitt cried out as he stood straight.

"Whoa! whoa! What's the problem here!" the bartender yelled in his scratchy voice.

"This guy's a fucking whack job!" Duff yelled back.

Sal swore back at Duff in a laughing flood of Western slang, curses from the coastal regions where the language was a meld of the modern and the Oriental tongues. It was a string of curses and jests that even Kayzitt only partially understood. A brick thrown about his mother and perhaps some more about the lack of honor in the man's anus. Kayzitt could only chuckle as the barkeep backed away from them as if he were staring at a witch.

"Get them out of here!" the bartender demanded.

Two large men were summoned from the back of the room and shuttled the three of them out the doors, creaking hinges slamming open.

Outside the air was cool but humid and the smoke from the tanner's fires was still strong in the stale currents.

"You three should probably go to wherever you're sleeping," said one of the burly men coated in furs and with a beard much like Juno's. He even stared at Juno as if he were looking in a queer reflection of himself. Juno wore no furs, only the relaxed leather vestments and thick canvas pants that he always wore in a raid.

"Get going," said the other.

Kayzitt winked at Sal, who smiled her yellowed smile and laughed as she put her hand gently upon the short sword at her hip. The large men on the porch of the tavern frowned, they had no weapons on them.

In the blink of an eye, Kayzitt drew his right tomahawk, ran across to the steps, jumped to the side of the first of the large men and, while still in the air, buried its steel head into the forehead of the second. Sal kicked the other in the crotch, doubling him over, and Juno pulled a long knife and gored him through the chest.

"Hey! You mountain motherfuckers! I want to party tonight!" Kayzitt cried out as he crossed over to where the tanner had retreated from his fire.

Kayzitt waved the smoke away with his hand and retrieved a thin burning log from the edge of the fire, as well as one of the jars of fresh liquid tallow, hot to the touch.

Burn bright.

Out of the tavern emerged three more hunters, similar to the others but with tarnished medals on their breast that glinted dully.

"What is all this ruckus about?" the front man half-shouted. "If you don't find yourself quick, you'll be likely to spend the night locked in the can."

"I hope you can catch us officer, or else you're going to be spending the night with my boot up your backside," Kayzitt yelled back.

The three officers took out their weapons at that, one wielding a mace, another a long hunting knife, and the third a short sword. The short sword gave the one away as a former Eastern soldier. Kayzitt chuckled at this and walked toward the three with a heady smile. The mud sucked at his boots and the three that awaited him backed away slightly, glancing at the bodies of the previous two that lay in a growing pool of deep burgundy. Kayzitt threw the jar of tallow in a high arc, laughing as the three men ducked and covered their faces. When they heard it shatter upon the sloping roof of the tavern they frowned at Kayzitt and cocked their weapons with renewed zeal.

"What kind of crazy…" one of them said, interrupted when Kayzitt threw the burning log.

It hit the roof of the tavern with a solid thump against the thick thatch. A sharp crackling could be heard and then the roof was engulfed by bright yellow flames.

The three men were immediately disorganized and Kayzitt chucked his tomahawk ahead, splitting one's skull. Sal took advantage of the chaos, spinning her short sword around and knocking away one of their weapons before thrusting forward and stabbing him through the stomach. Juno caught the last by battering his opponent backwards with heavy blows from his large mitt of a fist, then kicking him to the ground and burying his axe in his chest.

The flames were now swarming over the roof of the tavern and the occupants were rushing outside amid shouts and desperate protests. Some came with weapons and tried to work their way toward Kayzitt. Others were too drunk and struggled to even walk over the uneven steps from the porch. They got in the way of the others and Kayzitt laughed wildly at the scene. The flames were beautiful and golden bright. The black smoke churned its way to the heavens where the setting sun made it look strangely pink. It was the most elegant fire he had ever seen and he felt happy that he had been the one to start it. What a beautiful coincidence with the tallow makers. He knew he would find a way of setting the signal. Eventually the street filled and the trio was slowly surrounded by angry onlookers. Juno kicked a man backwards who tried to hit him with a club.

"Look what these animals did!" yelled an onlooker.

"Let's hang 'em!" yelled another who tossed a glass, just missing Kayzitt's temple.

The trio stood their ground in a triangle.

"Wait for it," Kayzitt said.

Just as he did, there was a loud din from the edge of the forest where the trading post dwindled into the growing thickness of trees and underbrush. From that dark abode, the roar of his frenzied troop rushed like an avalanche. The rest of his men stormed into the mass of startled trappers and hunters. Crimson war paint streaked their faces, arrows flew and landed in whistles and thuds. The crowd yelled and dispersed like a herd of cattle startled by a pack of wolves. They trampled those that fell before them and fled helplessly toward the buildings and tied up horses.

Kayzitt spotted Duff scrambling away from the action down the space between the tavern and a mail officer's station. He pushed past the violence, hustling to catch up with his prey, which was bobbing into that narrow darkness. Before Duff could disappear into the shadows of a low-hanging pine tree, Kayzitt tossed a tomahawk with a perfectly honed arc of the arm and flick of his wrist. The cruel head hit Duff square in the back and he fell like a sack of lard. Kayzitt walked over and pulled the rough leather-bound handle from Duff, who twitched and howled upon the sparse grass. With his foot he turned him over onto his back. Duff's arms crimped in toward his chest in pain and his balding head wrinkled with twisting folds of skin and fat. To Kayzitt he looked like one of those bald and wide-toothed seals that would roll and slide along the beach when he was on the California coast, during his years in the camps.

"Like I said. It's much easier when the prey has no idea that there is even a predator," Kayzitt said, and he drove the head of his tomahawk again and again into the body of the dying man. There was yelling from Duff and yelling behind him, where his men were engaged in similar pursuits. As he emerged from the black, choking smoke of the burning tavern Kayzitt found Juno and pulled him aside.

"Head to the brothel immediately. Make sure that a few of the whores are left alive. They'll spread the word quickly. Whores always do."

"But usually—" Juno began.

"But nothing, go now!"

Kayzitt's troops took more oil from various sources around the tanner's shop and soon the few buildings that made up the trading post were on fire—many with people still trapped inside. From the lodges that stood behind the tanner's and the trader's, there could be heard a chorus of shouting and wailing alike. Three remaining prostitutes were brought before Kayzitt. They wore clothes that looked as if they had been fine dresses but a couple hours before. Their hair was messed and they did not look at Kayzitt or any of his men. Their undergarments were torn, and as they stood they struggled to keep themselves dressed. After Kayzitt watched them for a minute one finally began to cry and it was not long before the other two were joining her in quiet sobs of fear.

"Go tell your people," Kayzitt said quietly as he approached them.

The sacrament had long since come to its climax. Now their dresses twisted in his eyes like foam upon sea swells. Their breathing was the crashing of waves. His head felt full to the brim.

"Tell everyone you can," he continued, getting close to the faces of the three pale young women. "Tell them what will happen to the East if your leaders don't give in and end this pointless conflict. Tell them that this is what happens when an unstoppable force meets an immovable object."

He gave the women coats, along with horses, food, water, and some other supplies that had not been burnt. Then he sent them trotting away down the road, crying into the manes of their horses.

Chapter Fifteen

June 2717
Tennessee Fortress

Seneca

One monster is dead, and my friends live. But how many remain? Will Tavin's passion for war only be inflamed further? Glory is a tempting mistress and when one is solving problems with a sword, the world seems to be full of monsters. There's talk of another already, a darker and more cerebral monster. How do we know that we're not over our heads? We may suffer from the gambler's dilemma. One success does not guarantee another.

"Now, where is it? Where is it?" Seneca muttered to himself as he searched pensively across the disorganized shelves of the library at the center of the keep.

Praxis had promised that he had put back the most interesting of books high upon the fourth book case and left the binding out by an inch so, as to be a mark for Seneca's eye. Seneca had promised in return to check the book out himself and see if it measured up to such praise. The library was lit by three wide windows in the far thick wall of the granite keep. In the shafts of afternoon light, dust flitted like tiny insects as he passed his hand over long ignored spines in loose bindings. Seneca kept searching, peering across the high shelf before realizing he might have miscounted.

He was in good spirits today. The fortress had undergone a battery of assaults by the besieging Western forces but had been repelled quite forcibly by the defenders, who were freshly invigorated by their victory over Clades and his men. The wall was no longer attacked at night. The West had simply lost too many in the assaults. Tavin had been the benefactor of much praise over the past week. More often than not he had been inebriated through the donations of drink and smoke from fellow soldiers wanting to hear details of what exactly happened outside the walls. Seneca enjoyed stories, but had to roll his eyes when Thom ordered Clades' head to be placed in a box and launched at the Western camp in one of the trebuchets.

"Aha," Seneca expressed as his eyes spotted the protruding spine of a thin hardcover from the next bookcase over. "Apparently, Praxis meant the fourth bookcase from the left...."

With practiced diligence, he thumbed through the crisp pages, scanning the book for title, text, and proportion, like he had all his medical readings before actually reading them. It was a book about farming, specifically distilling seawater during times of drought.

Praxis the practical soldier. He does nothing without gain. Looks for knowledge everywhere. Seeks it from all places, quietly soaking up good habits.

It could not be called the most interesting book, but there was little upon the shelves that did interest him. There were few fictions he had not already read and there was more than enough excitement in his life for him to approach the military tactics section, which dominated the general's library. Historical non-fiction could be interesting, but they all came to the same dead-end, which was unavoidable speculation about the end of the Old World, and thus, no longer became historical.

Seneca took a seat in a high-backed, leather-bound chair with the sunlight to his back and opened the book on farming. It would disappoint Praxis, he knew, if he did not read it and it was not a book of intimidating thickness. He could finish it all in this day and have time before bed to discuss it still. Sitting in the sunlight, with his sword in the barracks and not lashed to his hip, was liberating. The chair was a welcome cradle and the sun a nurturing respite. He wondered if Chiara was reading now as well. They used to read books of fiction from the appreciable library of the clinic while they sat in a bench-swing overlooking Lake Cayuga in the summer. The breeze coming off the lake would tickle them and buffet her dark hair lightly around her shoulders and he would touch the inner part of her elbow, thinking about nothing. As he sat in the comforting sun of the library window, he could smell the warm air rising off humid grass and hear the call of gulls as children threw stale bread onto the rocky shore.

The nostalgia was becoming too much to bear and Seneca shook it from his head. There was something to be said for staying in the here and now. A man could spend his entire life in the past if he was not careful. Such a fate seemed dangerous to him. No matter how hard things had gotten, he was determined to not become engulfed by daydreaming. He smiled.

Tavin's optimism affects me still, but I think I'll allow it.

He stared at the book on farming, opened it. Time and a sigh escaped his chest without permission. He had turned only ten pages and the sun barely moved its angle through the wide windows when he was interrupted by the searching presence of Lieutenant Jans.

"General wants to see you."

"What is it this time?" Seneca rebuked, then realized this was a new haughtiness in him. It was not too long ago that he would have lacked any confidence in addressing an officer in such a way. But lately the line between their rank and the rank of every officer beneath the general had become quite blurry.

"I better let him explain. He wants to meet with you and the others of your, um, outfit. All of you."

Seneca begrudgingly followed Jans out of the library and was surprised to find him not the least affected by his surliness as they walked outside and up the steps to the main offices of the keep.

"Quite some business with Clades' head there, eh?" Jans joked as he nudged Seneca with an elbow.

"Yes, it was. Quite some business."

"It was my idea actually. I think it was hilarious. Really, can you imagine the look on their faces? They must have been waiting on him quite a while and then all they get is that fucked-up mug!"

The lieutenant laughed, his broad shoulders shaking and the percussion of his voice echoing off the far walls of the keep and the low wall of the stair.

"You should have seen him when he was alive," Seneca said.

Tavin had kept an even demeanor about the display, but Seneca had wondered what his true feelings were. Tavin could often appear the most Western of any of them. Every day he paid as much attention to the shine of his blades as he did the trim of his beard. He wondered if a bloodlust had taken Tavin prisoner.

Upon the staircase he bumped into the slender and tall frame of Kendo, who greeted Seneca with his usual cheery smile. The others were present as well and together they continued the climb to the fortress observatory. When they entered the inner sanctum—where Bok and Thom kept their working office—they found the two generals in the middle of a conversation, surrounded by a few of the lieutenants, who listened obsequiously to every word of the old veterans. As the six entered the room, the generals barely glanced up from their verbal fencing.

"The messenger could be wrong," Thom was explaining as Bok stood, a regal and dark statue in his military uniform.

"The one thing our Capital seems to do well is send messages. That much I'll give them," Bok replied.

"I can't believe there's still no reinforcements. I was promised I would have them in six months. It's been almost nine."

"I could take some cavalry out and scout eastward," Lieutenant Cody offered somewhat sheepishly from his place along the wall.

"No. We're not weakening this fortress's defenses for that," Thom scoffed, his olive skin making dark earthy furrows where his frown creased his face in the pale light from the doorway.

"We'll do it," Tavin said, and Seneca's spine tingled with anxiety. "We'll find your reinforcements. Maybe they just got lost."

Thom looked up from where he had been watching his own pacing feet wear a groove into the floor.

"I expected nothing less." He pulled out a pencil and set to an expansive map laying out across his desk and then stood straighter and taller as he addressed Tavin and Seneca and the others directly. "But that is not your mission. You have a different assignment."

Seneca noticed that Bok, barely moving the rest of his body, took a deep breath and watched Thom expectantly. It was a similar look that Seneca had seen in the clinic, usually amongst fathers who were awaiting the return of the doctor and expecting to hear poor news regarding their loved one.

"And what assignment is that?" Seneca asked.

"There's a Western marauder that the Chancellor has assigned to you personally. You can read your orders yourself if you like. I just got them."

The general rubbed the thick stubbles of black hair on his head as he searched the papers on his desk and then handed Seneca an opened letter. It had been sealed with the official seal of the Chancellor, a diving eagle upon green wax. The letter held the same instructions Thom had explained and beneath was the fluidly regal signature of Chancellor Garrett Carest.

"The marauder in question is thought to be named Kayzitt. Bok was trying to catch him around Nashville weeks ago, but by now he has made it through the front lines. We believe this man leads a fairly small contingent but has nonetheless been causing havoc that I care not to describe. He was last spotted in the central hills of West Virginia." Thom reached under the table and pulled out a thin roll of paper. "This is a map of his movements, at least to the best of our ability to project. Such projections have been made by our fine leaders at the Capital, who suspect this Kayzitt is merely hopping from village to village and avoiding the larger towns. And this time I tend to agree with their projections."

Seneca watched as Tavin took the map from the general's outstretched hand and perused it before bringing it over to him and the other four. In turn they examined where red ink had mapped out the marauder's known paths and victim towns. The gray of a graphite pencil traced out the suspected routes that might be taken: one leading northward to the Great Lakes, another through the heart of the Pennsylvania territories, and a last, fainter line, going eastward toward the capital.

"We do have hearsay that came with the messenger that this Kayzitt has possibly been spotted heading toward the more central projection, toward the ruins of Pitt, and then perhaps up into central and northern Pennsylvania. There are several manufacturing towns in that direction where such raiders could put a dent in our weapons supplies," General Thom explained.

Seneca saw Oil'ib paying uncommon attention to the general's words.

"Is anyone else looking for him?" Seneca wondered aloud.

"There are others. A larger group from the capitol was dispatched. But I've been ordered to send you as well. It seems whatever ties the capital has to Pennsylvania are strong enough to pull you out of Tennessee. I am sorry to take you from the front like this. I only found out last night myself. You must understand, I have to send you."

Again, Seneca realized the lack of the weight of his sword at his hip. Where only minutes ago it had been like the relief of a vacation to be rid of its shackles, now he felt naked without it. Instinctively he clutched at where the worn leather wrapping would rest below the pommel at the intersection of his hip and oblique, only to feel the rigid leather of his belt. There was a sharp pain of the nerves from the scar on his left flank and for a second he thought he would have to sit down. The poorly illuminated close quarters of the office were stifling. The lieutenants beside the mellow oil lamps were too close for comfort and there was nowhere for him to rest. But the pain was gone as quickly as it came and left his mind thinking only of the hulking Clades and the strength with which the man had disarmed him.

"So, when do we have to leave?" Gannon asked, sighing somberly.

"Yeah," Tavin said more enthusiastically, almost as if to cover for Gannon's demeanor. "When do we leave?"

"At nightfall. When it's safest to leave. We'll give you bows as well as the fastest horses we have and plenty of supplies," Thom replied. "Captain Franzen would you be so kind?"

Captain Franzen reached under the far table and pulled out six small drawstring sacks. He tossed one to each of them, Seneca caught his and immediately realized its contents from the solid jingle and thump with which the weighted pouch hit his hands. Looking inside he found a collection of gold coins, a handful of silver, and scattered coppers as well.

"You'll need it," Franzen stated.

"And you've earned it," Bok added.

The afternoon was spent collecting their belongings and fresh supplies. As the sun approached the horizon, they ate a merry dinner at the officer's table in the barracks and said their goodbyes, receiving much appreciation from the lieutenants, sergeants, and infantrymen. Seneca shook what seemed like hundreds of hands and smiled a fake smile at a sea of faces he knew he would never see again. They were ushered by the remnants of their short-lived friendships to the side of the barracks by the stables. There were a few more conversations and well-wishes to be had and then Seneca found himself strapping his sword to his hip once again, and patting his side to make sure he didn't forget his bowie knife.

As he slid the knife back into its sheath and clasped the copper buttons that held it in place, the weight of worry left him, and he realized for the first time that he was headed in the direction of home. As his heart elated with the thought, he stifled it. No need for high hopes. Still, excitement squirmed inside him like a child wriggling free from the embrace of a parent. There was hope, so much hope, in leaving the faraway front of the war. And for the first time he felt that an assignment meant something to him personally. Here he stood a chance to rid the world of a direct threat to his home. In his mind he pictured the red, graphite mappings of the generals. The thickest center line had led up through the center of Pennsylvania and though it had metered out rapidly he knew the line could be continued into the Finger Lakes region and into his own backyard.

"So, here we go again," Gannon said in exasperation, stamping his heels.

"Now you want to stay here?" Tavin posited.

"Here we have walls," Gannon retorted.

"Here we have nothing," Kendo disagreed. "Eventually they'll take this place. It could take them a long time. No one knows, but eventually, and even if we win there's just as much a chance we die here as wherever we go."

"Yeah, yeah that's right. I'd rather take my chances in the wild then—in, um—in here," Oil'ib added.

"Want to go home someday?" Tavin asked. "Then our place isn't here defending a siege. We're ants in a colony right now. Just six extra hands nothing more. We do what these guys want and maybe we have a chance to do something meaningful."

Tavin's words rung true in Seneca's chest. But he was still careful with the sensation. How many times had he merely interpreted false hope as predicted truth? His mind searched his past for examples and came up empty-handed, but he knew it had happened before.

"I trust you guys," Gannon replied, "but I can't help but feel there is another layer behind what you are saying. Our assignment is simple enough. But you read the letter. We are supposed to report to the capital upon completion of the mission. We're not free afterwards. We aren't going home afterward. You say you see rewards and a way out of this war. I see that in the varnish. Below it though, I smell exploitation, plain and simple. I smell an endless loop of assignments, taking us here and there and everywhere until we are dead," he cut off others replies. "Hold on! Or until we're drained of use. And every time we will be a little closer to someone's home. I'm telling you! Every time there will be a small but tasteful promise of an end. That's all I'm saying."

"I understand that Gannon, but let's be fair for a second," Tavin said. "They just paid us to leave the front lines. A place we've been bouncing around for a year. You remember when we were fighting in the open field with the battalion? Our lives were a random chance. You said so yourself. So, I don't care what Bok says about Kayzitt, we'll be out of the fire for a while. Maybe we're replacing the fire with a frying pan, but that's still worth leaving." He tested the withdrawal of his swords from the sheaths upon his back before replacing them again.

"We don't even know precisely where he is," Seneca said, having held the point in all day till the generals were out of earshot, "We'll be alone out there for a long time."

"One-hundred and fifteen miles to be exact," Tavin mentioned, which drew a few eyebrows.

The light from the rising moon was brighter than that of the fading twilight by the time Bok had brought the horses to them from the stables. They trotted in a pristine line at the beckoning of the stable masters and their aids.

Each was diligently fitted with new saddles and stirrups. One at a time, the battle-master—dressed in his ornate regalia of an Eastern general—handed each of the six their horse.

Tavin received a jet-black horse, a jumpy stallion that made a habit of stamping his hooves when not under a careful hand. The largest of the bunch was given to Oil'ib, a spotted brown and white destrier. It munched voraciously upon the gentle grasses that showed through the cobblestones. The horse for Praxis was a solid caramel-brown rouncey with a tawny mane and an unobtrusive nature. Bok seemed to linger at giving that one away Seneca noticed, and Praxis was able to mount the beast without a single shifting hoof. Kendo was gifted a yellow mare, so tall and strong that the stable master lamented giving away such a promising breeder. To Gannon, a black and white rouncey that had been the horse of a cavalry captain. Lastly, Seneca took hold of the horse Bok put into his possession, a sleek gray courser. Its coat was polished steel and its mane shone in the moonlight like a waterfall of fine silver strings. It was a sizable animal, and Seneca, himself of no diminished size, found mounting the beast to be quite the climb. The war horse bucked only slightly as Seneca put boots to the stirrups and craned its head to the left as if to look him over.

"What is your name, huh?" Seneca said quietly as he patted the horse gently upon the withers and felt the strong muscles relaxing to his presence beneath him.

"They have names?" Praxis asked aloud.

"You should pick them yourselves," Bok advised in his usual careful speech. "But take care in doing so. As soldiers you should be weary of your attachments. In giving something a name, you give it an altered life that will forever hold the mark. Be wary that life does not weigh too heavily upon your own."

They walked the horses down toward the rear entrance of the fortress, on the side that the enemy army had the least presence. Thom signaled down to a sergeant, who passed the signal up to Captain Keller on the wall for the portcullis to be raised and the doors opened. After a moment, Keller returned the signal, meaning there was no sign of enemies at the gate and the northern road seemed equally clear. Seneca thought how lucky they had been to make their escape upon the night of a full moon. It would be hard for an enemy to remain hidden beneath the walls tonight. Though there was some risk of having their escape followed.

Bok was not quite done with them however and before Thom gave the signal to open the gate, he watched his elder colleague approach the six men of the Chancellor. As Seneca waited, his grip tightened upon the woven leather reins—sweat already dampening the braids despite the cool night air. Bok approached and stood just off their front. As they were about to part, Seneca wondered how they had played into the story of this man's life. What part did they form? Were they somewhere in the ending climax of a great warrior's biography? Or was this but some strange epilogue, a mere tryst with grandeur following an age of victories?

"Be careful of your spirits on the road. Clades was a man of action. But this raider they have sent to the east, he is something much more, if you will allow me to be honest of my intuition. The waves of the West will test our strength now. They are heading for the mountains. They will try to break the back of your home. Remember there are some things in war that are taken. Either forcibly or slowly, there are pieces of you that will be taken. But there are some things that only you can give away. Your honor is what a man gives himself, no one else can take it. Don't give yourself away to a madman."

Thom gave the signal and the gate lifted with groans of heavy wood on rattling iron chains.

"Take the road north for about ten miles as hard as you can ride," Thom called to them above the sound of the rising gate, "That will get you out of harm's way. Get some sleep and ride hard the next day, turning east. It'll be at least a hundred miles until you start seeing houses again, but it'll be worth it. The steppe will take you where you need to go."

Seneca nudged his horse with a quick but powerful thrust from his knees and the six of them burst out of the fortress, Tavin leading the way. They rode hard, without pause, or to glance back at the shrinking lights of the torches upon the high wall. Up the steady incline of the northbound road, the world was hidden from view beyond the crest of the massive hill that housed the fortress and the sky-scattered stars upon a dark indigo horizon. Beyond, the road twisted in its grayness under the moonlit sky, sank into the dark and shadowy valleys. Seneca glanced behind him in time to see the last of the torches upon the high overlook of the keep disappear behind the hill as the road led down.

The night and following day rose and fell like the hills they traveled along. They stopped only to water themselves and the horses and to walk for a few miles in order to rest the backs of their friendly beasts. Finally, the following evening, they allowed themselves to build a camp and fire, thoroughly convinced of the lack of any followers. Despite the two days of riding and little sleep, Seneca was unable to find rest after their early supper and sat by the fire, turning the glowing coals onto the fresher logs with a stick. Tavin, Oil'ib, Gannon, and Praxis had managed to find the respite and were passed out upon their respective mats, not even setting up the fine canvas tents. It was a clear and still evening and the surrounding thickness of leaves pressed the sound from any breeze. Kendo couldn't find rest either, and so he joined Seneca.

"It makes complete sense that I can't sleep," Kendo said sarcastically.

"I think I might have started a bad habit when we were on all those night shifts," Seneca replied, throwing his stick into the fire, "Now whenever this hour comes, I find myself vaguely anxious without any cause. I suppose Clades still lives on in a way."

"I know how you feel." Kendo opened his canteen and took a sip. "What a strange year. This time last summer we were in Pennsylvania, and now we are headed back."

Before the others had gone to bed, they had all been discussing the most logical way to find Kayzitt. It had come to little conclusion and only furthered exhaustion. For Seneca it had the opposite reaction. His mind still turned over the various options. Should they try to reason out a location for Kayzitt and his men directly? Or should they merely try to predict his next target and surprise him in the defense of a town?

"We'll find him. We'll find people to help us and we'll destroy him," Kendo asserted, as if commenting on Seneca's thoughts.

Kendo was a tall man, with slender but strong limbs and a crop of short-cut brass hair. His skin was tan except where the sleeves of his outfit had kept it white. His round head nestled atop a sharp jaw and an easy smile, high above his lanky shoulders. Kendo had warm hazel eyes that spoke of inner timidity and a social patience that would outstrip even the most belligerent of attitudes. Sometimes this was more of a pain than a blessing; Seneca, or especially Tavin, could grow angry with Kendo for how easily he brushed aside the more intricate adversities that life presented or, blandly stamping it with a summative cliché, called the situation solved. He was an endearing person who was capable of an extraordinarily insipid naiveté that both garnered him easy acquaintances and could enrage his closest friends. Kendo never let on how much he really thought about any one idea or controversial opinion. Because of this, he was the easiest person to be friends with, but also the hardest person to get close to. It was as if he never took chances with losing a single person in his social circle. To Seneca, this was overly cautious and only made Kendo a more tempting target for unstable conversation. With Tavin distracted by sleep, Seneca gladly took his opportunity for a careful dissection.

"Why are you here Kendo?"

"Why do you ask?"

"Because there's no general in the next room. There's no sergeant listening in. We're not being followed. And I'm curious."

Kendo shook his head and smiled.

"I've told you. When we left Oregon, the East took us in. Never looked down on us or questioned our intentions. They made us feel at home."

"That's not why you're here though. I don't question your loyalty to the East," Seneca assured, trying to sound kind while still pressing the question. "And you're not a nationalist anyway. I know you well enough. Why *are* you here?"

"Why am I here?" Kendo reissued the question to himself.

"Your family had enough money to keep you out of this by how you speak of them. You could have avoided this life. Tell me what happened when you left your father's business."

"How long have you been speculating?"

"I think each of us gets speculated on every day; and none of us think you left your father's company on good terms."

"You're right. I didn't want what he offered me," Kendo explained. "It's that simple. I couldn't do it."

"That goes without saying, but why?"

Kendo sighed long and slow.

"I couldn't take advantage of people, take what didn't belong to me just because I learned a skill that would let me take it. My father, he wasn't the fairest of men. I didn't agree with some of the things he did. I know you will ask what, but it's hard to explain to someone who hasn't been in the ship-building business. Basically, he would overcharge people, but he did other things too. My brother swallowed that pill fine, but it made me sick."

"What kind of practices?"

"I'd rather not get into the particulars. It just made me uncomfortable that I couldn't be proud of my father or his business."

"Was he not liked among his customers?"

"Oh no. That's the thing. His customers loved him and thought that he was doing them all these favors and his stuff was high quality supplies. But he would find ways to trap his customers in debt."

"So, you just walked away?"

"I rejected it," Kendo clarified. "He offered me everything, the whole shipyard and business, and I said no. Then it got ugly. That's when he said I could never make him proud. He said I could never be what he expected me to be. Like I had failed to grasp all the lessons he taught me. So he sent me away."

"What do you mean?"

Kendo rubbed his hands upon his pants nervously.

"He didn't just let me leave. He had the staff escort me off the property. He actually did that to me. I've never seen him so mad. I wandered north with a group of traveling performers after that."

Seneca laughed, expecting the latter to be a joke. But

when he saw that Kendo was squirming beneath his own laughter, he allowed his friend to continue.

"I'm serious. They needed someone tall to stock the cages. I stayed with them until we reached the capitol, and when I saw the demand for soldiers, I realized I had to do it."

"Why didn't you tell us this when we first met you?" Seneca asked.

"I got drunk and told Praxis, but I guess he stayed quiet. Oil'ib has a wife that is sitting at home. You have a girl at home. You all miss your families so much, how can I complain when I didn't even get along with mine? I didn't want to bring it up."

"And just like the others you were good at it," Seneca stated.

"Remember, I was Western born. My dad's a business owner and even he was taught as a child to master a weapon. But not every Westerner is a skilled swordsman. Yeah, they train everybody out there, but it doesn't make them any more talented. That's all natural. You either have it or you don't."

"I'm finding out how true that is," Seneca agreed. "I'm sorry you had it rough with your dad. I can relate. My father—our relationship never came to a head like yours did, but it was a constant stress. He used to say that there is always room for improvement even if you are doing your best and that no one should ever be satisfied. Well, that's the medicine he practiced as a parent. My father never recognized talent or praised hard work." Seneca rubbed his face as he pictured home again and laughed a little at his memories. "By the time the draft sergeant came for us at the clinic I was almost torn. Don't get me wrong, I would not have left Chiara willingly. But another part of me was driven to go just to show him that I didn't need him. Some days in camp I would even feel bad for the apprentices still back with him. Though now they probably feel the same way about us."

Kendo nodded along agreeably and leaned backwards stretching as far back as he could. Seneca thought the conversation was over but Kendo was unusually talkative.

"What would you tell your father if he was here now?" his friend asked in a quieter tone.

Seneca was caught off-guard by the question but the answer found him.

"I'd tell him how people trust me, depend on me, and think enough of me to give me responsibility. That's all I ever wanted from him: respect."

Chapter Sixteen

June 2717
Ruins of Pittsburgh

Kayzitt

What lovely locations man chooses to settle. Three rivers meet together in the basin of beautiful hills. The hills themselves are welcoming and gentle. They must have grown complacent. Here in the decaying glory of its buildings is the lesson for humanity. Nothing matters more than the drive for continuous self-improvement and adaptation. Even if it means stepping outside of all your comforts.

Kayzitt squatted in the thick mud and poked at the paw print gingerly with his finger, upon the firm ridges where the mud has been pressed to the side by the weight of the beast. The pad of the paw had been wide and splayed beneath the flex of a massive foreleg, the hints of sharp claws showed as small divots toward the front. He sniffed the air; it was musty over the earthy tones of the drying mud. There was warning in the smell, and fear as well. They were not welcome here.

"This is the spot," Kayzitt said, standing and turning to Sal as he spoke.

Sal trotted off, springy in the step and electric in the wry heat of the day. The humidity showed in the pearls of sweat that had condensed upon her back between the leather straps of her vestments. Kayzitt knew his group would obey his every word. Commands were often unnecessary. Just as much could be done with a glance and a wave of the hand. But the Eastern prisoner, the lost deserter they found on the road, was not one of his men. And despite Kayzitt's insistence that he would die quickly, the prisoner resisted at every turn. His men drove a fresh poplar tree trunk into the earth behind him. There were uses for all things, Kayzitt mused. He stepped forward to meet his captive.

"Come on," Kayzitt said. "You might as well calm yourself. There's nothing you can do."

Above them, the sunlight glittered against a massive twisting and shattered steel skeleton, the ruins of Pittsburgh. Behind them the three rivers converged, their sloshing in the light breeze could be heard even from this distance.

There was not much time left if the ceremony was to be completed perfectly and Kayzitt preferred every ceremony to go perfectly. Somewhere in the dark underbelly of the sprawling mausoleum, the beast waited. There were pieces of old and broken things that caught the sun's rays at times, but he thought he saw the eyes that he had followed, glinting beneath the shrouded vestibules. From the heights, came the creaking of metal beams, the haunting music of the former city. The old buildings complained of their broken backs and waited for time to bury them beneath their own rust and dirt.

The prisoner stood before Kayzitt with panicked hatred on his pale face. He was strong and young, perfect for the ceremony.

"What honor is there in this?" the prisoner spat. "Do you Westerners have no respect for fellow men?"

"You misunderstand," Kayzitt replied coolly as he tied his own bright red hair up into a tight bun. "You are receiving the highest honor for a prisoner of war. And I am not going to kill you."

He made a motion with his head. The prisoner was making ready to speak again but was interrupted by Kayzitt's men dragging him—kicking at the mud— to the post, where they tied him. Kayzitt approach him again and ripped open the man's shirt. Sal handed him a small clay pot and brush, and Kayzitt began to paint a yellow circle on the prisoner's chest. The paint was bright and caught the sunlight. As the beads of it ran down the man's heaving chest, Kayzitt made sure to catch each runaway drop and feed it back into the growing image, until the symbol was painted thickly in the golden paint.

"Come on man! What is this?" the prisoner whined. "What gives you the right? You fucker!"

Kayzitt laughed.

"Well I'm doing it aren't I? If I'm not allowed, then someone should stop me."

The prisoner heaved against his bindings.

"I'll join you guys. I'll do anything. Just let me go!"

Kayzitt looked up at the prisoner, fascinated.

"You would give up on your people so quickly? You

would cast their honor aside and became one of us? You would do all of that for what? A chance to live a while longer? You sicken me."

Sal stepped forward with a small knife as Kayzitt stepped away, handing the paint and brush to Jun. The men watched diligently, awaiting the coming excitement with pacing feet. Kayzitt nodded for Sal to go ahead and she drew the small, but razor-sharp, knife from its short leather sheath and held it to the chest of the prisoner.

"Wait, wait, wait– stop please!"

She made a small cut on each of his pectorals. The blood ran in small streams over the yellow disk upon his chest. The prisoner shouted in pain, when it was done he seemed more confused. His mouth moved around inaudible words and puffed with his chest.

"It'll all make sense," Kayzitt stated.

He offered a brief smile and then signaled his outfit to walk past the prisoner, each one of them following his lead in quiet reverence. Kayzitt took his thumb and pressed it into the gently running blood of the prisoner and pressed it into a red circle upon his own forehead, so too did Sal, and Juno, and then all the others. They then stood at attention in an outcropping of cinder stone about fifty yards away.

"Wait. Please come back. Please! You can't do this to me! I'm a human being!" The words broke off, hoarse.

The prisoner struggled before proceeding to cry softly. There was no person in front of him to face any more. Kayzitt and the others sat behind him on the outcropping, but Kayzitt could see the ruins as the victim must have seen it. A twisted canyon of groaning giants. The sun and the wind the only presence for him now. It nearly distracted him from the beast that had emerged from the darkness.

Slowly the lion made its way from the depths of the jumbled rocks and vegetation onto the muddy plain beneath the steel mountains. Its blunt and burnished mane waved gently as the mighty shoulders flexed its form toward the prisoner. The prisoner was silent. He did not see the lion.

Behind him, Kayzitt's men held their breath as silently as the rocks themselves. Finally, the prisoner saw the beast as it stalked him, sniffing the air between them, its deep rumbling breath bringing forth the lapping pink tongue as it tasted the air.

"Help! Help!" the prisoner screamed, then stopped as the beast stared straight at him.

It continued its primal evaluation, sniffing around the man's crotch. Then the animal sat its hindquarters down and appeared at peace with their prisoner. For the briefest moment Kayzitt became concerned for the mission. Was this creature's mercy a sign? Was this mission not blessed?

Show me a sign.

Without warning the beast leaped forward from the ground in a swiftness that made Kayzitt recoil in his seat. It was around the prisoner's throat before a scream had left his lips and with a couple shakes of its head ended the man's life. Then, standing on its hind legs, at a height that dwarfed the sacrifice himself, the lion latched hold of the shoulder and drew the upper half of the corpse to the ground, the body tearing where the rope held it to the thick post. Blood splattered across the golden mane and the beast began to gorge itself on the entrails.

"Now," Kayzitt said, barely moving his mouth.

With bows and swords drawn, his men splintered off in scuttling footsteps and formed a ring around the great lion as he feasted upon his meal. When the beast finally noticed the men as they neared closer and closed the circle, it snarled and showed its long, blood-soaked fangs and dark purple gums. It bristled and clawed at the air, threatening to kill each of them as it turned and turned, searching for escape. But the raiders were already letting loose their arrows and the missiles hit with solid thuds into the flanks of the beast. It staggered and pounced in desperation, landing heavily on one of the raiders who had dared to get too close.

Kayzitt made his approach and, as the lion was backing off of his second victim, landed heavily on its back, sinking the long dagger in his hand deep into the beast's neck, between the shoulder and the jugular. Staggering, lurching, the lion tried to shake him off, but Kayzitt stabbed again, a third time, once more and it fell, wheezing its last breaths upon the thick mud as Kayzitt dried his brow on his sleeve. When it was dead, Kayzitt signaled for his men. They began gathering the wood and other pieces of earth on which to build a decent pyre.

At high noon the golden body of the lion was laid upon a pile of dry wood and kindling. Then Kayzitt took his long knife from the beast's neck and began to cut into the breast. As he dissected, he chanted an old prayer out loud so that all his companions and troops could hear.

"The horizon showed you where to go and you went. The clouds attempted to stifle. The darkness showed you your weaknesses. The light released you and you flourished. Those that stand in your way are blinded by your glory!"

"To the glory of Sol and to the glory of the West!" his troop replied in unison.

Kayzitt rooted around in the hot blood of the beast before he found the proper cords and cut loose the heart, heavy with fat and blood. Sal brought forth a bowl of salted water, deep in a dark bladder. In it, Kayzitt washed the heart and shook away the blood that he could. Then, he pulled it from the bladder and held it above his head so that the shadow of the heart blocked the intense sunlight from his eyes as he spoke.

"May the sun shine brightly upon us until we meet it at the eastern sea!"

The raiders cheered in reply and Kayzitt looked at each of them, forcing his stern eyes into theirs. Then he took a bite of the heart.

It was salty and tasted of iron and copper. The tough flesh slid around his mouth on a thin palette of fat. But Kayzitt was accustomed, hungry, and full of the spirit. He swallowed and felt the weight of the raw meat fall into his stomach. He felt strengthened and as he rose his face to the sun he could feel the tiredness of the past weeks leaving his joints. Behind him, Sal was lighting the pyre, as she knew to do. He handed the heart to her when she was done and kissed her on her forehead as she bit into the heart herself. She smiled at him as she did so, the sweat from her skin was salty and strangely sweet after the metallic taste of the heart.

One by one, each man took a bite of the heart and gave praise to the glory of the West and as they filled the canyon of the ruins with their raucous celebration, the flames grew higher and higher and engulfed the body of the lion.

The day of unity will come on the heels of a blood-soaked night.

Chapter Seventeen

June 2717
Canyontown, Pennsylvania

Dahli

Yes, my husband frustrated me. I shudder to imagine how much time was wasted in his deliberation, or how much annoyance I felt waiting for his thoughts to arrive at the conclusions I had already made, but those feelings do not summarize my time with him. He had a reservoir of kindness and patience I will never find in another human being. He had the majority of the traits that bring people happiness, but not all of the ones I craved. If only one human being could actually complete another.

The ornate brick oven at the heart of the kitchen drove Dahli's attraction to her new home. While touring the property with Mr. Avery, she had gushed over the heavy arch and stone-worked separations between the hearth, fireplace, and oven, and how the bowed cast iron of the stove had been shaped into a paisley pattern. After seeing the rolling yard that was now her garden and the short apple trees that were now her orchard, her heart sealed itself upon the house.

Now her kitchen was a mess of burnt crust, flour, and the oppressive heat from the coals beneath the oven. Outside, the day was sultry and gave no relief to the sauna that her house had become with her midday activities. Even after she threw open the windows, Dahli felt no cleansing draft and resorted to removing her shirt and skirt, relying only upon her tunic and a light pair of cotton trousers while she fanned her flushed face with paper.

Baking proved a modest distraction. Three loaves of bread—only one truly edible—had managed to shake her mind out of the gloomy spiral it had taken for most of the day. But now it was too hot and thoughts sank themselves upon her like the humidity of the house. She had been buying flour and sugar at the shop only a small walk away. Women of her own age were the principal attendants to the store, and a flock of them had congregated to gossip outside, their hands grasping the wide baskets full of their errand prizes. She had heard them turn their conversation to the war. Had one of them heard? The defenses at Illinois had fallen. Yes, quite so, and Tennessee was under siege.

One of their nephews had been sent to Tennessee, one of the ladies was pretty sure. But surely it would be okay, yes. The Eastern men would rebuff their opponent and reinforcements from the Capital would surely save the day. Surely, yes, yes, of course. No invader from the West, after all, had ever gotten past the mountains of Appalachia.

Dahli fled the gossip, feeling her heart sink, pulling the warm blood from her face. She had returned home cold, the words of the women nestling with the words of her father in her ears and breeding morose ideas.

Dahli glanced at her long counter top. At the end of it lay a pale yellowed envelope, the handwriting so familiar but the paper so obviously aged beyond the original date of its writing. She feared the letter for a bevy of reasons that she could not reiterate to herself, lest she feel deepened regret. Reaching down to touch it she made the slightest contact with the edge, recoiling her hand as quickly as it had landed.

In her loneliness she had allowed Jeremiah to invite himself over once again. The past week he had taken a flattering interest in her new house and its upkeep; she had not been able to resist telling him that he could come over and see the details of the inside. She had blushed over the memory of their kiss and how she had kicked him out but only a week before. His advances seemed obvious, but she thought it prudent to have it out with him once and for all. Maybe he planned on taking things further, but there was no other option than to tell him they must remain only friends. The planned conversation kept running through her head and it never got any more comfortable. Again, the yellowed envelope grabbed her eyes. She dared not touch it.

Cool water splashed over her face and arms as she found herself in the washroom. She dried and changed her clothes to a light summer dress and was shortly relieved of the oppressive heat. As Dahli reorganized the kitchen, she cut slices from the good loaf of bread. The other two she threw out for the birds. Perhaps she would visit some of her friends from the school later. It had been so long since she had seen the other girls of her age and so few of them were free enough or close enough to account for visits. The gentle rapping of knuckles upon the heavy oak door turned her toward the entrance. Jeremiah stood on the other side of the door with his smile on full display. He had a bouquet of spring daisies in his hand and a look of bright sincerity upon his face.

"I was going to lie and say I picked them. But it would be an injustice to the florist. He has such a fine eye for arrangements."

"The stems are already cut at an angle. I definitely would have called you a liar," Dahli responded as she returned the smile.

"I'm glad I didn't tarnish my record fruitlessly," he stated looking down at his shuffling feet a moment before locking eyes with her. "I know I took too much upon myself with my last visit, but at the risk of being thrown out again I just couldn't stay away. I hope you'll find some use for me. I would rather waste my own time than yours."

She stood aside and allowed Jeremiah to walk back into the house.

Given the little time she had, Dahli had managed to create a reasonably presentable home despite its limited furniture. All of her earnings of late had gone into filling the voids. Newly cushioned chairs and a gentle hardwood loveseat sat in the living room around the hearth.

One bedroom had been filled with her own belongings and another with everything she had that belonged to Oil'ib. That room was shut away, and she only visited it in times when her chest felt heavy.

"I am surprised that you wanted to come back. There is little here to see. I haven't quite finished decorating, and the garden is still coming into its own," Said Dahli.

"What are you saying? That I don't know it when I see a

beautiful home? Or a beautiful person?" Jeremiah replied.

"I'm saying I can't figure you out. And please, don't flatter me. I've warned you once already against flattery. My father taught me how to use it and be used by it long ago," she stated.

She was trying to sound serious, trying to ward off the impelling forces that she knew there was no defense for. But her words only came off as cheery and playful. Her cheeks burned.

"Maybe you can't figure me out because I'm not trying to do anything. Maybe it doesn't make sense to you that a man could just want to spend time with someone," he responded.

He took the vase from one of the countertops and replaced the old withered flowers with the fresh daisies. The kitchen was somewhat spartan and the flowers gave it a spark of life.

"What do you want though? You can't fool me into believing that a man goes about his days without a plan. Especially men like you. What do you *really* want?" asked Dahli.

"You want me to say I want you?" he asked. "Would that make it easier? Then you can just send me away because I was too aggressive."

"I want you to be honest with me is all," Dahli said, swishing back a pace. "I think I have earned that."

He frowned. "Have I ever given you the impression of dishonesty?"

"The impression you've given me is one I'm not sure you have the clout to keep. You act like a fine man, one that any woman would be lucky to have. But there's a catch, a couple catches. You haven't come out and said if it's true and that is as good as being dishonest. Afterall, I haven't had the luxury of seeing you pass any of life's real tests. You had an easy upbringing. You haven't had to face much difficulty in life. Have you ever had to tie yourself to a cause, or another person, and hold on for dear life; ride the ups and downs and show that you were capable?"

"That seems like a high-flying accusation from a woman who lived with one of the richest men in—"

"–Aha!" she pointed, "let me finish! You are right though 'lived'. Past tense. I managed to finally go out and do something on my own, though. Where do you think you are standing? This is not my father's house. And while I realize I may not be off fighting some great war or putting my life on the line for the needy or a cause, at least I'm doing something on my own. At least there's nothing beneath me but the ground I'm building, and if I fall, then I fall on my own knees and not on my parents. What about you? Have you done anything or said anything truly honest? Something that you and only you stand behind?"

There was a long pause as Jeremiah furrowed his dark eyebrows and looked off to the left. Outside, she could hear the chirps of birds swarming at the burnt and crumbling loaves of bread on the lawn.

"You're right. Maybe I haven't ever gone out on a ledge before. But I want to. I want to go out on a limb and say something that only I am standing behind. I'll be honest. And if you don't like it? Well, then we'll see. I suppose it'll be over then. But…." He put his hands akimbo as he looked down into her eyes. "I want you Dahli. I said it– I've wanted you for a while now and I've been afraid to tell you too soon because you might think I was just after your dowry or some meaningless crap like that. Now, I can see myself out if you like. Tell me I'm wrong and I'll go. I'll go and I'll never bother you again and it'll be strictly professional from here out."

The words beat upon her chest like a bass drum. The movements of her limbs were an existential phenomenon, and she felt that her body was propelled by some outside source. She turned from him and walked over to where the door was still open ajar. The warm sweet aroma of the outside spring air whispered. For a moment, she thought she was going to open it and hustle Jeremiah outside. Out where he belonged. Away from her safety, away from the coolness that she kept, insulating her worries and doubts. When she closed the door and turned her back on it, Dahli was sure she no longer knew herself at all. The freedom in not knowing, in no longer caring about the lack of her inward knowledge, was exhilarating. And for a second nothing existed but her and Jeremiah, his pale presence waiting in the golden light that shone through the kitchen window.

Yearning drove her direction, the longing to be wanted, to feel loved and to love, to give herself entirely and be reciprocated in full.

They were closer now, and before she could stop their lips were touching and she was moving them against his caressing. And she found her hand inside his own. And she was leading him blindly down the hallway, the blood rushing through her and warming the blushing skin upon her face and chest.

I need you... I need this...

"This is crazy," he said.

"I know."

As she moved over on the sheets, already warmed by her body, he climbed in beside her, his hands finding her naked frame and caressing her skin so that she squirmed beneath him.

She moved her hips up and down against his own as he lowered himself down upon her. His lips were on her then, kissing down her chest and nuzzling her nipples until they felt like firm peaks of electric tension on her skin. She reached down to where she knew he was and accepted him easily, undulating and arching her back as he slipped in and out of her senses.

Her hands gripped blindly against the pillows and downy mattress, hanging on as she whipped over and found herself nestling into the kisses that he lay upon her neck, tingling and jolting, making her pinch his face between her own and her shoulder and rolling her eyes back in the spinning moment. When it was over, her body hummed and her skin was hot, cool where stripes of sweat navigated with gravity.

"I never expected that," Jeremiah said while slowly massaging her shoulders.

She said nothing, hardly registering in her mind what he had uttered. Her gaze continued on the painting upon the wall. The leaves overlooking the lake were orange and red with the beauty of their wilting. Sadness was growing quickly in her now and she felt that if she moved, she would break the seal that kept it inside her. She dreaded the thought of him seeing her weep after making love.

"You should go," she told him.

"I'm sorry?"

"Don't be sorry. I just need some time alone. Just go. Please, don't make me say it again."

Jeremiah dressed gracefully and left in the same manner. He paused only to lay a gentle kiss upon her forehead. A show that broke the tiniest seal in her walls and forced a tear to drop warmly down her cheek when she blinked. There seemed to be an understanding when he followed her gaze to the painting on the wall. He stood there, attempting to start a sentence but found nothing. Then he was out of sight and she could feel him standing in the open doorway and the gentle change in the movement of the air as he left and closed the door again, so quietly that the latch hardly made a click against its iron.

When her sobs had passed and she regained control of her grief she crept to the counter and again stared at the yellowed paper of the letter. It bore only her name and the address of her father's house. She wondered how long her father had held it before he gave it to her. Without anything left to gain or lose, she opened the letter. The creases of paper giving way easily to her hasty and frantic strength. She unfurled it and felt sad that the writing was not as long as she had hoped.

Dahli,

I've begun to enjoy writing as it seems to be easier for me when I can put everything on paper. I can throw my words away until they sound right. And my friend Praxis can check my spelling. Anyway, we just made it to Greensboro, somewhere in Kentucky. It's the biggest town I've ever seen. It seems every frontiersman, miner, and trader arrived here a hundred years ago and built a small empire.

I am only able to pen this letter because, for the first time in months, we are not in the wilderness protecting our main army. We've been given the job of protecting this town instead and I've never been happier. Not counting being home with you of course. We're eating like kings and the townspeople have accepted us. I'm hopeful as the war progresses, reinforcements will arrive soon and

I'll be able to come home and rejoin you.

I'm saving every penny I can, and the life has been more difficult at times than I thought possible. Fear not because I have had my share of good fortune. We survived the frontier, including three battles. For the time being they've made me head scout for our local area. The best news, however, has been my friends. There are five especially that I couldn't have made it this far without. Maybe one day you'll meet them.

For now, it's beginning to get warm again, and we're alive. I can't ask for anything more except to see you again.

I love you,
Oil'ib

Dahli read and re-read the letter several times before lowering it from her gaze. Again and again she observed the curve of the ink in the letters underneath the stroke of a hand that was unfamiliar to her. Then she gripped it against her bosom as she heaved. She enclosed herself within the second bedroom, amongst the trappings and furs and instruments. She got into the bed, took the letter against her again and fell asleep.

Chapter Eighteen

July 2717
West Virginia

Gannon

I am terrified. I feel eyes on my shoulders everywhere I go, but then I look around and I'm alone. There is no immediate danger, but the tension refuses to leave. I suppose, in war, tension is better than relaxation. After all, a relaxed man is a dead man. But now I fear it will never leave. It's becoming too deeply ingrained. It is as much a part of me as my smile. I wake up and it is waiting for me.

Gannon lapped the remnants of cool water from his canteen with fervid gulps, a thin stream seeped from the corner of his mouth and into his thickening stubble.

"Just ahead?" he questioned Oil'ib.

"Umm… should be,"

"Trust him, there've been tracks massing more and more

frequently in this direction. We're closing in," Praxis stated.

Gannon chuckled.

"Now we have two scouts?"

"To be fair he is a distinguished graduate of Oil'ib's apprenticeship program," Tavin deadpanned.

Gannon recalled how Oil'ib and Praxis had managed to find them in Tennessee after the sacking of Greensboro. Without those tracking skills, he and the others would have certainly been killed.

"Stellar marks too," Oil'ib quipped.

They rode their steeds gently down into the broken entrance of a village. It looked to be the place that they had been promised. A day earlier, they talked with an accommodating hunter who had seen the movements of a band that met their target's description. The air still smelled of burnt thatch and lard. Darkened buildings and homes were deserted and lay ruin on their stone foundations. Not all was destroyed, but it was enough that Gannon held out little hope for the next move in their chase. The village ruins stunk with the gloomy threat of a dead end. One thing had become obvious in their time picking up the trail of this Kayzitt and his path of violence: rarely did he and his troops take the main road. Instead, they seemed to lurk in small numbers through the forests, sometimes making multiple trails that circled back upon each other. Gannon felt that they were chasing the heels of death itself.

"Well done, Oil'ib," Tavin congratulated, patting his friend on the back. "If the coast is clear, we can search for any survivors and then try to pick up the trail before they get ahead of us."

They paused a moment at the entrance to the village, idly waiting as the wind buffeted them gently with the smell of death. The smell left a lingering taste of vomit in Gannon's mouth.

"I think we're good," Seneca surmised.

"Two columns. Right down the middle," Tavin advised.

The others nodded and Gannon lightly spurred his rouncey onward. They crossed the boundary into the village itself and Gannon felt like he had passed through a screen of icy water. Turkey vultures obscured the bodies in the street beneath piles of greasy black feathers. He struggled to imagine the audacity of the people who attacked such a small and meaningless village, likely devoid of even a militia, let alone any true Eastern forces. Fear and hatred broiled in his stomach.

What are we to each other?

"We'll have to search the houses," Tavin offered when they had reached the end of the village without the fortune of something finding them.

"For what?" Praxis responded.

"Survivors, obviously."

"This is a bad mission," Gannon stated aloud which drew an agreement from Seneca.

"I still think charging into a hoard of Westerners on the front lines is a worse mission," Kendo added, to which Tavin vehemently motioned his own agreement.

Tavin always expressed his patriotism the most fervently. Gannon had, on more than one occasion, been persuaded to accept Tavin's views of life. Still, Gannon knew that they desired different things. Gannon's ideals would have them living on the beach while Tavin's led them to this village of death.

Their attention was diverted by the sudden appearance of cavalry moving from the east. Horses and their riders converged over the main road in a long line of four columns. About sixty by Gannon's count. He clutched at the quiver of arrows upon his back as the apprehension jolted through his body in a sudden electric surge, making his eyes widen and his ears prick. He watched as the mass of soldiers move toward them along the village road like a surging wave off the coast.

"Looks friendly," Oil'ib said.

They turned and drew their bows, nocking arrows just in case.

"We fire and scatter off if they aren't—they can't hit all of us," Tavin replied, speaking out of the corner of his mouth.

"I think they could," Seneca disagreed.

As the cavalry grew closer and the leader slowed its mass to a gentle trot as it entered the village road, Gannon lowered his shoulders. There was no mistaking it. The leader was a woman. The face made Gannon relax, demanded her own line of thinking. Female leaders and even infantry were not a completely uncommon thing in the Western legions, but in the east, there was a more dubious view on the subject and women rarely attained or even sought military stature. Not since Solly died in the sacking of Greensboro had he seen such a creature. Somber green banners of the Eastern Republic could be seen dominating the force behind her. She sat atop her ride with a strong and slender pose as if posture came easily to her. A long blonde braid across her shoulder. Holding her hand aloft and motioning for her men to stop, she alone continued forward on her black horse. Gannon made out the full curves of her lips and the sharp angled blue eyes that decorated her pretty face. Her skin was pale, fine silk and she moved with a showy purposefulness that made every minute gesture seem deliberate.

"I didn't think anyone else would show up," she said as the horses behind her came to a thumping stop. "My name's Hemma. I'm the captain of this outfit."

"I'm Tavin and these are my fellows," Tavin responded before Gannon could even summon the breath to do so. "We're agents of the Chancellor, and at the moment we're looking for the man who led the sacking of this village. Are you also on the trail Kayzitt?"

"You've guessed correctly," Hemma said, "And there's supposed to be two other groups from Ohio that should be in this area, but I haven't heard a whisper." She kicked her horse ahead to get closer to the six. "I'm impressed, I thought I'd be the first one here."

"Maybe an issue with your map?" Kendo said with some sarcasm.

"No, I think it's with my men who seem to take longer to piss than I do, even though nature gave them every advantage in that department."

"Well, you only lost by ten minutes so don't feel too badly," Tavin stated.

Gannon noticed a certain giddiness in Tavin that he had not seen in a while. It was quite different than his usual energy for action and swordplay.

"Fellas," Gannon stated with expressed annoyance, finding it odd they were being so sociable given the setting.

"Yeah—right," Tavin acknowledged. "We were about to search the buildings."

"We'll help you," Hemma replied. "Gentlemen! Split off and search, report anything living or unusual to me."

The Eastern cavalry split up in pairs, with precision suggesting that this type of reconnaissance had been practiced in the decimated remains of similar towns. Gannon felt sour and split off, mentioning so to Kendo before hitching his horse to a post in the main road.

"You sure?" Kendo asked softly.

"Yeah. I'm already tired of this place," he said back.

He followed a trail of emptiness for a while, walking wherever the other soldiers were not. Seeing Tavin in the presence of this woman captain had taken the remaining spirit from him and he wanted to be alone for as long as the process would take. He felt that a sense of ceremony was lacking, some due diligence to the awful crime that had been committed there. Gannon was not a religious man, but he could not shake the feeling that some prayer needed to be said for the people that were slain.

Like so many earthworms after a rain.

Gannon continued to the far house and pushed the door forward on creaking hinges with the length of his morningstar. If there was an ambush, he hoped he might have some time to center his thoughts.

The house was empty and the air still. The only movement was the swirling of dust motes in the sunshine that splashed through the smashed windows. Blood stains trailed along the compacted dirt floor to the back door past the fireplace. Upon opening the garden door, he found two mounds. Gannon closed the door before his eyes could stare, but his mind had already processed the shadows and knew them for a man and woman lying dead. The woman was naked and both of their heads were smashed in.

He turned back into the house with the familiar pit in his stomach. He made feeble attempts at calling out for survivors.

"Hello," he called softly. "Is anyone alive?"

He worked his way slowly around to the staircase and climbed it, the creaking of the wood startled him at first. As he gained the top of the he peeked over it. A few feet down the hallway was the arm of a young child, stretched across the entrance to a room with the hand just in the ray of light from a window in the room. Gannon froze and nearly vomited. He rushed down the steps and sat at the bottom, collecting his head in his hands.

"I can't do this," he uttered to himself.

As he walked back through the settling dust and shadows however, the corner of his eyes saw a scuttling form. Gannon whipped around as his heart leapt into his throat and his muscles tensed around his handle. The shadow had been small, only the size of a dog, but he knew he had seen human eyes disappearing behind the corner of the large fireplace. He crept slowly around the corner and back into the kitchen, trying to garner the courage to call out to the thing that he had seen. He hoped it was merely a dog or a rat, but the courage failed in his throat and only his mindless legs carried him. Finally, gaining the corner, Gannon peered into the far back of the fireplace, to where the ashen remains of a wood fire graced a clay oven. There, within the depths were two quivering human eyes, a child.

"Hey," Gannon hardly whispered. Then, a gentle touch

louder, "Hey, I'm from the capitol. I am Eastern, like you. We're here to help."

Gannon put away his morningstar on his back and reached out a gloved hand toward the oven, attempting a sheepish smile. But as he grew closer the child screamed and began to kick at the ashes that lay across the oven opening. The piercing note of the scream startled him and he raised up and bumped his head loudly off a lamp that hung from the mantle. He seethed in pain and patted his head and the child made a dash from the oven, exposing her frail frame. The soot and ash smudged and streaked on her dark skin, giving her the appearance of a ghost. But Gannon collected himself and did not miss the opportunity. As the young girl exploded from the oven he managed to catch her in his arms and, with a gentle forcefulness, brought her to a cradle there.

"It's alright. It's alright."

She tried to fight his strength, but she had none to give herself. By the cracks in her voice he knew she had been without water and she quickly collapsed into a shaking and silent cry. Gannon soothed her and made gentle cooing noises and he petted her short black hair, grimy with the dirt of her concealment.

"We're here to help. It's alright. You're alright. My name's Gannon. What's your name?" he finally said. There was no answer, even after the girl no longer shook and he pumped her some water from the large water pump beside the oven.

The girl had no words to give, though she no longer struggled and drank greedily from his canteen.

"I'm sorry about what happened. My people and I are here to help you and get you somewhere safe."

Footsteps could be heard coming from the entrance to the

house. Again, the small girl began to struggle against Gannon's cradling arms. Her efforts shook a warm tear from his eye and it slid quickly down to drop where the ashes had gathered upon her shoulders. As if immediately noticing the moisture, the girl stopped her meek thrashing and finally looked into Gannon's eyes. Her own were dark, darker than the blackness from which she had emerged as a fleeting shadow. Grief hid in the sleepless sagging and hollowness that surrounded those eyes. Yet within them, Gannon saw the light of youth fighting for its life. A candle in an endless cavern.

"No, no that's okay," Gannon looked to the door as a silhouette appeared in the glaring light. The voice that spoke his name was familiar and he turned back to the girl, who appeared to be fighting between sleep and panic. "That's one of my friends. It's okay we're going to get you out of here."

Seneca approached with a gentle scuffling of his leather boots across the earthen floor. Gannon was glad that it was Seneca, who was more sensitive and empathetic than the others in their group, which certainly resembled a group of ruffians.

"Hi," Seneca said as he knelt to the child, his voice paternal, and he touched the girl gently on the forehead, compared her temperature to his own. "Are you hungry?"

The girl nodded carefully, the shock in her eyes retreating slightly with the promise of food. Gannon noticed that the pantry in the kitchen was hanging open and that not a crumb of food was present. But he rejoiced that the child had shown even the slightest sign of communication.

Outside, she gazed at the other soldiers and the braying horses with silent alarm. Gannon was able to procure provisions from his own sack and was soon feeding the girl small pieces of apple that he cut with his knife. She curled away in the presence of his knife at first. But Gannon made lamentations and then showed her how he could feed her the slices. To this she became accustomed. And Gannon lost three of his apples to her before she fell asleep. Feeling a sentimental wreck, Gannon carried her around with her head resting on his shoulder while she slept. He was pleased that they had come to the village.

He remembered the woman leading the cavalry. In times like these, he felt reassured in deferring to the more thoughtful sex. He walked as hurriedly across the street as he could without waking the girl. He waded toward the cavalry captain through the soldiers gathering corpses to an intact shed.

"We didn't find anyone," Hemma reported before spotting the girl. "Oh my God. Is she okay?"

Gannon only shrugged, and Hemma cheerily accepted the girl into her own arms, stroking the sleeping child's hair with her gloved hand. After promising to return, Gannon left to meet with the other five of his companions who had isolated themselves from Hemma's people.

"We need to move quickly," Tavin stated. "Obviously they're going to follow the woodland trails into Pennsylvania. No sense waiting here."

"Is there nothing we can do for her though? She is just a little girl," Gannon asked, letting his voice grow a touch pleading without challenging his friend's consciences directly.

Praxis' voice was firm however, "There's a problem. This town has no supplies. Nothing. We were checking cupboards, cellars, everywhere. They cleaned this place out."

"And we're looking at two days of provisions at most," Seneca added.

"We're on a time crunch," Oil'ib said suddenly.

"Oh, really? We're on a time crunch Oil'ib?!" Seneca said, earning a laugh from Kendo.

"What about Hemma?" Gannon asked. "We could try to convince her to take the girl."

"Can we focus on one thing at a time?" Tavin pressed back with the response that Gannon had expected. "This village was massacred and we need to determine our next direction before we do anything else."

"He's right. Every minute we're standing here these savages are putting more ground between us," Kendo said, rocking back and forth on the balls of his feet.

"Well I'm trying to get us moving!" Oil'ib said with uncharacteristic fire in his voice. "Pennsylvania is—is—it's where my family lives. We are headed toward my hometown!"

"Look, Hemma said there's a town fifteen miles northeast of here," Tavin said, "Oil'ib, what directions are their tracks going?"

"Umm…"

"Quickly Oil'ib," Tavin pushed.

"North, sort of northeast," Oil'ib pointed in the direction.

"That'll be close," Praxis said. "Worth a shot."

"We can drop the girl off if there are people there," Gannon said, preparing to walk back to Hemma and check on the child.

But Hemma was already upon them.

"I'm having the sergeant fix up one of the wagons for her.

Condense some supplies and all. It won't be the smoothest ride, but she will be as comfortable as we can make her. Then hopefully someone in the next town will take her in."

Gannon was relieved that she had taken the initiative.

"Thank you for doing this. And for understanding our position."

"It's not a problem. We should travel together though, there's strength in numbers," she replied.

Hemma had a generous grin with fine straight teeth. Even Gannon found himself disarmed, unsure whether to smile or salute. They hastily agreed to her offer and welcomed the company on the open road.

"We need to move fast. Hemma, you mind if I take the front with you?" Tavin asked.

"I'm not your captain. Unless you want me to be," she replied.

"Sorry, I can be a terrible control freak sometimes," Tavin said with a wink.

The sun was racing to meet them on the horizon, and Gannon looked back at where the cavalry moved along behind them. He saw the cart that held the sleeping child.

Will she keep a flame inside her? Will she scrape a meaning in this world?

"What's he doing?" Hemma asked him, moving her horse in between Tavin and Gannon and motioning ahead to where Oil'ib was racing his large brown and white destrier ahead at a gallop. Then, after gaining a distance, stopping to inspect the road and tracks as if reading a letter written there in the dust.

"That's Oil'ib. His methods are a little unorthodox," Tavin

replied to Hemma.

Oil'ib continued riding ahead out of earshot before the group could catch up. The cavalry men snickered as if watching a show-off.

"The key is to ignore him and then he'll come back and start explaining everything to you. Direct questions only make him clam up. With Oil'ib, one has to learn patience in its quintessence," Tavin added.

Hemma laughed. "He's an agent of the Chancellor?" she wondered aloud.

"One of the finest," Gannon said with a sly smile.

"Where are you idiots from?" she asked with a laugh.

"All over. I'm from North Carolina. Gannon here is from New England," Tavin mentioned.

"Cape Cod actually, but everyone just says New England," Gannon explained.

"Seneca, the one with the lovely beard, is from the Finger Lakes. Praxis, the blonde with the trustworthy face is from Florida. Kendo, the tall one, originally Western but now fiercely loyal to us. And of course, our frolicking friend here is from the great territory of Pennsylvania," said Tavin.

"Going home," Hemma replied.

"Starting to look that way."

As a teenager playing in taverns, Gannon had learned the art of flirtation enough to teach a class on it. Sometimes he had jested that his career was traveling the Eastern shore and picking up local girls. He considered womanizing to be the most noble of the animalistic pursuits. Yet he found himself unwilling to play or get between Hemma and Tavin, who were continuing a flirtatious conversation. Since showing their rank as men of the Chancellor, the captain had become more languid and sociable. She did not seem like a military woman at times, not until she addressed her own men, who acted with complete dignity at her every order.

"You guys look kinda young to be agents," Hemma stated. "Gannon how old are you now?"

"I was born in the spring so I'm twenty-three."

"And he's the oldest," Tavin replied.

"That's fairly impressive. My uncle didn't become an agent until he was in his thirties."

"How many agents are there?" Gannon inquired.

"I don't know. Not many, despite the war. It used to be more back in the day."

"I wonder why?"

"My uncle only lived to b-"

Just then Oil'ib, who had been out of view far up the road, circled back. He rode his horse hard.

Just then Oil'ib, who had been out of view far up the road, circled back. He rode his horse hard.

When he approached, the horse's nostrils flared as he sucked in a huge lungful of air. "That town is up ahead. It looks untouched," he reported.

"Any militia?" Hemma asked.

"A lot."

"Explains why Kayzitt left them alone," Tavin added. "Now we know a little more about our enemy's limits. Let's move."

Around the village prickled a thick fencing with only a small entrance for wagons to fit through. Militia immediately swarmed from the buildings and formed a defensive position behind the fencing. As their group approached however, Hemma signaled for the Eastern colors to be shown. As if relaxing, the green flag with the eagle emblem was raised and the militia backed away from the entrance, allowing a single leader to move forward. The cavalry, Gannon, and the others flooded in around the crescent of militia men before coming to a sliding stop.

"There's a war going on you know. What are all you people doing here?" Hemma questioned.

Increasingly it was becoming obvious that her manner was brash as a leader. Gannon could see Tavin smiling to himself.

"There's a war right here!" said the militia leader, a barrel-chested man with equally brash tone. "Raiders went by our town two weeks ago. Us here's the only thing that kept them moving."

"How many were there?" Tavin asked.

Gannon held his breath awaiting the man's answer.

"I don't know for sure. Maybe fifty or sixty."

"That's who were pursuing. What direction were they headed?" Hemma asked.

"Northeast. There's only one more village that they could hope to find between here and Pennsylvania. Them's mountain people up yonder. They'll never find 'em."

"He's in Pennsylvania by now, I bet," Tavin stated. "He'll start slowing down as the population clusters."

The militia leader continued. "In case you wondering, that village I'm talking about is only ten miles north. We saw smoke coming up over the horizon and went to investigate. That's when we found one of their wounded they left behind."

"One of the raider's men?!" Gannon asked.

"That's right."

"Where is he being held?" Seneca asked.

"Keeping him in the barn."

"I'm shocked they didn't dispose of him before they left. He could tell us everything," Tavin surmised.

"Can we see him?" Seneca furthered, reaching their front.

"We need to see him," Oil'ib added.

The militia laughed to themselves. A chorus of chuckles.

"He's a little rough around the edges right now. You can do what you want tomorrow, but in these parts we spend an evening with folks before they up and go running around everywhere. Don't know yet if we can trust y'all. Seein' how it's getting late, why don't y'all set up a camp out here within the fences and meet us in that big building for dinner. It's Saturday, that's the day we spend together as a town. In the morning, I will see to your wishes with the raider."

The sun was now beginning to sink beneath the dark outlines of trees far off in the rolling hills. There was little room left for travel in the day and it was decided to acquiesce the wishes of the militia leader and to take advantage of hospitality as it was offered. There was little ever offered to soldiers. After setting up his sleeping mat and tent with the others, Gannon saw to the proper adoption of the young girl before joining the others in the town hall. It was much easier than he had even hoped and the child was taken in by the town doctor, who insisted he would have the child cared for in the small ward he ran before finding her a new family. This delighted Gannon to tears and he had found himself hard pressed to keep composure as he thanked the doctor gratuitously.

As the town began to swell in its evening excitement, Gannon found himself seated at a long table in the town hall amongst the warm bodies of his fellow soldiers, and beneath the bright candles of the hall's iron chandeliers. The antlers of deer, elk, caribou, and even a giant moose crowned the high seats at the rear of the long building. Lion and bear skins were flung over the rears of the chairs of the town's leaders. The militia leader, the same man from before, sat to the right of what appeared to be the town's main leadership, a man of sixty or so years, who had a hard, lined face brightened with years of living generously. It was kind, though tough, and his gray hair seemed to shine. Music was playing in a far corner and Gannon tapped his foot along to the rhythm of a hide drum as skilled guitar and mandolin players plucked a light lively theme. He sipped upon a large mug of a brown stout and ate heartily of braised pork, softly cooked potatoes with garlic and butter and vegetables like small miracles. It had been months since he had eaten so well.

"Why'd you do that?" Gannon heard Hemma exclaim.

"I had to! He kept climbing over the wall," Tavin replied.

"That's the craziest thing I've ever heard," Hemma said, leaning in closer to Tavin, who was flushed with laughter as he boasted.

"Gannon."

Gannon was drawn out of his wandering stupor by the repetition of his name.

"Gannon play something," Seneca was saying loud enough for the table to hear.

Gannon glanced to where the musicians had stopped their music and were now shopping around their instruments to those who might want to play next.

"No. Come on," Gannon said trying to ward off his friend.

"Seriously. Go play something," Seneca insisted.

The others started goading him as well. Soon, even strangers were insisting that he take the guitar from the small rise and play. They stamped their feet and Gannon knew that Seneca had sealed his fate. Conceding, he sauntered with a smile from the table, approaching the old man who was putting down the guitar.

"Hey, there. Mind if I play?"

The hall was somewhat quieter as the tables of children and their parents and grandparents watched Gannon tune and strum the guitar. There was still the laughter and conversations of those who continued to eat and jest with each other over their food. But Gannon found the gazes of his friends and of the cavalry men who had joined them. A childhood song sprung with the least effort to his mind and without attempting to remember another option he began the first series of chords, his fingers sliding along the rigid copper wire, and sang:

> Love is the closest thing to sadness.
> Sleep the closest thing to death.
> Time is all that lies between.
> Our lives measured by its breadth.
> We often cry when we are happy.
> We weep when we are sad.
> The former tears, minus the latter, is all we've ever had.
> A lover's voice may be a blessing. An enemy's, a curse.
> But upon a mother's loving breast, were both these voices nursed.

Chapter Nineteen

July 2717
West Virginia

Tavin

Am I a child again? What else can explain the fluttering wings in my stomach? Suddenly my words are heavier and stick in my throat, my tongue struggles to get them out. I'm careful to consider every phrase. I truly admire this woman. She is completely unshielded in her personality. If it was a soldier, it would carry two swords.

"Was I wrong to seem happy tonight?" Tavin asked, opening the door for Hemma, as the two of them exited the warm atmosphere of the town hall and entered the lighter air of the summer night.

"Why would you think it's wrong?" she replied.

"I don't know. Just with everything that's happened. Sometimes I feel like I'm heartless if I don't seem beaten up all the time."

"You should feel however you want to feel," she replied, locking eyes with him for a brief moment.

Tavin cheeks grew warm. He was glad the night was dark and his body language would not distract from his words. The heavy door closed softly behind them and muffled the music and laughter to a gentle hum.

"Does it feel like a storm is always over your shoulder?" Tavin asked her.

She turned, pushing her strong jawline forward in a contemplative stare. He admired the way she moved and thought. Nothing was taken for granted to her and conversation never felt idle or wasted.

"Are you talking about death?"

Tavin laughed. How simple she could make things.

"Isn't that what we're always avoiding. Even when we talk?"

She nodded with a sad acceptance.

"Ever since Jon died, I've felt like I'm waiting my turn," she continued, and, as if feeling his expression dropping. "He was my brother. He led this group when we were the main cavalry. They broke through and we had to retreat home after he fell. The storm found him a long time ago."

"I'm sorry."

"Thank you," she squeezed his hand for a moment before pulling back. "You should be thankful for your friends. I've never seen such a close group. It's like you guys read each other's thoughts."

"That's an apt description," Tavin scratched his beard.

"How long have you known them?"

"Almost two years."

They walked farther from the town hall and past an oak tree where a bench sat. They took the opportunity to sit down. His body inched closer to hers. Her beautiful golden braid drew his eye with the way it draped over her shoulder and caused him to stare.

"You keep looking at me like I'm a painting," she said.

Tavin laughed out loud.

"I don't think I've ever seen someone as lovely as you. I hope you'll forgive me for staring."

"You must have grown up in a cave," she quipped with a laugh.

"I'm just a country boy, but I've seen enough faces to know yours is special. And you talk intelligently. Even if you looked like Oil'ib's female doppelganger I'd still be talking to you."

She pursed her lips and hit his arm softly, causing his cheeks to flush.

"You're terrible," she said. "But you're funny."

A cool breeze floated between them and drew their bodies closer until their legs were touching.

"Don't take this the wrong way, but when we were running from Clades all I could think about was how far away I was from anything good, and now that I'm here I really have nothing to complain about. I mean, it feels like I have been so lucky to survive."

She smiled at him, a fine glimmer in the velvet of the night air.

"You are sweet. And it's interesting, how random life is. That we crossed paths at all is a chance, but to be hunting the same man…"

Tavin felt himself grit his teeth. There was a path he did not intend on taking the conversation. His mind raced for a path to divert it.

"You can't predict anything. Life moves too fast. That's the positive to look at. There's no room to get bored or become complacent. Seneca and Gannon complain, but I like the fact that I've slept under so many skies the last few years. My world is always changing, so it never stops fascinating me."

They stared at each other a moment.

"You're too nice to be a soldier, Tavin. What are your real goals? Why join up willingly?"

"One might ask you the same thing."

They both laughed. The moon was rising and its light showed the road. They decided to walk around the grass toward the area of the tents. Tavin knew he had little time remaining in their conversation. He could see the end in the words as they left her mouth. A yearning desperation was filling his chest. A regret housed there as well. *We could have left the hall earlier and had more time together alone*, he thought.

"I don't want to hear everybody else's stories and not have any of my own," Tavin looked at her with an earnest truthfulness. "This will be the event that defines this decade, perhaps this century. To not see it with my own eyes would have felt so empty."

"And you wouldn't have had a marvelous evening with me," Hemma smiled again and touched his arm.

Her touch was both strong and delicate, it was endearing and encapsulating without possessiveness. There was no coy invitation in how her fingers melded around his arm for a brief second, only a quiet acknowledgement of all that was being unsaid.

As they approached the light of the torches and lamps in the small tent city of Hemma's forces, her long hair flashed like burnished gold and he could see that at some point she had released her braids down onto her high shoulders in rivulets. In their short time together, she had managed to excite him in every way. Her conversation during their dinner had been apt and witty without lacking in the latent humor that bloomed at the end of each point they covered. How quickly he had become infatuated. Giving his own emotions such attention seemed dangerous. There was such a slim chance for real happiness considering the circumstances.

"And if we catch Kayzitt, we'll have a story of our own. Bigger than anything you might have heard from another," she said with a hidden sadness.

He realized he had been devouring her words without chewing them. They were at the tents now and they had paused before entering the invisible sphere that separated the military canvas from the rest of the quiet village. Tavin searched for her eyes and upon finding them, deep wells of dancing blue light in the perfumed air of summer, quoted the plea that had been forming on his lips.

"Stay with us. You and all your people. We can find him together," he tried to look stern but knew he was not. "I mean it. There's no sense splitting up. It's the same mission."

Then a gruff voice appeared from the tents.

"Captain, one of the Chancellor's men has made the

prisoner talk. I didn't see what happened, I just heard."

They both turned abruptly to where the tall shadow had appeared beneath a torch.

"What has he said?" she asked.

A second silhouette appeared behind the first, walking out from behind the corner of one of the larger tents. Without seeing his face, Tavin recognized the outline of Praxis.

"He just needed a reason to talk," his friend said, like a man who had just fixed the shoe upon a draft horse. "He'll be fine."

"What happened?" Tavin asked. "How long have you been at this?"

"He got worked over last night. When the militia handed him over, he was already weak. Only took half an hour to get what we needed," Praxis explained. "Come on, we're wasting time."

Gathering the others from the town hall proved difficult. Oil'ib and Seneca had gotten fairly drunk, and Gannon had been hard pressed to leave the barmaid he was buttering up with kisses and compliments. Kendo had been of some support though, and with his and Praxis' starkness they managed to pull the group together in the main hall to hear the report from Praxis, who seemed eager to leave. Tension emanated from him in silent waves that made Tavin pace anxiously, his eyes on the growing light in the eastern horizon. Tavin lamented that Praxis had not waited a single night to see this prisoner of war.

"Alright, just be out with it so everyone can hear," Hemma ordered.

"The man admitted everything he knew, I'm pretty sure of that," Praxis prefaced. "Essentially, Kayzitt is headed through Pennsylvania to attack the canyon region. There's a major armorer up there without a local militia. Apparently, his force isn't robust. I think it's obvious their goal is chaos, make the East afraid of fighting and force a surrender. They use the mountains and old ruins for hideouts, avoiding Eastern forces on the roads. After they finish in Pennsylvania, they will likely cross the great lakes to hide in neutral land for the winter."

Tavin, in a moment of intense dread, looked over at Oil'ib, whose face was sinking and growing pale as the moon.

Life's tectonic shifts.

"W-w-we have to leave now!" Oil'ib slurred. "We'll ride until we collapse. We must go. Now!"

"Yes, we will," Tavin asserted. "But we're fifty miles from Pennsylvania. He could be half way through the territory by now. The good news is, with Hemma's people, we will have no problem matching a force like that."

"Yes, but we leave now. As in right now," Seneca pressed, glancing at Oil'ib, who was struggling free of his drunken stupor. "Our horses, we need to go get our horses immediately."

"Sen, we need to wait for Hemma's people, of course," Tavin replied.

"No chance, we travel much faster as the six of us. We can't wait for cart… burdened—burdened horses," he garbled. "We have to go alone."

"You think the six of us are going to stop him? We need her numbers to have any chance in a fight," Tavin rained back.

"Tavin that's ridiculous," Praxis' stoic voice added. "We need to make all possible haste. Our only option is to beat him north and get the locals to safety. There is no fight to be had."

"We all have horses, I don't see your point," Tavin

replied.

"God damn it, man! Stop thinking with your dick. The six of us can, without question, move much faster than a group of sixty and that isn't up for debate," Seneca shouted.

Tavin's heart sunk. His chest felt buried beneath the silence of the group as the eyes of his friends all settled upon him, awaiting his rebellion or acceptance, ready to squash the former if it raised its head. It did, but he did not let it show. He looked down the circle of men to Hemma, who was whispering orders to her lieutenant. The lieutenant took off running toward the tents. Her face showed none of the vague sadness that he felt must be so obvious on his own. Perhaps she had not heard what Seneca said. All the pleasantness of the drinks and merriment had left his body like water from a fall.

"Come on. If we're going to leave let's fucking leave. Don't you stand still on me now!" he said to his friends and walked toward the stables. "Gentlemen, let's go! As you said, time is of the essence. We can't wait for sentiment!"

With brisk steps they reached their horses and stocked their saddlebags with fresh provisions some of the locals provided.

"I know this isn't easy Tavin, but we have to go," Seneca whispered to him.

Praxis patted him on the back before climbing atop his horse.

"Even from here I can find the way. I-I-I need no… map," Oil'ib spurted.

Tavin patted his own horse upon its mane. He swallowed bitter disappointment then nearly regurgitated when a familiar hand touched his shoulder. Without hearing her approach, Hemma's presence caught Tavin by surprise. She was smiling. He longed to do something, but did not know what it was.

"Just go. We'll follow behind as soon as we can. Maybe we'll head for the Lake Road and we can cut him off."

Tavin nodded.

"Tavin we *must* go," Seneca asserted, already upon his steel gray horse. His friend looked at him with hurried sympathy.

"This isn't the last time you'll see me," Tavin promised.

Chapter Twenty

July 2717
Southern Pennsylvania

Seneca

I wish sincerely that every person who would raise his hand to murder another would have his arm fall off on the spot. Every man who is abusive to a woman—I wish that their eyes would melt before they could lay a hand upon one. For all those who beat children, I wish that their own anger would make them burst into flames. Then we would have some damn peace on Earth. That's using omnipotence effectively.

"It's getting late," Seneca said, walking back toward their campfire after emptying his bladder on a nearby tree. "We have twelve hours of riding tomorrow, if we're efficient."

A day of riding had put them well into the Pennsylvania territory. The horses needed resting, and darkness had found them again. Seneca, after recovering, barely remembered the daytime.

Soon he would welcome sleep.

"What if this Kayzitt is setting a trap for us," Praxis pondered. "I mean how can we be sure of anything?"

"Come on, he doesn't even know we're hunting him," Gannon replied.

"I would," Oil'ib stated from across the flames.

"Alright maybe you would. Would he really waste time with traps?"

"I would," Oil'ib repeated.

Gannon looked exasperated.

"Just read some more Praxis," Gannon motioned from where he reclined upon his sleeping pad. "I'm serious. I don't want to think about him anymore."

Seneca found his own seat while a racket of coyotes in the valley below worked up. They had obviously caught something by the way they yelled and screamed in the sinking twilight. The noise made Seneca anxious. It was going to be a loud night; he could tell already. His legs ached, unused to riding. He feared he may be too exhausted to sleep. Seneca stretched out and warmed his feet by the fire while Praxis continued to read aloud. In his friend's hand lay an old and dusty book, its pages barely illuminated by the low flames.

The tempest howled its rage against the mast. All around us the seas sang praises to the storm. The deluge crashed and broke, refusing to yield its applause to the thunder and shock. Whipping, dragging, slipping, the wooden beast bent to the tempests' will. Foul winds screamed out again over the decks. Hope slipped away with its whistling song as the clouds above

broke open for a moment, allowing the moon a brief glance at
gravity's destruction.

"Hold fast!" shouted the captain, refusing to give up the
night. The sails pivoted desperately, reaching for a break in the
strength of nature. With an aching belch the hull slapped down
upon the swelling void. One wave, another, cresting high before its
rapid descent.

"Pull together!"

The captain screamed, inwardly begging the winds
forbearance. He glanced upwards seeing the shimmering moon
once more and let loose a final prayer to the God above.

Oil'ib was nodding and Seneca noticed Tavin laughing
quietly to himself.

"Why do you laugh at God?" Oil'ib asked timidly.

The sound of Oil'ib's sullen drawl made Seneca raise his
head. Oil'ib had been quiet throughout the riding of the day and
even during the preparation of camp. Praxis put down the book and
rested it on his chest, bemused that Oil'ib should break now from
the trance that had pulled him all day.

"Why shouldn't I? I've never seen a God, or talked to a
God or known anyone who has. I don't think that anyone ever has
at all."

"Some, um… people say that they have. There's no
reason to think he doesn't exist."

Seneca rolled on his sleeping mat and braced himself up
on his elbows. Oil'ib made no eye contact with Tavin when he
spoke from his seat on a smooth stone. He stared only at the fire,
his eyes alight with worry. They had barely convinced him to stop

for the night. Had they not succeeded in that, Oil'ib might have run his horse into the ground. The threat of the marauder was an invisible plight on their minds, but the embodiment sat on Oil'ib's shoulder, weighing upon him.

"Well," Tavin continued, "the burden shouldn't be on me to prove he doesn't exist. You have to prove that he does. You can't prove that there *isn't* an all-powerful snapping turtle that controls the universe, or that there *isn't* a reunion on the moon when we die. It doesn't mean we believe in those things."

This drew a laugh from Kendo but sunk Oil'ib back into his quietude.

"So, if there's no God what happens after we die?" Gannon asked. "Surely there can't be nothing. I can't imagine not existing."

"I don't know, and that's the point. We talk about God like we have any idea, but we never will," Tavin assured. "There's an ocean of responsibility down here and people looking to a higher power are just pretending that responsibility isn't theirs."

"I never really considered it until Clades," Seneca added, "Not existing, that is. It's like trying to picture infinity. The mind warps. I suppose it's like before you were born. Neutral non-existence. But once someone stabs you, not existing becomes a terrifying idea."

"Sen, you don't believe in God," Tavin told him. "You only believe in nature; you've said so yourself."

Seneca smirked. "That's true. Any explanation for a god without a creator can be used for a world without a creator. But that nothing in us is intransient? I just can't believe that. Look at the way nature recycles itself. The living things are fed from the soil and the soil is fed by their death. Nothing is wasted, everything is used. People speak of God as if he is a person in the sky that knows all the hairs on your head. I think it is *nature* that is worth worshiping. It *is* the hairs on your head, and some day each one will feel a dandelion."

"Reincarnation," Praxis summed up. "That's what you believe?"

Seneca smiled wider and sat up to face his friends and put his hands over the fire.

"Not completely, but I think that's closer to what's real than anything else I've heard. Think of it like this. When you burn something it doesn't go away it just becomes ash, right? You can't completely destroy anything. So perhaps our mind burns when we die, so to speak, but it's not gone. It's just something else. All the excess weight burns away."

Seneca watched the smoke disperse above. The starry sky twinkled.

"I think to cling to anything but what's right here, right now, is wasting hope," Tavin brandished. "Maybe you're right about the mind, or maybe Oil'ib's God exists, but what's *definitely* real is right here. My flesh, my swords, my voice, you guys, you're real. And if I spend a moment counting on something else, I'm not putting all of my trust and energy into something real. I can't take that kind of risk."

"I don't think about that stuff. I really don't," Gannon said. "Except when I hear an especially inspiring piece of music. Then, sometimes, I don't think a person could make that by themselves."

Seneca nodded, "I am similarly sentimental."

"Okay... then on the other side maybe there's a reason

we're doing what we do, and I mean us specifically," Kendo said from where he laid. "Maybe we'll find out something no one else has ever known. Maybe we'll fix things, and make something right. We are doing something, but not doing it alone. If we stand up for something and somebody's life is better for it, then… Maybe *that* is God. Not an actual guy but an *idea*."

"That is a comforting thought," Seneca admitted, "But, as Tavin might say, it assumes a lot. It might even be narcissistic. It could be the opposite. Maybe we are part of the problem. Maybe we have a gift and we're using it wrong."

Energy was seeping from his mind as if a leak of it had sprung from his legs.

"Then sometimes I think it's broken for good, and maybe all we can do is fade away and hope for something new," he said. "Things have to reach the deepest level of bad before they can ever be good again."

"That's cold," Kendo replied with a laugh. "In the West, they believe only the sun can destroy them. They believe nothing else can defeat them. They base their entire religion on that aspect. That someday the sun will devour them in the ultimate red glory of death, *but* only after they have conquered all the world can it happen."

"So, they wish for the end of days?"

"Doesn't everyone?"

"Clades seemed to," Praxis mentioned.

"They'll learn their lesson I'm sure," Kendo stated. "Like you said, such thoughts stink of narcissism."

"While we learn *our* lesson no doubt," Seneca added with some sadness. "I can only wonder what that might be."

"It'll all go away eventually." Praxis sighed and laid on his back. "The West wins. We win. It doesn't matter. I'm waking up every day and trying to put my head down at night. I don't know what I'll do when it's all over. I don't care. They took me from my home, and I couldn't stop them." Praxis looked unusually pale in the face as he spoke. "Mom was crying her eyes out. My dad couldn't do anything, and even if he could it wouldn't matter. We're not in control of anything. Whether we die from a sword or a stroke it doesn't matter. You're only free to choose what you were always going to choose."

Seneca, usually quick to formulate a rebuttal was halted by the bleakness of Praxis's words.

"So, what matters in life then?" Gannon asked.

"I guess just living."

"I never told any of you guys about my grandfather, did I?" Gannon said, looking straight through the fire as he spoke. "Well, he was in the first war. He wasn't anything special, just a regular guy. He was definitely old for a soldier at that time but he went over in place of my dad who always had trouble walking. Anyway, they were out on patrol one night— this was when all the battles were happening near the big river—it was the dead of night and all around he started to hear noises. There were some arrows fired. Anyway, he had a crossbow on him and held the line with the rest of his comrades. All of a sudden someone bursts out of the bushes and he fired without thinking."

"It was an innocent, wasn't it?" Praxis asked.

"That's right. That's right. It was a little girl. The Westerners had experimented with sending children through the lines as reconnaissance. Someone who the enemy would refrain from targeting. This time it didn't work."

"So, you agree with me?" Praxis stated.

"No. No, I don't. Because the action may have meant nothing, and the outcome was unfair. The act though, all of it encompassing three seconds, changed my grandfather's life forever. The way he behaved, the way he carried himself, the care he showed children, the devotion he gave his family. He stopped taking care of himself. He loved other people still. He listened to every person when they spoke, and let others share in what he had. But life became too simple to him after the pain became a part of him. He drank himself into an early grave after giving all his remaining life to charity."

Gannon leaned in toward the fire, the golden light shadowed over his thick eyebrows.

"My father. brother, and uncle were sitting around him when he died. At the end he couldn't even see, but he made a point to tell that story, and then he was gone. Yeah, he killed someone innocent and that loss can't be reasoned with, but it absolutely meant something in as profound a way as I've ever seen."

There was silence for a time. The crickets seemed loud in the absence of all else. In their white noise Seneca thought he heard a woman's voice, or perhaps a song. But he fought the hallucination and returned to the crackling of the fire. It was several minutes still, and Seneca might have thought that he was already asleep, when Oil'ib spoke again, fluttering his mind obnoxiously from its resting. Seneca resisted the urge to berate him for his timing, he knew it took Oil'ib longer to form his thoughts.

"The reason I believe in God is because deep down there's a presence out there that I can't explain, but it feels real.

Something following me everywhere I go and I can feel it telling me I'm okay. You know—y-you know—what I mean?"

"I wish I could," Tavin replied sleepily. "I wish for that above all things."

Seneca dreamt he was back at home in the vineyards along the lake, picking grapes. A woman wore a white linen dress. She turned to talk to him but he could not make out her face.

Chapter Twenty-One

August 2717
Canyontown, Pennsylvania

Dak

His fur is my coat. His flesh is my food. His antlers hang above my mantle so I will not forget his gift.

Dak's knees creaked like the worn floorboards of his family's modest country home as he walked in circles about the house. The sun had only been up a short time. He knew there would be a catch in the traps. His gut instincts were usually correct. The feeling had rolled him out of bed and sent him pacing around the cool musty air looking for the clamp he would need to unhinge the traps. Dutifully, his wife, Jule, had rolled out of bed shortly after he awoke and he could hear her in the kitchen arranging the wood in the hearth. Dust scattered lightly as Dak opened the door to the closet that housed his trapping instruments, the dust of his family. Pieces of him were in that dust, his father, his father's father. No matter how much Jule swept there would always be dust. And no matter how diluted it became over the years, the lives of all his ancestors remained there. Such thoughts made smiles deepen the wrinkles of Dak's face. He was in his fifties, lined and slightly stooped by the work of his trade and the desperations it could bring upon him, but still lean and strong. He ascended to the top of the steps where he met his wife.

"You scared me!" Jule exclaimed. "I didn't hear you coming."

"Knee's been bothering me. I took it slow."

"Where are you going?"

"I found the clamps Oil'ib bought before he left. I prefer mine, but they'll do."

Jule examined them with a loving eye.

"He was always getting every new thing he could find. There's barely a scratch on them."

"He loves the business. I hope he can take it over when he gets back. I'm ready to stop working any day now," Dak said as he moved toward the door.

"Oh, stop bitching." She winked at him.

He was already dressed for the walk, his patched canvas pants and high leather boots, broken in, comfortable, every fold, seam, and curve of the sole known to his skin and heel. They smiled at each other before Dak exited outside, bringing with him his crossbow and hunting axe. He first checked the drying of the previous week's pelts from where they hung on light iron chains. They were still in need of more time and sunlight but would be ready to come down by the time he was ready to hang the fur of whatever poor creature had been trapped by him last night.

He could make the walk blindfolded, and attempts at changing his habit in any way had failed years ago. By now his routine had already worn a thin dusty trail in the sloping hill of his property. He walked down the fields of alfalfa and sparse beech trees in his usual loping manner, his head swinging at each coming landmark. First the fire pit and the edge of the low grass where he boiled the water from the stream and soaked his hides; where his son Oil'ib had spent many a night learning the trade by his own teaching, and where Dak's own father had taught him to start a fire. There was another pit of memories under the dark ash and dust of that fire circle. Many of the stones he knew like his own feet. The landmark passed behind him as Dak continued his trail into the forest, his eyes on the tree-line and instinctively searching for any dry sticks that he could bring back.

At the tree-line Dak slowed. The lush green plant life parted gently to the touch of his hand and the nudge of his axe. Dak's instincts as a hunter made him slow down for the last quarter mile of the walk. The silence of the forest broke only occasionally by the accidental falling of a twig or cone, or the brushing of a breeze. In the forest even the passing of an insect was heard. And so Dak moved quietly. He was death to the beast that he would find. Its paw or leg trapped in the iron jaws of his business. Dak felt hurried to have it over with. It was respect that made Dak slow down when he entered the forest, for life itself and the deal he made with it. He did not rush to the gain, for he did not rush to lose what he must trade inside himself when he looked into fearful eyes and knew that apologies were of no use.

This morning however, Dak's stomach twisted in a wry way. He moved even slower than before. It had been with him since he had woken up that morning, thinking it was merely the familiar feeling—something was caught in his trap. Now, as the sunlight was hidden behind the thickening canopy and his stomach mirrored the growing dimness, he was sure that something was wrong. Still there was no reason to stop, and he considered himself a fool despite the feeling.

I'm too old for this? That's such a cliche. But God, it's truer every day. My knees are killing me. My back isn't springing back like it used to. The soles of my feet ache by the evening time. I used to run these woods like a deer, and now I feel I have more in common with an opossum.

A small echoing, as if from the soft reverberation of the moss and trees, broke Dak's train of thought. Like a muffled howl or a loud whimper that had barely made it to his ears. The sound was gone before he could listen to it. And Dak found himself standing still, his face and limbs motionless in silence, waiting again for the sound, narrowing down what trap he should check first. But the sound did not come again and Dak continued on his way, feeling more and more uneasy. The sound replayed itself differently in his head each time, until he was certain it was an alien sound to his life in the forest. The shaking of the high leaves in the breeze brought a sudden chill to his spine and a prickling to his skin. He pressed on. His loping pace returning as he now wished to be done with this chore and to be back at home tending to the garden. The silent fear prodded him on, no longer aware of the pain in his knees. And then he reached the next landmark, a large oak tree near a thicket of mulberry bushes. It was then that Dak heard the sound, startling him despite his expectancy. A deep and painful moaning not far from him.

Dak's heart dropped into his stomach and he hurried through the low ferns and herbs to where his trap had been set. The moaning growing louder with each step. A man in desperate pain. Dak cursed and shuddered as he jogged around trunk and branch, until he finally spotted the helpless person. His long hair was ragged in a painful thrashing. The man fell to the ground, the teeth of the iron grip twisting at his ankle.

"Oh god! Hang on I'll get you free!" Dak plodded forward to help him but was violently pushed away.

The trap was meant for a bear, whose prints he had seen in these parts over the past week. He wondered if the poor man had been hungry and after the berries that Dak had gathered there.

"Get away from me you devil!" the trapped man shouted, frothing at the mouth and cursing with an accent that gave Dak pause.

The accent was surely a Western one, and Dak measured the victim anew, long blond hair and scruffy beard, a sword in a scabbard at his hip. Dropping the clamp in his hand, Dak searched for the words to address his victim with. The iron clamp landed with a clank upon the ground just as a hoard of armed and nasty looking men appeared from the gaps of the trees around him. They moved so quietly for being a band of forty-some souls. With a reflex Dak reached for the crossbow at his back, managing to pull it around to his front. A shout from his flank stopped him before he could point his weapon upwards. The voice was so close, so strident that it made Dak freeze in his joints. It sounded more like a demon than a man, but the voice, when it spoke, was fine and punctuated by expression.

"Don't even try it."

From behind Dak stepped a shorter man of average weight, with wavy red hair and two cruel tomahawks straddling each hip. The clean-shaven face held sharp and wild eyes that made the newcomer look mad. There was dirt, or the remnants of a red clay or paint about the cheeks and temple and he walked in a way that spoke of hidden reserves of energy and strength. Dak knew his type. Had seen it in the first war.

The leader walked up and examined the maimed leg and then stood and contemplated the thing as if it were merely a simplicity. Before another word could be spoken he had his tomahawk in the poor victims head. There was a spurt of blood and several spasms and then the trapped man was dead upon the ground, his moaning diminished to a dying wheeze. The leader then looked at Dak directly, his unwavering eyes forcing Dak's to look away.

"The war's made it this far east?" Dak asked while scanning the ground.

"Well we have anyway. The rest of our people are catching up."

"I have no quarrel with you men."

"Yes, you do. Everyone in this country does."

"What you do with your men is your concern, stranger," Dak stumbled with his tongue as he spoke. "But I have no business with you. I will return to my home now."

Dak made to step away, but the quickness of the leader's reply kept his feet from moving.

"From the moment we were born this has always been our business. Is this not your trap, trapper? Is that not a part of your business? Do you know what my business is, sir?"

Dak's mouth made empty movements. The leader's laugh was loud and cackling in response. It brought forth the laughter from the large men that gathered all around them. Dak felt like he was surrounded by a thunderstorm and that he was trying to reason with the lightning. Somewhere there was the laughter of a woman as well, like a gleaming hope in the stormy night. He clung to it. Hopeful to reason his way out of this situation.

"I apologize trapper, my name is Kayzitt. I would like to formally get your own name."

"Dak."

"Pleased to meet you Dak. I don't hold you personally responsible of course. You seem an honest hard-working man," Kayzitt clarified. "So am I."

"What are you doing here?"

"Setting things right." The woman's voice sounded again. And Dak spied her as she assumed a place near Kayzitt. She was pretty, with toned and cord-like muscles under ebony skin. Her voice was strong and gave him less hope for his predicament.

"Tell me, Dak, do you know what I fix?" Kayzitt asked him, a predator's smile on his face.

"Unless you brought my son back to me there is nothing here that needs fixing."

Kayzitt smirked a longer smile still and some of his soldiers laughed again. Dak felt a lump growing in his throat. He longed to be back at home and wished that he had listened to his gut more carefully.

"You don't seem frightened of us. Is it because you've seen our type before?"

"I remember your people."

"A soldier," Kayzitt smiled. "I thought so. I always know a soldier. It's a gift I have. We carry a certain weight when we walk, figuratively."

"What do you want?"

"Sal just told you. We're setting things right," Kayzitt motioned with his hand. "Now keep in mind your town. This whole area is going to burn, and we're not going to be kind unfortunately, but you're different. You're like us."

"I'm not like you."

"Oh, don't get sentimental on me Dak. You know what I mean. We're both men of action—fighters. We treat men of action with a certain amount of leeway. In fact, I'll make a deal with you, as a means of some recompense. If you can kill me, my men will leave you alone. I can promise you that. I can't guarantee anyone else's safety but they won't touch you."

Kayzitt snapped his finger at one of his men who stepped forward.

"Give him your sword."

Someone handed the weapon to Dak.

The pummel was not foreign to Dak's hand, though he wished it was. A slim and well whetted war blade. Its handle slightly curved. Its blade was sharpened to a razor's edge. In Dak's mind two powerful forces were waging now. A wave of animalistic fear was numbing his limbs as he became aware of what was happening to him. It scraped over his bones like a dull blade and made his insides squirm. But beyond that, there was a lapsing acceptance that surprised him. He acknowledged it like a familiar stranger. A person both old and new to him. It was something that his own father had spoken of upon his death bed. But Dak had not expected the visit so soon.

The ending was so clear to him now that the acceptance of its truth penetrated and permuted the fear that gripped his chest. He longed to be home again, wished he would have spent a little longer with his wife that morning, though he cherished the years he had been beside her. The acceptance, the fear, both wrestled within him. Dak was too tired to protest. But he was strong, he knew he was still strong. And he flexed his old back with its muscles of steel cable. His arms accepted the weight of the sword casually, though he was sure his eyes were crying.

Kayzitt drew one of his own weapons. The spring in the young leader's body as he paced sideways, looking Dak up and down, was shocking. An impossible adversary. But Dak saw the seriousness of the way the Western man eyed him. He knew what Dak was. He was a trapped animal, fighting for his life against impossible odds.

"My God!" Dak whispered to himself.

"Begin," Kayzitt beckoned.

Dak feigned to walk away, and then when he felt Kayzitt approaching he spun around, swinging wide and momentarily forcing Kayzitt backwards. He picked up a rock and chucked it, just missing a dodging Kayzitt who charged forward and battered the man backwards. Strike, strike, strike. The wood handles of the tomahawks batted and cracked and echoed amongst the trees. The sharp iron heads hooked around the blade and swung young and old opponents around in their force.

How easily the way of the soldier returned to Dak. He felt the surge of adrenaline, fear-induced euphoria. Yet the limbs did not respond like they should. He felt slow, and his elbows did not bend as fast. His knees no longer bounced beneath his weight.

Kayzitt spun out and then danced sideways. The look on the younger man's predator face was keen, aiming, and clear. The eyes were wide and wild, almost frantic in their pursuant gaze. Dak's mouth was dry and he gasped for air. He felt sweat pooling in wet pockets around his stomach and back. It ran in a rivulet from his underarms and threatened to slip his weapon from his grip. His leather boots dug and scuffed at the ground desperately. Kayzitt pounced forward again and caught the front of his upper leg with his blade. Dak stumbled and turned his forward momentum into a lunge, throwing himself forward, releasing the strength in his leg and locking weapons with Kayzitt in a heavy collision. The blow blew them both back onto the dead man in the trap. Dak felt the corpse still warm beneath his hand as he rose himself to his feet. The searing pain in his leg made him wince and stumble again. Kayzitt was already standing however, and with a flashing maneuver disarmed Dak, sending the sword scuttling away across tree roots and beneath a wide fern. Then there was a flash of blackness and pain as the hilt of his opponent's weapon struck Dak in the head. He dropped to his knees convulsively.

"I admire your courage Dak. I really do," Kayzitt said, dropping to a knee and putting his wild face and tangled red hair in front of Dak. Eye to eye with his destruction, Dak could only murmur. Kayzitt's words barely made it through a ringing and thick cotton sound in his ears.

"You'll die a clean death," Kayzitt continued, "Your neighbors won't, unfortunately. The East raped our lands and now they play the innocent. The problem is no country cares about its dead soldiers as much as they say they do, but you know what does scare them?" Kayzitt leaned in closer, whispering, "Seeing its citizens dead in their beds. We do what we have to."

Kayzitt stood tall.

Dak looked up at the sun beaming through the leaves. The brightness hit his eyes softly as Kayzitt swung his weapon down. Dak drifted into a sea of swirling lights.

Chapter Twenty-Two

August 2717
Canyontown, Pennsylvania

Dahli

I'm tired of thinking about the consequences of my actions. For a change I would like to just enjoy the actions themselves. So many people are so quick to judge, but for every heart that is broken, lie that is told, or life that is lost, life itself goes on. What about my time and my life? How many people's opinions do I have to chain it to? I say none but my own. I will deal with consequences as they arise and with a smile on my face.

The eggs on Dahli's plate were as bright yellow as the sun as it peaked early over the hilltops. She watched as Jeremiah punctured his yolk with his fork, letting the yellow ooze around onto his plate, then he soaked it up with his bread and ate. Dahli felt a strange pleasure in feeding him, in providing a house and good food for their breakfast. It was something she had never truly done before for anyone. They finished their meal and sat smiling awkwardly at each other and out the window in turn. At this point, Dahli was happy just to have her emotions in check. The awkwardness was a small price to pay.

They had agreed to go on a hike today into the canyon after work, to escape the heat. Summer days like this made the canyon a perfect oasis. They would hike down the hills and end at the cool clean creek at the bottom. If the water was not too cold, she looked forward to a swim.

"Are you ready?" Jeremiah said from the living room.

"Almost."

She finished packing her lunch with a deep breath and looked up to see him standing there.

"You alright?" He asked.

"I'm fine."

He gave her a look that said *I'm not convinced.*

"I'm just having a lot of thoughts," she continued. "But it's not anything linear enough to share."

Jeremiah offered her a hug that she accepted, and being nestled in his warm chest was a brief reprieve.

"I know," he said with signature warmth. "We knew this would be hard, and if you need me to go away for a bit at any point it's—"

"I already tried that in my head and it never works," she said. "Having you around is too much a positive thing to give way to the negatives. But I have all these other feelings and I want to make sure I don't hurt you in the process."

"It's okay," he assured. "Remind me again. It's supposed to be busy at the factory today, right?"

"Extremely busy. We're short on everything."

"Exactly, so we're going to have a lot of other things to think about, right?"

She nodded.

"Then let's enjoy our ride there at least, and get our minds out of our emotions for now, yeah? We have a nice hike to look forward too."

They embraced again and she gave him the gentlest peck on the lips, and then departed the house hand-in-hand.

Once on horseback Dahli's train of thought did change. As they started their ride to the factory, she thought about the cavalry that had come through the town the day Oil'ib had left for the war. The horses had been so much bigger and serious then her own mild mare.

"You ever thought about joining the fight?" Dahli asked Jeremiah.

He laughed.

"I don't find the honor in fighting people that others attest to," he replied.

"Is that so?"

He shook his head.

"That's what I tell myself."

"I don't blame you for not going, but I also can understand why so many would."

"Do you think less of me?" he asked meekly.

"For not wanting to die?"

"I didn't say that was the reason," he replied. "It's more complicated than that. I'd like to think it's more that I don't want to kill people."

She nodded to herself.

"Oil'ib used to take me out on hunts when he was still here. The first couple times he would kill the animal in front of me, and I couldn't handle it, but eventually I saw what he was doing. I saw the mercy in it. The deer would overrun those hills," she said pointing off the West. "The predator population up here is thin so the deer were becoming too plentiful. They were starving in the winters. He did their population a service."

"So, it's okay to kill people as long as you're helping their species?"

"It depends on how you do it," she replied. "If someone kills with anger and hatred then it isn't the same. Oil'ib had respect for the animals. He loved them. He cared for them in all ways. There was no hatred in his act."

Jeremiah seemed gloomier now.

"I don't mean to assume so much. It just felt topical."

Dahli tried to think of a way to steer the conversation but her train of thought was abruptly interrupted by a pillar of black smoke billowing suddenly over the horizon.

Jeremiah pointed ahead. "That doesn't look normal."

"Oh my god what if there was an accident?" Dahli's panic clear on her features.

"Let's go!" Jeremiah shouted, kicking up his horse.

They raced down the road at a full gallop, Jeremiah a little ahead of her. Dahli knew her father would already be at the factory. There had been small fires before, but each one had thrown her father into weeks of frustration. She rounded the last corner of the road, past the houses of the laborers and hurried down the stretch to the factory. Her heart quickened and her hands felt numb on the reins when she saw he building being eaten by flames, numerous bodies strewn throughout the street.

"No!" she screamed.

The doors to the factory burst open as two of the blacksmiths appeared, chasing a third man who was shirtless and covered in what looked like dark red blood. The two smiths proceeded to beat the man to death with their long hammers but then were set upon by more men of the same red-soaked garb. They were running in and out of the factory and more appeared from the road out of town past the southern road.

"Felix! Roman!" she shouted.

But the smiths were cut down by the marauders before they could respond to her calls and then stabbed over and over while lying prone in the dirt.

"We need to go now!" Jeremiah insisted as he turned his horse.

At first Dahli's voice stuck in her throat and her eyes stayed fixed upon the scene, unable to tear themselves away. Her feet did not respond to her mind's wish to flee.

"Dahli!" came the call from Jeremiah, as he tugged on her reins and brought her face to his. "We must go now!"

She followed him then, kicking her own horse into a frenzy as her mind raced along the road with the beating hooves.

What is happening? Who are those men? What do they want with—

Then she swallowed as the possibility arose in her head. *Dear God, the war... we're losing the war...*

"Where should we go?" Jeremiah yelled from beside her.

"Back to the house!" she shouted as they rushed onwards

in terror. Behind them there was the sound of metallic thunder and she imagined the roof of the factory collapsing under the flames and a cry threatened to break from her lips.

She dismounted just outside the door to her house; they tied the horses loosely to a tree before running inside and holding the door closed with their backs, panting. Already she was drenched in sweat and her extremities cold. Numb.

"What do we do?" he asked her.

"Take what we can and leave. Nothing else we can do," she said. "Follow me."

She led him into the workshop and took Oil'ib's saddle bags off the wall.

"Take this one into the kitchen and fill it with anything we might need," she ordered pushing the bag into his stomach. "Quickly!"

She turned her attention back to the supplies hanging on the wall and grabbed two of Oil'ibs dirks, lashing one around her waist. She took the last tomahawk he left behind, some rope, two large furs, flint, fishing wire, hooks and hats. She stuffed the bag and then rushed into the kitchen.

"How're you making out?" she asked him.

"I got what's left of the apples. All the salted meat. I have bread. It won't last long, but—," he started before she cut him off.

"We have to go. Take this," she said tossing him the other dirk.

"Where are we going?" he asked.

"Anywhere."

Frantically they strapped up, dressed in hardier clothes, and were ready. They each carried one of the bags and Jeremiah wore some of Oil'ib's old hunting clothes. Seeing the tall leather vestments filled out by a body again made Dahli feel weepy. But she gilded herself. She knew they would have to camp out a few days before it would be safe to come back and search for their families. There would be no room for emotions now. Jeremiah moved toward the door and put his hand upon the handle of the dirk, but she saw that his hands were shaking.

"You know what to do with that?" she asked him.

"I can manage."

"You're looking at it like it's on fire."

He laughed nervously.

"Come on," he said as he clutched the door handle.

As the door opened a force from the outside threw it inward with a startling crack. There was a sound of meat being cut and from Jeremiah came a whimper. Dahli blanched. A marauder stood in the doorway like a red demon. And from his hands a short sword protruded all the way through Jeremiah. The marauder chuckled and lifted up on the hilt, cutting up Jeremiah's gut and into his chest as Jeremiah dropped everything, his mouth leaking blood.

Dahli screamed at the top of her lungs. The brigand pulled out his blade and threw Jeremiah aside with a lurching swipe. Before he could hit the ground Dahli whipped her bag around and smacked at the sword. Her effort paid off and the sword flew from his hand and she turned to the kitchen. But before she could make it far, terribly strong hands grabbed her around the waist. She was being dragged to the ground. As he turned her around she could see that he was caked in red down to the whites of his black and dilated eyes. Eyes that were empty as death. The red clay, spattered with blood dripped and flaked as she struggled against him. When he got close enough she used her only remaining leverage and slammed her forehead against his nose.

"Fucking bitch!" he howled, spitting blood as she freed herself.

With her arms now free, Dahli pulled her tomahawk from its sling and swung it at the demon's throat. But he blocked her with his forearm, leaving a cruel gash. She swung again but missed and her assailant smacked her arm hard, sending the weapon flying from her hand. So, she kicked hard at his crotch, the lessons on fighting rattling around her head in Oil'ib's voice.

Don't fight clean. Use every advantage. Go for the soft spots. Stay aggressive.

She tried to kick him again, but this time he caught her leg and swung her down. She reached for her knife but saw stars as he clocked her across the face. She was lifted from the ground and slung over his shoulders. The blood rushed to her head and lights danced in her vision, the world spinning. She vomited.

"I'm gonna fucking take my time with *you*," the red devil said in a voice like a rasp as he dragged her back to the bedroom. "I'm going to fuck you until you bleed."

Finally, terror helped her world come back into focus. She began kicking and flailing, sending all her limbs shooting at whatever she could hit.

"Fuck you!" he shouted as he slammed her down on the bed.

She felt the mattress shutter beneath her weight as she collided with it and her breath left her body. Dahli gasped for air and sent another kick at his crotch only to have it caught and the leg pinned beneath his knee. Then he was on top of her and ripping at her clothes. She could feel the stitching give then hear it tear away and the air felt cold on her skin. She clenched her fist and socked him in the face, then closed her eyes as she saw his own fist shooting toward her and again cold blackness filled her vision.

Her shirt was gone, his slimy and bearded face roughly fondling her exposed breasts. Then she felt his hands at the top of her pants. Dahli squirmed and tried to distract him by pushing up with her left hand as her right reached for the dirk on her hip. Her pants gave way then and ripped in half but the leverage allowed her to draw the weapon from a greater angle. With a deep breath she drove the blade into his side while letting loose a blistering cry.

"Ah! Fuck!"

The dirk came loose from his side and she gripped it tightly as he retreated slightly. But then he had his own blade and before she could react, he had slipped it forcefully into her side: the same place she had stabbed him. She gasped and her heartbeat tripled in pace as her mind blanked. There was not so much pain as there was cold and weakness and her muscles turned rigid around the wound.

With the adrenaline pumping through her at full speed she pulled her knife back and shot it forward again with a fury. She buried the blade into his flank again, and immediately drew it out again. Before he was able to respond to her second attack, she buried the dirk in his abdomen again. The demon responded to her attack and stabbed her again as he stumbled, the knife sinking into her left side between her lower ribs. His grip on the blade loosened and he hit the floor.

The world was drowned by the rushing in her ears for a

time. And then she could hear him whimpering on the ground. He was choking and coughing.

"Please," he murmured.

Dahli withdrew the knife from her side with a seething pain and then threw it onto the bed beside her. She pressed a wad of blankets against her wounds as the blood soaked her hands and she made a small sob. Struggling against the pain, she turned her head and looked at her attacker. He seemed like a child then, the way he was huddled in on himself, his blood pooling onto the floor. His pallor was white, the edges of his lips turning blue as if he were freezing.

"Why?" she asked with diminishing strength, tears running down her cheeks. "Why would you do this?"

He tried to look up at her but his eyes were vague and distant, the red was dripping down into his eyes and his large pupils quivered as they found her voice. He began moving spasmodically.

"Mother," he muttered. "Mother, please."

He reached out his hand for her, but not in a threatening way. His eyes looked more human as they searched her face, terrified and lost.

"Help me."

"Look what you did," she whispered.

He was choking on his blood.

"I'm sorry."

She felt such strange pity for him then, rage as well, but pity all the same. Weakening and scared, she reached out and took hold of his cold and slippery hand. He cried.

"I've done badly," he said to the void.

She could no longer answer, her strength gone. Their hands stay interlocked a few more moments and then fell apart.

Chapter Twenty-Three

September 2717
Canyontown, Pennsylvania

Seneca

The hopes and dreams of childhood have largely been replaced by one all-consuming hope that is dashed again and again only to resurge with the same meager entreaty. Please, may the world not give me any more reasons to hate humanity.

They followed Oil'ib like a pack of dogs upon the heels of a buck. Seneca pressed his knees in against the heaving ribs of the horse. As they climbed the final hills along the ridge of the great Pennsylvania canyon, the terrain grew rougher with oblong stones about the poorly kept road. A rainstorm had risen the level of the river high enough to make the valley road impassable. Instead, they were forced to take their horses along the trails that followed the curve of the precipice beside them.

Oil'ib was desperate to see them to Canyontown. He had

been quiet and had only stopped to rest his horse twice the whole day, never fully recuperating. Seneca understood. The fear that gripped Oil'ib was palpable.

At last the road flattened out into a marshy plain with a ring of rounded green mountains like a crown. At the bottom of the slope, Oil'ib slowed his horse, or perhaps it could not go any longer. The froth upon its brown lips had thickened there and its mouth hung open in the hackamore, panting from the heat of the work.

"Oil'ib where are we?" Seneca urged, but he received no response.

"Oil'ib where are you taking us?" Gannon pleaded, but again no response was offered.

"Home."

They had only time to glance amongst themselves before Oil'ib again urged his horse forward along a road that encircled the plain like a ring. He led them along a curve in a thickly bushed stream and then again up another steep hill. Here Seneca caught up to Oil'ib, who had slowed noticeably, more than the hill required. His eyes were cast only upon the horizon of the hill itself, where the gray casting of the sky met the beaten brown road. When they finally crested, Oil'ib let go of the reins and their horses stopped alongside his. There, nestled into the side of the hill, the alfalfa grass lower down upon the slope of their property waved lightly in the air that rose from the valley. And above that field was the charred skeleton of a family home. Seneca's heart seemed to miss several beats. Without asking, he knew what this meant, to Oil'ib and to the future of their mission. He saw it etched clearly in his mind. He saw the weeks of grief, anguish, revenge, and hatred. He saw the poverty of obsession that would now brand his friend's life.

This will be forever.

"No!" Oil'ib finally screamed, leaving his horse, which teetered slightly from his shifting momentum before continuing on in a mad sprint down the road.

They followed, running, but not sprinting. They gave their friend his due distance. Dread still filled their hearts. The road gave way to other burned houses, black soot blowing against the trees. Passing them without much thought, they followed Oil'ib to the one nestled above the alfalfa field.

A smell of smoke and wood fire, of acrid sulfurous soot and ash filled Seneca's nostrils. He thought for sure that the air still had waves of terrible heat emanating from the house. Yet it was cool enough already for Oil'ib to enter. He began throwing away the ominous black beams of fallen construction. Lifting and searching, they helped him. The fine black powder covered Seneca's hands. The house was unrecognizable except for the squat stone hearth; in it, a kettle full of black water.

"Hello? Is anyone here?" Seneca shouted, begging with the quiet hills. "Anybody?"

Oil'ib paced. He searched frantically under the burned logs and fine gray ash of the thatch roof. He stopped. He sat and stared at nothing for a long moment. He got up and ran through what would have been a wall, jumping the remnants and running along the perimeter of the house. Sitting again outside, he cried and beat the ground with his fists. Oil'ib kicked and clenched his teeth. His expressions changed at a staggering pace and then he was still again. Lying upon his side—his face covered with smears of soot, his eyes wide. Oil'ib became a statue.

"Oil'ib. We should start checking the main of the town," Seneca offered applying his gentlest energy as best he could.

His friend stammered.

They returned to their horses, Oil'ib still leading but not seeing.

The road grew wider and cobbled as they turned a bend around a thick grove of trees. The town was as the last town had been, and the one before that. Ashes caught in Seneca's mouth, blew gently in the sparse breeze like snow flurries, collecting in pockets on the green grass and in the crevices between cobblestones. At last, a huge manor revealed itself along the road. Largely intact, it presided over the ruin of the town with an ominous height. It was brick and slate. Its glass windows had been smashed outward from the top floor, the empty eye sockets of a skull. The air around the walls had a hollow feel as they followed Oil'ib inside. This time, their friend walked with a fearful slowness.

Seneca's mind went back to his first encounter with death.

Dad why isn't that man breathing?

A door was open. Inside, strewn along the hardwood polished floor were two men, dressed as servants. Their throats were cut and congealed black blood spilled over their jackets. Oil'ib ran to the staircase beyond the foyer. Its twisting iron rails guided him around and up onto the second floor, where they could hear him bursting through closed doors and battering furniture out of his way. Seneca stood with the others in the lofty foyer, numb with failure.

Tavin slipped past him then, hurriedly searching the

cupboards and storerooms for food.

"This is worse than I ever imagined," Seneca uttered.

Tavin only nodded.

"You have nothing to say about this?"

"I'm thinking."

As the pounding sounds of Oil'ib's footsteps reverberated down the twisting staircase, the others gathered again in the central foyer. Seneca noticed that the corpses of the servants had yet to start stinking, though the sticky smell of death was upon them.

"She's not here," Oil'ib stated with manic energy.

"Where would she be?" Gannon asked.

Oil'ib did not answer but rather ran back outside to where they tied their horses at the hitching post. In uncharacteristic haste, he mounted his ride and tore out again, so fast that the others almost lost him in pursuit. The clatter of the hooves upon the cobblestones echoed against the high walls of the desolated manor as they rode away, the only sound in the ruins of the town. Oil'ib led them back through the main road, back through the thick soot and ash-strewn street, past the bodies that had not been collected. Bodies that would not be collected at all. He led them to a glen at the end of a side road at the edge of town. There at the end, before a green expanse of grass spotted with a few trees still stood a cottage. Its roof was freshly tarred and still smelled of pitch. Its windows were shattered and quiet.

"Oil'ib what is this place?" Gannon asked, incredulous.

"Dahli's old room at her parents' house was empty. She isn't there anymore. She either got away somehow, or she's here."

"Why would she be here?" Tavin inquired.

Oil'ib sniffed back mucus and spit upon the ground. His

eyes were still wet and red with grief behind his mask of black soot. "We talked about buying this place before I left."

They all dismounted and approached the house gingerly. Seneca put a hand on Oil'ib's shoulder and squeezed, unable to look his friend in the eye as he allowed him to pass.

Oil'ib took a step into the house and then pushed forward.

"Dahli?" Oil'ib said in a voice barely louder than a whisper. "Dahli?"

They walked together into the side bedroom of the modest house. It was the first room that Oil'ib led them to and the last room that he ever saw in that place. He collapsed on the floor in tears. Only after several body-shaken sobs did Oil'ib sit up against the wall, unable to touch her. She lay prone on the bed. A red bloom of blood staining the linen sheets near her heart. On the floor beside the bed was a dead raider in a pool of his own blood. Seneca saw that it had been a slash to the abdomen, the wound was ragged and the skin was white as paper around the deep red of the wound. Oil'ib simply cried in a heap, while the others leaned in to carry him away.

Seneca fought the lump in his own throat but found that every breath snagged upon its weight and drew water to his eyes. Every thought of pity for his friend led to a frantic fear for his own loved one who was only a few days ride away in the finger lakes. From Oil'ib, he inherited the frantic hurry and at the same time knew he must try to console an inconsolable man. His throat felt too thick to breathe and he strained against the weight of Oil'ib as they carried him back outside and into the gray light of day. They huddled around Oil'ib and tried to comfort him. He pushed them away and fell back against the ground.

"Leave it," Praxis said pulling the others off of Oil'ib.

They left him alone, lying in the soft green grass outside the back door to the cottage. The rustling of the trees was the only sound. Oil'ib lay there like a corpse himself.

Hours later saw the angle of the gray light in the sky shifting lower, but still Oil'ib did not move. Seneca sat farther away, nearer the house to keep a watch of the horses that grazed voraciously on the tender green sprouts in the yard. Gannon alone sat with him, as Tavin, Praxis, and Kendo had gone back into the main of town to search for survivors and tracks by which to follow the demons they hunted.

"I never wanted to face Clades," Seneca mentioned to Gannon quietly, both of them having given up on watching Oil'ib's catatonic trance. "Even despite all the things he did, I never wanted to find him. I just wanted to survive… but this is different. I want this Kayzitt son-of-a-bitch to bleed out in front of me so I can know it's done."

"I agree."

"But that's a terrible thought to have. No one should want such things."

"If only we were so advanced," Gannon reasoned. "But we have to do it, and not just Kayzitt, but all of them."

"Your mood has certainly changed since camp. All I heard from you was damn this life, damn this army, damn our existence. Now you're gunning for a fight?"

"Nothing's changed. Except this. This is personal. My feelings otherwise are the same."

Just then a loud crash came from inside the cottage.

Seneca and Gannon leapt to their feet, startled, with hands on their knives. They turned and ran inside, stepping over the corpse of another civilian to where the sound had exploded from. They were stopped at the doorway by a chair flying across the entryway. Seneca backed out, ushering Gannon behind him. Inside, Oil'ib was destroying the house with a splitting maul.

Chapter Twenty-Four

September 2717
Canyontown, Pennsylvania

Gannon

It is so obvious that I'm different. They either fail to see what's right in front of their faces, or they simply care for me too much to ever agree. I don't belong here, and still I wish I could give them the same reservations. They deserve better than this. They deserve to know what it's like to create and not just destroy. To be an artist is to feel your life transcending itself. I would give anything for them to feel it too.

The six men of the Chancellor rode north along the high canyon road at a miserly pace, slowed by the necessity of keeping Oil'ib on his horse. After destroying much of the inner part of the cottage, Oil'ib had succeeded in bruising his own ribs when part of the roofing came down upon him. He had grown so deaf to reason that he had smashed a support beam in his raging blows. Had

Gannon not tackled him out of the way, Oil'ib might have been dead already. Instead he was in the stupor of opium that Seneca gave him to deal with the pain, barely upright in the saddle, barely steering his horse. Tavin finally tied the horse to his own, keeping their band in pursuit of the raider.

Gannon sighed as he felt the tender bruise forming on his chin, the only thank you that Oil'ib had given him in his mute rage for saving his life. He winced, touching where Oil'ib's heavy fist had pushed him away. Regretfully, Gannon almost wished they had left Oil'ib there. What use was he now? He glanced behind the rear of his own horse to see Oil'ib, eyes half closed, lost in a strange nexus of ecstasy and grief. The fool had taken too much opium, he was a reactionary hedonist when it came to drugs. Always getting too high, always over treating the symptom. No one dared to admonish their slow and quiet friend, but Gannon knew that each of them still felt the weight of his anchor, and worried how long it would drag at them, or if their friend would return at all.

If I had done a few things differently, I would not be here right now. Kayzitt would mean nothing more to me than a passing tale of a far-off boogeyman. I would care little at all for what he did to Oil'ib's town, nor would I even know any of these men to begin with.

Seeing Oil'ib's desperate grief and hearing the breaking chords of his muffled cries had struck Gannon. He realized he had never felt this badly for anyone in his life. It was the first time that tears came easily for someone other than himself, with or without the soreness of the bruise on his chin. He had imagined his own home town and returning there only to find it in ashes.

They had searched all day for survivors and bathed in the

soot of homes in hopes of finding something but it had all been for naught. Eventually, they realized they must hurry and leave in hopes of saving the next town on the marauders' path. They had stayed as long as they did because of Oil'ib. Not only was he outside himself with grief, but they had hoped that finding one survivor might negate his suffering, if only slightly. But it was not to be. The factory and manor that were Oil'ib's in-laws they found to be nothing more than black shells of brick. The bodies they found only added to his friend's grief. Now Gannon wished that he possessed something, anything that might help his friend recover.

The love of friends means little more than the love of family. More than birth is required to earn it.

"We're running out of time. Do you guys understand that?" Tavin said aloud.

"Tavin, that's not helping," Seneca retorted, "He's moving at the pace he can move."

"Well I'm not the one that gave him opium," Tavin said loudly.

"If I didn't, the pain from that fall would have slowed him just as much."

Oil'ib's eyes opened a little wider, and he mumbled something.

"What did he say?" Praxis asked from the front of the group.

"He didn't say anything," Gannon replied.

Oil'ib cleared his voice and his sullen sloth-like words came out louder.

"I'm sorry I hit you."

Gannon slowed his horse and allowed himself to come

alongside Oil'ib.

"I'll give you a pass this time."

Oil'ib lifted his head, widened his eyes as if to fight himself out of the grip of the poppy. Gannon looked at the others, who had returned their attention to the road ahead. In turn, he quietly resumed speaking to his desolate friend.

"You remember in camp when Captain Vencin flogged you?" Gannon asked, "What stuck with me about that beating was how stoic you were. It was like he wasn't even there, and you could just think about something else. I still don't get how you did it."

"What?" Oil'ib inquired.

"Shut off pain. No one can do that like you can, and now I see you trying to do it again."

There was a moment of silence but for the clomping of the hooves as they reached a muddy point in the road.

"Don't," Gannon urged. "Don't try and do it because that task is insurmountable. You need to let it be real for however long it has to feel real."

"Then… then it'll never stop," Oil'ib replied quietly.

"That's fine. I didn't say it would go away. I'm going to think about this forever, so I highly doubt you'll do better. But one day. Maybe, one day it won't stay with you all the time. One day you won't wake up to it anymore. Gradually, it'll take up less of your thoughts. You can't try and defeat this thing any other way."

"My axe could fix-" and Oil'ib's speech slurred into mumbling once again. Gannon took the reins.

"Well, we may still have these bastards under foot yet. When the time comes, I want whatever is in your mind to unleash itself. Let *them* pay for it."

Gannon saw that the thought sunk into Oil'ib's mind and lodged there. The faraway look in his friend's eyes was no longer vague. It searched the distance as if there was something to be seen upon the horizon, something that he wanted, needed desperately. Behind the eyes glazed with opium and sadness was a small flame, a pitiful flame, but one that burned still. It would grow with time, with immense heat and threaten to engulf the object of his searching in hellfire.

"Tavin's right, we need to pick up the pace. We still have a job to do, and now it's more personal than ever. If you need to take it easy for a while—I won't blame you for a moment—but I'm telling you we'll need you in this fight."
Gannon said nothing for a moment. He waited to see if Oil'ib would respond the way he hoped.

"When I first met you in camp you were a quiet, frustrating, meandering person, but you had a spark. I respected the hell out of that. You are still a quiet, frustrating, meandering person," Gannon smirked. "But all your goals can still be in front of you. We just have to live to see this war end. Can that be good enough for now? At least until we kill these men?"

"Untie my horse," Oil'ib finally replied, quietly but with conviction like a stone wall.

"You got it," Gannon said, returning the steely look of resolution, and nudged his horse forward to catch up with Tavin's.

"Hey, what's this?" Tavin asked, startled as he saw Gannon undoing the rope that tethered Oil'ib's horse to his own. "Is he ready?"

Gannon's answer was to throw the end of the rope back

to Oil'ib. Oil'ib snatched it out of the air and in a second had the loose end secured around the saddle.

"Shall you lead then?" Gannon asked him.

Oil'ib nodded and kicked his horse into a frenzied gallop, calling back as he raced the others down the stretch of road.

"I know the way!"

Chapter Twenty-Five

October 2717
Port of Lake Erie, Pennsylvania

Tavin

I can think of only one fate worse than death and that is humiliation. If we combat a great evil and fall valiantly, I can at least stomach that thought, but to combat a great evil and be outclassed is worse. If I cannot hold the mantle of victor let me at least hold the mantle of a worthy opponent.

Another town was on the horizon, beset by the great mass of Lake Erie as it rose to grandeur. The vast expanse swallowed up Tavin's mind in its azure reflection of the sky. Blue on blue, the motes of the wakes of ships coming into port like a distorted mirror.

Since finding Oil'ib's home burned to the ground and burying their friend's wife in the same black dirt, Tavin had barely slept, despite exhaustion. Tavin worried instead. Their target was a platoon of at least forty men if they had measured the tracks correctly; they would be impossible to conquer alone. For the first time in his life, he was hesitant to rush into battle. What would six men do against that force? He thought about employing traps, but he knew even the most well laid plan would lead to their deaths.

Tavin shook his head. They simply needed more men, and he hoped that the port-town would hold the key. They carried the Chancellor's medallion, sure, but they were grungy now, their new uniforms stained and soiled by the weeks on the road. Their hair was long and pulled back, their clothes dusty, and their beards were growing tangled without proper keep. When they entered the town, he expected people would keep their distance.

We must look more like pirates than soldiers, Tavin thought.

As they descended the final foothills, they lost view of the lake, the thatch roof houses and slate shingles of the larger buildings blocking the shore from view. The breeze blew strongly against them from the north, bringing the smell of fish and humidity. When they reached the entrance to the town proper, a guard awaited them. They were greeted with pointed spears and men on horseback emerged with ropes and shackles, surprising their own horses and making Tavin's buck and fuss underneath him.

"What business do you have here?" said a hefty man with a thick mustache. He stepped forward, close enough to not need to shout over the wind, but far enough away to be safe from Tavin's sword.

"The Chancellor's," Tavin replied.

"Oh? Men of the Chancellor, you say?"

"We've been chasing a clan of Western raiders. They're led by a man named Kayzitt." Tavin pulled his medallion out from under his shirt and flashed it to the militia, the gold emblem of the eagle flashed in the sunlight. "He's heading this way. That much we're sure of."

The head guard nodded.

"The war wasn't supposed to be here this soon. But what you're saying does explain some recent events." He pinched at the bushy hair on his upper lip. "What is your name and who do you bring with you?"

"Tavin," he replied. "These men here are agents, too. All of us. Who runs this town?"

"The Baron. I will take you to him. He might find your timing convenient."

The spear wall was lowered and the agents of the Chancellor were escorted down the road into a bustling fishing town. Everything had the look of being quite temporary. The houses and places of business looked to be assembled quickly from wood and cheap thatch. It was in the boats where the wealth was obviously stored. There were small boats with nimble sails and sleekly painted cabins, boats of fine pitched wood, and boats of ornate decor. Then there were the ships. Large and lording over the smaller docks. The sails flapped and rippled in the wind like the fine white sheets of a giant hung out to dry. The wood creaked and moaned under its own weight, rattling its chains and slapping its ropes against the waves that were blown to shore.

Tavin had always loved the sea and managed to visit the ports in Carolina a few times with his father, though he had never been fortunate enough to board a ship bigger than a rowboat. The sight of the ships excited him.

"You folks don't mind the old buildings?" Gannon asked looking over at some of the dilapidated structures of the town in the distance.

"We go where the fish go. We've been here for almost ten seasons," the man said. "This spot has been good to us."
They rode past a fish market and leather tanning shop down toward a large cabin with smoke billowing out its chimney.

"Wise of you to have a militia," Kendo added.

"You'll have to forgive us, we're not usually on high alert, but times have changed," said the head guard who introduced himself as Trenton, though Tavin and the others did not return the favor. "A boat of ours went missing a week ago, and that's not all."

The agents looked at each other with affirming glances.

"Hey Dani. Can you and your brother take these men's horses?"

As they dismounted at the cabin, two teenagers emerged from a wigwam and tended to their horses.

"Thank you," Tavin said as he passed the reins to a young girl, who smiled and led his horse off with cooing noises.

Trenton then led the group into the cabin, opening the door for them and ushering them into the hallway where craftsmen were leaning over large swaths of paper, sketching the designs for hauls and talking vigorously. Outside one of the windows more fishermen were coming and going while others were busy planning long sections of timber with smooth reaching motions. The smell of sawdust danced through the hallway, and they moved through it to a room down an opposing hallway that was dank and dusty and smelled of old leather. Upon entering the room, they were greeted by a short and thin man who was covered in flecks of sawdust and drinking something strong from a canteen. His eyes were bright and merry, and his voice was more forceful than one would have expected from a man of his stature. The Baron greeted them heartily, shook their hands with his own hard-worked palms, offered them beer—which they graciously accepted—and removed his hat to reveal close cut hair.

"Working today?" Trenton asked him.

"Well shit, we're a boat short. It's all hands-on deck," the Baron replied. "Now, who might you gentlemen be?"

"These men claim to be agents of the Chancellor," Trenton stated.

The six men each pulled their medallions revealing the Capitol crest.

"Am I in trouble?" the Baron asked.

Tavin shook his head.

"We're looking for a clan of Western raiders. They're supposedly on the lake road to Canada, which would take them past your place. Besides the missing boat, has anything strange happened lately?" Tavin asked.

The Baron sighed and, after Trenton handed them their frosted beers, he closed the door. They sat upon an eclectic mix of wooden furniture as the Baron leaned back against a wide table strewn with ledgers, he coughed to clear his throat.

"Some of our hunters said they saw tracks in the woods. Lots of tracks. We didn't think anything of it, but there was a fire in one of our storehouses late one night. It took almost all of us to contain it, and by the morning we realized one of our newest ships had gone missing. Big fucking thing too. Must've been the same people. Last we knew it was headed north-northwest, but we haven't seen it since, and we have too much work to go chasing it. Might have to wait until spring."

"You guys should consider yourselves lucky," Seneca replied. "They've done—" he caught his voice and glanced at Oil'ib, but Oil'ib was silent and his eyes were distant, off in another realm of thought. "They've done far worse."

"Well, they killed two of our dockworkers. Whoever it was. It's not been easy around here. Men keep wanting to sail off and look for the bastards but I don't think it'll help. You can call me LaMare. The Baron is a gag more than it is my name. I know Trenton would love to hear you keep calling me that, though."

"Did anyone possibly see them taking the boat?" Tavin asked.

"Just one," LaMare replied.

"May we see him?" Tavin asked.

"Trenton, bring him here please."

Trenton exited the room.

"Sir, do you mind if some of us ask around, maybe get a feel for the area? Anything could help," Gannon said. LaMare nodded.

"We'll catch you up," Tavin said as Gannon left with Kendo and Oil'ib.

Just as the three were leaving, Trenton and a gangly young man with curly black hair walked in.

"Hey boss," the young man said.

"Kaleb, these men are here on behalf of the Chancellor and they're here to help us with our problem. Just tell them what you told me, please."

Kaleb looked a little shocked to be put in such a spot and Tavin felt some sympathy for him. He was sure that the town was rarely visited by men of the Capitol except for the purposes of taxes.

"It's okay," Tavin said. "You're not in trouble. Just tell us what you know."

"Like, just tell you what I saw?" Kaleb clarified.

"Whatever you saw—make me see it."

"I had guard duty on the docks that night with Brenner and Toby," The young man explained as he ran his hand through his oily black curls. "One of our lanterns ran out of oil and we didn't have any on us, so I ran back to the boathouse to get some more. It took me a while to find it, but when I looked back through the doorway a bunch of guys were approaching the docks. I was… *paralyzed*. They just… they… they grabbed my friends and I don't know what they did, but they all got on the *Esmeralda* and sailed away. I don't know how many there were. Maybe ten, or *fifty* even. I was too afraid to watch. They were terrifying. Their faces were painted with red and black and they smelled like… like ashes."

"The *Esmeralda* was our most prized ship," LaMare interjected with a regretting tone. "Big, but fast for its size."

"Did you go tell anyone?" Tavin asked, turning to Kaleb again.

"I ran back toward the houses but the storehouse was on fire and everyone was working to get that under control. By the time we got back to the docks the ship was already almost out of sight."

"Were they armed?" Seneca asked.

"They had weapons. Lots of weapons."

"You couldn't see how many there were at any time?" Praxis pressed.

"Couple dozen maybe—hard to tell in the dark. But they had many footsteps going up the gangplank."

Tavin, Praxis and Seneca looked at each other, knowing that they must have followed the right trail. But a slight bewilderment was behind each of their eyes. Tavin felt it himself, twitching in the background of his assuredness. What to do now?

"Did you expect less?" Seneca asked them.

"It is what it is," Tavin replied. "Anything else stand out about them?"

Kaleb shook his head no.

"Kaleb what are you working on today?" LaMare asked.

"New rudder."

"Okay. Good luck, I'll be out to help you in a bit."

The door closed behind Kaleb and the room was quiet but for the sliding of the blade outside.

"That's who we're looking for," Tavin said. "How fast was that boat he took?"

"We only have one ship faster."

"We'll need it," Seneca replied.

"That's right," Tavin and Praxis added together.

"You'll need my boat?" LaMare wondered. "So now we can be down two vessels in fishing season? You're crazy."

"I think he's going to the north side of the lakes. The winter is easier there and the bastard probably knows that there are Eastern forces on his heels. But the war is not in Canada," Tavin explained as he looked LaMare dead in the eyes. "The war is in the East. He's not going to stay up there for very long. Probably just the winter. You really want him hanging out until he comes back in the spring?"

"What do you suggest we do?" LaMare mused. "What would the Chancellor have of us?"

Tavin could not tell if it was sarcasm or desperation that lit the last question. He thought LaMare to be a strange leader, one that might not cooperate so easily.

"We take the boat, and as many people as will join us and we go find them," Seneca stated.

"Shouldn't we wait for—"

"No. If he gets across that lake, he's gone. This is our only chance," Praxis replied.

"If we asked the men of your town, would any join us to avenge those boys? How many would come?" Tavin asked.

LaMare shook his head and smiled at them.

"What about our defenses? I would not leave us open to another robbery. As it is, we have extra guard duties every night now."

"An Eastern cavalry is following us as we speak. A few days behind. Their leader's name is Hemma and she'll be here any day now. They'll watch over your town," Tavin bargained.

When he said Hemma's name Tavin's voice felt

weak and out of breath. His throat felt thick and his chest heavy. He was so surprised by his reaction to thoughts of this woman that he had to take a deep breath, drawing an eyebrow from Seneca.

"How big is the militia?" Praxis asked.

"You're not taking all of them," LaMare pressed with scrutiny.

"Fine. How many?" Tavin asked.

"Enough to fill that boat I'm giving you. But I need your word that we will be protected by this cavalry."

They all smiled and Tavin let out a sigh.

"Thank you. I give you my word as a man of the East, your town will not see any more danger. That might as well be the word of the Chancellor himself."

"We will see," LaMare mused seriously. "We will see just how good that word is. But I can promise you men one thing," the Baron of the shipping town pinched at the skin around his nimble chin, "if you bring me back my ship, with or without the head of the man who stole her, then I can promise you that you will be welcome in this town for a long time. With all the fish you can eat and beer you can drink."

LaMare was excited when put to a task. Though his body was lean and his muscles ropelike, he moved with a great strength and his people followed his enthusiastic charge with similar gusto. Once he had shown them the ship, by which the six men of the Chancellor would give chase to Kayzitt, it was little over two hours before it was fully stocked with food stuffs and weapons. The small force of local militia that had volunteered for the mission of revenge had proven ample enough—twenty-four strong men. He was beside himself with excitement and the desperate hope that they could finally have it out. The wind was picking up in their favor, snapping the billowing sails in its gusts and filling his heart with a wild feeling. He decided to put himself to work and found Kendo helping to fix the riggings of a jib sail.

"You got this?"

"I've been around boats all my life," Kendo replied.

"Well, I wouldn't expect to have to do much of the sailing," Praxis added.

"Speaking of which, are we ready to set off?" Seneca wondered while helping stock barrels full of arrows.

"Here's Trenton now," Tavin mentioned, noticing him lumbering toward them from the boat house.

Trenton gave a few loud orders and the gangplank was lifted and sent clattering to its space on the deck. Then, there was a sound of iron chains gathering and Tavin felt the first lurch of movement beneath him as the ship was freed from its tethers. Trenton, captain of the guard of Presque, approached them with a wry smile beneath his mustache. His hair was like black wool bordering his rosy-cheeked, wind-kissed face. A simple cape of fur was the only thing that distinguished him from the other men of the militia, who all wore buckskin uniforms and brought old cutlasses and new bows as their weapons.

The bows were freshly strung with sinew, and the wood still smelled faintly of its cutting. But the swords were something different, more like family heirlooms than the weapons of a soldier. Yet Tavin did not doubt that the blades in their scabbards were sharp. He could tell that Trenton was a man who took pride in his job.

"You like it?" the captain asked him as the shouts of the sailors sounded their departure.

"You should ask him, he's the sailing man." Tavin said pointing at Kendo

"A sailor and a soldier? A man after my own heart. She's a beaut, eh?" Trenton said, turning from Tavin to Kendo's tall stature and back again. "Strong keel, plenty of deck space, everything is state-of-the-art."

"It's lovely," Kendo replied. "My father built ships his whole life, but not quite like this one. It's impressive."

"We're lucky they didn't take it," Tavin added. "How many men is that?"

"Twenty-nine, at the last count, and myself makes thirty."

Tavin was happy that he had remembered what Kaleb had said earlier. Kayzitt could have as many as fifty men if the upper guess was correct. And all of them savages, certainly.

"Thirty-six," he mumbled to himself before shaking the man's hand. "I want to thank you for the help."

"Well now, it didn't take much to rally these boys. Brenner and Toby were some of our brightest young builders. They were born in our group and would've run their own boat one day. We were not going to rest well with the grief of their loss. But when you men arrived... Well, we won't rest until they're answered for."

"LaMare mentioned bringing the boat back too," Tavin said, noting the more obvious motivation.

Trenton smiled and offered a sigh.

"You can't take a fisherman's most prized vessel."

"He's not coming, is he?" Tavin said suddenly, noticing the young craftsman Kaleb amongst the rigging with the others.

"Oh yes, he is," Trenton retorted. "The boys they killed were his best friends. You just try and send him off this boat. Watch what he'll do."

Tavin nodded and let it go.

"Very well."

As the expanse of water grew and grew around them and the wind picked up speed across the glass-like plane of the lake, Tavin looked back across the water to where the people on the shoreline were holding hands to their eyes to block out the sun. His eyes searched the last hill, which they had descended upon entering the town, hoping that he might see the horses of Hemma's cavalry stepping down its rocky embankments. But there was no such movement. Only the trees waved in the breeze and played tricks upon his eyes. He needed her. The thought alarmed him. Never before had a woman captured his feelings so quickly. There'd never been anything standing between him and leaving, nothing pulling him back from the open road or the horizon before. And Tavin worried. It felt so much like a weakness.

Chapter Twenty-Six

October 2717
Lake Erie

Gannon

I was born to play music, but now I find I have inhabited the role of an actor. I must become something I am not. I must train myself to think differently if I am to survive. The role is far more grotesque and inhuman, but at least I can say I'm still an artist.

Not until they were a good distance from the docks did Gannon notice the leaves on the hills in the distance were turning their autumn colors. And now he could smell the change of the seasons in the cold wind that blew off the lake and caught their sails as the ship tacked its way upwind. He shivered and pulled his fur coat closer around him as he walked under the swoop sail and past the foremast. A gentle spray of mist coated his face as he approached the bow of the ship. It smelled of the icy water, of fish, and the plants of the depths. Again, he shivered. The air over the expansive lake was cold and humid, making his skin feel tacky with a moisture that sank into his skin.

Gannon was happy to be out on the ship. It was a large caravel, similar to the likes he would see out upon the ocean from his family's lighthouse on the cape of New England. A fantastic build, he thought, with fresh, strong wood. The main and foremasts were sticky with fresh pitch and the sails were still a pristine white. There was more than enough room for their thirty-some men, and he was glad for it. *LaMare*, Gannon thought to himself, *must be a quality shipbuilder*. It was no wonder that he wanted the stolen ship back from the monsters they chased.

At home, such a ship would be worth a fortune. He had never felt so close to home in the entire time of his enlistment. The marine smell was so familiar. The air was saltier in New England, and the tackiness more poignant, but it was similar enough. He wondered what his family was doing now. It was about the time to be extinguishing the fire in the mirrors at the top of the light house. The sky was clear where their ship strode out upon the lake.

There had been some excitement in the morning as Trenton spotted the ship they sought through the spyglass some miles to the northwest, beating slowly upwind. Fortunately, Kayzitt seemed an inexperienced sailor for despite their late start, their caravel was gaining on the marauder, and Trenton was able to identify their target beyond a doubt.

The celebrations from the crew had been raucous and had drawn Gannon to the upper deck. Without the spyglass, the enemy was just a mote on the silvery morning horizon, but it was there and Trenton was a master sailor. He was already boasting just how he would come around right on top of her. But soon the cold air had chased Gannon back down into the lower cabins again and Trenton followed him, keen on discussing the plan of action.

It was dark and musty in the lower deck and the creaking ladder welcomed them into the glow of candles and oil lamps against the shadows of men moving about their work. Gannon's eyes were slow to adjust and he guided himself carefully down the narrow corridors and through the shallow-ceilinged decks to the officer's quarters. There, some of his friends awaited them, seated on crates about a large spool of rope that served as a table for a simple oil lamp. The flickering light illuminated the familiar faces and several papers that were scattered about the rough-hewn wood. Gannon sat down by Tavin, whose face was sharp and angular in the low light despite the mass of cinnamon beard that bordered his face.

"So, you don't know what the fighting will be like then?" Trenton asked as he sat on an empty crate. It was a question he had already asked earlier and Seneca sighed to himself from a shadowed seat further back on sacks of grain.

"Unfortunately, we've never seen them fight in person, but in all likelihood, they'll be trained well beyond typical Western ranks," Tavin replied. "When was the last time any of your men were in a fight?"

Trenton scratched his head and pulled at his heavy mustache.

"I left some guys behind. I couldn't convince everyone to come, but the ones that did, they're ready to go. Well, I mean the older ones were in the first war, but the younger ones are strong. They build boats all day. They train as often as they can. They can drag a mast tree a mile through the mud."

To Gannon, Trenton seemed unsure. His eyes darted away after he spoke and glanced nervously about the sketches on the table, designs of the ship they chased, maps of the Canadian shoreline. The way his eyes moved away made Gannon uneasy. Instinctively, his fingers drummed and tapped against the tabletop, scratching his calloused skin against the rough surface. He made eye contact with Seneca. The gleaming green eyes were mere cuts in the shadow as his friend coughed and leaned forward, and Gannon ceased his drumming.

"Trenton, I respect what you men are doing, and I know what it means to your village being out here," Tavin continued, "so here's the deal. As long as we're chasing these bastards, it's your call. You do whatever it takes to get up alongside them, and along the way we want to help in any way we can. I don't care if we have to get out and row."

This made Seneca chuckle from the wall where he sat and sent a wave of snorts through their circle. Even Praxis could not help but smile. Then Tavin pursed his eyebrows again and leaned back as his nostrils flared, "But once we're alongside them, you and your men have to take our instruction. They have to do exactly what we say when we say it. If we can keep them in the water we'll have to try to board *inevitably*. Speaking of which, how close is land?"

"Very close," Trenton replied. "And I am plenty familiar with pirate tactics."

The sailor and captain of the militia seemed annoyed but not offended.

"As long as we can keep the fight on boats the advantage is with us," Tavin concluded.

"Quick question. How much food would have been on board that boat they stole?" Praxis wondered.

"Almost none. Maybe some rations that got left behind in a locker, but we take everything off after we sail, especially food."

"So, they're sailing around likely living off just their provisions. That's certainly an edge," Seneca stated. "They've been traveling around for months. They're on unfamiliar waters, and all of your men are fresh. This isn't an impossible mission."

"And clearly they're not well versed in sailing. Look how quickly we caught up," Trenton added. "We'll be able to outmaneuver them. I'll bring us around right on top—"

"You'll be right in the line of fire if you insist on manning the wheel," Gannon stated, having already heard Trenton's promises enough. He wondered if the master sailor could actually imagine the necessities of a battle.

"No one takes that wheel away from me. Especially not tomorrow."

"You think we'll overtake them by then?" Seneca inquired.

"I know that ship. We'll have them soon."

Gannon felt feverish, though he was not ill. The closeness of the quarters was too much and the lighting too low. He felt like he was breathing his own hot breath in a wooden coffin. All at once he felt the urge to be out of there.

"I'll go up top. I'm overdue."

Kendo made a small noise as if to ask his meaning, but Gannon was already out of reach, overdue for nothing but fresh air. He followed the pale daylight at the end of the corridor along the lower decks, passing the stolid figures of several men along the way. The rungs of the ladder were under his hands. Then, hefting his weight upward, he broke his head into the rushing air and the light of day. All around him on the deck, the men of the militia worked tirelessly at the lateen sails, jibing them around at angles with the wind and calling out "bearing away!" and "jibe-ho!"

Gannon sauntered along the top deck trying to be unnoticeable. Gulls were calling from the main mast and he avoided them, not wanting to be dropped on today. A sign of bad luck would have broken his spirit. Upon climbing the quarterdeck, he nodded to the helmsman, who did not see him, his stern and level eyes keen on the horizon and the angle of the jib sail. So, he kept walking to the poop deck, where the railing ended with a doused lantern. Gannon peered over the rear of the ship and stared down at the wake that foamed and sloshed behind where the ship cut its way through the gentle water, dark slate and blue-green. He felt a presence behind him then, familiar, not one of the strangers in the militia or the helmsman.

"What is it Praxis?" Gannon said.

"How did you know it was me?"

"Because you're the only person I've ever met who makes no noise."

Praxis joined him at the railing, inhaling the fine air deeply, a corn-cob pipe in his hand.

"You've also never seen me smoke, so I guess now's the time, right?" Praxis said.

Gannon laughed.

"Thank you."

He took the pipe from his friend's hand and puffed gingerly on the mouthpiece. The tobacco was sharp, fresh, and flavorful. He assumed Praxis had traded for it with one of the militia men. He was sure that they no longer possessed tobacco this fresh in their own group. He let the smoke slip from his mouth as he opened it, the wind sucking it out like a ghost leaving his body to dissipate in the turbulence above the water.

"You've been really vacant the last couple weeks," Praxis said.

"I think after Canyontown we all have the right be a little vacant."

"I worry about you most of all though," Praxis stated. "You all think because I don't say much that I don't know what you're thinking, but I do, and your mind troubles me."

"Why? Oil'ib has far more on his mind than I do."

"No, he doesn't," Praxis scoffed. "He knows exactly what he needs to do. He needs to kill. Oil'ib is a hunter. That's all he's thinking about."

"He's got a broken heart."

"You have a confused one."

"Get out of my head Praxis," Gannon spit into the foaming lake below. They paused awhile, not saying anything. "Don't you think I got enough from Bok already?"

The feeling that had started at the sacking of Greensboro was still there and sinking into him with tenacious persistence. He had thought that the burning of Canyontown and seeing Oil'ib in such agony might have changed all that. That revenge might stoke the fire that had gone out. But it had not. The fire was truly ashes, and there were no more coals to burn.

"You don't want to fight Kayzitt?" Praxis asked.

"No. I've come to terms with that. He shouldn't be allowed to live anymore, and the same for all his people. I want to see them dead just as much as you or Oil'ib even." Gannon took a puff and passed the pipe back. "That being said, this whole thing we're doing... I can't do it. I'm not like the rest of you."

"I never feel negatively about this business. Maybe I don't feel emotions like I should. Maybe you're the only one that's normal."

Gannon wished his friend could not sound so calculating.

"I think I'm the only one honest enough to admit it. Seneca's close. But even if I could ignore my feelings there is the practical matter at hand." Gannon reached again for the pipe from Praxis' hand, puffed on it nervously. The fragrant smoke filling his sinuses until he coughed. "Eventually I will get in the way. I know it. And I won't be the cause of anything happening to any of you."

"Your anxieties are so odd."

"Come on Praxis. I'm so fucking lucky to be here still, and I don't think I can bear the thought of one of you having your throat slit because my luck ran out. And at some point, I have to stay true to what I believe in. I'm an artist. That sounds absurd and selfish and weak, but I can't keep pretending I'm anything else. That's all I'll ever be."

"So, what's your plan then?"

"After we finish with these people I'm leaving…"

"Fuck that, Gannon. You're not leaving alone," Praxis replied.

"I have to. I'm going to follow the road between Ontario and Erie. I'll find shelter with some of the tribes in the area. It won't be a problem; I've traded my music for housing and food for years. Then I'll work my way back to New England. If I die out there then that is my business, but it will be on my terms." He turned to make sure his friend understood he was serious this time. "Please Praxis, please don't tell the others. Not yet. I want to tell them in my own way, and when you guys get back to the Capitol you are free to tell the Chancellor I died or deserted or whatever."

Praxis finished the tobacco. His face was furrowed with thought as he tapped the bowl of the pipe against the hardwood railing, knocking the ashes out into the water as the breeze carried them away.

"I have a feeling you'll change your mind, but just in case, you need to promise me when the time comes that you'll give me one chance to argue you out of it."

Gannon smiled. It was a better reaction than he could have gotten from the others.

"I can do that."

Still, Gannon wrung his hands as the day passed. He alternated between being below deck, playing card games in the low light and swaying of the ship on the water, and rushing back up to the fresh air to check on the progress. Each time the enemy ship was a little closer and Trenton was growing more and more boisterous as he led the calls of "bearing away!" When the sun finally met with the horizon and the warm pink light of evening spread across the sky, Gannon felt more at peace. Darkness swallowed the chase and he returned to the lower decks, offering himself up to sleep in the clutches of his burlap hammock. The oil lamp in the quarters was doused and complete darkness took hold. Gannon slipped into sleep without knowing when his eyes had closed.

For a moment of indeterminable length his great consternation was abated in a profound slumber. He slept deeply and did not wake till the sounds of a great panic shook him from his rest. The light of day could already be seen dimly from the reaches of the corridor and through the few cracks in the deck above. There was shouting and loud voices giving orders as feet clamored above and below him. Gannon was startled and clutched at the sides of his hammock. For a moment he forgot where he was and thought for sure that he was back in Greensboro, that the sacking of the town was still going on and that he might not have ever escaped—might never escape. Steadily he remembered his surroundings and, lunging to the floor with a swinging dismount of his hammock, was glad to see that he was still fully dressed and ran his hand through his thinning hair as he collected himself.

"What's going on?" he yelled over to a few militia doing likewise.

"No idea."

Gannon slung his morning-star to his back, strapped on his sword belt and ran up on deck, following the pale light to the ladder. The cool morning air greeted his head with fresh gusts and blew his hair about. Feet ran by him as he climbed and the shouting was even louder above the sound of the sails catching the wind. The jib sail was swinging about and the ship rocked to one side as the wheel was turned sharply by the helmsman. It was all Gannon could do to keep his balance as he gained the main deck. Tavin was shoving past him then, and Gannon moved to keep up with his friend as Tavin shouted orders to the militia.

Then he saw the boat. He knew it immediately though he had never seen it so close. A thing of beauty, the size of its prow and thickness of its hull were intimidating. The captured ship was keeling over to one side as it made desperate attempts to steer itself to a greater distance. And for the first time, Gannon could see the enemy, moving about the deck with a great hurry. Their faces indistinguishable.

The mere visualization of the presence, the finalization of their existence, and the inescapable validity of their mission struck Gannon to his core. He was filled with a paralyzing nervousness and heard the loud voice of Tavin shouting ferociously above the sounds of the rigging being pulled taunt.

"Spread out! No easy targets!" he bellowed.

"Here," Kendo said appearing by Gannon's side, handing him his bow and quiver.

At the helm, Trenton had taken the wheel and was pulling on its polished spokes with great stretches of his arms down and down again toward port, following Kayzitt's ship in its wake as both ships turned tightly, veering toward the approaching shoreline. Gannon noticed it for the first time then, a broken line of pebbles and rounded rocks leading to scruffy jack pines and the golden leaves of beech trees that thickened into the distance. The sun was poking its light through the clouded skies, and the sudden warmth brought sweat to Gannon's torso. He took the bow and quiver from Kendo, nodding, and slung both around his shoulders.

"In position!" Tavin shouted over the surging mist. Oil'ib and several men wielding crossbows and spears took a low position on the deck while militiamen with longbows stood in back.

Gannon nocked an arrow and tested the tension of the bow. His eyes searched the enemy vessel for signs of a leader. But they were indistinguishable, muddy and tattered like men of the wild and—Gannon squinted to make sure he was seeing correctly—their faces appeared to be painted various shades of red.

"Hold!" Tavin shouted, followed by echoing calls

from Praxis and Seneca.

Trenton was screaming down at the men around the masts. To Gannon it was loud but indistinguishable, but the sailors pulled at the riggings and moved the foremast around, beckoning the jib sail to a new angle. The ship gained speed as it caught the wind off the lake again and began to catch on an even keel with the enemy ship, pulling up along her starboard side. Both ships were racing along the trajectory of the shoreline, following it eastward to where it became less jagged and opened to a gray beach. As they became even with the other ship, Gannon saw that the enemy was also preparing to fire hell down upon them. The narrow tapering of slender bows could be seen standing at attention along the deck. Before he had time to fret, Tavin roared again from the forecastle.

"Longbows fire!"

The archers ripped off a volley to which Gannon offered a delayed contribution. The arrow sprung from the tension of his bow and disappeared into the cloud of darts that raced away from their deck. Kayzitt's ship offered a response, and Gannon winced as he saw the needles slipping gracefully toward them through the silver sky. Neither volley met pay dirt, the sound of the missiles breaking off the haul gave him a temporary respite.

"Second volley!"

Trenton ripped the wheel hard, bringing them even closer. Gannon held his breath as he notched another arrow to the sinew string. He closed his left eye and stared down his target, aiming a little higher than the quarterdeck of their sister ship. They fired again. This time several shots hit, but Kayzitt's return volley also found success and the opposing arrows came thudding in amongst them. Several men were hit and called out in pain, though no one fell.

Gannon breathed heavily, his heart pounding in his chest. A constriction was binding his torso. For a moment he thought he might just as well dive off the ship and take his chances in the cold water. But his feet stayed their place and he notched another arrow to his bow. The ship got closer still until Trenton leveled off the approach and Tavin ran along the portside main deck, where the men with crossbows crouched behind the crates and riggings by the railing.

"Crossbows, now!" he shouted dropping to the deck as the bowman let loose their projectiles.

Gannon saw Oil'ib amongst those in the line of crossbows. Their levers were pulled and the bolt actions collided with the crossbars with a loud thwack. They shot excellently, and he could see the men on the opposing ship fall away from the front. Their group seemed to be enjoying the advantage, consistently holding the high ground. Yet the return fire from the opponent was successful and three men fell from their weapons. Oil'ib still stood, crouched as he was behind a thick coil of rope that caught a cruel missile that might have killed him. The wounded squirmed in pain like caught fish until they were pulled away.

Gannon dropped low, reloading his bow with an arrow from the quiver on his back. One of the younger militiamen was running along the ranks and stuffing their quivers with fresh arrows, the reassurance of the new weight on his shoulders gave him a renewed strength. Trenton took an arrow to the shoulder, wavered and stumbled but then gripped the rungs of the large wheel and steadied himself, shouting new orders to the sailors below.

At that point, the volleys degenerated into wild firing. Arrows whistled wide overhead and some clattered to the floor near Gannon's feet. Men squatted in safety and then resurfaced to take shots at the opposing deck. The two ships were so close that one might have jumped between the two and at least touched the boards of the opposing deck with a hand. Gannon crouched low and waddled his way toward the cover of the main mast, putting his back to it as the wind and arrows whistled over his head. Not far from him, nearer to the stern, he saw Seneca grab a spear from a fallen militia man and toss it in a rainbow arc of a javelin throw. The spear curved elegantly through the air and came to an end in the belly of one of Kayzitt's soldiers. Gannon hoped that it was the leader himself, that the mission might be one large step closer to completion.

"Ah-Ha!" Seneca cheered as the target hit the deck, the spear sticking through him awkwardly.

There was desperate shouting from both ships now, and men were racing to the riggings and the quarter deck. Gannon stood tenuously, testing the safety of the air with every inch gained. He saw the cause of the alarm. High rocks were approaching quickly toward the front of the ships. The entire weight of the opposing ship jerked dangerously away to port in avoidance. The move was successful, but it ran the ship aground. Gannon could hear the scraping of the hull upon the round pebbles of the shallow shoreline. There was a pause and he feared that they were going to hit the rocks, so hastily were they approaching without a reaction from the ship. Then, their ship followed suit and Gannon was tossed to the ground again as the ship grounded to a stop upon the shore.

Men shouted, collected themselves and their weapons, and ran along the deck, rousing those that were ready. But one voice rose above them all in its desperate questioning.

"Trenton!" it shouted.

Gannon followed the mass of militiamen up the steps to the top of the quarter deck and there found Trenton, dead on the floor with six arrows in his heavy torso. Tavin was above them before there was time for the loss to sink in. He scrambled to the top of a nearby rigging, his finger pointing accusingly at the enemy ship nearby.

"We must go! We must follow them!"

Gannon followed the direction of his friend's gesturing hand and saw that the enemy was emptying their ship, spraying out onto the shoreline like rats.

Chapter Twenty-Seven

October 2717
Shores of Canada

Oil'ib

Out on the hunt, in the winter, I remember being a child and my fingers going numb from the cold iron. When I came home mom soaked my hands in warm water. It had not hurt until then.

Oil'ib loaded another shaft into his crossbow, pulling back the lever until it latched with a heavy click. Then he was over the side of the ship, rappelling down the thick hempen rope and landing on the rough beach. He hit his head against the mast of the lateen sail during the excitement and his ears were still ringing. The voices of the men around him were muffled as they crested the dune of pebble-riddled sand that walled in the beach. Underneath his leather boots, the loose footing gave little traction and sounded strange in his ears, like sandy cotton. As the grassy field beyond the dune came into view, Oil'ib caught a glimpse of the enemy.

They were standing in slowly retreating lines, with bows taut and waiting. A tackle from behind crashed Oil'ib to the top of the crest just as the arrows let loose.

When the arrows sailed overhead Oil'ib turned and pushed Tavin off him.

"You hear me?" Tavin said, slapping him on the shoulder. "Get down!"

The group of twenty-two readied their bows with their remaining arrows and fired down upon the Western marauders who maintained an intermittent retreat, occasionally taking shots of their own. Oil'ib lay still upon his stomach then rolled back down the crest. There, he saw that the others were kneeled down in a circle making a plan of attack and he crawled toward them as the militiamen continued to exchange shots with the enemy.

"What now?" Seneca asked.

"All-out assault," Tavin said.

Gannon grumbled something that Oil'ib could not make out.

"Yes," Tavin replied. But there was a hesitation. "Why else are we here? It's now or never. They're tired. Much, much more than we are."

"How do you know?" asked one of the sailors.

"Because they'd be charging us right now if they weren't. They're on the defensive for a change, so we have to strike now. If we let them retreat to the wilderness, we will have missed our window."

"I want their heads," Oil'ib finally said. It was the first time he had been able to put away enough emotion to find his voice and even to him it sounded like the voice of a stranger. His voice was deep and ominous, shrouded in something terrible.

"Let's finish it right now," Praxis said with cold finality.

"Alright," Tavin whisked some sweat from his brow. "How many of us? Twenty-two? Let's split up into two groups and try and flank down the east and west of the dune. I think they expect us to stay here so at least we'll surprise them. Oil'ib, Gannon, Praxis take eight of the men with you. Kendo, Seneca, and myself will take the remaining eight. Kaleb!" he called and the young militia man came over carrying a spear and an old cutlass at his waist.

"Give Seneca that spear," ordered Tavin. "He's the best thrower. Everyone fire, throw whatever you have and then charge. I promise you they are more exhausted than we are."

"Focus now," Seneca reassured his friends. "Think of nothing but the blade in your hands. Let fate worry about the rest."

They followed Tavin's plan and split off into two groups, hoping to lose themselves from the enemy's view for a time as they rounded the dune. When Oil'ib's group rounded the far edge and came out from the trees, he could see that they had beat Tavin's group to it by a few seconds. This garnered the attention of the leader of the Western platoon, and Oil'ib found his target.

"Fire!" yelled a man in the central rear of the Western group.

He was a shorter man, lithe but strong with wide eyes and an eccentric face beneath the splashes of war paint. His hair was a copper red and its tangled lengths coiled down to his shoulders. Beside him was a black-skinned female. Her presence surprised Oil'ib. He pushed her from his mind and focused all of himself upon the leader, the man that Oil'ib had trailed with the last of his life's meaning. Now that his target was standing in his view his sadness was diminished, his legs and arms felt stronger, a frenzy threatened to take hold of him. He bit at his tongue as he raised his crossbow with his final arrow notched in the mechanism.

The arrows from the Western platoon buzzed toward them like angry hornets and stuck and clattered off bark and flesh alike. The Eastern group returned fire and Oil'ib held perfectly still, waiting for his opportunity. Kayzitt stopped moving for a second as the arrow volley dwindled. Oil'ib held his breath and lined up his crossbow with Kayzitt's head, pointing the barbs of the arrowhead directly on the copper red hair. He felt his heart beating and there was a pain in his calf that he pushed from his mind. One beat, two beats, then the space in between heartbeats, and in the perfect stillness of his limbs and body, fired.

The bolt shot out of his crossbow with amazing speed, his finger having barely touched the mechanism. But the shot went wide and glanced off the shoulder of Kayzitt. Oil'ib cursed and for a second the red leader was surely looking at him. Oil'ib threw down his crossbow, useless. As he reached for his axe, he gathered the positions of the others around him. From the far side of the dune he saw the others emerge and watched Seneca let loose his javelin, which found its home through the thigh of an enemy, dropping him to the ground.

A sharp pain rang out of his calf again. Oil'ib looked down to see an arrow jutting from the flesh behind his leg. With calm steadiness he reached down and broke off the tip, seething as the movement wiggled the shaft in his flesh. Then he extracted it slowly. Tired, shaken, sweating, exhausted, he regained himself and found his blade. One by one the others in his group drew their swords as well and the Western platoon answered in kind. Oil'ib's eyes never left the red hair of his enemy, and he watched as Kayzitt pulled twin long-handled tomahawks from their simple thongs at his waist.

There was a twitch, a spasm of his muscles, and then Oil'ib was flying over the ground, his feet hitting with delicate ferocity as he sprinted forward, vaguely aware of his compatriots following behind him. As he ran there was a familiar feeling—a glazing over of the realms of higher thought, his inner voice silenced. There was an instinctual awareness, instinctual in its velocity to the forefront of his mind yet simultaneously without space. He was aware of the positions of Praxis and Gannon behind him. Time was a non-sequitur and his outer and inner worlds melded into one understanding. The tingling in the forehead and a slight burning ecstasy throughout the body, he felt like he was outside of himself, both watching and controlling.

He kept his eyes locked on Kayzitt. His enemy was emerging, stepping forward and twirling his twin tomahawks. Oil'ib picked up speed. The dust of the earth kicked up as he pushed himself as hard as his body would allow. Men descended upon each other. Oil'ib was cut off by a Western warrior and kicked his heels back, bringing his momentum looping forward and flinging his battle axe end-over-end into the man's chest. A spray of blood escaped the torso of his foe painting, briefly, the air around him. He did not pause, pulling forth his fighting axe from his belt.

Another attempted to connect on a downward chop but Oil'ib deflected it. The man, tall and built like an ox, returned a cross swing that would have felled lesser opponents, but instead it sliced hollow air as Oil'ib backpedaled. The Westerner used the momentum to spin around and backhand Oil'ib, but Oil'ib had already seen it coming and dropped low, swinging for the knees. The man recoiled in time and as Oil'ib approached, he hit Oil'ib's face with a heavy kick. Oil'ib spat the pooling blood out of his mouth and answered the kick with one of his own. Stumbling, he pushed his enemy backwards.

On his left a pair of men were hacking away at each other with dwindling ferocity as they collapsed. Oil'ib closed his eyes a split second as blood splattered his face. The warm droplets blended amongst the beads of sweat. Then he brought his axe down, knocking away his enemy's attack. Three parries and his opponent overstepped a lunge. Oil'ib's sharp downward chop separated the man's left arm from his shoulder with disgusting efficiency. Oil'ib delivered a head butt that broke bones, pulled the axe back and chopped him through the forehead.

Out of the corner of his mind he saw Kendo fall hard only for an aggressor to underestimate the length of the sword staff and end up with the blade through the stomach. Another feeling disturbed him for a moment. Panic, coming from Gannon. It was not immediate danger, but his friend felt out of sync. It was as if there was a drum that the six of them were dancing to and Gannon was overreacting, over-thinking, out of rhythm. He could not turn and help, though.

His eyes scanned only for Kayzitt. Grass shuffled under his soles. The wind fell silent offering no mask for the carnage, the sounds of steel cutting into flesh and bone and the screams of rage, agony, and fear. There was nothing to blow away the stench of death and blood. An enemy stepped in front of him then, a maniac of a man, missing all his teeth.

"I'll kill you, bird boy!" the grotesque man screamed while taking measured swings at Oil'ib's head with a rusted sword.

Oil'ib backpedaled, avoiding a wide swing from his enemy, and spun around catching the Westerner in the flank with the edge of his axe. A follow-up left the man's skull in two hemispheres. Turning again, he looked for Kayzitt. At last he saw him, finishing off one of the militia before he began to backpedal, obviously sensing as Oil'ib did, that the Eastern forces were winning the ground. Screams reverberated all around him, the air smelled metallic. He pressed on, kicking up his heels and taking off like a dog on a scent. Ducking a spear thrust and twisting past one of his own men, he lunged forward to intercept the leader.

An unexpected swing from the leader's right hand sent a tomahawk scarily close to his temple. His quick reaction managed to avoid disaster but Kayzitt was suddenly upon him, and now pressed him backwards, swinging with chop after chop. A perturbing smile was on the man's face, despite the strength that propelled his blades. Oil'ib blocked one after another but they came too fast and too well placed. Each attack was a predictable shot at an area he had left open.

Finally, one of the attacks found home, cutting his right quad. Oil'ib saw an opening as the blade slowed in the flesh of his own leg and sent a hard punch forward, connecting with Kayzitt's nose and drawing blood. He reached downward and pulled forth his own tomahawk. They paced around each other like rabid dogs. Oil'ib could not feel his face.

Hatred brewed and sloshed out of him. His mind skipped around to the things that were destroyed. His home burnt to the ground, the taste of ashes still upon his mouth, the sweet smell of death, and the rose of blood—Oil'ib gnashed his teeth and spat.

"Come on," he growled.

Kayzitt stopped pacing then and leapt ahead, achieving several feet of air and coming down in a cross-swing. One strike after another, Oil'ib blocked them away backpedaling but could not find the opening to take the offense. Kayzitt was quicker than him. He was gaining leverage with each parry, working Oil'ib downhill. A tomahawk whispered death past his ear as it barely missed Oil'ib's head. He dropped low and cut a wide swing that sent Kayzitt stumbling backwards. He breathed, surprised he had found that opening. He struggled to keep calm, to keep the state of mind that the vision of battle required. His rage was blinding. His moves were becoming jerky and predictable, his arms were tired, so tired. The hefting and swinging of the axe had become nearly too much. He was drenched with sweat and his mouth was dry as a bone. Still he locked his feet against the burning wound in his calf, and drove forward again.

Gannon shouted, appearing suddenly from the right to join the fray.

Kayzitt showed no fear by the surprise, however, and reacted elegantly picking up Gannon's strike with a simple upwards parry and then following through with his second tomahawk to slice Gannon's triceps. Oil'ib saw the cut and leaped in, sending Kayzitt backwards again. He swung with three heavy attacks that battered the tomahawks of his enemy away and pushed Kayzitt up the hillside. But just as it seemed he could break, Kayzitt caught himself on the ground and spun up high, kicking away Oil'ib's tomahawk and roundhouse kicked him in the head.

Oil'ib's eyes broke open the moment his back touched earth. He expected to witness Kayzitt finish his life.

Instead Gannon was again above him, having caught up from the pain of his injury and was attempting to subdue the warrior. Gannon gave Kayzitt a moment's hesitation and a swinging block disarmed his friend. Gannon stood still and silent for an eternity in time's cruel grasp. The world slowed as the sword was twisted away, hanging in the air. Then time caught up to gravity and in a singular act of cold savagery Kayzitt spun around and swung his right-handed weapon into Gannon's flank.

Blistering pangs shot through Oil'ib's nerves as Gannon plummeted to earth. Kayzitt withdrew his weapon as Oil'ib struggled to his feet. For a brief moment the marauder looked into Oil'ib's eyes. The smile was gone. Instead he seemed to be looking past Oil'ib. Indeed, Oil'ib could sense that the Western forces were nearly destroyed. He would have him still. But then Kayzitt ran, sprinted up the hill like a mountain lion running from a whip.

Oil'ib made to run but his calf gave out. His enemy made it up into the rocky hill of beech trees, their golden leaves making a tawny carpet on the ground. Instead of chasing, Oil'ib hurried to where Gannon lay wheezing upon his back and lowered to his knees. With desperate strength he gathered his friend in his arms.

"Oil'ib help me."

He looked to his right and saw his friends killing the remainder of Kayzitt's forces. Tavin, his face covered in a mask of crimson and an eye swollen shut, was beating a defeated enemy into the ground with one punch after another. Kendo noticed Oil'ib's desperate look first and finished sliding his knife across his foe's throat before tossing him like a cracked egg shell.

Gannon's desperate words pulled his wayward gaze back to where it belonged.

"You're stronger than this life. Please... please... believe that," Gannon gasped. "I'm sorry that..." he seethed through his teeth as he gasped in pain. "Fuck! I'm sorry that I fucked up. I was going to..." Gannon coughed. Oil'ib held his head with his right and put pressure on the wound with his left. "I wish we could have seen the end together. I wish we could have celebrated something."

"No god, please d-don't say that. Gannon, I... I'm sorry that I hit you. I-I-I... I'm sorry. What w-w-what do you need?" Oil'ib blurted through tears forming in his hot eyes. He could feel the warmth of his friend's lifeblood beating out in steady pulses through his fingers as he tried to staunch the wound. He knew that this was the last time he would ever see him alive or hear his voice and know his thoughts.

The desperation paralyzed him. Oil'ib only gazed into the paling face of Gannon and began to cry. Gannon was beginning to convulse with the pain and his eyes were shuttering.

"Gannon, l-l-look at me."

Gannon's focus had already left him. His eyes could follow only the rays of the sun interrupted over and over by the passing clouds.

"Gannon say something," Seneca instructed as he arrived, helping turn Gannon to better see the savage wound.

Seneca placed a hand on the side and removed the clothing, checking the wound before offering a solemn look to everyone. Oil'ib had felt it too. Life had left their friend.

"We got them," Tavin was chanting to himself with frantic tears mixing into the blood that had painted his face. "We got them."

Oil'ib stood. He held the crimson mess of Gannon's blood before him, glistening red in the cold sunlight.

"No," he took a deep breath and released the last of his tears, his body shuddering as he tore himself away from his friend. "We didn't."

"No. Goddamnit, you're not doing this," Seneca blurted. "That's not how we handle this."

"I love you all," Oil'ib wiped blood from his face.

"Stop. Oil'ib, stop. Give this some time," Seneca said with a stern sadness. "He is just one man, it is over. He won't survive the winter by himself out here."

Oil'ib only offered a soft smile before retrieving his tomahawk and fighting axe. He walked back to the first body he killed and wrenched his battle axe from the chest. His mind felt free. It floated along like a ship unhampered by an anchor, all sails open, let loose upon the wind. It was as if he had already died and passed into pure existence. There was nothing left to be. There were no strings pulling him toward one life or the other.

"You're right. He won't survive the winter. I will hope to see you all again."

His friends sat in silence. The cooling body of Gannon cradled between them. Not one could stir to chase him. He knew they were too exhausted. But he had all the strength in the world again. The weight of the soldier had slipped away. A loathsome coil to him now. He was the hunter again. And his prey was out there, close but fleeting, dangerous but fleeing. His feet carried him with renewed energy as he found the trail he sought.

A branch broke. The dirt pushed aside from the edge of

running feet. The wind carried the embrace of the wilderness. He accepted it fondly, like a hug from a parent. With tears in his eyes, Oil'ib did not look.

Chapter Twenty-Eight

October 2717
Shores of Canada

Seneca

What we did was necessary. The act itself can be explained. It was not heroics. Heroics are done after what is necessary. They are extra. Feeding your child is necessary, but it is not heroic. Oil'ib does what he feels to be a necessity. And I respect his heroism.

"I thought that we might be invincible," Tavin said as he wiped his nose.

"I believed it, too," Seneca agreed.

Seneca was still holding Gannon's lifeless body. He looked out at the carnage in the grassy sand. The dead lay strewn across it in silence but for the breeze that blew off of the lake and pushed gentle waves onto the stony sand. The sun was high now and there was warmth in its rays. It highlighted the pallor of Gannon's complexion, his eyes now closed and his body cold. The militia had been spent. Only Kaleb, the youngest of them all, survived. The young man had been pacing around in the field amongst the dead for a while now. His bloodied sword still unclean and dragging lines in the ground behind him.

"We should take care of his body," Seneca said.

"What about all the other bodies?" Praxis asked, softly enough that Kaleb would not be able to hear. "He probably cares about those people too."

There was silent agreement. Then Seneca roused himself and stood, placing Gannon's body gently on the sand.

"Kaleb," he called down the hill.

Surprisingly the young man answered with haste and came running up the hill as if he had remembered that other people in the world were still alive. When he reached the top and saw the four of them, he became cognizant of his sword and cleaned it upon his pants before sheathing it. His voice was quiet when he spoke and it seemed to Seneca that his mind was elsewhere, and only the first layer of Kaleb was answering him.

"Yes?"

"Which one of these ships would LaMare rather see returned to him?"

The boy looked at where both ships were moored upon the silt and sand. The larger ship was to the right and more stooped upon its side, but the smaller one was run farther aground. Both would take some work getting back out to deep water. Thankfully, the tide was still coming in, and Seneca could see from the waterline of the beach that both ships could be afloat by nightfall.

"One of them, you see, is going to have to stay here

through the winter. We'll make a pyre of all its extra contents…."

Kaleb's eyes widened a little with thought and Seneca was glad to see that he had woken him from his stupor, if but a little.

"The *Esmeralda*," Kaleb replied, pointing at the largest of the two, which had been absconded with by Kayzitt and his platoon.

"That one is easily the finest ship we have. It's named after his wife, so I think the Baron would like to see that one coming home. It's a shame to leave the *Harbinger*," said Kaleb as he glanced between the boat and the bodies of the men whom he had come here with. "But they deserve a good pyre. And we can come pick it up in the spring when the ice has thawed."

There was a cracking in the boy's throat that almost made Seneca lose his composure again. Instead, he put his hand on Kaleb's shoulder and thanked him. Together, the five of them lifted Gannon and brought him down to the shore.

By the time night had fallen, and the milky way glittered in the sky, the deck of the *Esmeralda*, now fully out to water and sitting with anchor down, housed the five survivors. They watched as Kaleb came swimming from the shoreline. He splashed in the darkness and looked like a pale sea creature in the light of the stars. Only his ripples on the sky's reflection were truly visible. Then Kendo threw him down a rope and the four of them brought the boy on board with great heaves. They offered him blankets and he took them up greedily as he stripped off his wet clothes and sat with his hands over the glow of the lantern on the forecastle deck.

"Were you able to light it?" Praxis asked.

"Yes," Kaleb replied, shivering. "It should go any second now."

As if on cue the pile of tables, casks, chairs, barrels, and other flammable wares went up in a great fireball, its boards and planks having been drenched in pitch and oil. The blaze burned so brightly that it wiped the stars from the sky and illuminated the forest farther off on the beach.

They stared out in solemn silence as the remains of their friend burned atop the pyre. Seneca wondered if Gannon could see them from somewhere and appreciate the light.

Goodbye friend, if you can hear me, Seneca thought. *If you can see us, watch over us.*

The prayer made him feel foolish and asinine, but emotion hardened in his throat. He wanted to pull himself away from the blaze, and walk down to the riggings. He could not do it. He stared into the blaze, consumed.

Soon they would be headed toward the Capitol. Seneca knew this was not the end of their time in violence.

I must not think of it. This conflict has my body. It has my time and my attention. Is that not enough? It will not also have my mind. It will not have my heart.

His mind turned toward Chiara helplessly. All thoughts led to her. All roads led to the Capitol.

Seneca was disturbed to realize that he could not completely remember her face. He knew it, yes, he knew her face. But it was blurry now and transient. It was in his mind then gone, ushered aside by Gannon's death mask and by the bloody rose blooming from Oil'ib's wife. He fought to picture the dark auburn hair and the olive skin, but her face eluded him.

"We should have followed him," Tavin stated suddenly, then snorted back sadness.

Seneca noticed that the others were lifting the chains and letting loose the sails behind them. He could hear the clinking of the iron and the unfurling canvas being thrown open in the darkness. Kaleb was at the wheel.

"I think Oil'ib was right this time," Seneca replied as the boat began to drift out into the open water.

Seneca blinked; the bright light of the pyre made him feel warm. He kept his eyes there until he could no longer see the shore.

The End

About the Authors

THADDEUS YEISER & CONRAD BAIR

Thaddeus Yeiser was born in Butler, Pennsylvania and later lived all over the Keystone state including Erie, York, Selinsgrove and Harrisburg. He studied broadcasting and film in college and helped run a sports radio station. He now works in Sales Management in Delaware. When he's not writing, you can find him soaking up nature or following his favorite sports. He is a student of history and a lover of scotch.

Conrad Bair was born and raised in Wellsboro, Pennsylvania. He studied biology and philosophy in college and has worked in Healthcare ever since. Primarily he enjoys hiking around the country, but visiting family in Pennsylvania is a close second. He lives in Arizona with his long-time partner and two spoiled house cats. He loves writing, painting and music.

Follow their writing journey on Twitter w@SCBair and @thadyeiser!

ठ

CPSIA information can be obtained
at www.ICGtesting.com
Printed in the USA
LVHW110333220720
661196LV00003B/201

9 781947 578371